"

# To Whatever End

ECHOES OF IMARA BOOK 1

CLAIRE FRANK

Copyright © 2014 Claire Frank

All rights reserved. This book or any portion thereof may not be reproduced or used in any manner whatsoever without the express written consent of the copyright holder, except for brief quotations for the purpose of reviews.

This is a work of fiction. Any names, characters, places, events or incidents are products of the author's imagination and used in a fictitious manner. Any resemblance to actual places, events or people, living or dead, is purely coincidental or fictionalized.

First printing, 2014

Mad Wizard Press
PO Box 4266
Everett, WA 98204

ISBN-13: 978-0692348932

ISBN-10: 069234893X

Edited by Eliza Dee of Clio Editing Services

Cover Art by Trevor Smith

Map and chapter icons by David Frank

Printed by CreateSpace

For David

Always have.

# CONTENTS

| | |
|---|---|
| 1. A Journey | 1 |
| 2. East Haven | 12 |
| 3. Orders | 22 |
| 4. Halthas | 27 |
| 5. Family Matters | 36 |
| 6. Of Wars Past | 50 |
| 7. Companions | 58 |
| 8. Life Tree | 67 |
| 9. A Pebble in the Road | 75 |
| 10. On the Run | 82 |
| 11. Solace | 87 |
| 12. New Lodgings | 96 |
| 13. Aid of the Crown | 104 |
| 14. Ale Stone | 111 |
| 15. Gathering Friends | 118 |
| 16. The Lyceum | 130 |
| 17. Conditioning | 138 |
| 18. Black Masks | 146 |
| 19. Smoke and Hinges | 152 |
| 20. The Quarry | 161 |
| 21. Transference | 169 |
| 22. News Unexpected | 179 |
| 23. Confrontation | 186 |
| 24. Finding Control | 196 |

# CONTENTS

| | |
|---|---|
| 25. Guildmaster Stellan | 206 |
| 26. Into Mist | 217 |
| 27. Keys | 227 |
| 28. Watchtower | 232 |
| 29. XIV | 241 |
| 30. Breakout | 249 |
| 31. Absorption | 258 |
| 32. Revelations | 264 |
| 33. Truths | 273 |
| 34. Consequences | 282 |
| 35. Return | 288 |
| 36. Paragon | 297 |
| 37. Sending Messages | 305 |
| 38. Trust | 311 |
| 39. Collapse | 318 |
| 40. What Once Was Lost | 327 |
| 41. Cutting Losses | 338 |
| 42. Chains | 346 |
| 43. To Whatever End | 354 |
| 44. Aftermath | 374 |
| 45. Choices | 380 |
| 46. Watching | 386 |
| A Note from the Author | |

# ACKNOWLEDGMENTS

First and foremost, to my husband David. This book is the result of many hours of brainstorming, world-building, note taking, idea-bouncing, discussing, and even a bit of arguing. Thank you for challenging me to think through the difficult parts, for tugging on each thread of the story to make sure it wouldn't unravel, and for sharing your endless stream of ideas. Without you, this story never would have been written. The time spent with you, planning, plotting and bantering ideas has been amazing and I look forward to many more stories to come.

To the beta readers who shared their valuable time - Dan Bogh, Jane Brooks, Alice Finch, and Josh Wedin. Your insight, comments, and criticisms were immensely helpful. The time you so generously spent pouring through that first draft has done an enormous amount to help me grow as a writer and make this book far better than it would have been without your thoughts.

To Trevor Smith, responsible for the stunning cover. Thank you for putting up with my pickiness and requests for changes, and for bringing Cecily to life.

To Eliza Dee, thank you for your thorough revisions and suggestions. A good editor not only polishes a manuscript, but helps the writer grow and I certainly learned from your expertise.

Last, but most certainly not least, to all my family and friends who have cheered me on, you are all incredible. Your belief in me means more than I can say.

THAYA
NORTH WATCHTOWER
MADRONA
NORCROST KEEP
COMPOUND
WESFELL
EAST HAVEN
HALTHAS
HALTHAS
SAHAAR

## IMARAN MARRIAGE RITE

*Mynas feorh singende eower cweoan mynas son*

*Aet-samne wea a-feagen*

*Ge-treowsian o arian ealdor be-innan eowa*

*An-standan neah eower siid*

*O aeg-hwaet endian*

My soul sings and yours answers my song

Together we become one

I pledge to honor the life within you

And stand by your side

To whatever end

## 1 : A JOURNEY

CECILY CLOSED HER EYES, her breath fogging in the cool predawn air, and opened her Awareness. She felt it reach out from her core as it spread across the forest floor, picking out every pine needle, branch and stone. In seconds, she had a mental map of the surrounding terrain. She could see the forest debris between the trees and the rise and fall of the land better than if it had been full daylight. The clearing was flat, but she could feel the slope to her left where the hill descended toward her home. He was coming, and she would be ready.

Although he was adept at hiding his movements, she felt his careful footsteps before she could hear them. She marveled at how softly he could step, despite his size. He could take her unaware if she wasn't expecting him. She also knew that his strength made people underestimate his stealth. She would not make that mistake.

As she focused on the feeling of his feet on the forest floor, Cecily almost forgot she was standing in the clearing, in plain sight. With a sharp intake of breath, she sprinted, keeping her Awareness spread out as she ran. Immediately, he gave chase. He was faster than she was, but she could see where she was going in a way he could not. His speed defied the darkness, and as he gained ground, she wondered how he could see well enough to move so fast.

As the ground plunged downhill, she turned sharply and almost lost her footing. Dirt cascaded around her feet, and she pushed her heels into the ground to keep from falling as she stumbled down the hillside. He would be within sight of her now, but she did not feel him follow her down the slope. The vibrations of his footfalls veered to the right. Once she reached the bottom of the hill, she'd have a direct route home and he would be left behind. What was his game?

He ran farther away and disappeared from her mental sight. The branches rustled in the breeze as Cecily slowed, scattering a few pine needles at her feet. She couldn't risk the effort to push her Awareness out further to follow him. She'd have to slow down and keep an eye on her edges, waiting for him to get close.

The image of the terrain sharpened in her mind while she crept forward, feeling the tingle of anticipation run up her spine. She scanned the forest and darted forward, choosing her steps carefully. Her tall leather boots hardly made a sound, even amongst the twigs and pine needles. *Where is he?* She picked up her pace and before long, she could see smoke curling from a chimney. Home. She was almost there, and still no sign of her pursuer.

His huge form burst into the quiet clearing, stunning her with his speed. Dropping her Awareness, she ran, sprinting down the gentle slope toward her home. The terrain was open, but she knew she couldn't make it. No longer trying to hide, he ran toward her at full speed. Her breath came in gasps and her legs burned but she pushed harder, determined to make it to her house.

The sound of his footfalls rose and his hand brushed her back. She threw herself forward and tucked into a roll to evade his grasp.

Turning and Wielding as she skidded across the ground, she used her Reach to grab his feet and make him stumble. He lost his footing as she scrambled to her feet. She Reached again, Pulling his legs so he crashed to the ground and landed hard on his back.

She turned and ran, pushing her legs as hard as she could. She was almost there, but his feet pounded behind her. He clutched the back of her shirt, pulled her to a stop and flung her to the ground. His strong grip held fast and he caught her leg with his other hand before she could kick it away. He pulled her across the ground as she struggled and turned her onto her back, pinning her under his weight.

She stopped struggling. Her breath came fast and she shook her dark hair out of her eyes. He held her down by the wrists, his hips holding hers flat to the ground. They stared at each other for a few seconds, his silver-gray eyes intent on her face, his grip on her wrists firm but gentle.

His face broke into a wide smile and they both began to laugh.

He leaned his forehead down to hers as his shoulders shook. "That was well-played. I didn't think I would have time to circle around you."

"You shouldn't have had time. I slowed down too much at the bottom of the hill. If I had just kept running, I would have been inside brewing our tea by the time you got here."

"I counted on that. You always think too much."

She rolled her eyes but grinned back at him nonetheless. "You could let me up, you know."

His eyes narrowed and his mouth turned up in a sly smirk. "I could. But I rather like this position."

With a heave, she tried to thrust her hips up, but he was too big to budge. "But the ground is cold," she said, sticking out her lower lip.

"Fair enough," he said with a laugh and helped her to her feet. They brushed each other off and walked side by side into the comfort of their home.

Her husband, undaunted by the dirt on his clothes, went straight to the kitchen. He uncovered the glowstone lanterns, flooding the kitchen with light, and she heard the sound of pots and pans rattling around as he set about making breakfast. He always worked up an appetite after their little games. They often spent their early mornings in a mock chase through the forest, in order to keep their skills sharp.

Cecily stood in front of the river rock fireplace and picked bits of twig out of her long braid. After brushing a few pine needles from her tunic and leggings, she poured herself a steaming mug of tea, and wandered out to the porch to enjoy the quiet. The sky glowed with the promise of the sun, blazing purple and red as the darkness retreated. Closing her eyes, she once again let her Awareness spread. She felt the boards of her house, logs she and Daro had felled themselves, each stone hauled from the riverbed with their own hands. Daro's movements in the kitchen were comforting and she allowed the calm of the moment to soothe her thoughts. The clanking of pots in the kitchen broke her concentration and her Awareness shrunk back suddenly as released her Wielding Energy. The world seemed to fade, as if it had dissipated into mist and nothing was left but the small patch of ground underneath her feet.

She strolled in to check on Daro. His large frame blocked her view of the food, but the smell awoke her hunger. He was a tall man, well-muscled and strong, his shoulder-length brown hair a little unruly, as always. He wore a dark green tunic with a long leather vest that belted at the waist, and loose brown pants tucked into thick leather boots. She stood in the doorway and watched as he carefully took an egg out of the basket and cracked it into a pan. Someone who did not know Daro might be surprised at his ability to handle something as fragile as an egg with such gentleness. His large hands appeared suited to swinging a sword, rather than handling a cooking utensil. But Cecily knew there was much more to the man she'd married than the muscles that knotted his arms and back, or his ability to do heavy lifting.

He turned and smiled at her, his eyes shining in the glowstone's light. Although Daro's mother had been from a Halthian family, his father had been an Imaran, a little-understood race of people who lived far to the southeast. Daro resembled his father's people, with his tall stature, unusual eye color and olive skin.

"Hungry yet?" he asked over the crack and sizzle of the potatoes and eggs. A flick of the pan in his left hand flipped the egg over. "Shouldn't take too long to finish."

"It smells delicious." She sidled up next to him and threaded her arm around his waist while she tucked her head under his arm. He was much taller than she, but somehow she never felt small next to him. Although Cecily was Halthian, she and Daro shared an Imaran marriage bond, a subconscious connection they barely understood. It drew her close to him in a way other Halthians didn't experience.

She eyed the food and the mess on the stove. He might be gentle, but he was rarely tidy. "We should hurry, though; we have a long day ahead of us."

"Would you mind telling Edson that breakfast is ready?" he asked as he began spooning food into bowls.

"Mmmm," she said and trailed her fingers down his arm. She paused in the doorway and used her Reach, brushing him with her Wielding Energy. She wrapped it around him, feeling the contours of his body, and nuzzled him with Pressure. He glanced at her over his shoulder with a smile as she walked away to find their young charge.

Edson was out in their workshop, up early to do his chores. He reminded Cecily so much of her husband: tall, well-muscled, with a quiet demeanor that hid a whirlwind of thought inside. They had met him in East Haven, a town a couple days' ride from their home.

Although he was only fifteen, he had been on his own a long time. His parents had passed when he was just a boy. Daro had been drawn to take him in; he had also lost his parents as a child and the two seemed to understand each other. Edson was a Wielder, with abilities similar to Cecily's own, and she had resolved to help him gain entrance to the Lyceum, the prestigious academy of learning in Halthas.

"Good morning, Miss Cecily," he said with a flourish when he noticed her. He swept his arm back as if he had a cloak to brandish. "I trust the night kept you well."

"Yes, thank you," she replied formally. "I am gladly refreshed." She had been introducing him to the basics of court manners, helping prepare him for life at the Lyceum. "Would you care to join Master Daro and me for some refreshment on this fine morning?"

"The pleasure would be mine." He touched his left hand to his chest and bowed at the waist.

"Use your right hand when you bow," Cecily corrected.

He raked his hand through his dark hair. "I should know that. I can remember the words easily enough, but I always seem to forget the motions. It would be easy to get yourself into trouble with the wrong people, I expect."

"You have no idea. A little head jiggle could get you married off to the ugly fifth daughter of a Baron if you aren't careful." She winked at him.

He chucked. "I don't know, the ugly fifth daughter of a Baron is still the daughter of a Baron. That wouldn't be half bad."

"True enough. But you'll be better off finding yourself a nice merchant girl. There will be plenty of them at the Lyceum. It isn't only the nobility who attend. Believe me, you don't want anything to do with the Halthian nobility." She turned around to go back inside.

"They can't be all bad," he said. "You know how to speak well, but you're not half as wicked as you say the nobility is."

Cecily stopped and rested one hand on the doorframe. "They're not all bad, no. But their world is wicked. Power can do that to people." *And I am as wicked as I say they are. But hopefully you'll never have to know about that.*

They ate their breakfast and got straight to work preparing for the day's journey. It was time for their annual trip to the capital city of Halthas, something Cecily both looked forward to and dreaded each year. She'd grown up in the city and in many ways, it still felt like home. But it held conflicting memories that made it difficult to go back. She did look forward to seeing their old companions. Five years prior, Halthas had been embroiled in a civil war. Daro, Cecily and their group of companions had been instrumental in defeating the former king and helping King Rogan take the throne. After the conflict ended, the companions had drifted back to their lives. They still met once a year in Halthas, a welcome chance to reminisce with old friends who felt much more like family.

Daro was outside loading their wagon with his goods. He was a skilled craftsman whose work had become extremely popular with the Halthian nobility. He created beautiful items, and although he was not a Shaper, someone who could work with and manipulate a particular material, his work was lovely. Unlike Shapers, whose ability allowed them to work with just one material, such as metal, wood or stone, Daro was able to craft with numerous materials. He created beautiful wood chests, delicate metal jewelry, and carvings of stone.

The popularity of Daro's work had grown as it became fashionable to own a piece with his distinctive scripted *D* on the piece. Noble ladies wore their Imaran-inspired jewelry to all the most important society functions, and his beautiful wood chests had become mainstays in many Halthian homes. She and Daro had left Halthas the year prior with so many special orders, she had wondered if he would have time to fill them all. She knew it puzzled her husband that his work was so prized. She, however, was familiar with the temperament of the nobles. Once something caught on, its popularity would spread like wildfire, each noble wanting to outdo the others. After a few noble ladies had taken a liking to his work, his name had circulated, and soon they were all clamoring for their own original pieces.

She had her own goods to bring and she checked the contents of her large, wooden chest. She made books, beautiful illuminated manuscripts, painstakingly illustrated by her own hand. She ran her fingers over the stamped leather covers. She almost hated to part with them. She'd spent the last year copying and illustrating historical works, teaching manuals, and books of poetry. She picked up a volume of poetry. The gilding on the pages sparkled and her finger traced the tiny flowers she had painted in the margins. She smiled, knowing the book was to be a gift for a young Halthian girl on her eleventh birthday. She hoped the girl would love it as much as she did. She put the book down and closed the chest, leaving it for Daro to take to the wagon.

Outside, Edson was hitching up the horses. He rubbed down their necks and talked to them in soothing tones. Daro loaded the last of their goods and baggage, taking special care with Cecily's chest. She helped secure the cover over the back of the wagon.

The three of them swung themselves up onto the seat and Daro took the reins. They bounced as the wagon started down the dirt road that led out of the hills to Norgrost Keep. Norgrost was the last outpost guarding a pass through the Eastern Mountains. Cecily found the town friendly and charming. This far from the capital, the pull of court politics was weak and she and Daro had made a quiet life a few miles from town. Sometimes she could even convince herself the outside world no longer existed, just the mountains, their valley, the rushing river and a bustling little frontier town. It was a nice fantasy.

They reached the main road before long. Even this far from the capital, the road was paved, huge slabs of stone fitted together precisely in a way only Stone Shapers could craft. It made traveling swift and relatively comfortable.

After riding in silence for some time, Daro spoke. "Ceci," he said, "are you planning to see your parents?" She saw Edson's head turn toward her, then quickly away. Her family was not often discussed.

She sighed. "Yes, I suppose I will."

Daro nodded and kept his eyes on the road. "Will I be joining you?" he asked, enunciating each word carefully.

She hesitated. Her family were high-ranking nobility who disapproved of her marriage to Daro. It had been over seven years and they still hadn't forgiven her for marrying without their consent. Daro's family was of humble origins, his mother from a merchant family and his father from Imara. His parents' own marriage had been a scandal, an unprecedented union between a Halthian and an Imaran. The taint of the gossip and the low position of Daro's family had been too much for her parents, and they'd never accepted him. Her mother was particularly adept at making Daro uncomfortable when they visited. As much as Cecily preferred to have him by her side, it was easier for everyone if he stayed away.

"I'm sure your business in the city will keep you occupied. But I'll send your deepest apologies," she said.

He looked at her, his eyes soft. "I'll come if you want me to," he said, his voice gentle.

"I know you would," she said as she leaned against his arm. "It will be fine. My mother will run out of things to complain about eventually."

Daro laughed. "I suppose. Don't let her get to you."

"Easier said than done. You know what she's like." Cecily looked out at the passing landscape. "I just hope she doesn't mention children again."

Daro wrapped his arm around her shoulders and held her close. They would both have loved a child, but after seven years of marriage, Cecily was beginning to give up on the notion.

As Daro leaned down, he spoke low into her ear. "That has nothing to do with them." He kissed the top of her head. "Someday, love. Someday." He squeezed her shoulders and pulled his arm back around to take the reins in both hands.

"I know." She adjusted in her seat and smoothed out her clothes. She wore a long-sleeved tunic, dyed dark blue, under a wide, brown leather belt. Her pants were simple black leggings, tucked into knee-high brown leather boots. After leaving her family, she'd adopted a casual style of dress, more common among craftsmen and merchants than nobility. It remained a sore point with her mother, but Cecily much preferred the practicality of her clothing over the stuffy formality of Halthian high fashion.

She decided to change the subject. "I haven't heard back from Magister Brunell," she said. "Not since his last letter, which was months ago. I was planning to meet with him while we were in the city to talk with him about Edson's petition for admission into the Lyceum. But he hasn't written back."

"That is odd," Daro said.

"Can you just go see him?" Edson asked.

"I'm not exactly their favorite former student," she said with a laugh. "Magister Brunell is on a very short list of people from the Lyceum who will still talk to me. But he has clout. I'm certain he could put in a good word for you."

Daro flicked the reins. "Did he say anything about leaving Halthas? Maybe he's away."

"No, but his letter was strange," she said and paused for a moment. "He went on and on about how the Lyceum had changed and there were things he must do, all in the name of progress. I wasn't sure what he was talking about. But that's how some of the magisters are. They have a tendency toward melodrama, especially when it comes to their research."

"It is a strange world you lived in," Daro said. "I won't pretend to understand it."

Cecily smiled and leaned her head on Daro's arm, letting the motion of the cart relax her. She hoped her old magister was well but decided not to let it worry her. The Lyceum wouldn't open its rolls for new students until next spring, and it was only late summer. She had plenty of time to help secure Edson's entrance. She sighed, enjoying the warmth of her husband's arm as the wagon rumbled down the road.

## 2 : EAST HAVEN

THE TWO-DAY JOURNEY PASSED quickly. They made their way south toward the river, stopping for the night at the home of friends, where they were happy for the welcome of a warm meal and a safe place to sleep for the night. Daro left them with a few gifts, as he always did, delighting the children with small wooden bears, complete with pointy claws and fangs, before they continued on.

The sun was close to the horizon when they came in sight of East Haven. The low wooden buildings sprawled out away from the river's edge in a tangle of curving streets. The town wasn't very big, but if you didn't know your way around, it would be easy to get lost in the streets and alleys, backyard gardens and storefronts. East Haven had a tilted quality, almost as if the ground under the buildings had shifted in places, leaving them uneven. But studying them with a steady eye seemed to show the lines precise and straight. The effect was endearing, rather than jarring, and made East Haven seem shabby in the way an old grandmother is—worn with years but warm with welcome.

Daro led the wagon toward the river in as straight a line as possible through the jumble of buildings. The streets were well kept and relatively clean, most of the buildings in good repair. East Haven seemed to be thriving in peacetime, although the war hadn't touched the outskirts of the kingdom the way it had the city of Halthas. Trade had picked up again, and trade was East Haven's reason for existing. Poised on the banks of the mighty Bresne River, it was the easternmost of many towns along the way, a port for the great riverboats and a popular destination with merchants and traders.

Their favorite inn, the Floating Abode, affectionately known as the Float, stood on one of the large piers jutting out into the wide waters of the river. Cecily's heart warmed at the sight. They had been staying there for the last several years on their trips to Halthas, and it had become a welcome stop on the journey.

They pulled their wagon up to the pier entrance as two boys came running from the stables; the inn itself was situated further out over the water. Daro flipped them each a coin and gave them instructions as to the horses, while Cecily asked Edson to go fetch the innkeeper. As Edson hurried in on his errand, Cecily gave her cargo a perfunctory glance and took a deep breath of the fresh night air. She had considered settling in East Haven when they'd left Halthas, but it was still too populated for Daro's taste. He preferred the solitude of their mountain home, and she enjoyed it as well, though she did have a fondness for the river.

The innkeeper appeared, his sure stride forcing Edson to hurry to keep up. He was tall, sporting a full head of salt-and-pepper hair. His crisp white tunic and dark blue vest were clean and well-tailored, but not ostentatious, although Cecily knew his inn did good business.

His eyes crinkled at the corners when he smiled. "Cecily!" he exclaimed. "The sun goes down, but the world is a little brighter this night."

She held her hands out to him and he took them in his own. His hands were warm and strong, calloused over from years of work. "It is lovely to see you, Mr. Fielding. I trust all is well."

"Yes, yes, my dear. Busy as ever." He dropped her hands and gestured at the pier behind his back. "We're nearly full this evening, but we have room for you, of course. We always have room for our favorite guests."

Daro strolled over and shook hands with the innkeeper, exchanging pleasant greetings. Cecily left her husband to arrange the details of their goods with him. Their wagon would be stored for the night and loaded on the riverboat in the morning. With a wave, she beckoned to Edson to follow her to the inn.

The wooden planks of the pier creaked under their feet as they walked out over the water. The inn was several stories high, a patchwork of floors and small balconies that looked as if it had been built up over the years in a haphazard fashion. Soft lights glowed in many of the windows and although it shared the tilted character of all the East Haven buildings, it was in good repair. Cecily and Edson pushed through the large wooden door and were greeted by the smells of cooking meat, wood fire and ale. She found a fairly private table at the edge of the room and gestured for Edson to take a seat across from her.

He slid onto the bench and looked around the room. "I've never been in the Float before. Never had the coin."

Cecily smiled. "It's one of my favorites. The food is good and the rooms comfortable."

Edson looked around again. "To a kid like me, this place is downright luxurious. But isn't it a little, I don't know, ordinary for you?"

She furrowed her brow and pursed her lips. "What makes you say that? Do I put on such airs?"

Edson shrugged. "No, not like that. But the way you've been explaining all about Halthian court manners, I get the feeling you're used to a certain level of comfort."

Cecily cocked her head to the side. "Comfort and costly elegance are different things. I lived long enough amongst the nobles in Halthas. I chose this life."

His face reddened a little. "Of course, that's not what I meant, Miss Cecily." She was briefly pleased that he shifted to a more formal address when he thought he was in trouble. "I've never been to Halthas, and people out here, well, you know, they tell all sorts of stories about the important folk – kings and lords and ladies. Meeting you, I've just never been able to figure out how it makes sense, you being a noble, but being, well, you."

"I'm just me, Edson." She shrugged a little. "I grew up in Halthas, I went to the Lyceum, and I fought in the war. I guess I'm not much like most of the nobles. I probably never was. But this is who I really am."

Daro appeared and sat down next to Cecily. He nodded to the serving girl and she brought three mugs of ale. "Our things are in order. The riverboat will be off in the morning." He took a swig and set his large mug down, sloshing a little out onto the table. Cecily wiped the drops away with her hand.

Edson looked around again, drawing Cecily's attention to the rest of the room, which had gone quiet since Daro's entrance. Heads turned in their direction and quite a few people openly stared. Sighing, Daro took another swig of ale and looked firmly down at the table.

Cecily wanted to stare right back, but she tried to ignore the eyes. Edson looked around in confusion, then leaned closer to his companions. "What's everyone staring at?"

"Us, I suppose. Daro is a bit"—Cecily paused—"distinctive."

"I never asked for this," Daro said. Cecily sighed. She hated when his mood turned. It would take her a while to coax him back to sociability.

"It is you!" A man's voice carried across the room. There was no mistaking whom he was addressing. Cecily gripped her mug a little harder as the man made his way across the busy room. Dressed in bright colors, he wore a long red cloak that marked him as a traveling minstrel. He was the last person Cecily wanted to see at that moment.

He approached their table with his head held high. "The heavens truly smile on me this night," he said, loud enough for the room to hear, and bowed with a dramatic flourish. "I travel far from my home, the great city of Halthas, and yet I have the privilege of encountering heroes of the realm."

"No such heroes here," Daro growled without looking up.

Cecily's eyes darted from her husband to the minstrel. She hoped he would take the hint and leave them alone. The minstrel smiled broadly and her heart sank a little. Apparently, he lacked the sense to walk away, or was too enticed by the boost to his reputation his little display might bring.

"Ah, Master Daro, don't be so modest! The realm owes you and your lovely wife a debt of thanks! Please, allow me to perform a song in your honor. It is the very least I can do." He bowed again and turned to address the crowd in the room, tossing his cloak over his shoulder.

"What say you? Shall we have a ballad of our heroes?" Many of the patrons began to clap and the minstrel flashed a wide smile.

"Why should we?" came a voice from across the room. A middle-aged man with a balding head and a full beard slammed his mug on the table. "Caused enough trouble, that lot." Most of the room went quiet, save for a few grumbles of agreement from the others at his table.

The minstrel's hands flew to his face in a dramatic gesture of surprise. "Good sir! These people are heroes! Surely a mere song is far less than they deserve."

The man stood. "Nothing but trouble. I figure if it wasn't for them and their friends, we never woulda had a war in the first place. New king," he said, nearly spitting out the words. "New king and a pig's eye, not gonna get you nothin'. Shoulda left things alone."

Cecily groaned inside. Some called them heroes; not everyone agreed. She knew there was little point in trying to convince malcontents that the former King Hadran had been a vicious murderer. The details seemed to matter little. She looked up at Daro. He traced the lip of his mug with a finger.

The minstrel was going on again about their virtue and heroism. "Why, Master Daro himself, he saved many who would have perished in the fires of the Madrona Massacre! How could one fault such heroic efforts?"

"Here's what I'm thinkin'," the man said as he walked closer to their table, exaggerating each stride and striking his boots hard on the floor. "I'm thinkin' this lot put one king on a throne, why don't they go kill him now and put me up there? What say you to that? I'd do a damn fine job of it too, if I say so." His friends at his table laughed. The man kept walking and stopped in front of the minstrel.

Cecily wanted to stop this before it went too far. "You shouldn't speak about that which you know nothing," she said, only loud enough for the man to hear. "We're not here for attention. We'd just like to sit and eat in peace, so if you'll kindly take your seat."

The minstrel was attempting to regain control of the situation. He flipped his cloak and raised his hand, but the man cut him off before he could begin. "I'll not take orders from the likes of you. What're you still doing with this Imaran beast anyway? The way I hear it, you come from noble blood. Maybe you're headin' to the city to have a bit of a thing with the king on the side, eh? That's why Rogan's king, folks! This little lady had a romp in a stable and rewarded him with a crown!"

Cecily's eyes narrowed and her mind darted quickly through a list of unpleasant things she could do to him. The sound of a chair scraping on the floor stopped her and she saw Daro slowly get up from his seat. He stood a head taller than both the minstrel and the heckler. He straightened his back and glared at the man with an icy stare. "You will not speak to my wife like that," he said, his tone low and even.

The man paled slightly but stood his ground. "I'll take my seat when you folk move on. You're not welcome in this town."

Daro stared at him, unblinking. The man looked back at his friends and two others stood and walked over to join him; both men fingered knives at their belts. One side of Daro's mouth lifted in the slightest smile. Cecily recognized the look of his body relaxing, his arms loose at his sides. He wasn't one to charge into a brawl, but he was ready to coil up and spring at the men.

The room had gone still. The other patrons leaned away, and a few even scurried to the outskirts of the room. The innkeeper stood near the door, wringing his hands. Edson stayed in his seat and darted nervous glances between Cecily and Daro.

Cecily desperately wanted to avoid a fight. Reasoning with these men was not going to get them anywhere, though, so she decided to take a different approach. She stood, her movement slow and deliberate. The minstrel moved aside and watched with his mouth slightly open.

Cecily lifted her chin and took a step toward the men. She brushed Daro's arm with her hand, hoping to keep him back. She knew the second Daro made a move, the men would attack. "You would do well to keep your ignorance to yourself and refrain from speaking ill of others," she said, her voice carrying across the room. "I suggest you do as my husband asked and take your seat."

The man in the center rested his hand on the hilt of his knife. Cecily Reached with her Wielding Energy and applied Pressure, a tight grip on the man's wrist. His eyes went wide, and he snatched his hand away, shaking it. She gripped tighter, keeping her eyes firmly locked on his. The two men next to him furrowed their eyebrows in confusion. One drew his knife and Cecily grabbed his wrist with Pressure, tightening it so his blade dropped to the floor.

"We don't want a fight," she said, keeping her Pressure grip solid. "And you don't want to fight us." She kicked the knife across the floor and it skidded to a halt near the wall. She squeezed them both with Pressure again and held them until they both winced.

Daro put his hand on the small of her back. Cecily held their gaze for a moment longer before she dropped her Pressure grip and turned to take her seat. Daro followed, deliberately turning away to dismiss them. The men shuffled away, their faces flushed, and left through the front door rather than returning to their table.

The tension gradually melted from the room. The chatter of conversation rose in a low crescendo and the bustle of activity resumed. The minstrel backed away a few feet from their table and scanned the room with a neutral expression. Cecily caught his eye and gave him a hard stare. *Don't even think about it.* He cringed and went back to his seat.

Cecily glanced around. Most of the patrons had gone back to their food and drink, but a few still turned their way. No one else had joined in the threats, but no one stood up for them either. The people here seemed to be indifferent, at best.

"Bloody minstrels, can't ever keep their mouths shut," Daro grumbled. He rose from his seat and walked to the stairs without another word. Cecily sighed.

Edson shifted in his seat and scratched his head, his eyes still darting around the room. "Does this happen a lot?" he asked.

Cecily shrugged. "No, not a lot. But this isn't the first time. It's hard to know what the mood of a place will be. More often than not, the crowd cheers and calls for the song, and then sings along." She chuckled to herself. "Once they tried to hoist us up in our chairs and carry us around the room. Daro hated that just as much."

"Not sure how they'd lift him anyway," Edson said with a grin. "But, and sorry if it isn't my place to ask, why does he get so upset?"

"The war wasn't what most people thought. It wasn't all glory and honor and heroics. We didn't make Rogan the king. He was king by right, after Hadran died." She deliberately said "died," rather than "was killed." It somehow made the whole thing seem more honorable. "Daro didn't want to be involved, but we did what we felt was right. Now he just wants to be left alone."

The innkeeper came to their table, bringing their dinner himself. "My dear, please accept my apologies for the, uh, incident. I cannot thank you enough for ending it peacefully. My inn is not a brawling tavern. I'll see to it those men aren't welcomed in my establishment again. They had no right!"

"Please, Mr. Fielding, it's all right, truly," Cecily said, her voice gentle. "Sometimes these things happen."

"Be that as it may, there will be no charge, of course. And Master Daro, will he be joining you, or would you like his dinner sent up to your room?"

"I believe he would prefer to dine in his room this evening. If you would be so kind as to send mine as well, it would be most appreciated." Cecily smiled.

He nodded and waved frantically for a serving girl. "Yes, yes, that will be fine. Come Betsy, this will be going to the large room upstairs. Hurry, on with you now."

Cecily rose and left the innkeeper to arrange for their dinner. "Edson, we'll expect you up early to help with the cargo, but you're welcome to enjoy the Float tonight if you wish." He smiled and nodded. She guessed he was relieved he wasn't being banished to his room for the night. The minstrel had taken to the small stage and begun to play a soft melody on his lute as Edson dug into his dinner.

*Bloody minstrels indeed*, Cecily thought as she alighted the stairs. She knew Daro would be in a foul mood. No matter, she knew plenty of ways to draw her husband out of a bad mood. She paused on the stair as the minstrel's song grew louder, his voice added to the strumming of his instrument. On a whim, she quested out with her Awareness and brushed the strings of his lute, then Reached and broke one of them with a quick snap. A discordant twang cut across the room as the minstrel almost dropped his instrument. He fumbled to keep it in his hands and looked around in surprise. A few patrons laughed into their drinks.

Cecily smiled to herself and went upstairs to join her husband.

# 3 : ORDERS

THE VOICES WERE FAMILIAR. He awoke to them each day; they told him he was still alive. At first, the constant chaos in his mind had threatened to take his sanity. Day after day, the grind in his head had worn him down, taking away his will. Until he'd accepted the chaos. He'd embraced it, owned it, made it a part of him. Now he couldn't imagine living without it. It gave him something to hold on to; an anchor for his being.

He brushed back his long hair and tied it at the nape of his neck. His mask and hood sat next to his bed. He rubbed his bare face, feeling the night's growth. He wondered what he would look like if he let it grow. Of course, that was a silly idea. Not shaving each morning was unthinkable. It was required.

He stood and left the mask on the table. He felt exposed without it, the air prickling his bare skin. His dark, windowless room gave him no indication of what time it might be; he guessed before dawn. He didn't sleep much anymore. Closing his eyes was dangerous. There were too many voices in the dark.

He sat back down on the edge of his bed. There was little else in the room: a bed, just wide enough for him to sleep on, and a small table next to it. A normal room might have a window, a dressing table with a bowl of water for washing, hooks for hanging cloaks or clothing. This room had none of those things. Just the bed, the table and the chains.

His eyes flicked over to the dull silver fetters and his fingers clenched, turning his knuckles white. Four chains were bolted to the floor, manacles for wrists and ankles at their ends. He could remember the cold bite of the metal, his skin rubbed raw to bleeding. Absently, he rubbed his wrists. He hadn't needed to be bound in a long time, but they kept them in his room nonetheless, a constant reminder.

He sat for a while in the dark and stared at nothing. He'd learned to embrace these moments of silence, cling to them. In the beginning, the silence had been his enemy. He'd paced around his room and walked in circles, trying to escape it. Now the early morning before they came for him was his time. It was the only thing left that belonged to him.

He dressed, pulling on the loose black pants and tugging the black shirt over his body. The soft fabric hung from his lean frame. He slipped his feet into his black boots and fastened the silver buckles.

Eventually, the door swung open, intruding on the silence like an unwanted guest at a dinner party. A servant came in and washed his face and hands, then shaved the stubble from his chin. He complied like a penitent child, sitting motionless and staring into nothing. It was easier this way.

She left him to put his mask and hood on by himself. It slipped over his skin, close and warm. His breath was hot inside it, but he was used to the feeling of warmth over his mouth. It covered his face, the supple fabric clinging to the contours of his jaw, nose and forehead. A slit in the front allowed him to see. He adjusted the fit, pulling the mask into place so it didn't intrude on his vision. It was a comfort, the pressure against his face and head. He had fought the mask in the beginning. He could no longer remember why.

The wait wasn't long. He was never sure what would happen when they led him out of his room. He'd memorized the labyrinthine hallways, the numbers of doors, the turns to each place they took him. They could cover his eyes and he could still find his way. His heartbeat rose; it felt like rebellion somehow, knowing the hallways. He briefly wondered if he was supposed to know them, and what they would do to him if they found out. Surely they realized. He had been there so long. Not that he could say how long; his sense of time had long since disappeared. He kept walking, following his guide, and pushed thoughts of time out of his mind. Thinking about time always led to thinking about the before, and the before couldn't exist anymore.

His stomach turned sour and his heart beat faster as the route became clear. One more hallway branched off to the left and he willed his guide to keep going straight. *Don't turn, please don't turn.* He didn't want to go there, not today. A few more steps and he would know. His urge to flee was overwhelming, but he buried it, pushed it down with everything he had. Sweat dripped down his temple, soaking into his mask.

His guide walked on, straight. He let out his breath and the tightness in his back and shoulders began to ease. As they passed the hallway to the left, he forced his eyes forward. Don't even look. It was easier that way.

His guide led him through a door into an open air courtyard at the center of the compound. A stone fountain crumbled in the middle, the water long since having stopped flowing. Ivy and moss crept through the cobblestones, nature working hard to retake the ruin. The cloudy sky was visible high above, towering over the sprawling building. He briefly wondered what this building had been, when it had been whole.

"Number One," a voice barked, and he snapped to attention, standing erect and staring obediently ahead.

He heard footsteps behind him. Slow, patient. He knew the sound of those footsteps, the precise click, click, click of the shoes on the stones, the swish of the robes on the ground. The mere sound of those footsteps made his stomach clench with renewed fear. He held himself still and suffered the inspection, the scrutiny, as Nihil circled him, looking him up and down. Deep inside, he wanted to scoff, to turn up his nose at such treatment. He pushed the feeling down so hard he almost gasped. Such thoughts were dangerous.

"I have orders for you, Number One," Nihil said.

Number One gave a brief nod, otherwise keeping still.

"There is another guest I would like to invite into our"—he paused and gestured around at the crumbling courtyard—"home. This person will be a valuable contributor to the work we are doing here. I have very high hopes for him; high hopes indeed." Nihil took a few steps toward him. "Inviting him here, however, is likely to prove... complicated. This situation requires great care and certain precautions."

Number One nodded again, a brisk up and down of his chin. Whatever questions he may have had never made it near his lips. You didn't ask Nihil questions.

"I need you to take Number Four and Number Five with you. Number Two will follow behind to clean up your trail. Sindre will give you the details. As I said, this is an important task. I trust you will keep things well in hand."

Who was Nihil after that he deemed so important? And why send four of them? Number One often extended Nihil's so-called invitations alone. Curiosity, a long-since-forgotten sensation, rose in Number One.

"Preparations are already underway," Nihil continued. "I expect our new guest will be available in a few days' time." He crossed the distance to Number One in a few quick strides and peered into the slit in his mask. Nihil's eyes were unnerving, a swirl of blue and green. Number One did his best not to flinch at his gaze. *Do my eyes look like that now?* "I expect you to bring our guest here and I expect him to be very much alive and in good condition when he arrives. Is that understood?"

Number One gave another brisk nod.

Nihil walked away, his careful stride clicking on the cobblestone. Number One reached to scratch the back of his neck as he awaited Sindre. Another new guest. If there had been any room left in him for pity, he would have felt it for whoever Nihil was sending him after.

## 4 : HALTHAS

Cecily awoke shortly after dawn. She stretched her arms over her head and breathed deeply. The open window let in the chill morning air, but she didn't mind. The sound of the river was so soothing, she'd slept better than she had in months. She rolled over and curled up next to Daro. He was warm and she pressed her cold feet against his legs. He flinched a little in his sleep, but relaxed as she tucked her head against his shoulder and draped her arm across his chest. Breathing in his warm scent, she wished they could spend another day at the Float, rather than get up to board the riverboat.

But get up they both did, if reluctantly. After a hearty breakfast in the common room, thankfully uninterrupted by minstrels or other guests, they made their way down the road to the riverboat dock.

The dock was a bustle of activity, the dockworkers moving cargo and sailors preparing for departure. The riverboat was designed to ferry passengers and goods up and down the Bresne River. Its wide deck and deep hull had cabins and sleeping quarters, as well as a large cargo hold. At the back of the vessel, an enormous wheel towered over the deck, dripping water that sparkled in the pale light of the morning sun. Cecily marveled at the power it would take to turn the wheel. Halthas was downriver, but on the return journey, Wielders would generate the force to make the giant wheel turn and move the huge riverboat against the strong current of the river.

Daro took care of the arrangements for their cargo and when all was set, the riverboat departed. Cecily and Daro were situated in a small cabin overlooking the water. Edson had felt uncomfortable taking a room for himself and opted for a hammock in the larger communal sleeping quarters.

It took a week for the boat to make its way downriver toward Halthas, stopping at several port towns along the way. The large vessel slipped through the water as the river wheel turned under the clear summer sky. Cecily always enjoyed the trip more than Daro. His subtle wildness and inability to sit still for very long made him look a bit like a pacing animal as he wandered the deck each day.

As they approached the city, Cecily and Daro stood with Edson on the forward deck, their hands resting on the railing. The wind swept through their hair as they squinted in the sun. The city of Halthas drew into view and Cecily glanced at Edson's face, wondering what he would think of his first glimpse of the city.

Halthas had been settled several hundred years before by Wielders and Shapers from the west, who had sought to escape the oppressive Attalonian Empire across the sea. The concentration of people with Wielding or Shaping abilities meant Halthas had grown into a kingdom where the majority of people had some degree of ability. Known across the world as the City of Wonders, the entire city had been built by Stone and Wood Shapers who were masters of their craft.

"The palace is there on the hill," Cecily said to Edson as she pointed toward the towering spires of the seat of the Crown. The streets flowed out from the palace in a starburst pattern, the estates of the oldest Halthian families spread out around it. "It looks even more amazing up close." She pointed next to a hill on the other side of the city. "That's the Lyceum. It's a marvel in its own right. The library is incredible. You've never seen so many books."

"Cecily and her books," Daro said. "But she's right. The Lyceum is impressive."

Edson stared. "Everything is so grand."

"I think the Shapers who built the northern city were doing their best to outdo each other with their craftsmanship," Daro said.

As they drew closer to the city proper, the natural banks of the river gave way to docks, piers and buildings that lined the water on the south side. The riverbank sloped down to the water in front of the city wall, housing a crowded mass of warehouses and docks, busy with ships and vessels of all sizes. The northern city was surrounded by a thick stone wall that plunged directly into the river, with towers at regular intervals.

"The wall was built after the Attalonian Empire attacked," Cecily said to Edson. "It's hard to imagine, looking at the defenses as they stand now, but Attalon nearly crushed Halthas. After the attempted invasion, the next few kings poured enormous resources into building the wall and the towers. Fire Wielders still patrol the wall, although we've been at peace with Attalon for as long as anyone can remember."

"Attalon seems like it must belong to another world," Edson said. "Hard to believe anything exists across the sea. Is it true that they enslave Wielders and Shapers?"

"Some of them," Cecily said. "One of my classmates at the Lyceum was from Attalon. His family fled to Halthas so they wouldn't have to hide his abilities."

"I've been all over the continent," Daro said, "but never to Attalon. Can't say I ever wanted to."

As they came in sight of the first of the three spans, Cecily pointed to the huge bridges. "The spans are the only way to get between northern and southern Halthas. The older part of the city is on the north side of the river. After the invasion, as they were rebuilding, people started settling the south side. Without the skill of Shapers and some specially trailed Wielders, it wouldn't have been possible to build those bridges. The river is half a mile wide here."

Edson's mouth opened as his head turned to follow the line of the first span. It soared across the river in a gentle arc.

"Only in Halthas, or so people say," Daro said. "There isn't another city quite like it."

"What do you think?" Cecily asked Edson with a smile.

"It's so big," he said, his voice soft.

Cecily just nodded. It was big. Although she'd been born and raised in the city, the size of it still impressed her each time she visited. Towering buildings, sprawling streets, enormous gardens. So much of the city defied reason.

Daro looked unimpressed, as usual. He raised an eyebrow and shrugged. "Too many people."

Cecily laughed. "For you, certainly, mountain man."

He made no move to argue. "The city is not my place. But don't worry, Edson, I won't let you get lost. Let's go." With a clap on the back and a smile, he turned from the railing to go collect their things.

Cecily paused and leaned into the railing to look up at the city beyond. Halthas always brought mixed feelings, reminders of the complications she had left behind. From her vantage point she could still see the palace, the tips of its towers glinting in the sunlight. The Lyceum was hidden behind the wall. It seemed like a lifetime ago that she had lived in that world.

However, most of her tasks in the city were pleasant ones, so she tried not to let her thoughts drift too far into the past. She set off to find her husband and help him with the unloading of their cargo.

If the docks in East Haven were a bustle of activity, the docks in southern Halthas were absolute chaos. Yet it was a controlled chaos, with dockworkers and sailors, merchants and passengers all intent on gathering their belongings and cargo and dispersing into the city. The wagon and horses were led off the riverboat under Daro's watchful eye. Edson stood to the side, doing his best to keep out of the way, with minimal success. Cecily felt a momentary pang of pity for the poor kid as another dockworker barked at him. She didn't have time for more than a quick consoling glance in his direction. The dockworkers tended to be gruff, and the best thing for them all to do was to get their cargo off the dock as soon as they could.

"There you are!" a familiar voice called out above the din. Cecily turned to see the bearded face of her old friend Griff. She hadn't seen him in months, but he always seemed to look the same, his auburn hair short, his red beard neatly trimmed. He wore a leather vest over a crisp linen shirt, the sleeves rolled up over his thick forearms, with dark pants and sturdy black boots. As with all merchants, his belt gave an indication of his status. Made of supple leather and encrusted with more than a few shining jewels, it showed Griff was doing well.

Daro walked forward to greet him. They clasped hands and made as if to shake before grasping each other in a sturdy hug. "It's good to see you, old friend," Daro said as he stepped away.

Griff's smile was warm. "If I didn't know better, I'd think you got bigger since the last time I saw you. Must be that wild Imaran blood," he said with a chuckle. Daro smiled at him and shook his head at his friend's jest. "Well, at least we know that wife of yours is feeding you." He turned to Cecily and held his arms wide. "Cecily, my dear! It seems putting up with that brute of a man hasn't left you any worse for wear."

She smiled and stepped into his embrace, letting him crush her against his barrel chest. "I manage to hold my own." He squeezed her arms and let her go. "Griff, may I present Edson. He is planning to enter the Lyceum next year. We thought it would be good to give him a taste of the city ahead of time."

"Good, good, another set of hands," bellowed Griff with a laugh. "Will he be joining us tomorrow night?"

"Of course," Cecily said.

"Excellent. Do we have some stories for you, my lad. You want to hear about the rages of war? We can tell you all about it. The battles, the blood, the heroism," Griff said, and he swung his hand as if brandishing a sword.

Edson's eyes were wide and Cecily patted Griff's arm. "Don't get him too excited, Griff, you're going to scare him."

As she checked the contents of their wagon, Cecily noticed another familiar face, quietly inspecting the hitch and lashings. She caught Serv's eye and smiled. Griff and Serv had been friends and business partners as long as she had known them. Daro had worked with them as a merchant guard for years before he'd met Cecily. Serv had short sandy-blond hair and light blue eyes, and he kept his face clean shaven. He wore a vest that came to his waist in front and curved to trail down past his knees in back. Beneath was a long tunic of muted green and loose brown pants tucked into tall boots with brass buckles. He always wore his worn leather sword belt, and his curved northern-style blade hung at his hip. His Wielding ability was small but effective. A quick flick of Serv's hand and an enemy would find their foot stuck to the floor or their blade stuck in its sheath. He gave her a slight nod and touched his hand to his forehead.

They made their way up the low incline away from the docks toward the city gates. The huge walls towered above them and the guards at the gate checked all who passed through. Daro and Griff led the horses in front. Cecily could hear their voices but couldn't quite make out their words. Speaking of business, she assumed. Griff and Serv were well-respected merchants, both in Halthas itself and in the neighboring kingdoms. Most of the goods Daro intended to sell would go through them, although Daro would deal with some of his customers directly. Most of Cecily's books would be sold through them as well, particularly the ones bound for the Lyceum. It saved her the trouble of dealing with the administration of her former school, as she hadn't exactly left on good terms. She sighed as she thought about the bridges she'd burned in the city.

Serv walked alongside the wagon, his hand resting lightly on the side. He wore his sword with the assurance of someone who knew how to use it. Edson walked next to Cecily at the back of the wagon, his head darting back and forth as he took in the sights, smells and sounds of the city. It was impressive, even in the less affluent quarters near the river. The buildings showed little wear, despite their age. Cecily often wondered if there were Shapers alive who could reproduce the long-lasting architecture of the older structures.

Griff and Serv's warehouse wasn't far from the riverfront. The air hung heavy with the scents of fish, horses, and crowded bodies. Daro drifted to the back of the wagon and fell into step with Cecily. She tucked her hand in the crook of his arm and squeezed him gently. He didn't love being in the city, but she could sense his greater ease at being off the riverboat.

The streets were busy and Cecily noticed signs of festivities. Floral wreaths decorated doors and garlands hung along the rooflines and over windows. She and Daro always visited Halthas during the Feast of Sovereignty, a late-summer festival celebrating the triumph of Halthas over the Attalonian invasion.

Their wagon lumbered ahead and Daro leaned in to Cecily. "I'll catch up," he said and veered off to the side. The crowd parted for him as he walked.

Edson fell into step with her as they turned up a side street. "Where's he going?"

"He probably smelled food," she said.

They continued toward Griff and Serv's warehouse, and Daro met them after a short while. He handed a small bundle to Cecily and tossed one to Edson, who held it up to his nose and sniffed.

"What is it?" Edson asked.

"Meat pie," Daro said. He held a crisp brown pastry wrapped in a thin cloth. He took a bite and closed his eyes, chewing slowly. "This makes it all worthwhile."

Cecily laughed. "I told you he smelled food."

The streets were lined with tidy two-story buildings, shops on the ground floor and living quarters above. The party paused at a crossroads and Daro conferred briefly with Griff. Their goods would be taken to Griff and Serv's warehouse for safekeeping overnight. Daro would begin distribution of many of his special order pieces the next day, delivering to some of his more prominent clients personally. She knew his reputation as a war hero only added to his popularity, but she was careful to keep that to herself. He bristled at the thought that people valued his work for his name over his craftsmanship. She wondered if her family had any of his work displayed in their home. It made her smile to know her mother must be torn between her disdain for Daro and her desire to keep up with current fashion. Maybe she would bring a piece for her mother when she visited. It would either please her mother because she could brag about her relationship to the artist, or it would rankle her, which Cecily had to admit, would certainly be pleasing to her.

As they walked toward their usual inn, the Rising Sun, Cecily resolved to visit her family in the morning and bring with her a token of Daro's craft as a gift. Maybe not a token; perhaps something large that they couldn't help but display. Yes, something large would do nicely. For the first time, she actually looked forward to her visit with her family, if only to see the look on her mother's face.

## 5 : FAMILY MATTERS

CECILY CLUNG TO THE bedpost and sucked in a deep breath while Daro worked the cords of her corset. He pulled the strings tight and she let out a little "ouch."

Daro loosened the strings a bit before tying them. "Sorry. You know I hate fastening you in this contraption. I'm terrible at it."

"Aw, don't you like dressing me?" She looked over her shoulder and pressed her lips together in a smile.

"I'd rather be *undressing* you," Daro answered and pulled her in close. "You do look rather delicious in all this finery." He leaned down and kissed her while his hands slid around her waist to her corset strings.

She pushed him back with a gentle nudge. "Oh no. I'm not going through all that cinching again. Not today, at any rate."

Daro smiled and reached out to brush his fingers across her bare collarbone. Her hair hung loose around her shoulders, cascading down her back, and he pushed a few loose tendrils away from her neck. His touch sent a pleasant tingle down her spine. He leaned in and kissed her shoulder, and she let him lay her down gently on the bed. *Maybe it wouldn't be so bad to have to re-dress.*

Half an hour later, she was dressed and thought she had her hair under control. She spun around and fluffed her skirt. The corset was deep green and plunged to a low 'v' in front, emphasizing the shape of her hips. The top was straight and pushed her breasts up, an effect she found dramatically uncomfortable, and Daro obviously found alluring. Her blouse was cream-colored with a small ruffle across the neckline and black ribbons sewn into the long sleeves, making it appear as if they tied down the sides. The floor-length skirt had wide, deep green stripes alternating with pale green. Brighter colors were the current fashion in Halthas, but Cecily would only go so far to please her mother's sensibilities.

"Well?" she asked and looked to her husband for approval.

His mouth turned up in a lazy smile. "You look incredible, as always. Of course, you could be wearing brown burlap and you'd still look wonderful."

"I think brown burlap might be more comfortable than this ensemble."

"Then why wear it?"

"It's one less thing for her to complain about, I guess," she said. She turned and moved her hair out of the way as Daro draped a necklace around her neck and fastened the clasp behind her.

"And this doesn't give her cause for complaint?" he asked as he ran his fingers along the chain at her throat and cupped the blue stone in his large hand.

It was simple at first glance, a winding chain of silver with a deep blue sapphire that dangled at her neck. The setting for the stone was an intricate lace of woven silver holding the sparkling gem in place. Daro had made it for her, painstakingly weaving each thread of silver around the sapphire. It had been Daro's bridal gift to her; there was nothing she valued more.

Cecily fingered the necklace at her throat. The low-cut blouse that was so fashionable in Halthas ensured her Imaran-style necklace was visible. "If she complains about my necklace now she's just being petty. She's commented on it enough times in the past. But I can see it in her eyes, she knows it's beautiful."

Daro ran his fingers along her temple and down to her neck. She met his eyes and smiled. "You need to wipe that grin off your face," she said and gave him a playful nudge. "Edson will be looking for you soon and you can't go out looking like that."

"Looking like what?" He brushed his hair back from his face. Giving her another lazy smile, he traced his finger across her collarbone again. A knock at the door made Cecily start and she felt her face flush.

Daro narrowed his eyes at her. "What?" he asked with a laugh. "Your aristocratic sensibilities come out at the funniest times. We're married, love. We have been for a while now and I'm pretty sure everyone knows it." He gave her a knowing look.

She tried to brush him off as he went to answer the door. "I know. The knock just startled me a little."

He raised his eyebrows and smiled before he opened the door. Edson was waiting on the other side and his eyes went wide when he caught sight of Cecily. He stared at her openly for a moment before Daro gave an exaggerated cough.

Edson blinked before he regained his composure. He walked in the room, nodding to Daro, and approached Cecily. He took her hand in his and bowed forward, gently brushing her fingers with his lips. Releasing her hand, he paused with just the slightest hesitation, his eyes flicking up to the ceiling. "Lady Imaran, it pleases me greatly to make your acquaintance this morning," he said finally.

"Well done, Edson. That was very proper."

Daro gave Cecily a wicked smile. "Sorry to keep you waiting. Cecily looked far too tempting in that dress." He winked at Edson, then looked back at Cecily, sizing her up like a predator would his prey.

Her mouth dropped open. "Daro!" she said and felt her face flush anew. These things were simply not for open conversation, and she didn't care if he thought it was her stuffy aristocratic manners showing.

Daro laughed and patted a rather uncomfortable-looking Edson on the back. Turning back to Cecily, he asked, "Do you want us to see you to the bridge?"

She glared at him for a few more seconds before answering. "No, I arranged for a carriage."

He walked back to stand in front of her and gently ran his hands up and down her arms. "Are you sure you don't want me to come with you?" he asked.

She met his eyes and smiled with resignation. "No, I'll be fine."

He nodded and kissed her before leading Edson out the door, on their way to attend to their first day of business in the city.

Cecily took a deep breath and steeled herself for her first task of the day, then made her way outside to await her carriage, secretly hoping her family might be out of the city when she called.

The carriage ride wasn't long and as it slowed to a stop, Cecily felt her heartbeat quicken. Her stomach was tight and she chided herself for being so agitated. This had been her home; it shouldn't send her into such spasms of anxiety. With all she'd faced in the war, it seemed ridiculous that a simple visit to her own family would be cause for such trembling.

She took another deep breath as a footman opened the carriage door. He took her hand and helped her down the step onto the walk in front of her family estate.

Although situated in the heart of Halthas, her childhood home gave the impression of a country manor. A large, imposing building bordered by trees and large shrubbery on all sides, it was isolated from the surrounding cityscape. Stone steps led up to the oversized double wooden doors. Cecily had bounded up and down those steps countless times in her youth, greeting friends and relatives who came to call.

She had sent word early that morning so that her parents would be expecting her but wouldn't have time to prepare much of a spectacle. She thought back to the earliest days of her marriage, when she hadn't been welcome here at all. It had been a bit of a relief to know she simply needn't see them. There were no decisions to be made or guilt for not visiting. But after the war, when her name had spread amongst the ranks of the heroes, her family had rescinded their disownment and publicly boasted of their famous daughter. She knew her parents saw her as a means to furthering their own cause, and it dug deep.

She gave instructions to the footman to bring Daro's chest inside. It was exquisitely crafted, the dark wood inlaid with light in a pattern of curved lines weaving in and out of each other. She chose it because it was so distinctly Daro's design. Any one of her family's acquaintances who were familiar with his work would recognize the craftsmanship. Plus, it was large and worth a hefty price. Her mother would be unable to refuse such an extravagant gift without seriously violating the rules of propriety.

She carefully picked up her skirt as she walked up the steps, and another footman opened the door. She felt herself falling back into her noble posture with ease, her left elbow bent as if waiting for an escort to take her arm, her right hand clutching her skirt with the tips of her fingers. Part of her wanted to rebel, to come calling in her normal clothes, her hair undone. She'd done just that, in her first visits after the war. She hadn't the strength or patience to pretend to be Cecily Graymere anymore. But she'd learned over the last few years how to make her visits more cordial, and therefore more tolerable. Dressing up and putting on aristocratic manners seemed to improve her mother's mood.

"Milady," the footman said as he led her into the sitting room. "Lady Graymere will receive you shortly." A few refreshments sat on a gleaming silver tray. The room was pleasantly warm and Cecily had to suppress a chuckle. Her parents had installed a hearthstone in their fireplace. Similar to the glowstones everyone used for light, hearthstones were an Imaran wonder, something even the most skilled Halthian Wielders at the Lyceum had been unable to duplicate. They were smooth stones, fairly large and heavier than they appeared. Their mix of pale green and cream color was not particularly eye-catching, but what made them remarkable was their ability to regulate the temperature of a room. If it was cold, they emanated heat. On a warm day, they cooled the space, keeping the room at a comfortable temperature. They had been popular in Halthas for years and Cecily was sure the Imaran traders made a substantial sum for them.

Two figures appeared in the doorway and Cecily turned to greet them. Her younger sister, Liliana, bounced into the room and grasped Cecily with a squeal. She was slightly taller than Cecily, with the same dark brown hair and alabaster skin. Her cream blouse was cinched with a lavender corset, her voluminous yellow skirt arcing wide around her hips, embroidered with small birds and flowers in shades of lavender and blue. Her hair was swept up on top of her head in current Halthian fashion, held up with sparkling clips and pins topped with small pearls.

"Cecily!" she exclaimed as she gripped Cecily's hands in her own. "It is so marvelous to see you! I wish you wouldn't stay away so long. What a lovely dress! The colors are a little dull though, don't you think? How long have you been in the city?"

"Liliana, please contain yourself," the other figure in the doorway said, cutting off Liliana's unbroken stream of chatter. Lady Martessa Graymere was a stately, imposing woman, dressed immaculately in a long burgundy-and-gold brocade overdress, with gold laces up the front and a collar of lace spilling out the top for modesty. Her gray hair was pinned back, every piece smooth and precisely in place.

Liliana stepped dutifully aside as their mother glided into the room. Cecily dipped into a low curtsy as her mother approached. Martessa reached out to grasp Cecily's hands as she straightened, and gave her a forced smile. There had never been much warmth between Cecily and her mother. Martessa's cold eyes glinted as she regarded her daughter, and her gaze swept the room behind them. *She's probably making sure Daro isn't here.*

"My daughter, how lovely of you to think of us on your visit." She squeezed her daughter's hands and dropped them a little too abruptly.

Cecily bit back a sharp remark and smiled. "I am pleased to see you again, Mother."

Lady Martessa swept past, lowered herself deliberately onto the edge of a chair and picked up a cup of steaming tea. She did not invite Cecily to sit. Liliana took a seat on the other side of the refreshment table. As a resident of the house, Liliana was permitted to sit without invitation. Cecily had to wait. Struggling for patience, she clasped her hands in front of her and resolved not to speak first.

Liliana seemed oblivious to the standoff in front of her. "Will Father and Royce be joining us, Mother?" she asked. "I know they're terribly busy, but I was so hoping they would come see Cecily."

Lady Martessa turned her chin toward her younger daughter and took a careful sip from her delicate porcelain cup. "No, Liliana, your father and brother will not be joining us this morning."

Liliana sighed with obvious dismay. "Mother, really, they must have time for this. We're just having a bit of tea."

Martessa's jaw clenched. "That will be enough, Liliana."

Cecily rarely saw her father and older brother. Her Lord Ellis Graymere had been largely absent even when she was still in the family's good graces, frequently engaged with the family's business dealings. Her brother Royce had never forgiven her for marrying Daro and leaving the Lyceum. He treated her with cold indifference whenever he saw her.

Finally, Martessa motioned for Cecily to sit. Cecily nodded to her mother, determined to remain the picture of decorum, and sat down on the edge of a chair, folding her hands neatly in her lap.

"Well, then," her mother continued, appearing to have decided some conversation was in order. "How is your health?"

*My health?* "I'm well, thank you for asking," she answered, not quite sure how else to answer the question. Liliana took a cup of tea and sipped it, peeking out over the top of the porcelain.

Martessa motioned for her servant to hand Cecily a cup of tea and continued. "Good. And you are still living out in"—she paused and waved one hand around idly—"wherever it is you live?"

"Near Norgrost Keep," she answered.

"Yes, yes," she said with a dismissive flit of her hand. "Did you hear that Calden Dover recently completed his training at the Lyceum?"

Cecily tried to look interested but wondered how her mother thought she would hear about the minutiae of the Halthian court. The Dovers were another noble family and had always been close allies of the Graymeres, but she couldn't recall Calden specifically.

"I don't suppose you remember him," Martessa continued. "It has been quite some time since you left the Lyceum so rashly. I don't know how you ever expected that scandal to subside. You had everyone talking about it for months."

Cecily willed herself not to roll her eyes. "Yes, Mother, I realize that. We've spoken of this before, I'm sure you recall."

"We saw the Dovers recently and Calden spoke very highly of his experience at the Lyceum," Martessa said.

"I'm pleased to hear that."

"Unlike yours, I suppose," Martessa said. "As if you were too good for the Lyceum. You were their star student in your day. I still can't fathom how you could throw that all away to run off and marry that Imaran."

Cecily let out a small sigh. Her mother complained about her leaving the Lyceum and ranted about her choice of husband on almost every visit.

Martessa continued. "Your father is arranging a match between Liliana and Calden. He is set to inherit his father's title and has very strong prospects."

Liliana nearly bounced in her seat, her eyes bright with excitement. Cecily smiled at her sister. "Lily, that is wonderful news."

"Yes, well, fortunately your sister has enough sense to agree to a suitable marriage. We had hoped to improve the family's fortunes with a match for you, but apparently the prince was not good enough."

Cecily's neck tightened. "That was a long time ago."

Martessa's eyes narrowed. "It may have been years ago, but a marriage to a prince is not something one can simply throw away."

She sighed, some of her frustration leaking into her voice. "Prince Pathius is dead, as is his father. Rogan is king now. What do you think would have become of me if I had married him?"

Martessa pressed her lips into a thin line. "Perhaps things could have turned out differently."

Cecily fumbled with her cup and nearly dropped her tea in her lap. "Mother, Prince Pathius went missing during the war. He probably died in battle. I doubt his lack of a marriage to me had anything to do with it."

"Didn't it? How different would things have been if you hadn't been involved?"

Cecily's voice hardened. "We have been over this too many times to count. I didn't start the war. Hadran did. You have no idea what he was really like. All you saw were the parties and processions, the face he showed the world. Hadran was awful, Mother, and Pathius was probably just as bad. I got involved in the war against him because I had to do what I felt was right. Even that didn't make up for the things I did before, all in Hadran's name." Her voice trailed off and she turned away. She didn't want to think about that.

Martessa clicked her tongue. "Such dramatics. I only meant a prince is a good choice for a husband. Pity Rogan has no sons. He certainly has a long line of women waiting for the chance to be his wife. He isn't too old yet, you know. Are you still on friendly terms with the king? You should urge him to settle on a wife. A single man as king is unseemly."

Cecily sighed and let the matter drop. She had argued with her mother too many times about the Lyceum and the war. Once she had even tried to tell her mother the truth. Cecily had been handpicked by the former King Hadran to enter the Lyceum of Power, a secretive wing of the institution. They had helped her hone her Wielding abilities, but Hadran had expected her to use them for his own dark ends. Eventually, Cecily had been unable to stomach the tasks she was given, and she'd left the Lyceum completely. Her mother had brushed off her explanation, choosing to believe Cecily had only left to marry Daro.

She blinked as she realized her mother was watching her. "I brought you something," she said in an effort to change the subject. Her mother's eyes lit up in surprise. "I had the footmen bring it in when I arrived."

"All right, then, bring it in," she said and waved to one of the footmen standing silently just outside the door.

It took two men to bring in Daro's chest. The wood was polished to a shine and the distinctly Imaran design was the height of Halthian fashion. The scripted $D$ was featured on the lower right side, and Cecily was pleased to see the footmen carry it in so her husband's mark was clearly visible. She stole a glance at her mother, hoping to read something in her expression, but Martessa's face was a stoic mask. She narrowed her eyes as if scrutinizing the chest as the footmen set it down in front of her. Liliana's empty teacup hung in her limp hand and she gaped, her eyes wide.

Cecily suppressed a feeling of satisfaction. Her mother was trying desperately to hold her emotions in, but Cecily could read her expression. She had not expected this.

"As you can see, the design is completely unique. There isn't another piece that can match its beauty." She paused and saw an inkling of emotion cross her mother's face. "I thought it would look perfect just over there," she said, gesturing to a space below a window. "It will make a remarkable conversation piece."

Her mother looked at the space Cecily indicated and nodded to herself ever so slightly. Cecily could see her calculating the social value of such an item. Would her friends find it enviable, or would they remember the artist in question was the rogue her daughter had run off with?

The social boost of owning the piece seemed to win out over her mother's disdain for Daro. She motioned to the footmen. "You heard her, put it over there. I suppose that will have to do. It is a bit dark, but one can't argue with what is fashionable."

Cecily smiled. "Daro will be so pleased that you like it."

Her mother's face snapped back to her. "Where is he? Surely you have not been abandoned in the city?"

"He sends his regrets, but business keeps him occupied." *You treat him like refuse every time he comes here so it's not likely he will ever visit again.*

Martessa pressed her lips together and turned to address Liliana. "Improper, if you ask me, that a husband should leave his wife to go roaming around the city. At least he has the decency to dress you well these days."

Cecily couldn't suppress a smirk as she recalled her husband undressing her earlier. She decided it would be best to cut the visit short. Despite her mother's attempts at unpleasantness, the visit had been rather painless. She didn't want to stay too long and risk it turning sour.

"With that, I'm afraid I must depart," she said. "Lily, it was lovely to see you, as always. Mother, thank you for your hospitality on such short notice. I hope you enjoy the gift, and please give my best to both Father and Royce."

Liliana sprung up from her seat and embraced her sister. "It was just wonderful to see you," she said as she pulled away. Cecily smiled and turned to the door.

"Cecily." Her mother's voice made her stop. "I'm glad to see you are in good health. Although your choice of clothing tells me you have no news of a growing family to share with us."

And there it was. Cecily should have run for the door the moment she got complacent about the visit. She'd thought her mother had run out of things to hurt her with, but of course, Martessa always seemed to know what to say to cut her deep. "No, I'm afraid I bring no such tidings," Cecily said without turning around.

"Hmm. I suppose it will be for the best, given what that man is. Liliana, I trust you won't be married for quite so many years before starting a family of your own, dear."

Cecily didn't answer, nor did she wait for her sister's reaction. She simply walked away, down the hall and out the door. A footman scrambled out after her, offering to send for the carriage, but she ignored him and kept walking. A carriage would suffocate her.

She walked to the street and turned, fumbling for the strings of her corset to loosen it. Of course her mother would ask *that* question. Better she had asked for details about the war, something Cecily rarely discussed even with those closest to her. Her heart beat too quickly and she felt panic rising to constrict her throat. She shouldn't let her mother do this to her, but starting a family was the last thing she wanted to discuss with her. She wished she could have turned around and told her mother they were choosing not to have children, choosing to wait until a later time. But as tears sprung to her eyes, she knew she wouldn't have been able to get the words out, because they certainly weren't true.

She set off, knowing her shoes were unsuited to the walk. She needed to escape this world and push all thoughts of her mother aside. She needed to feel Daro's arms around her, but most of all, she needed a large goblet of very strong wine.

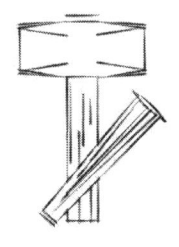

## 6 : OF WARS PAST

Daro sat at a large round table in the back room of the Rising Sun Inn. He leaned against the chair and stretched his legs in front of him. After spending the better part of the day delivering items to his more prestigious clients, his legs were tired.

He thought about his wife and fidgeted in his seat. He hated letting her face the wolves by herself, but he knew that his presence at her family home only made things worse. Funny, there had been a time when he'd thought the Graymeres might be coming around to him; the father, anyway, and her mother had seemed a little less acidic for a while. That certainly hadn't lasted. It was a relief to know he could avoid them, although he felt selfish for having the thought. He didn't care whether they thought him a backwoods savage or not, but it bothered him that it was hard on Cecily.

"Should we go looking for her?" Edson asked. He'd spent the day with Daro, helping with his deliveries and gawking at the city.

"No, she'll be here before long." He took another swig of ale.

"What if something happened to her?"

Daro smiled. "Trust me, she can handle herself."

Edson laughed. "Yes, but this is a big city and I've heard all sorts of dark things happen in the streets. I was just wondering if we should be worried about her is all."

"If someone tries to hurt my wife, they picked the wrong target." So maybe he was bragging a little. He couldn't help but be proud of her. And it was certainly true; concern for her physical well-being hadn't occurred to him. "Maybe her visit went better than she expected. I'm sure she'll be here soon."

The door swung open, and Daro looked up, hoping to see his Cecily. Instead he saw a man dressed immaculately in a deep green doublet that bore the king's sigil embroidered on the chest. Daro rose from his chair as the man approached the table and reached out his hand to greet his old friend.

"Alastair," Daro said, and both men put a hand to their chests and bowed formally before sharing a friendly embrace. "It is good to see you, old friend."

Alastair smiled, the edges of his eyes showing just the faintest sign of age and his short dark hair made him look tidy and well-kept. "The pleasure is all mine. I'm glad to see you made it all the way back to our fair city." He looked down at the mostly empty table and added, "But you seem to have forgotten something rather important. Where is that beautiful wife of yours? You know I'm happy to see you, but she is a good deal more pleasant to look at."

"That she is," he said with a smile. Daro took his seat. Alastair followed and motioned to the serving girl. "She will be here shortly, I'm sure," Daro answered. "She had other business to attend to today."

"You shouldn't let that woman out of your sight in this city," Alastair said with a grin. "She might not want to leave."

"You'd have me play her escort? Come Alastair, you know her better than that. Cecily has a mind all her own."

"That she does, that she does," Alastair answered.

Daro introduced Edson, who seemed appropriately awed by the finery Alastair wore. "Alastair and I have known each other a long time. We trained together and traveled as merchant guards before he earned his current post at the palace."

"Did you fight in the war?" Edson asked, his voice low as if asking for a secret.

Daro frowned, but Alastair nodded. "That I did, young man. Fought alongside your master here, and his wife as well. It was a hard road, helping Rogan become king." He leaned forward and lowered his voice to a loud whisper. "Although, if you haven't noticed, the war isn't exactly Daro's favorite topic of conversation." Daro shot him a glare. "But still, we heroes have to stick together."

An uncomfortable silence fell which Daro did not attempt to break. Alastair shifted in his seat and looked pointedly at Daro, as if daring him to speak. He remained silent.

Finally, Edson rose and ran a hand through his hair. "I need to, uh…" He trailed off and walked away without finishing.

Alastair took a pull from his mug and nonchalantly set it down. "What?" he said finally.

"Don't go filling that boy's head with all that heroes nonsense," he said. "Yes, there was a war. I know this. But we didn't make Rogan the king and I don't like the insinuation that we did."

"Come now, I'm not trying to dredge up uncomfortable memories," Alastair answered. "I'm sorry for trying to have a bit of fun at your expense. But knowing you as I do, I'm sure that boy doesn't know half of what happened."

"And why should he? It happened. It's over. I just want peace."

Alastair rolled his eyes. "Peace. Is that it? Is that why you disappeared to the edge of the world?"

"I'd hardly call Norgrost Keep the 'edge of the world.'"

Alastair paused for a moment. "Daro, what are you doing?"

Daro looked around, feigning confusion. "Drinking ale, last I checked."

Alastair frowned. "You know full well what I mean. You ran off to the middle of nowhere to spend your days doing what—tinkering, making trinkets? You should be shaping men. Instead you're hiding out, and keeping her hidden away too. It's such a waste."

Daro stared at his mug for a long moment before answering. "There are two things I am good at. One is loving my wife. The other is killing men. Loving my wife doesn't cause nightmares. Leading men always led to death. When I was younger, I thought I could use my skills to protect people. But I did things in those days I'm not proud of, and I don't intend to repeat those mistakes."

"You're far too hard on yourself," Alastair replied. "What man hasn't done things he regrets?"

Daro met Alastair's eyes. "We all have our own ways of dealing with what we did. And I'm not talking about our days protecting merchant caravans. Your way was to stay here, be involved, serve the king. I'm sure the benefits of your newfound station don't hurt either," he said and gestured to Alastair's fine clothes. "I have my own way. I didn't want to be involved in the first place, but we did what needed to be done and that is the end of it."

Alastair sighed and lowered his voice. "You act as if we did something shameful—as if you want to sweep it under the rug. We did what needed doing, Daro. Plain and simple. King Hadran was insane, we all knew it. What he did out at Madrona Keep…" He trailed off and turned away. "You were there. You saw it. You saw how many people died, innocent people. And King Rogan is a good man. You know that too. We did what was right and the kingdom is better for it. You should be here, Daro. You could make a difference here, serving a good king."

Daro clenched his teeth and felt his anger rise. He took a deep breath. He didn't want to argue with his friend. He was about to reply when he realized another man was standing next to the table.

"Good timing, Callum," Alastair said with a hearty laugh. "I suspect Daro was about to throttle me. Please, sit down." He shoved a chair backwards.

Callum brushed his dark hair from his eyes. He was dressed in his usual long black coat with a wide collar turned up around his neck, a loose-fitting black shirt and trousers, and shiny black boots with the tops folded down. He sank down in a chair next to Alastair and flipped a gold coin along his knuckles.

Daro forced himself to relax and nodded to Callum. As always, he was struck by Callum's youthful appearance as the man peeked out from behind his slightly disheveled hair with a rather boyish grin. "Good to see you," Daro said. "We weren't sure if you'd be here this year."

"I live nearby, so it's convenient enough," Callum said with a shrug. His gaze swung back and forth between Daro and Alastair, one corner of his mouth turned up slightly. "So, what are we talking about? Clearly not the price of wine."

"I was simply trying to figure out why our friend here has run off to the farthest reaches of the kingdom and seems content to waste his life making trinkets for the gentry," Alastair said. He leaned back in his chair and set his mug down hard.

"I would hardly say I ran away. Besides, what do you know about my life? I trained for years learning how to hurt people under the guise of defending them. And what did that get me? A lot of blood on my hands. Now I need to create. I need to keep busy, and the things I make are hardly trinkets. I have something now that I can take pride in. I do good work and I've made a good home for my wife."

"You can't keep hiding her away, you know," Alastair replied. "She thrives here, you have to see that. She was born here, this is her home. She shouldn't be living out in the wild. She needs more to keep her happy."

Daro pushed his mug away and slammed his hand down on the table. "And what do you think you know about my wife?"

"Hey, easy, Daro," said Callum, putting a hand out toward him. "He didn't mean anything by that."

Daro glared at both of them. They didn't know the first thing about her, or how to make her happy. "Leave her out of this."

"Fine, fine," said Alastair. "But think about it. We both know Rogan wants you here. Why won't you at least consider it?"

Callum tossed his coin in the air and caught it with deft fingers. "You'd have better luck talking him into wearing one of Cecily's corsets."

They all laughed, even Daro. He had to admit, the image of himself cinched up in a corset was more than a little bit funny.

Alastair smiled. "Truly, Daro, I'm not trying to cause trouble. But you were both made for bigger things. You always say you don't belong, but you never saw yourself. How many people looked to you during those times of uncertainty, when things turned sour and we all feared for our lives? When we were out in the wilds, or on the streets of this very city, you led. We should have died many times over, but somehow you always found a way to pull through. It's a shame to see that all go to waste."

"He has a point, you know," said Callum. Daro looked at him in confusion. It wasn't often that Callum and Alastair agreed. Callum looked back and forth between the other two men again. "What? I'm just saying that it seems crazy for a man like you to be living out in the middle of nowhere making tables and chairs, or whatever it is you do." He leaned in and rested his elbow on the table. "I know this fellow who could really use a man like you. Completely legitimate, I assure you, and it would pay extremely well." He trailed off, raising his eyebrows at Daro.

"You know a fellow?" Daro said. "Thank you, Callum, but no, I'm not sure I want to know who this 'fellow' might be."

"Oh no, it's nothing like that," Callum said with a dismissive wave of his hand. "Completely legal." Alastair snorted. Callum smirked at him. "I'm fairly certain my offer would be a bit more enticing than that of our good king."

"You're both idiots," Daro said and shook his head. "What others believe isn't important to me. You can think I ran away or I'm hiding or whatever you want. I just want to live in peace and love my wife, simple as that."

The door opened as Alastair opened his mouth to reply. Cecily appeared in the doorway and Daro stood. Her long hair was windblown and her blouse hung loose around her body, her unbound corset clutched in her hand. She met Daro's eyes from across the room and he knew something was wrong. He pushed the chair away from the table and walked to her, no further thought for his friends. She took a few steps toward him and threw herself into his arms.

He drew his arms around her protectively and kissed the top of her head. "Cecily, what happened?"

"I'm okay. I don't want to talk about it here." He brushed the hair back from her face. She gave him a small smile and reached down to take off her shoes. "These shoes are terrible."

He rubbed her back gently and walked her toward the stairs as anger rose up like bile in his throat. He should have gone with her. He didn't know what they had said to put her in this state, but he was furious with himself for not having been there to protect her. As he mounted the stairs, he looked toward the friends he'd left at the table and had a passing thought for them and those still due to arrive. They could bloody well wait. Her face was so pale and her eyes red.

He hadn't seen her look like that in a long time.

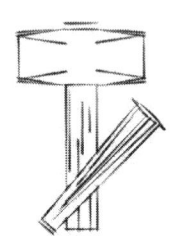

## 7 : COMPANIONS

Daro shut the door with a soft click, followed Cecily to the bed, and sat on the edge next to her. "What happened?" he asked, his voice soft.

She took a deep breath. "I shouldn't let her get to me like this. I don't know how she does it, but she always knows exactly what to say to get under my skin. She always did." She paused and Daro stroked her back, waiting for her to continue. "Everything was going fine, just the usual from my mother. My sister is getting married. I gave my mother the chest and she accepted it with a decent amount of grace. Then as I was leaving, she asked about having a family. She said it was 'for the best' that we don't have any children." She choked out the last few words, put her hand to her mouth, and breathed deeply to stop herself from crying. "I just left. I didn't say anything else. And I walked back here."

Daro closed his eyes and kept rubbing her back gently. *Damn that woman.* "Oh, love," he said. He never really knew what to say, especially about this. "She was just trying to upset you."

Cecily sniffed a little. "I know. I reacted badly. I shouldn't have let her see how much that hurt."

Daro shook his head and wrapped his arms around his wife. "No, it doesn't matter what she saw or what she thinks."

Cecily leaned into his arms and sat quietly for a moment. Then she pulled away to look up at him. "Is it terrible that I want to have a baby to spite my mother? Just to see the look on her face when I tell her that her precious noble blood will be mingled with that of a half-Imaran mountain man?"

Daro smiled. "Now, that's my girl." She smiled back and he relaxed a little. Her face had returned to its normal color and her eyes were bright. He brushed the hair back from her face. "Always remember, they can't take anything away from us. We're out of their power now."

Cecily smiled wider. "This is why I love you. It's impossible to stay upset when I'm with you." She kissed him quickly and got up to change her clothes.

He leaned back on the bed and braced himself with one arm as he watched her dress. He could sense her relief as she discarded her formal dress and donned her typical attire. Tonight she wore a cream tunic, cut to flatter her feminine shape. She pulled on her dark leggings and high brown leather boots. She added a wide belt and smoothed out her shirt. Her bearing still made her clothing look a bit regal; perhaps it was the ease with which she stood. Or maybe he was always a little drunk with her beauty. Cecily claimed she wasn't considered particularly beautiful, but he couldn't imagine anyone more so. She had a delicate jaw and a small nose, her eyes brown against her fair skin.

She straightened her necklace and brushed her hair back with her hands. She turned toward the small mirror and braided two small braids at each temple, pulled them to the back of her head, and pinned them in place. She fluffed out the rest of her hair, letting it hang down her back.

"There," she said as she turned to him. "I feel better."

He smiled again. "You look perfect."

"I suppose we should go downstairs. The rest of them will be there by now, I expect," she said. "Besides, I'm famished."

Their table was nearly full when they made their way down the stairs to the back room. Edson had returned and sat listening to Alastair with wide eyes. Daro wondered what rubbish Alastair was filling the lad's head with this time. Griff and Serv had joined the group, Griff's hearty laughs audible from the upper floor. Callum leaned in toward Mira, a tall and lanky woman dressed in the uniform of a king's guard, the king's sigil embroidered across her chest. Mira was a Precision Wielder, whose abilities made her an uncannily accurate archer, and had joined King Rogan's personal guard after the war.

On Callum's other side sat Sumara, a sultry woman with silky black hair and a full mouth. She wore a long, sleeveless white dress, with braided straps crossing her shoulders and a loose leather belt draped at her waist. Originally from Sahaar, a kingdom to the south of Halthas, Sumara had never changed her style of dress to adopt Halthian fashion. She was a Lightning Wielder and a former classmate of Cecily's at the Lyceum, now under the patronage of one of the high noble houses of Halthas.

Everyone stood at their approach. Daro placed his hand on the small of Cecily's back and led her to the table. They smiled at their friends, and Cecily stepped forward to embrace them each in turn.

They greeted each other warmly, no one resting on formality. These were the companions they had fought with, bled with, and trusted with their lives during the war—people who were much more like family than mere friends. Daro sat down, leaning back in his chair. It was good to see the companions again.

There were others who wouldn't be joining them for their annual gathering. Merrick hated the city more than Daro, preferring the solitude of his cabin in the woods outside the city. He and Cecily would pay him a visit on their way home. Rogan was king now. He had more important things to attend to than a gathering of friends at an inn. And Daro wasn't sure they could find an establishment large enough for his retinue of guards. There were others as well, those buried and gone, who had given their lives in the struggle against Hadran.

When everyone had settled into their chairs, their mugs and goblets refilled, Griff rose, mug in hand. "A toast to our king. To His Majesty, King Rogan!"

Everyone raised their glass in agreement. "To the king!"

Griff remained standing. "And to us. May we all live long and happy lives, free of the misery of war."

"Hear, hear!" came the reply. Daro lifted his mug and drank a heavy swig of dark ale. He could drink to that wholeheartedly.

The innkeeper and several serving girls brought out platters of steaming food. Daro dug in, filling his plate with a pile of tender pork ribs doused in a thick honey sauce, roast pheasant with herbs, and a chunk of soft brown bread. The sweet smell of the honey sauce and the juice of the roasted meat made his mouth water. As he bit into a piece of pheasant, the skin crackled and juice ran down his chin.

A serving girl leaned across the table and filled several mugs from a thick ceramic jug. She wore a long bright yellow dress that laced up the front over a short-sleeved blouse, with a clean beige apron tied at her waist, her cleaning rag tucked into the band. Callum caught Daro's eye and gave him a quick wink. He flicked the hair from his eyes and held out a coin between the tips of his two fingers. "Keep 'em coming, darling." She smiled and took the coin, turning to walk back toward the kitchen.

Callum's mouth curled up in a crooked smile as he held up her cleaning rag. Daro smiled over his food and glanced up at the girl. She stopped, patted her hip, and looked over her shoulder. Callum held his arm out, the rag hanging from his upturned hand. Her brows drew down as she walked back and snatched the rag from his grip.

"You seemed to have dropped this," he said as he looked up over his shoulder. She narrowed her eyes at him and started to turn away, but he stopped her, laying a hand on her arm. "Careful, darling, you seem to be missing something," he said and handed her back the coin.

Her mouth opened as she plucked it from his fingers. "How did you do that?" she asked. The conversations around the table quieted as their heads turned to look at Callum and the girl. Daro took another bite of pheasant.

"You really should be careful with your money," Callum said. He pushed his chair back and stood up with a smile. "There are a lot of unscrupulous folk who might take advantage." He lightly touched her hand, placing it palm up, and closed her fingers around the coin. He laid his hand on top of her fist. "I wouldn't want you to lose any of your hard-earned reward." He flicked the fingers of his other hand and another coin appeared, held between two fingers. The serving girl's eyebrows rose, and she smiled.

"I just want to be certain my friends and I have a pleasant evening. I find the best way to do that," he said as he closed his hand, flipping it open again and showing his empty palm, "is to keep the ale flowing." He smiled and lifted his hand off of hers. She opened it to find two coins, clinking together in the palm of her hand. "Don't worry, darling, I'm just having some fun with you."

She laughed and shook her head as she clasped the two coins. "Have a seat, sir. I'll be back to fill your mugs."

Daro chuckled to himself as he filled his plate with more food. The hum of conversation grew as the companions settled into their meal.

Callum looked across the table at Daro and raised his eyebrows. "What's that in your pocket?"

Daro lifted one corner of his mouth in a smile as he leaned back from the table and patted down his pockets. He felt a round disk and pulled it out. One of Callum's coins. Daro laughed, shaking his head, and flipped the coin back to Callum. "I don't know how you do that," he said.

Callum shrugged his shoulders, caught the coin, and made it disappear again with a flick of his fingers. Daro loved it when Callum showed off his sleight of hand. One might assume Callum was an Illusionist, with a Wielding ability that aided his tricks. He was a powerful Wielder, but his gift was Empathy, the ability to influence and control emotions. Daro didn't know how Callum had learned to fool people the way he did, but it always made for an amusing evening.

Daro turned to his wife and she smiled, the stress gone from her eyes. He lifted his mug and washed down his food with a long pull of the rich ale.

"Serv and I were in Madrona a few months back," Griff said and the table quieted at the mention of the town. "The Keep is fully manned again and the town is looking downright lively."

"Daro and I haven't been there in a long time," Cecily said. "I think they were still rebuilding the last time we were there."

Madrona Keep was where the war had begun, and where Daro had first met many of the companions. Fearing a rebellion, King Hadran had called together the heads of the noble houses he believed to be traitorous. He ambushed them under a banner of peace in what had become known as the Madrona Massacre. Mira, Sumara and Alastair were among the survivors.

Mira spoke up. "I'll never forget climbing over that wall, seeing Daro reaching up for me. I thought I was dead and then there he was."

"We all thought we were dead," Alastair said.

"How did you get out?" Edson asked, his glance roving around the table.

"It was chaos," Alastair said. "Hadran's men attacked without warning, killing people and setting fire to everything. I don't think Hadran expected anyone to get out, but a few of us did."

"Daro and I came running to help when we saw the smoke," Cecily said, her voice quiet. "We had almost left the town before the conclave began. As soon as I heard Hadran would be at the Keep, I wanted to leave. A problem with one of our horses kept us longer than we'd planned."

"There wasn't much we could do," Daro said. "We grabbed as many survivors as we could and ferried them into the woods. Hadran's men rampaged through that poor town, burning most of it to the ground." He put an arm around Cecily's shoulders. He knew it was hard for her to relive those memories.

"That was a dark day," Alastair said, nodding slowly. "But not without its bright spots. Daro here did manage to save a certain man by the name of Rogan, and that certainly had important ramifications later."

Edson's eyes widened. "You saved the king?"

"He wasn't the king yet," Daro said. "We helped whoever we could that night."

"I can't forget the night we were all holed up in that cave, north of the city," Griff said, shaking his head. "We were so sure Hadran's soldiers were coming for us, we must have jumped at every sound."

"Or the night Callum snuck us all back into the city," Sumara said. "I recall Cecily was the only one willing to trust you when you hustled us down into your underground hiding place. The rest of us wondered if we would end up worse off than before."

Callum smiled. "Cecily, you always were my favorite," he said with a wink.

Daro took another swig of ale and listened as the companions recalled moments from the war. The strange, the surprising, the frightening and even the amusing. No one spoke of the truly bad memories, particularly the night that had ended the conflict. There was something sacred about the memories of that night, as though there were a silent agreement to leave them unspoken.

"It was a shame we had to fight, but I'm certain Halthas is stronger for it," Mira said. "I hate to think of what life would have been like if Hadran had kept the throne. Or if his son had taken it."

"No telling what kind of a king Prince Pathius would have made," Alastair said as he put down his mug.

"I doubt he would have been any better than his father," Cecily said. Daro glanced at his wife. She stared at the table. "I didn't know Pathius well, but I know Hadran was preparing him for the throne. Hadran's influence must have been strong."

"What happened to him?" Edson asked.

Alastair shrugged. "He died in the fighting."

Callum gestured with his hand. "Which certainly made the question of succession simpler."

"Callum, that's a terrible thing to say," Sumara said.

"Perhaps," Callum said. "That doesn't make it less true."

It was well into the night when Daro lumbered up the stairs, his head swimming from too much ale. His heart was full, the recollections vivid, but no longer quite so painful. The companions were like a family to him, tied together by shared experience and tragedy. Reliving their ordeals together dulled the edges of his memories, while assuring him it had all been real. A part of him longed for the days when their lives had intertwined. He didn't wish for war, but it had been difficult for all of them to return to a normal existence once the conflict had ended. Spending time with them reminded him they also felt the pull of their companionship and the challenges of putting their lives back together after everything they had seen and done.

As he lay in bed, Alastair's words from earlier in the evening rung in his ears. Sleep eluded him and he pondered whether his friend might be right. Was he hiding Cecily away? Had they run from their responsibilities? He pushed the thought away. The kingdom could bloody well run itself now. Rogan had plenty of good men; he had no need for Daro. Or Cecily. They would spend a few more days in the city and return to the contentment of their home.

As he had assured his wife, no one could take anything from them. The kingdom didn't have power over them anymore. No one did.

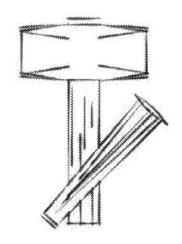

## 8 : LIFE TREE

DARO HUNG BACK AS Cecily ran her hands along a bolt of cloth. They were wandering through the central market in the north side of the city. Cecily loved to browse the stalls, searching for items to add to their home. She'd already bought a pair of silver candleholders that Daro had placed in his pack. He wasn't sure why they needed more candleholders, but he deferred to his wife on things of that nature. He didn't mind the market too much. It could get crowded, but Cecily knew how to keep him content. As long as he could stop and sample the sweetmeats, steaming meat pies, and other market delicacies, he was happy enough.

"What did you think of that one?" Cecily asked as they wandered away from the stall.

Daro popped another roasted nut into his mouth. "It was," he said with a pause, "nice?"

Cecily smiled and playfully hit his arm. "I'm serious. You're not paying attention."

"I'm running out of food," he replied.

She rolled her eyes. "Do you see what I have to deal with?" she asked Edson.

Edson walked alongside them. After several days in the city, he seemed to be getting used to the crowds and grandeur and had finally stopped gawking at everything. "Oh no, I'm not getting involved."

"Fine," Cecily said and tossed her hair behind her shoulder. "Neither of you are any help."

Something in a stall on the other side of the walk caught Daro's eye. "Here, what about these?" he asked, leading her to a table displaying beaded necklaces and other small ornaments. He took a set of hair pins with colorful ribbons attached to them. "These are pretty. What do you think?" He pinned a piece of her hair up, letting the ribbon cascade down the back of her hair.

Cecily touched the silky ribbon. "I don't know, they're a little girlish, don't you think?"

"I like them," Daro said and handed the craftswoman a coin.

Cecily fixed the hairpin, adjusting her hair a bit, and added the second one on the other side. "There," she said and turned around in a little circle.

She stopped suddenly and tilted her head to the side, looking past Daro, her attention on something further down the road. She met his eyes, nodding to where she'd been looking.

Daro turned to see three Imaran men walking past, a short distance away. They were far taller than any Halthian, taller even than Daro. They all had similar dark hair and olive skin and wore the customary Imaran clothing Daro remembered from his youth. Their hip-length shirts that wrapped around their chest, held tight with a tie around the waist, created an asymmetrical line down their front and left their muscled arms bare. Their pants were loose fitting and cinched at their ankles, showing their short, supple brown shoes. Loose cloaks hung down behind them, with wide hoods that hung down their backs. The colors were muted greens and browns, soft in comparison to much of what was worn by the Halthians. They looked at Daro and he could see their bright, silver eyes. Their gazes rested on him for a moment and they spoke a few, quick words to each other before moving on.

Cecily put her hand on his arm. "Do you think they know who you are?"

"Maybe. I'm the only Imaran I know of who doesn't actually live in Imara, so I suppose I'm a bit obvious," he replied.

"Do you have any contact with the Imarans?" Edson asked.

Daro shook his head. "Not for a long time. After I went to live with my Halthian aunt and uncle, one or two of them would occasionally come and ask about me. But after I left there, I didn't see them very often. Only times like this," he said, as he gestured in the direction they had gone.

Daro wanted to change the subject. He touched Cecily's elbow and gave her a light nudge. "Let's show Edson the Life Tree. There used to be that great bakery right across the way. We can't come to the city and not get one of those sweet buns."

"The sweet buns," Cecily said to Edson as she shook her head. "He remembers the Life Tree because of the sweet buns. Really Daro, I think you could navigate the city entirely by the food."

He grinned as she tucked her hand in the crook of his elbow. "Yes, my love, I think you're right."

They walked along the street, leaving the busy market behind, and turned onto a smaller side road.

The Life Tree was in the center of Northern Halthas, a short walk from the market. They emerged onto a large courtyard of stone, the tiles making a cascading pattern of lights and darks that emanated out from the center. In the midst of the courtyard stood the Life Tree, bordered by a low wall of stone that encased it in a large planter.

Edson's eyes widened and his mouth hung open. Daro smiled. Everyone gawked at the Life Tree, especially the first time they saw it.

For all intents and purposes, it looked like an enormous living tree. The first branches shot out about ten feet from the ground, curving downward at the tips, drawn down by the weight of their leaves. The leaves themselves were spread out almost like a hand, with five points on each, and they seemed to turn in the wind. The entire tree always appeared to be moving, rustling in the wind, swaying and shifting. The leaves seemed to turn color as the light hit them, making them appear to shift and move. But the Life Tree was not alive, nor was it a tree. It was stone.

"It looks so real," Edson whispered.

"Yes, it does," Cecily answered.

"Did the Imarans really make this?" Edson asked.

Daro nodded. "They did, hundreds of years ago. The stories say the Imarans brought the stone and carved it right here in the center of the city, as a gift to Halthas."

"How did they do that?" Edson asked, his voice still filled with awe.

"I wish I could tell you," Daro answered as he gazed at the Tree. The apparent movement of the leaves was almost hypnotic. He always tried to see the Life Tree for what it was, lifeless stone. But he could never make his eyes believe. The harder he stared, the more lifelike it seemed.

"No one in Halthas really understands how they did it," Cecily said. "I think even the scholars at the Lyceum gave up a long time ago."

They all moved closer to the Tree to get a better look. Edson walked around and peered at it closely. "I can't imagine how they made it look so alive. You said they brought in the stone? It doesn't look like any stone I've ever seen."

"No, it isn't," Cecily answered. "I'm no expert on stone, but it doesn't feel like anything I'm used to."

"Come closer, I want to show you something," Daro said as he beckoned to Edson. They all walked to the edge of the Tree's enclosure. The low wall surrounding it was the perfect height for sitting, and they all took a seat, following Daro's lead. "Close your eyes," he said.

They closed their eyes. Daro took a deep breath as calm washed over him. The Life Tree emanated a feeling of peace and tranquility that was even more surprising to most people than its lifelike appearance.

"That's incredible," Edson said quietly. "This is no Shaper trick."

"No," Daro said and took another deep breath. He could almost smell the fresh scent of wildflowers. "Imarans don't have Shapers. They don't have Wielders, either. They're just"—he paused—"Imarans."

"Am I supposed to feel so relaxed?" Edson asked.

"Most people do, especially this close," Cecily said. "Just another reason they call Halthas the City of Wonders."

They basked in the tranquility of the Life Tree for a while, looking up at the shifting leaves and studying the branches. The Life Tree was the one place in Halthas that Daro genuinely loved. Cecily always told him it must remind him of his earliest days, when he'd lived with his parents in Imara. Perhaps she was right, although he couldn't remember anything there that looked like this.

A smell tickled Daro's nose, and he remembered the sweet buns. As much as he enjoyed the Life Tree, it would be a shame to leave the city without one.

Daro licked the cinnamon off his fingers as they approached Griff and Serv's warehouse. His former employers came out to greet them. Griff's face lit up with his usual smile, and Serv gave a quiet nod.

"Everything is ready," Griff said and clapped Daro on the back in greeting. "You'll be leaving tomorrow?"

Daro nodded. "We have a long trip ahead of us. If we're lucky, the weather will be kind, but I'm not counting on it."

"As well you shouldn't," Griff answered. "Autumn is nearly upon us. Listen, Daro," he said as he came in closer and gave a half glance over at Edson. "I have a bit of a proposition for you."

Daro chuckled. He had spent many years working for Griff and Serv as the head of their merchant guard before he'd met Cecily. "Proposition? Should I be nervous?"

Griff put a hand on his shoulder as they walked into the warehouse building, leading him away from the others. "No, no, nothing like that," he said. "But I was wondering if you might be able to spare Edson for a while. We're making a trip north into Thaya and we could use another set of hands. We won't be going far past the Halthian border, mind you. Too chaotic up there these days. But two of my men quit just yesterday, and finding good replacements is a hard thing. A hard thing indeed." He turned to face Daro and put his thumbs in his jeweled belt. "I was thinking, perhaps your young man there might fancy a trip through the North Mountains. See a few things along the way. We both know how good travel is for a man, learn the ways of the world a bit better."

Daro smiled. He couldn't help but agree. He had traveled extensively with Griff and Serv, and those years had done much to shape the man he had become. "Doesn't sound like a bad notion," he said. "But we'll have to ask Edson what he thinks. If he'd like to join you, he's welcome to. I agree, it would be good for him."

"Excellent," Griff said. "And you know, there isn't a finer swordsman than Serv this side of the mountains. A little time with him and our young friend will be a force to be reckoned with." Daro nodded and the men shook hands. "Thank you, my friend," Griff said.

"Of course," Daro said, before walking away to find Edson and Cecily.

Edson proved to be enthusiastic about the idea, so the arrangements were made. He would stay in Halthas with Griff and Serv and accompany them on their next journey to Thaya. The group would travel east to Norgrost Keep after their journey and promised to bring Edson home along the way.

"I'm going to miss him," Cecily said as they walked back to their inn, the shadows growing long as the sun dipped low on the horizon.

Daro put his arm around her and nodded. "Me too. It will be a bit quieter without him around."

"I hope he'll be okay. Isn't there a lot of fighting in Thaya?"

"There might be, but they won't go too far across the border. There is a small city just on the other side of the mountains, Surat. I don't think they ever go farther than that. Serv won't go, at any rate."

Cecily looked up at him, her eyebrows lifted. "Really? Why? He's from Thaya, isn't he?"

"He is, but he never goes back. He's never talked about it, and I don't ask."

They kept walking and Cecily was quiet for a moment. "How did I not know that about him?"

Daro shrugged. "We all have secrets, I suppose." He felt Cecily stiffen, but he didn't ask what troubled her. He knew she carried a few secrets of her own and never tried to pry them out of her. He knew enough about her life before they met to realize that some things needed to stay in the past.

He hugged her close. She threaded her arm around his waist and they walked back to their inn, enjoying the comfortable silence. They had a long journey ahead of them the next day. Although their visit to Halthas had been a relatively pleasant one, he was more than ready to leave the city behind for the open road.

## 9 : A PEBBLE IN THE ROAD

Cecily swayed with the motion of the wagon as it traveled down the road. Puffy white clouds drifted across the sky, barely visible through the gap in the trees above their heads. The forest pressed in on either side, creeping toward the road as if it intended to overtake it. Tall moss-covered fir trees towered over them, their limbs crowded together to dilute the sunlight, and leafy ferns reached their fronds toward the gray stone of the road.

She reached her arms up to stretch. They had spent the night in a modest inn at a crossroads a day's journey from Halthas. The bed had been small and cramped, and her neck was stiff. She looked forward to spending a more comfortable evening at Merrick's cabin. His home was simple, but cozy.

"We're making good time," Daro said and glanced at her as she stretched. "The turnoff to Merrick's isn't far from here."

Cecily rubbed her eyes and leaned against Daro's arm. "We could cut south tomorrow and catch a riverboat to East Haven," she said. "It would cut some time off our journey."

He shrugged. "We'll be home before you know it."

The overland route took longer, but she knew Daro preferred it to the confinement of the riverboat. She sighed and looked out over the thick forest. The branches closed above them, creating a tunnel of green and brown. She had to admit, the view was lovely.

A loud blast rang out and the force of the explosion tossed Cecily through the air. She rolled as she hit the ground, then sprang to her feet. Dust and bits of rock flew everywhere, obscuring her vision, and her ears rang. She shook her head to clear it and slammed open her Awareness, searching for the source of the attack. She could sense Daro on the other side of the road, picking himself up and looking around.

She couldn't feel anything with her Awareness, just the trees, the underbrush and the terrain. Their wagon was upturned, leaning against a tree on the far side of the road. One of their horses was dead, the other already gone, running down the road. She backed up, stepping one foot behind the other to put a tree behind her.

A ripple in her Awareness caught her attention. Someone was there, but they were managing to hide from her. A Sensory Wielder, and a powerful one. He was Shielding his presence. Now that she knew what to look for, she could sense two more ripples. There were at least three of them.

Something flew toward her and she used her Reach to Push it away. A glowing-hot piece of rock exploded where it hit, sending up a spray of dirt. She could see the Wielder now, across the road just behind the tree line. He was masked and dressed all in black. With a strong Push, she slammed into him with her Reach. He stumbled backward but didn't lose his feet, and he raised his arm to throw.

Another rock, glowing orange and red, sped toward her and she barely managed to Push it aside. Debris flew as it exploded and she threw up her arms to protect herself.

Daro ran toward the masked rock Wielder, his sword drawn. Sensing movement on her side of the road, Cecily drew back into the trees. The ripples in her Awareness coalesced into figures as the Sensor dropped his Shield. One was near the rock Wielder, hanging back in the trees. The Sensor himself was up the road from her, standing in the low brush just off the side of the road. She peeked out from behind her tree. He was also dressed in black, his face hidden by a mask. He held a bow, the string pulled back.

The arrow raced forward and she could feel the air it displaced as it sliced toward her. She ducked back behind the tree but the arrow curved, arcing around the tree trunk in an impossible path. She Pushed it away with her Reach and it stuck into a tree trunk. *How did he do that?* He was a Sensor—he couldn't be using Precision. It wasn't possible.

He proved her wrong as he shot another arrow that wound through the trees. She Pushed it, trying to knock it off course, but it didn't veer away as a typical arrow should. It pushed back against her, the other Wielder's Precision vying with her Push to keep it on course. She managed to make it miss, but it brushed by her face so close she could feel the whoosh of air as it sliced by.

Cecily could sense Daro across the road, crossing swords with the rock Wielder. The third man still hung back; she briefly wondered why he wasn't attacking when she caught a glimpse of the Sensor as he darted amongst the trees. *Fine. I can play this game.* Ducking behind a tall fir tree, she put her back to the rough bark and centered her Awareness on him to quickly feel him out. As he lifted his bow again she Reached, using Pressure to weaken his grip. He shook his hand as Cecily breathed deep to keep her concentration. Finding his wrist, she applied Pressure again. His hand convulsed and he nearly dropped his bow.

He cried out as she Pushed harder. With a quick flick of her Wielding Energy, she hit his knees with Pressure. As she held him she could feel his energy set against hers, Pushing back as he tried to Shield himself against her. If he could wedge her Awareness back far enough, she'd have to let go. *How is he doing this?* He cried out again as she Pushed, tightening the Pressure on his knees.

His grip on her Wielding Energy tightened and she could feel him Push back against her. Sweat beaded on her forehead and ran down her back. She threw more energy at him, Pushing him down, but he surged back, breaking her Wield.

As soon as her Pressure was gone, he jumped to his feet and nocked another arrow. It flew toward her, darting around the trees. She Pushed at the arrow, fighting its enhanced momentum. He shot again and she tried to Push the arrows off course as she ducked behind another tree. One arrow swung wide, but the other sliced across her shoulder, ripping through her flesh in a sharp ribbon of pain.

Fury and pain surged inside her and she Reached for the Sensor and hit him with a Push before he could fire another arrow. With a tight grip on his wrist, she clamped him with Pressure. He cried out, dropping his bow, but slammed her with a Push of his own. The blow made her falter, and she lost her Pressure grip, her shoulder burning. His Wielding Energy wrapped around her chest and squeezed, the Pressure from his Wield crushing the air from her lungs. She gasped for breath and Pushed back, assaulting his grip and forcing him to let go.

Gritting her teeth with the effort, she grabbed his knees with Pressure and Pushed as hard as she could. The Pressure made him stumble and she hit his ankles with her Reach, sweeping his feet out from under him. He landed on his back with a grunt and she hit him with another Push, smashing the air from his lungs. With a gasp, he tried to get up but she hit him with another Push, slamming his head onto the ground, knocking him unconscious.

Another explosion rang out and she flung open her Awareness. The third man still hung back in the trees. *Why aren't you attacking?* Daro was on his knees, picking himself up, his sword still in his hand. Cecily darted for the road, breathing hard. The rock Wielder threw a hot rock and it exploded near her feet, leaving a small crater in the road. As shards of rock blasted by her legs, the sharp pieces tore her leggings and embedded into her skin. Blood trickled down her arm, and her legs stung with pain as she stumbled backward from the force of the blast.

Daro charged the Wielder and their swords clashed with a metallic ring. Daro thrust, and the Wielder blocked while he dug into a pouch at his waist. He tossed another rock, which Daro smacked with his sword, sending it flying as it burst apart with a loud pop.

Cecily Reached, gripped the Wielder's sword, and Pulled to send his arm swinging wide. He stepped around and threw another rock at her, rotating his sword in time to block Daro's strike. Cecily dove back into the brush as the rock exploded, hitting her with debris.

She got up and lurched back to the road as a crackling line of frost raced across the stone toward her. The third figure stood against the tree line, black against the brush behind him. His face was covered, nothing showing but the slit around his eyes. He lifted his hand and the air around him shimmered, the frost spreading wide. The plants at his feet withered and turned brown, their leaves curling inward. Daro and the rock Wielder still fought, the clang of their swords ringing in the air. He threw another rock but Daro jumped to the side and came down with his blade, hitting the other man hard.

Cecily hesitated and watched the man across the road. The plants around him continued to wither, crusting over with frost. She'd never seen anything like it. Was he some kind of Absorption Wielder? She'd never seen one so strong.

Daro spun, and his sword smashed against the rock Wielder's blade. He drove the man backward as he swung relentlessly. Cecily's eyes flicked back to the man across the road and she shot her Reach toward him.

He lifted his hand and she flew backward through the air. It felt as if something had exploded in her chest and her Awareness came crashing in. She hit the ground in a blast of pain that was quickly swallowed in blackness.

Cecily heard muffled voices, distant, as if heard through a closed door. Someone was saying her name.

Her body felt watery, useless. She couldn't open her eyes, couldn't make sense of what was happening. Her mind was fuzzy and confused. Where was she? She heard her name again, but it sounded strange, like it should belong to someone else. She struggled to breathe. Her lungs felt seared, but not by heat. They felt frozen, burning with cold as if they were caked with ice.

She opened her eyes, her mind groggy, and her breath misted out in a cloud. She blinked against the light and winced at the pain. Something in the back of her mind told her to look, to Reach out, to see. But she was too weak to Wield, to open her Awareness even a fraction of an inch.

She tried to move, but something was on her chest, holding her down. A boot. *That's odd. Where did that come from…?*

"… won't hurt her… weapon down… come with us…" Snatches of words broke through the haze, but she couldn't understand what they meant.

As she turned her head, she was finally able to focus enough to recognize who she was looking at. Daro. He slowly lowered his sword, laying it on the ground, his arms outstretched. "Just let her go."

The boot lifted off her chest. She couldn't see anything and realized she'd closed her eyes. The blackness felt so nice, so quiet. Maybe she would stay here, just a while longer.

"Cecily!" Daro's voice again.

She forced her eyes open. Things were starting to come back, make sense. She blinked and looked at Daro.

"See? She will be fine. In an hour or so, she'll be back on her feet. Just come with us, and she goes free." A man was standing over her, his face covered with a black mask. He looked down at her, his eyes an unnatural swirl of colors, brown and blue mixed with green. She blinked to clear her vision, but his disturbing eyes remained the same. They seemed to shine from the blackness of his cowl. "Or I can finish her now." He held his palm outstretched over her.

"No," Daro said, his voice thick with alarm. He held his hands up in front of him and locked eyes with Cecily. "No," he said again, barely above a whisper. His face was pure anguish. Cecily had never seen that look on his face, and it terrified her.

Other figures swam into view, two other men in masks. One approached Daro and placed a hand on his arm. The blackness threatened to overtake her. Her lungs burned and her eyes went in and out of focus. Nothing made sense. She blinked, her eyelids heavy. Someone was speaking again but she couldn't make it out. Daro gave a small nod. Panic arose deep inside, but she was too weak to move. Daro looked at her, his jaw clenched tight. He squeezed his eyes shut and turned away, letting the man lead him out of her sight. She tried to take a breath and cry out but her lungs burned and she felt herself slipping down, back into the dark, into nothing.

## 10 : ON THE RUN

Cecily looked up and blinked. Tall trees crowded above her, bits of sunlight peeking through. Everything looked unnaturally bright and she raised her hand to her forehead to shade her eyes from the light. Her arm felt heavy and awkward, and her mind swirled with confusion.

Panic seized her and she struggled to sit up. *Daro. Where is Daro?* Vague images flashed through her mind: Daro putting down his sword, his face full of anguish; someone leading him away. She sat up, pressed her palms to her face, and fought through the weak, sick feeling. She took a few deep breaths, her lungs still burning as if they'd been frozen and were taking their time in thawing.

She glanced around and turned her head to look up at the sky. The forest was thick but she could see the sun glinting through the boughs above. She hadn't been unconscious long—it was still midday. She took another breath to calm herself and opened her Awareness. Even with just a small circle, the image was fuzzy and uncertain. What had they done to her?

As she struggled to her feet, she looked around again. Little lines of blood ran down her stinging legs and her left arm was heavy with pain. Her bloody shirt stuck to her shoulder. She tucked her injured arm close to her body and left the road, seeking the relative shelter of the trees.

Holding her Awareness open took effort, and her body felt sluggish and frail. She pushed it out, desperately hoping to find some sign of Daro and his captors. The Sensor would be hiding their movements, so she concentrated, looking for any signs of rippling, but found nothing. A knot of fear grew as she realized Daro was gone. She leaned her back against a tree and closed her eyes.

Strength seeped back into her body, and her mind drifted into focus. Instinct told her to move. She could still be in danger. Someone might be coming back to finish her off. It was what she would do—send someone back to tie up the loose ends.

She limped through the trees, heading east, and held her Awareness open as far as she could. Her circle widened as her Wielding Energy gradually returned. Her breath came easier and she moved quickly through the brush, fear pushing her on.

A figure appeared at the edge of her Awareness, as if materializing from nothing. Instinctively, she dropped to the ground. Three arrows sliced past and stuck into a tree behind her, each with a dull thud. She crawled across the ground on her belly and scurried behind another large tree. *Loose end, indeed.* She had him in her Awareness, could sense him readying another arrow. He took a few steps toward her, his bow raised.

Keeping still, her heart pounding, she barely dared to breathe. She was still weak and wasn't sure what she could manage against this strange adversary. Another arrow flew by, followed by another as he kept moving toward her. *He's trying to draw me out.* As she felt him move closer, she waited.

With a flick of her Reach, she snapped a twig behind a nearby tree. Her pursuer stopped and turned in the direction of the noise. She held her breath and kept silent. After a pause, she Reached again and Pushed down on the underbrush, making the leaves rustle. He was in her vision now, angling off toward the sound. Holding her position, she waited for him to get closer.

As she Pushed a pile of dead leaves, she swished them across the dirt and cracked another twig behind the next tree, hoping it sounded as if she'd dashed to a new hiding spot. Seeming to follow her ruse, he took careful steps toward the sound. She could see him clearly now; he wasn't ten feet away.

Springing from her hiding spot, she threw her Wielding Energy around his throat and squeezed, slamming him with Pressure. She grasped him as tightly as she could, squeezing with all the force she could muster. He dropped his bow, and his hands lurched to his neck. She Pushed harder, clenching her teeth against the pain in her shoulder.

She was too weak to keep her grip on him and he rounded on her, snarling behind his mask. He had unnatural eyes, several bright colors swirling together around his black pinprick of a pupil. As he lunged toward her, she jumped to the side to avoid his wild advance. She struck him with her elbow as he passed, but he turned and grabbed her arm. Twisting, she gripped his wrist with Pressure. With a shout, he let go of her arm, but swung with his other fist, striking her hard across the face. Pain erupted in her cheek as her lip split open and blood ran down her chin.

He grabbed her from behind and wrapped his arms around her. Throwing her head backwards, she hit him in the face. Despite the blow, he held on, so she threw her weight forward and bent over as far as she could. He slammed his Wielding Energy into her but she Pushed back, making him lose his footing. They both stumbled and rolled over each other on the ground. With a kick, she broke his hold, then scrambled back to her feet, dirt and dead leaves clinging to her. She tried to pin him down with Pressure, but she was too spent to hold him. He struggled up, growling in frustration.

Without a thought for direction, she turned and ran. Darting in and out of the trees, she knew her pursuer was close behind. As she looked ahead, she grabbed random bits of forest debris with her Reach and tossed them behind her, hoping to make the Sensor at least stumble and put more distance between them.

With gasping breaths and burning legs, she leaped over a fallen log and Reached to toss another branch behind. The footfalls of her pursuer still followed. She didn't risk a look behind and was too weak to open her Awareness. It felt like running blindfolded.

The sound of rushing water roared nearby and she veered toward it. Something hard pelted her in the back and nearly sent her sprawling, but she kept her feet and pushed harder as she ran toward the water.

The forest opened up and she skidded to a halt at the edge of a ravine, the churning water of a river below her. The drop was twenty feet straight down. She darted a quick look over her shoulder and saw the Sensor. He'd picked up a straight, pointed stick and drew his arm back to hurl it at her.

She pushed off the edge of the drop and leaped into the air, her feet slipping on the loose soil, sending rocks and dirt falling. As the water rushed toward her, she desperately Wielded, using every ounce of energy she had left and Pushed against the water, hoping to slow her descent. She pulled in her legs and gripped them with her hands as she splashed into the icy water.

The freezing glacial melt knocked the breath out of her as she plunged downward. Trying to kick up, she pushed against the riverbed to the air above, but her legs barely moved. The freezing water assaulted her, sucking the heat from her body. She struggled to the surface and felt the rushing water pull her downstream. Her head broke the surface and she took a gasping breath. As she turned to look, she could see the Sensor still standing on the cliff side, watching her until the river quickly took her around a bend, out of sight.

## 11 : SOLACE

Cecily dragged herself from the water onto the riverbank, shivering uncontrollably. She'd ridden the current downstream until the sides of the ravine sloped downward, gradually lowering to meet the level of the river below. As the river widened, the current slowed and she was able to struggle to the side and haul herself up onto the muddy bank.

She coughed and spit up water as she crawled out of the mud on her forearms and knees. Her fingers were stiff and useless from the cold, her body convulsing with violent shivers. With chattering teeth, she turned over and sat on the dirt a few feet out of the water. Her clothes hung off her, wet and heavy, and water dripped from her hair, onto her face and down her back.

She hoped the Sensor had been left far behind, but she couldn't be sure. She'd stayed in the river as long as she could stand, moving faster than someone on foot. As she stood, she stumbled on her numb feet. She needed to get warm, but as she looked around, she wasn't sure how.

With a shuddering breath, she wrapped her arms around herself and opened her Awareness. Despite her freezing body, her Wielding Energy was returning, her image of the surrounding area sharp. Though she couldn't feel any sign of her attacker, she didn't assume he was gone. If he was tracking her down the river, he'd be Shielding. She pushed outward, looking for anything that might help her. There was nothing. The forest spread around her, only tall pines and ivy, low ferns and moss.

She felt an overwhelming desire to lie down and close her eyes, but something told her she wouldn't get up if she gave into that dark temptation. Her first thought was to get away from the river, so she dragged herself along on numb feet, arms tucked into her body. Her vision grew blurry and her knees would scarcely bend, leaving her feet to scrape along the dirt as she walked.

One step at a time was all she could do. She was sure each stride would be her last, that her leg would slide forward, only to crumple, and she would fall to the ground. Somehow she kept her feet and continued forward, step after painful step, away from the river.

Her mind felt numb and nothing seemed to exist but the dirt under her feet. She forced herself to keep moving despite the violent shivers that wracked her body. A noise in the distance caught her attention, the sound of running feet, a body brushing past leaves and underbrush. She dragged her foot forward and leaned into her step. Her leg finally gave out and she collapsed to the forest floor. The footsteps raced closer, but her hazy mind was too weak with exhaustion to Wield.

A sharp bark rang out through the trees. She pushed herself up to her hands and knees as something darted in front of her. She blinked hard and looked up through her bedraggled hair. A large dog jumped around her, dark brown with a bushy black tail, tall pointy ears, and a long muzzle topped with black. He barked again, turning as if he called to someone, and circled back around to sniff at Cecily's face.

"Beau?" she said, her voice hardly more than a breath.

Beau barked and shuffled around her on his huge paws. He leaned in to sniff her again and let out a low whimper in his throat. She clenched her teeth and lowered herself to the ground, still shaking. "Good boy, Beau," she whispered, her voice rattling with her shivers. "Go get Merrick."

Beau barked again and she heard a voice calling back to him through the trees. "Beau!" Footsteps rushed toward her and she forced herself to keep her eyes open. "Oh gods, Cecily?"

She felt something soft settle on top of her and strong arms pull her up off the ground. "Merrick?" she said.

"Stay with me," Merrick said. "I've got you."

"Daro," she whispered.

"Okay," he said, "but we have to get you warm."

Cecily tucked herself into him, leaning her head against his shoulder, and rocked to the brisk rhythm of his footsteps. She drifted in and out of consciousness as he carried her. Occasionally, she felt him shift her weight in his arms and he spoke to keep her awake. After what felt like an eternity, they stopped and he slowly lowered her legs to the ground, keeping one arm around her. As she wavered on her feet, he opened the door to his cabin and ushered her inside.

Her teeth chattered painfully and her body shuddered as he pulled a chair up to the fire and draped it with a thick blanket. He unfastened her belt, helped her pull her freezing wet clothes off, and tossed them to the side. She winced as he pulled her tunic over her injured arm. He quickly wrapped the blanket around her and lowered her into the chair.

"Where's Daro?" he asked.

She tried to sit up. "I don't know," she breathed and clenched her teeth to keep them from chattering.

"Okay, sit back now," he said, his voice soothing as if he were speaking to a nervous animal. He gently pressed her back into the chair. He tucked the blanket around her and tossed more wood on the fire. Leaning her head back, she closed her eyes.

She heard the sounds of Merrick bustling about the cabin as she warmed next to the fire. Her shivering subsided as the heat melted into her body.

Merrick crouched down next to her and lifted her injured arm from inside the warm blanket. She felt his fingers gently press the skin around the wound but the effort to open her eyes was too great.

"This is going to hurt," he said. He held her arm out straight and gripped her wrist with a firm hand. She felt liquid trickle down her shoulder and flinched. "I know," he said, his voice gentle, "but I have to clean it." Her eyes fluttered open as he dabbed the wound with a cloth and the blistering pain began to dull. He pulled out a needle and she closed her eyes again. "It's deep. I have to stitch it closed." She nodded, set her jaw and held her arm still.

He dabbed a poultice over the stitches and wrapped her arm in a bandage. Her tight muscles relaxed as the heat of the fire soaked into her. Her shoulder ached, but it was no longer the searing pain of an open wound. He leaned down in front of her face and touched her chin to inspect her cheek and split lip. "This is going to look bad for a while, but it isn't serious." He gently probed her jaw, touching his fingers to her cheek and nose. "Nothing is broken."

He sucked in a breath when he saw her legs. "What in the name of the gods happened to you?" He picked up one leg and balanced it on his knee to pick out bits of stone. Cecily couldn't yet find the strength to answer. She let him dab her wounds with poultice and wrap her legs in bandages.

When he finished, he poured her a cup of hot tea. She held it in her hands and relished the warmth, keeping the blanket tucked around her. Beau laid down at her feet, watchful, his tall black ears twitching toward her. Merrick pulled up a chair and leaned forward, his elbows on his knees.

Relief and gratitude flooded Cecily as she looked at her friend. Merrick had a sturdy frame, chestnut hair and a light growth of stubble on his face and chin. His brown eyes had faint lines at their corners. Beau sat up next to him and Merrick reached out with a calloused hand to scratch behind his ears. His clothes were homemade, a beige tunic under a worn leather vest, dark brown pants and heavy boots. His brow furrowed in concern and he leaned forward. "What happened?" he asked.

Cecily adjusted the blanket and flexed her fingers, feeling the blood flow through her hands. "I don't know," she said, her voice quiet. Her lip hurt when she spoke. "We were attacked on the road. Something exploded and we both went flying. There were three of them, I think, powerful Wielders." She closed her eyes, and images of the men in their black masks floated through her mind. "They were dressed in black, their faces covered with masks. I couldn't see who they were."

"Do you know what happened to Daro?"

"They took him." Tears sprang to her eyes and a knot of fear tightened her stomach. "They left me behind and led him away."

Merrick hesitated, scratching his jaw. "But he was alive?"

"Yes. They said they would let me go, but someone came back and tried to finish me off. I lost him by jumping in the river." She took a shuddering breath. "These men weren't normal, Merrick. They could do things I've never seen before." She slumped in her chair and leaned her head back, her exhaustion overwhelming. "How did you find me?"

"I didn't. Beau found you. We were here at home, and he started barking and pawing at the door. I let him out and he took off toward the road. I followed and I hadn't gone far when I started hearing something, booming sounds, coming from the road. By the time I got there, no one was left, but I could see someone had been attacked. I read the signs and followed your trail all the way to the river. It wasn't easy, but I could still see your trail of energy in the water. We followed the river until Beau finally caught up with you."

Cecily shook her head. Merrick's Wielding ability allowed him to sense the energy signature of any living thing. He was the best tracker she knew. "We need to find Daro's trail."

"I know, but you're hurt. You need to lie down," Merrick said. He helped her up and led her toward his bedroom. Her legs felt shaky and she leaned on him for support. He laid her down and covered her with blankets, tucking them in around her.

"No," she said, her voice weak, "I can't sleep now. I have to find him."

"I know," he said softly. "We'll find him. But you need sleep first."

She fought to keep her eyes open but her body betrayed her. She lay back onto the soft pillow, her eyes fluttered shut, and she sank into an exhausted sleep.

Something cold and wet tickled Cecily's face. She awoke with a start, greeted by the snuffling nose of Beau. He laid his chin on the bed in front of her face, and his black eyes looked at her. His large black ears moved around, twitching toward her and turning behind. She smiled. "Hey Beau, good boy." He sniffed again, made a throaty noise, and sat up, as if he expected something.

Cecily cringed as she hauled herself up. She shrugged her shoulders and carefully rolled her arm backward. Her wound ached and the stitches pulled against her skin. Although her legs were sore and wobbly, she swung them around the side of the bed and stood up. Her head hurt and she reached up to touch her face, probing her lip and cheek. It was swollen and tender. She briefly wondered what she looked like, but decided she'd rather not know.

Her clothes were clean and dry, laid out on the end of the bed. She dressed, carefully pulling her tunic over her bandaged shoulder. She pulled the wrappings off her legs. The wounds were shallow, the worst ones already scabbed over.

Beau stood and stepped in front of her, his ears straight up, bushy tail wagging. "Where's Merrick?" she asked. Beau barked once and led her out into the main part of the cabin. The fire crackled and Merrick had left food sitting out on the table, but he was nowhere to be seen. She peeked out the window and wondered how long she'd been asleep. Sunlight filtered down through the trees. It looked to be midmorning.

Worry for Daro rose in her mind. She assured herself that Merrick must be out looking for him and forced herself to take care of necessities. Her stomach felt hollow and raw, as if it had been days since she had eaten. She ladled a bowl of soup and tore off a chunk of brown bread. Beau lay down next to the table and kept his eyes on her.

Beau's ears perked up and he lifted his head toward the door. "Is he coming home?" Cecily asked. The dog barked and a few seconds later, the door opened.

"Good, you're up," Merrick said as he walked in and shut the door behind him.

"Did you find the trail?" Cecily asked, unable to find patience.

"How are you feeling?" he said.

She waved her hand. "I'm fine. Did you find anything?"

Merrick unfastened the clasp of his cloak and tossed it to the side. "No."

"Nothing? No sign of where they went?"

He sat down in a chair across the table and Beau laid his head in his lap. "Not only was there no trail, there is no sign of you ever having been there. I saw the road the day you were attacked. There were holes and chunks of rock missing, the remains of your wagon, plenty of evidence of what happened there. Today, there's nothing."

"That doesn't make sense," Cecily said.

"No, it doesn't. I've been searching for two days and I can't find a trace."

Cecily dropped her bread. "Two days? I slept for two days? Oh gods, Merrick. Daro could be anywhere by now."

He put his hand out. "I know. Don't panic yet."

"How could there be nothing? There has to be some sign."

Merrick shook his head. "The road smells like it's been Swept clean. There's a gap, as if nothing touched the road for an entire day. That isn't normal. Even if there was no foot traffic, something would cross; bugs, small animals. Whoever did it was good. Very good. If I didn't know to look, I wouldn't have noticed the anomaly. I've met Sweepers before, but never one who could erase that much violence."

Cecily's mouth hung open and her stomach turned over. She pushed her bowl away, her appetite gone. She stared down at the table, unsure of what to do next. It hadn't occurred to her that Merrick might not find the trail.

"I don't know what I'm going to do," she said.

Beau trotted over and put his head in her lap. She scratched the top of his head.

"Beau wouldn't leave you alone, you know," Merrick said. "He sat there and watched you, the whole time you were asleep. Wouldn't come with me when I left."

She smiled and scratched his ears a little harder. "Sweet boy." The scabs on her legs itched and her shoulder ached. She sighed and looked around the cabin as if it held the answer. She couldn't follow the trail if there wasn't one. Even if she could, she didn't know what she'd find at the end of it. She needed help.

"I have to go back to Halthas," she said.

"Cecily, you're still injured, and I don't just mean that shoulder wound. Whatever they did to you, it knocked you out for days. You have to be careful."

"I don't have time to be careful. The longer I wait, the farther away Daro could be. I have to find out who took him, and why."

Merrick stood up. "I'll take you back to Halthas. Tomorrow, but only if you're strong enough." She opened her mouth to argue, but he put up a hand to cut her off. "No, don't argue. I won't risk your life on a hard ride back to the city. We can leave at first light. Not before."

Cecily sighed, feeling felt like a chastised child. Merrick turned and grabbed his cloak. He left out the door, Beau at his heels, leaving her no room to argue.

She had to admit, he was probably right. She still felt weak. She wasn't certain she could ride a horse, let alone make the two-day journey back to the city. But the waiting felt like it might kill her. She pulled her bowl of soup back in front of her and took a sip. If she was stuck there, she ought to do what she could to get her strength back. It would be a long ride back to the city, but she knew who she needed to see when she got there.

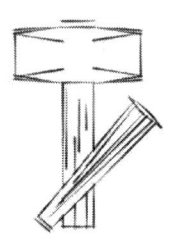

## 12 : NEW LODGINGS

DARO SQUEEZED HIS EYES together, and his stomach swirled with nausea. His head ached, and his mind was fuzzy. He breathed in slowly through his nose, and out again, finding his inner calm. His stomach still protested, but he felt in control of his body.

He moved with care, but he didn't seem to be injured. He wondered where he was and hesitated to open his eyes. Panic began to rise as Cecily sprang to his mind, the image of her lying in the road burned in his memory. He forced himself to relax when instinct insisted he get up and try to find her. He could feel through their bond that she was still alive. They'd held to their part of the bargain. That was something.

His hands and feet were bound and he tested the bonds, pulling his arms as far as they would go. The clink and scrape of metal told him he was in chains. He lay on his side, the surface beneath him hard. A dungeon, then.

He opened his eyes a crack and was surprised to see he was not in a cell. He was chained to the floor, but it was finished wood, not dirt or stone. The walls were paneled wood and the door looked ordinary. He turned his head and found a simple pallet bed with drab bedding and a pillow. It looked more inn than dungeon, aside from the chains bolted to the floor. Where was he?

His abductors hadn't given him a chance to discover who they were or where they were taking him. After he'd lost sight of Cecily, someone had touched him on the back as he walked. He'd felt the brief sensation of the breath being pulled from his lungs before everything went black. Then he'd woken up here, nauseous and sore and increasingly confused.

He turned toward the door at the sound of the lock clicking. The door eased open and Daro saw a pair of brown leather boots enter the room, the door closing behind. The light was dim; he couldn't see any windows. A woman knelt down next to him, holding a tray of food. He blinked slowly and looked at her, noticing her dark blond hair, tied back at the nape of her neck, and her sleek brown clothing.

She cocked her head to the side and looked at him. Her eyes were a swirl of brown mixed with blue, the two colors mingling around her dark pupil. Daro didn't like the way she looked at him, like a predator with captured prey. The corners of her mouth lifted in a smile, but her eyes remained cold. He would have to tread carefully with this one.

She set the tray on the floor near his face. He already knew the length of his chains; there was no way he could reach the food. He wasn't sure he wanted any. His stomach still protested, but the smell of the food woke hunger behind the nausea. He wondered how long he'd been unconscious.

The woman stayed motionless, watching him. He wondered if she expected him to speak but decided to stare back and remain silent. He buried his burning concern for his wife and his flurry of questions and let his mind go blank. Focus. One task at a time. She held all the power in this situation and he doubted demanding answers would avail him much. *Here I am. Your move.*

"Hmm." Her voice was deep, yet still feminine. "Are you injured?"

He couldn't place her accent, but she didn't sound Halthian. "No." Simple, direct. No more.

"Good." She sat down, crossing her legs, and scooted the tray out of the way. "I am Sindre, and you and I are going to get to know each other very well. Here is what we are going to do. I am going to let you eat today, but you have to be good for me." Her eyes flicked to the door. "None of that now. There is nowhere for you to go." Daro remained silent. "I would like to unlock your chains, but you have to be good, or I'm going to chain you up again. It is very difficult to eat with your hands bound."

Daro debated what to do. He had no idea where he was. He could be at the top of a tower, or deep in an underground cavern. If he did overpower this woman, he didn't know what would be outside the door—guards, weapons, a maze of hallways? He needed more information. And something told him he ought to eat. It would be more difficult to create an escape plan, let alone execute one, if he was weak from hunger.

He nodded once and waited.

She unlocked his chains. He sat up and rubbed his sore wrists, then silently ate the food she gave him, taking his time and trying to ignore her disconcerting stare. She sat across from him, motionless, watching with her strangely colored eyes. When he finished, she moved the tray to the side.

"We are so pleased you could join us," she said and pulled a necklace from inside her shirt. A flat disc of gray-and-green marbled rock hung from a thick silver chain. She fingered the rock, turning it over in her hand as she gazed at it. "We are doing important work here and your contribution will be extremely valuable. But for that, we need your cooperation." She met his eyes. "Your complete cooperation."

Daro remained silent. He had no intention of cooperating, but saw no reason to say so.

She continued rubbing the rock between her fingers. "I want you to understand from the beginning that it is not a matter of whether you will cooperate. It is only a matter of when. It would be easier for both of us if you come around quickly. But I don't think that will be the case, will it?"

She looked down at the dull rock in her hand and closed her grip around it. A spasm of pain shot from Daro's neck down his spine. He arched his back and clenched his teeth to keep from crying out. The pain vanished as quickly as it had hit and Daro sat, breathing heavily. The woman watched him with dispassionate eyes.

Something on the back of his neck felt warm and he reached behind his head, expecting to find blood. His fingers brushed something hard and cold at the base of his neck. As he probed with his fingers, his heartbeat quickened with alarm. A small, hard disc was embedded in his skin, the edges flush as if it had grown from the inside. It felt like a smooth stone but was shaped like an elongated diamond, the two shorter sides coming to a point at the top. He looked up at the woman. "What is this? What have you done?"

Her lips curled in another cold smile. "The means of your cooperation," she said. "And the way you will further our work."

Daro's fingers clutched at it, trying to find a way to dig it out of his skin. It was embedded too deep. His fingers brushed along the surface and scratched his skin.

"I suggest you stop," she said, her voice casual. "You will only hurt yourself."

Daro grabbed at it with his other hand, to no avail. Heat began to spread down his back, although the stone in his neck felt unchanged. The heat built and sweat began to bead on his forehead.

"Lower your hand," she said as she clutched the necklace in her fist.

Daro locked eyes with her, his hand still behind his neck. Her strange eyes narrowed and the heat intensified, sweat running down his back. He stayed motionless, refusing to give in.

"Fine," she said, and another stab of pain shot down his back. He flinched, grinding his teeth and grunting. The pain built, and he toppled to the side and writhed on the floor, clutching uselessly at the stone in his neck.

The pain disappeared and he was left panting.

"The faster you learn, the more productive our time together will be," she said. The pain spiked again and Daro cried out, despite his clenched teeth. The spasm was over in seconds but left him gasping in the wake of its intensity. "If you are good for me, I won't have to do this."

"What do you want from me?" he asked, between panting breaths.

"Cooperation," she said. "With time, you will learn to obey. And then, when you are ready, we will tap into the power inside you and unlock it."

"Power? I don't have any power."

"Oh, but you do." She trailed her fingers down his arm. "Whether you realize it or not."

Daro cringed at the woman's touch and struggled to sit up. "You can't keep me here."

"No? I think you'll find it exceedingly difficult to leave. Without me, and this," she said, holding up her medallion, "your implant will kill you. If you did get out, you might last a week, but no more." Daro's neck prickled. "The sooner you accept things the way they are, the better. You will learn. And I am afraid I don't have nearly as long as I would like to get you ready. I will have to accelerate our program. But I have high hopes for you. There is much work to be done, so best we get on with things, yes?"

She pulled some black fabric from inside her jacket. "We find it helps our subjects progress if we take certain steps. It helps them to accept their new life more readily."

"I don't care what you do to me. This is not my new life."

She smiled and smoothed out the fabric in her lap. "As I said, you will learn. Typically I wouldn't start with this, but the nature of things requires a certain haste." She held the fabric out to him. "Put it on." He stared at her, unmoving and silent. She hesitated a moment, her arm outstretched.

"Very well," she said.

Sharp pain flashed down Daro's spine again, radiating out into his arms and legs. It was intense, but he held his ground. He clenched his fists and locked his jaw. The pain vanished and the woman held the fabric out again.

"Put it on."

Daro said nothing and locked eyes with Sindre. She twitched and the pain returned. Heat spread from his neck and beads of sweat trickled down his back. He stared at a point on the wall and took deep breaths through his clenched teeth.

The pain ended and she once again held out the fabric. She spoke slowly, enunciating each word. "Put it on."

Daro remained still and his heart raced in anticipation. The pain hit like a blow from behind and he fell sideways, crying out despite his attempts to remain silent. He writhed on the floor, as agony spilled through his body. The sensation ended and he lay on the floor, panting.

"We have much to explore together, you and I," she said, her voice smooth. "It seems unpleasant at first, but you'll grow to appreciate what I do for you. We have so much to show you, so many gifts to give you. One day you will thank me." She stroked his hair back from his face. "Now, you will put this on."

Anger mingled with fear as Daro caught his breath. He sat up, set his jaw and stared at the wall. His muscles were tense and he waited, knowing the pain would come back. *I will not give in.*

She let out a heavy sigh. "You try my patience. I don't think you understand the position you are in."

Daro's body went slack and he slumped to the ground. He tried to move his arms to catch himself, but they wouldn't respond and he hit his head on the floor. His body was twisted in an awkward lump, but he couldn't move. His eyes darted around, and his breath came in quickening gasps as panic built. It was as if she had detached his body from his mind.

"You see," she said as she began to move, twisting him around to lie flat on his back, "I am in complete control. If you are good, you will be allowed to move freely. If not..." She paused and gripped the necklace again. "I do what must be done."

Daro's eyes strained to look sideways at Sindre. She leaned over him, picked up his head with one hand, and pulled the black fabric over his face. It was a mask that covered his head to his shoulders, with only a slit for his eyes. She adjusted the fabric so he could see, plucking at it with her fingers until it was fitted properly.

Daro struggled, desperately trying to force his arms and legs to move. He could feel the hard floor beneath him, his warm breath on the mask, but he couldn't move anything but his eyes. He blinked, as if moving the one responsive part of his body would somehow coax the rest into cooperation. But he couldn't so much as wiggle a toe.

"There, that wasn't so difficult, was it?" She sat back on her knees, almost out of Daro's field of vision. "Trust me when I say this is for the best. It will help you adapt." She leaned in close to his ear, her voice a soft whisper. "I mean it when I say I am looking forward to our time together. You are a most interesting subject."

She moved away from his face and the room went black. Daro blinked, squeezing his eyes shut and opening them again, to no avail. He saw nothing. His breath came in rapid gasps and his mind filled with a cloud of panic. His eyes darted up and down, but there was nothing, no light, form, or shadow. Only darkness. His unresponsive body lay limp on the floor, his mind desperately trying to regain control.

"I will leave you for now and I trust when I return, you will be ready to work together."

Inwardly he beat against the unyielding wall that bound him, and his mind was drenched in a soundless scream.

## 13 : AID OF THE CROWN

CECILY PULLED IN THE reins of her horse as she approached the palace gate. Merrick had accompanied her to Halthas, riding by her side and keeping her to a reasonable pace. The wait drove her mad. She knew each day that went by increased the chance of something horrible happening to Daro. But she was still recovering, and pushing herself to exhaustion wouldn't help. Merrick peeled off, leaving her at the gate, and headed toward the southern city to find rooms at an inn.

Two palace guards stood on either side of the Shaper-wrought black gate. One stepped forward and held his tall spear upright. "State your business."

"Lady Cecily Imaran, here to see the king," she replied. She kept her chin up, turned away and nudged her horse forward, as if there was no possibility of being denied entrance. Her body ached but she refused to let it show. She needed to be Lady Cecily, someone with every right to see the king without question. She didn't have the patience to explain herself to every guard in her way.

The guard nodded to someone on the far side and the gates swung open, revealing the inner courtyard. She kicked her horse forward.

The immaculate courtyard spread out before her. Master Garden Shapers had spent years cultivating the trees and plants, training them into intricate designs. The trees flowered year round, blossoms in shades of peach and white adorning the branches. Ivy trailed up stone pillars and over delicate arches. A wide stone walkway led to an enormous fountain in the center of the courtyard. Behind the fountain was a maze of hedges, trimmed to perfection.

The palace loomed above the courtyard. The central building was gleaming white stone, tall spires rising from the top. Gigantic stone lions stood at the four corners of the main structure. Legend held that the hill on which the palace complex stood had once been a mountain. Shapers had spent a hundred years training the rock, Shaping the palace out of the raw stone of the mountain. Cecily didn't know if that was true, or even possible, but even in her haste she couldn't help but admire the beauty of the imposing palace.

She dismounted and a groom took her horse's reins. She nodded to him and walked to one of the outer guards. "Lady Cecily Imaran. I am here to see King Rogan."

The guard glanced her up and down but opened the huge wooden door. "Wait here, milady," he said as they walked in.

The cavernous entry hall had a tall ceiling and a gleaming tile mosaic floor, the pale green and blue stones laid out in a circular pattern, the ancient symbol of Halthas. Cecily had stared at the pattern dozens of times on her visits to the palace, trying to find where it began and ended. It tricked the eye, seeming to be several different lines and one continuous line all at once. The ancient Shapers had apparently loved designs that appeared impossible; the old architecture was full of them.

The outer guard spoke with another man in uniform. "This way, milady," the second man said and gestured for her to follow.

He led her through a hallway and up a staircase, stopping outside a half-open door. "One moment, milady."

She crossed her arms and waited as he ducked into the room. He emerged and gave Cecily a polite nod as Alastair followed into the hallway.

Alastair's eyes went wide when he saw her face. "Cecily, what happened?"

"Please, I need to see the king."

"I believe he is in his study, but he may be occupied. Come in," he said, waving to his door. "Let me help."

"Someone took Daro. Alastair, they attacked us on the road and they almost killed me."

His mouth held open for moment before he spoke. "Yes, I daresay we need to see his Majesty."

She followed Alastair up another set of stairs to a set of closed double doors flanked by two uniformed guardsmen. In Hadran's day, they would have been in full armor, helmets and all. Rogan was a bit more practical, and far less paranoid. His guards wore swords at their sides but were without their heavy armor.

Alastair nodded to the guards, opened the door, and leaned his head inside. Cecily glanced down at her travel-stained clothes and wondered if she should have cleaned up before coming to the palace. Not that Rogan had never seen her in such a state; they had been through enough together in the war. She smoothed out her tunic and tucked her hair behind her ear as Alastair waved her inside.

Rogan's study was a large wood-paneled room with thick velvet curtains lining the windows. There were upholstered chairs set near the fireplace and a sturdy wood desk on the far wall. The tabletop was strewn with maps and papers and a round tray with a teapot and cup balanced precariously on one corner. Rogan himself sat behind the desk, in a beige doublet trimmed with gold. His dark brown hair was cut short, a sprinkling of gray showing at his temples, and a neatly trimmed beard framed his mouth. A winding circlet of gold sat on the desk.

He stood as they entered, folding a piece of paper and tucking it under a large map. "Cecily, this is a surprise."

"My apologies for disturbing you," Alastair said with a bow, "but the need was urgent."

Rogan walked forward and clasped Cecily's hands. "No need for apologies." His eyes rested on her face and his brow furrowed. "What happened to you? Please, sit down." He led her to an upholstered chair and she sat while he pulled up two more chairs for himself and Alastair.

"Your Highness, I know I didn't leave on good terms the last time I saw you. I want to apologize," Cecily said.

"Don't think about it another minute," Rogan said. "We will leave the past where it belongs. What's happened?"

"Daro and I were on our way home, about two days outside the city, when we were attacked on the road. There were at least three of them, dressed all in black and masked. I couldn't see any of their faces. We fought them, but"—she paused, unsure how to explain what she had seen—"they were very powerful Wielders. They did things that shouldn't be possible, things I've never faced before. One of them incapacitated me. It felt like he sucked the life right out of me. I was helpless. Daro was still fighting, but once they had me down, they threatened to kill me if he didn't leave with them. So he did." Her hands shook as she spoke, reliving every moment. "They led him away and I blacked out. Not long after I woke up, someone came back to kill me. I lost him, but I only survived because Merrick found me. As soon as I was strong enough, he brought me here."

Rogan's brow was drawn down and his lips turned in a frown. "Cecily, I am stunned." He got up, walked over to a window, and peered outside. "You did the right thing in coming to me," he said as he turned back to look at her. "What did Merrick find?"

"Nothing," she said, and his eyebrows rose. "He was as surprised as you are. They must have a Sweeper. They erased all signs that we'd been there. Our wagon was gone, and there wasn't the faintest hint of a trail. These men weren't normal, Rogan. There was something very wrong. I saw one of them up close and he had these eyes." She paused, trying to find the words to describe them. "They were unnatural, the colors all mixed. And they were bright, like a cat's eyes in the dark." A shiver went down her spine as she pictured the strange swirl of color.

Rogan rubbed his jaw. "This is quite troubling."

Alastair stood. "Should I assemble a contingent for a search?"

"No," Rogan answered. "I will handle this personally."

Alastair glanced at Cecily. "Of course, if that is what you think is best," he said.

"I do," Rogan said. He stepped in front of Cecily and offered his hand. She took it and rose from her seat. "You and Daro are among my most loyal friends. I will do everything I can to find out what happened to him."

She smiled, and some of the weight lifted from her shoulders. "Thank you." He let go of her hands and walked back to his desk. "Would you like me to send for Merrick or any of the others?" she asked. "Griff and Serv are likely still in the city. We saw all the companions just days ago. I'm sure they would be willing to help."

"That won't be necessary. I have men who can handle the details." He smiled. "You've been through a considerable ordeal. Alastair, could you please see that Cecily has proper accommodations? And ask the guards to be sure I am not disturbed until dinner."

Alastair touched Cecily's elbow and led her from the room. She followed in silence. Rogan had made no secret of his desire that she come back to Halthas, and the last time she had seen him, they had argued. She hadn't spoken to him since. His offer of help was a relief, but she walked away feeling unsatisfied. She'd thought he would send for their old companions to begin the search. His vague promise of help was less than what she wanted to hear.

She stopped in the midst of the hallway. "I won't need a room, Alastair. I won't be staying."

He turned to look at her and tilted his head to the side. "You're hurt and you've been through too much in the last several days. You need rest."

"I need to find my husband," she said. "I won't find him here. Besides, Merrick already went ahead to find rooms for us. I'll send a message once we're settled."

Alastair looked her in the eyes. "Cecily, you need to trust the king. He will find Daro."

She laid a hand on Alastair's arm. "I do trust him. That's why I came here. But I can't linger in the palace, waiting. It will drive me mad. Don't worry about me, I won't do anything rash. Merrick won't let me. Send word immediately if you have news."

He sighed and nodded. She turned away and took brisk steps down the hall, ignoring the soreness in her legs and the pulling in her shoulder. She needed to find Merrick, but more importantly, she needed more help. The Crown wasn't the only power in Halthas, and she wouldn't stop until she had the entire city looking for Daro, if that was what it took.

## 14 : ALE STONE

CECILY SPENT A RESTLESS night at the Boar's Head, a simple but clean inn near Griff and Serv's warehouse. Her injuries still nagged her and her dreams were troubled. She woke up several times, covered in a sheen of sweat, strange visions hovering just beyond her memory.

After leaving the palace she had visited a tailor to purchase new clothes, including a dark blue cloak. The nights would soon grow cold as autumn approached, and she had lost most of her traveling clothes when they were attacked. She dressed and braided her hair back, fastening Daro's necklace with extra care to ensure the clasp was secure.

She left the inn on foot under an overcast sky, the air thick with humidity. She kept the hood of her cloak drawn over her head to cover her face from gawking onlookers. She had inspected her lip and bruised cheek in the small looking glass in her room. The bruising was fading from purple to a sickly yellow, and the swelling was gone, but it was fresh enough to draw attention.

She made her way through the busy streets to the Ale Stone, a rugged tavern with an awning that drooped over the front door. Day or night, the Ale Stone was crowded with a mix of merchants, mercenaries, and many others whose professions Cecily didn't wish to uncover. It was one of several locations Cecily knew to be connected to the Halthian Underground, a loose network of criminal bosses and their various crews that operated within the city. They were said to be ruled by someone only known as the Count. Much of the trade that flowed in and out of Halthas went through the Underground, legal and illegal alike, making them a force the crown had to reluctantly ignore.

She stepped inside and was assaulted by the heavy aroma of smoke, meat, and cheap ale. A few girls loitered around the stairs, dressed in tight corsets and dingy chemises that left little to the imagination. The tables were full, and a low hum of voices hung in the air. A man with a thick beard bumped into her as he passed, sending her shoulder into a spasm of agony. He grumbled as she pushed past him. She gripped her shoulder and clenched her teeth.

She scanned the room from behind her cowl, looking from table to table. Most had men, and a few women, hunched over worn mugs, leaning in close and shooting furtive glances around the room as they spoke. Cecily was careful not to let her gaze linger on anyone too long, lest someone think she was staring. These weren't the sort of people to trifle with.

Off to one side, she found who she was looking for. Callum sat with his back to the wall, almost buried in a corner at the back of the tavern. He blended into the shadows in his black clothes, the collar of his long coat turned up around his neck, his tousled hair hanging in his eyes. He leaned back in his chair, and his hand rested on the table as he flipped a coin across his knuckles. Another man sat across from him, dressed in a shoddy gray tunic and worn leather vest. Callum tilted his head to the side and spoke, shaking his head. The other man gestured, threw his hands out wide, and pointed his finger at the ceiling. Callum shrugged and spoke again as the other man stood up and knocked his chair back onto the floor. He turned and stormed toward the front door, his face flushed red.

Cecily approached the table and bent down to pick up the chair. Callum raised his eyebrows. "Well, isn't this interesting. It isn't every day we get a distinguished Lady such as yourself in this poor excuse for a tavern." He paused and gestured at her hood with a quick flick of his wrist. "But perhaps you aren't yourself today?"

She lowered herself into her seat and drew her hood back. His eyes widened and he leaned forward. "What happened?"

She took a deep breath. "It's a long story, and I need your help."

His eyebrows rose. "Sounds interesting."

The tension melted from Cecily's shoulders and her breathing relaxed. She hadn't realized she was clenching her fists, but she opened her hands and flexed her fingers, as the sense of urgency that gripped her drifted away.

She met Callum's eyes. "Stop it."

He lifted his hands and raised his eyebrows. "What?"

"I can feel your Projection. You're trying to Calm me. Stop it." She didn't like it when Callum manipulated her emotions. He usually knew better.

"Okay, I give," he said and the strange sense of calm drifted away. "Sorry, you just look like you need to relax."

"Callum, this is serious. Daro is missing," she said.

He stopped flipping the thick gold coin and let it clatter to the table. "Your Daro?" He held a hand up in the air, gesturing Daro's height. "He's a little bit hard to lose."

"He was abducted." She explained what had happened, filling him in on the details of their attackers, Daro's abduction, her narrow escape, and the disappearing trail. Although she kept her face serene, she couldn't suppress a growing sense of dread that spread through her each time she thought of her husband.

Callum leaned back in his chair and picked up his coin with deft fingers. "Obviously we have to find him."

Cecily smiled with relief. "I was hoping you'd help me."

He tilted his head to the side. "Of course I'll help you. A fine, upstanding citizen like myself? What else did you expect?" She smiled again and Callum continued. "Tell me about the Wielders."

"One of them was definitely a Sensor. I could feel his Shield, and it was strong. I almost couldn't see through it. But he had Reach too. His arrows were enhanced with Precision, I could feel it. I didn't even think that was possible."

"No," Callum said, shaking his head. "I've never heard of a Sensory Wielder with Reach."

"The other one was throwing rocks at us. They glowed red and exploded when they hit."

"That one's new to me too," Callum said. "I dislike them already."

"The third one was even stranger. If I didn't know better, I'd say he was Absorbing, only massive amounts of energy. Hadran had Absorption, I saw him use it, but that was nothing compared to this. The plants around him were dying and it looked like he was freezing the road."

Callum's mouth hung open as she spoke. "Now I know I dislike these guys," he said.

"That isn't the worst of it. He hit me with something and it felt like…" She paused, uncertain how to explain what she'd felt. "It felt like he sucked energy out of me, only he was standing across the road. He didn't get close. It knocked the air out of me and made me feel like my lungs had been frozen. I barely got out of there alive. After Merrick found me, I slept for two days."

"So you're telling me Daro was abducted by a group of Wielders that do things we all know are completely impossible, and even Merrick couldn't find their trail. And you want me to help you find him."

Cecily winced. "Yes, I suppose that is what I'm saying."

Callum sucked in a deep breath and looked away. He rubbed his chin, his fingertips moving up and down his smooth jaw line. It made Cecily nervous. Callum was almost impossible to surprise. She didn't like the idea that this was as perplexing to him as it was to her.

"Very well," he said. He flipped his gold coin in the air and caught it with a quick flick of his wrist. "Who else knows about this?"

"Besides Merrick, just Alastair and Rogan. I went to the palace yesterday."

His lip curled up in a smile. "You came to me next? I'm flattered. You might say I'm almost as important as the king."

Cecily smiled as a young boy darted up to the table. His face was dirty and his clothes looked too big for him, a loose-fitting pair of trousers with an oversized tunic, a thin belt at his waist. Callum's gaze moved lazily to him and he raised his eyebrows at the boy. The boy hesitated as his eyes darted toward Cecily. He handed a folded piece of paper to Callum and said, "From the Count," before he turned and darted away, disappearing as quickly as he'd come. Callum opened the scrap and let out a low chuckle as he read the contents.

"Sorry about that. Nothing important."

Cecily looked at him and tilted her head to one side. "Not important? He said it's from the Count. Moving up in the world, are we?"

He shrugged. "No, it isn't important." She realized he'd already tucked the note into a pocket somewhere. She hadn't seen him do it.

He leaned forward and said, "I don't know who these guys are. I want you to know that up front. Whoever they are, they don't have anything to do with what I do."

"I know. That's not why I came."

"What I can't understand is this: why Daro? If I was in the kidnapping business, I'd wager you are the better target. You have a name, a family who might pay ransom money. It looks like they wanted him, specifically. That was clearly a planned ambush and they were after him, not you."

She'd been mulling over those very questions and had come to the same conclusion. "I wish I understood. If I knew what they wanted from him, I might have some idea of where to find him."

"Was he injured?"

"I don't think so. I couldn't be sure at the end, but if he was, it wasn't serious. He walked away."

Callum's eyes narrowed again. "He walked away? You mean, he went with them?"

Cecily nodded and fought down the tears that suddenly welled up in her eyes as the image of Daro's anguished face danced in her mind.

"I see. They had you down and threatened to kill you, unless he cooperated. Something like that?"

She nodded again and gritted her teeth as a flash of anger burned through her.

"This isn't your fault," Callum said, his blue eyes looking more honest than usual.

Cecily looked away. "I know. I just can't stop thinking about the look on his face. And every day that goes by makes it harder to find him. They could be halfway across the world by now. What if they took him down the river? They could have gone out to sea. They could be anywhere."

Callum put his hand on hers. "We'll find him. It doesn't matter how powerful they are, there will be a clue or a trail somewhere. We just have to find it." He sat back, resuming his casual posture. "I don't like finding out someone is pulling stunts like this in my territory. I've had a lot of that lately, and quite frankly, it's beginning to get on my nerves. Where are you staying?"

"The Boar's Head."

"Good. I know the owner, it's a good place. I'll meet you there in a few days. I need some time to see what I can discover. In the meantime, let the others know what happened. We're going to need their help."

Cecily nodded and pulled her cowl over her head again. She got up and headed for the door. Glancing back, she saw Callum had already disappeared from his seat. She looked around the room, but he was nowhere to be seen. It wasn't an unusual trick for Callum. She just hoped his network of less-than-savory contacts would prove helpful. She was starting to feel desperate.

## 15 : GATHERING FRIENDS

GRIFF POUNDED HIS FIST on the table, sloshing ale out of the fresh mugs. "What are we doing here? We can't sit around, eating and drinking!" He gestured out the window. "Our friend is out there, somewhere. And here we sit." He sat back in his chair, crossed his arms, and looked from person to person.

Cecily sat at the head of the table in the back room of the Boar's Head. She'd sent word to her friends several days before, asking them to meet her. Griff and Serv had arrived in what felt like minutes after her missives went out. It was an enormous relief to see Griff bursting in the room, wrapping her in his arms and assuring her they would drop everything until Daro was found. Serv brought tears to her eyes as he clutched her hands and dropped to one knee, pledging his life for his friend. Edson wrung his hands with worry and Cecily found herself reassuring him that everything would be fine, a sentiment she desperately wanted to believe herself.

Sumara had come shortly after, assuring Cecily she would do whatever she could to help. Mira arrived next, still wearing the deep blue uniform of the king's guard. Merrick was tolerating the close quarters of the city without complaint, although he often took Beau outside.

"Does anyone have any idea where to begin looking?" Mira asked. "What do you suggest, Griff? Should we march off into the woods and hope we stumble across some clue?"

Griff frowned, but Sumara spoke up. "We all want to help, but arguing will get us nowhere."

"I'm not arguing," Mira replied. "I'm just being realistic. Besides, we can't all go running off without any knowledge of where we are going or when we might be back. I have duties to His Majesty."

"You have a duty to Daro!" Griff bellowed. Cecily put a hand on Griff's arm, but he continued. "Without Daro, most of us would have died in the war. He saved my life more times than I can count, and I know that goes for you too."

Mira answered. "Don't question my loyalty, Griff. I am simply saying we need more information."

"Information without action leads us nowhere," he replied and pounded his fist on the table again.

"This is ridiculous," Mira said as she pushed her chair away from the table and walked to the window.

Cecily rubbed her temples. Watching her friends argue was nothing new, but without Daro there to interject, she wasn't sure how long it would go on. He had a knack for smoothing things out and finding ways to bring everyone to agreement. She missed him desperately.

"There has to be something," Griff said. "We've faced worse odds than this. Men don't just vanish without a trace."

"This one did." Merrick's voice was quiet, but his words cut through the room. "I spent two days walking the road and the woods beyond. There was nothing. It is as if it never happened."

Cecily knew Merrick was frustrated, but the concern in his voice was frightening.

The door opened and everyone looked up to see Callum. He smirked, sauntered over to the table, and pulled out a chair. "What are we talking about?" he asked as he reached to fill a plate with a chunk of brown bread, cheese and sliced apples.

"Please tell me you found something," Cecily said. She'd been anxious as she waited for Callum to arrive, hoping he would bring some new information.

Callum took a bite of bread. "Well," he said as he chewed his bite and dipped another piece in a pot of butter, "I have some good news and some bad. A lot of rumors and stories, for one. People vanishing without a trace? That isn't new, apparently."

Cecily wasn't sure whether that was the bad news or the good. Callum kept eating as everyone watched him, waiting for him to continue.

He swallowed another bite. "I can't be certain they are all connected, but there's a story going around about people disappearing. In a city this large, people vanish all the time, mind you. But usually there's an explanation. A man with gambling debt, an angry mistress, or a kid going off into the wilderness, trying to become a hero. Either they turn up, or their body does. This, though, this is different."

"Different? What do you mean?" Cecily asked.

Callum gestured with the chunk of bread in his hand. "Like Merrick said, these people vanish and there's nothing. No trail, nothing left behind, not even a reason. And the crazy thing is, these stories go back years, before the war, even. So it's likely Daro isn't the only one. That's the good news."

"The good news? How is that good news?" Griff asked.

Callum rolled his eyes. "The more people involved, the harder it is to keep something quiet. If you're talking about a handful of people kidnapping one man, that's hard to trace. But I'm telling you, this is big. These guys have resources and whatever it is they're doing, it's been going on for years. You can only hide that kind of thing for so long. Trust me."

"These aren't people you know?" Mira asked, one eyebrow raised.

Callum's mouth dropped. "I'm hurt, Mira. How could you insinuate I had anything to do with this?"

Mira sighed. "I'm not suggesting you were involved. I just thought there might be some connection to, well, your connections."

Callum shook his head. "That's the part that really rankles, truth be told. Someone is operating on our turf and the Count isn't happy about it."

"You said that was the good news. Does that mean there's bad news?" Cecily asked.

"Maybe not bad news, but troubling news, I suppose. I can't prove this is connected to what happened to Daro, but I have very strong suspicions. I've been investigating some smugglers out of Sahaar for the last few years. A sly group, I'll tell you that. They've been avoiding me for years."

"Why investigate? I thought smuggling was, how shall I say it, part of your business?" Sumara asked.

Callum shot her a crooked smile. "I won't say if you are right or wrong there, my sweet. But these guys, they're not just smuggling. I think they're moving people."

"You mean, slaves?" Sumara asked, her voice low.

"Something like that," Callum replied. "I have reason to believe they're trafficking people into the kingdom. I've been trying to find who's buying, but it hasn't been easy. I've followed a lot of false trails, and quite honestly, these guys are starting to make me angry."

The room went quiet as they looked around at each other. The founders of Halthas had been slaves, Wielders and Shapers who had fled the Attalonian Empire. While the neighboring kingdoms might deal in slavery, it had long been considered abhorrent by Halthians. Cecily knew even the Underground drew their line at slavery.

"You think the people that took Daro are buying slaves?" Cecily asked.

"I don't have enough proof yet, but it looks like they might be the same people," he said. "The real question is, if these people are moving as many slaves as I think they are, where are they winding up? The trail just disappears, much like Daro's trail did. I don't have a tracker who is nearly as good as Merrick, but I'm talking about hundreds, maybe even thousands of people crossing our borders. And then poof"—he flicked his fingers and the bread in his hand disappeared—"they're gone."

"If you suspect slave traders, why haven't you gone to the king?" Mira asked.

Callum flicked his hair from his eyes. "Who says I haven't?"

"I say, for one," came a voice from the door. Alastair walked in, looking official and tidy in his deep blue embroidered doublet. "Cecily, please forgive my lateness, but I had things to attend to before I could break away from the palace."

"That's quite all right, Alastair. Thank you for joining us," Cecily said.

Callum raised an eyebrow. "I'm sure you bring news of the great lengths our magnanimous majesty is undertaking to retrieve our honored friend?"

Alastair glared at him. "King Rogan is, of course, doing everything in his power to help."

"Really?" said Callum and looked around the room. "Where is he, then? Did he send you in his place? Or will another stand-in be along shortly?"

Alastair frowned. "Honestly, Callum, he is the king. He has many demands on his time. Surely you didn't expect him to come here tonight?"

Cecily shifted in her seat. She had expected, or at least hoped, Rogan would come. She wondered if he'd received the missive she'd sent, or if some underling had deemed it unimportant.

"I thought he might grace us with his presence," Callum said with a shrug. "In any case, what is it, exactly, that Rogan is using all his power to do?"

"I'm afraid I have little to report," Alastair answered and turned toward Cecily. "His Majesty asks me to tell you he is most distressed, but as of yet we have found very little in our search."

Cecily sighed. "Thank you for coming, anyway," she said. Callum snorted and she rolled her eyes at him. "Is the king aware of these stories Callum has heard? People disappearing, or this band of smugglers dealing in slaves?"

"To be truthful, I'm not certain. The king has a great many issues to attend to."

Mira nodded and the others looked around the room uncomfortably. "Of course," Cecily replied.

The room got quiet and Cecily stared down at the table. Callum kept eating his bread.

"Cecily," Alastair said, his voice breaking the silence. "I hate to bring this up, but, in light of the difficulty we've had finding Daro, I have to ask. Have you considered that perhaps Daro has been killed?"

All eyes swung to Cecily. Callum turned toward her and dropped his food. She slowly raised her gaze to meet Alastair's eyes. "I know he is alive."

"I want to believe that as much as you do. But none of us can be sure, and unfortunately, we have to be realistic about this."

"No, I know he is alive," she said and held Alastair's gaze. He opened his mouth to reply, but she continued. "How much do you know about Imarans?"

His brow furrowed. "Imarans? As much as anyone, I suppose."

"Did you know that the Imaran language has no word for mistress or adultery?"

Alastair's eyes shifted from side to side and his brow deepened. "That's fascinating, but I don't see how—"

She cut him off. "They don't have words for those things because those concepts don't exist. An Imaran would no more cheat on his spouse than kill her. It simply isn't done." She paused, everyone quietly watching her. "The Imarans believe that everyone has an inner energy, what we might call a soul. But they see it as something even deeper. They call it the *feorh-aelan*. We would translate it as 'soul fire' or maybe 'life energy.' When an Imaran meets his mate, his *feorh-aelan* is said to sing to hers, and if their souls are compatible, her *feorh-aelan* will answer back. And when they marry, their energies meld, bonding together to become one. Once they are bonded, it lasts for the rest of their lives."

"That's very interesting, but I'm not sure where you're going with all this," Alastair said.

"When I met Daro, something came alive inside me. I didn't understand what it was, and neither did he. Somehow his soul, his *feorhaelan*, sang to mine, and mine answered. And when we married, our souls melded, inseparably. The spirit inside me changed. We became like two parts of the same person." She glanced around the room at her friends. "I know he is alive because when he dies, his soul will sever from mine. And that hasn't happened."

A hushed silence settled over the room and Alastair looked down. "Well, that is good news, at least." He looked back up and glanced at their other companions. "I did come to tell you that King Rogan is doing all he can. He implores you to use caution and to allow him to handle this unfortunate situation."

Callum turned his head lazily toward Alastair. "Are you serious? You came here to tell us to sit tight because Rogan is handling it?"

"You're experienced in the art of espionage," Alastair replied. "You, of all people, must understand the delicacy of these matters."

Serv spoke up. "In other words, Rogan doesn't want us interfering and fouling up his plans."

Griff sat back and crossed his arms. "I don't like it. How is it that Rogan's plans don't include us? Who else could he possibly trust for this?"

"I agree," Sumara said as she brushed her dark hair away from her face. "Why hasn't he entrusted this to us?"

"These aren't the old days anymore," Alastair answered. "We all have our own lives. His Majesty couldn't assume you would all be here, ready to jump into action at a moment's notice. Griff and Serv are only in Halthas a portion of the year, isn't that right? Merrick, we seldom have the pleasure of seeing you. Sumara, you yourself have obligations, as do the rest of us." He gestured around the room. "King Rogan is doing his best, of that you can be certain."

Cecily looked around at her friends. "Alastair is right. I spoke with Rogan myself and he assured me he would help. I know he's doing everything he can."

Serv patted Griff on the shoulder as he crossed his arms and grumbled under his breath. Callum kept eating his food, hunched over his plate and pointedly ignoring Alastair. Sumara nodded at Cecily, and Edson looked around uncomfortably. Cecily felt bad for the poor lad; he was caught up in something he probably didn't understand.

"I'm afraid I must be off," Alastair said. "I'm sorry I am unable to stay longer. Mira, the guard will have need of you this evening, I believe. Cecily, I will send word as soon as I have news to report." He touched his right hand to his chest and bowed. Mira nodded and followed him out of the room.

An uncomfortable silence settled over the companions. Cecily stood and moved to stand by the window. They were on the ground floor, the busy street bustling with activity outside. She watched a woman walk by carrying a wicker basket of flowers, a baby strapped to her back and another child tagging along behind.

Callum eased in next to her and spoke in a low voice. "So that's it? We wait for Rogan?"

Cecily sighed. "Yes. We wait for Rogan."

Callum shook his head. "You trust him that much?"

"We both fought by his side. I trusted him with my life more times than I can count."

"Believe me, I remember. He's a decent enough king, even I have to admit that. But do you trust him with *this*?" Cecily looked at him and he held her gaze. "This isn't the king's world we're talking about. We aren't dealing with heads of noble houses and foreign dignitaries. This is abduction, smuggling, maybe slavery and who knows what else." He darted a quick glance around the room and leaned in closer, his voice quiet. "This is a little more my domain than his, if you catch my meaning."

"What do you suggest I do, then? Do you have a plan in that crafty head of yours?"

"Not yet. But I'm working on it. And when the time comes, I don't think we should sit around waiting for Rogan's errand boy to tell us what to do."

Cecily chuckled. "Alastair is not that bad. He's a good man."

"Maybe he is." Callum shrugged.

"How much do you know about what's happening up at the Lyceum?" she asked. She wanted to change the subject.

"They don't exactly enjoy my company, at least not out in the open, but I have connections. Why?"

"I have a contact at the Lyceum, and he sent me a rather odd letter before we left home. It doesn't have anything to do with Daro, but I'm concerned."

Callum's face erupted into a wide smile. "Cecily Imaran, you sly thing. You have a secret contact at the Lyceum?"

"Magister Brunell—he was my mentor at the Lyceum of Power. I don't know that I'd call it a secret, although he probably doesn't broadcast our association. The gods know, there isn't anyone else there who would even speak to me," she said.

Callum raised his eyebrows. The Lyceum of Power was a clandestine wing of the Lyceum, little of which was known to outsiders. During King Hadran's reign, the Lyceum of Power had worked closely with the Crown, and Cecily had been amongst those the king had used to carry out his orders.

"I do recall you left the Lyceum rather abruptly. They're still holding a grudge?"

Cecily shrugged. "I haven't been there in a long time. I've kept in contact with Brunell over the years. He's too much of an academic to hold a grudge if there's something that interests him. And he was always intensely interested in what I could do."

"You do have some good tricks," Callum said.

"I suppose. I don't know if he ever understood why I left, but he never shunned me for it. And he was one of the few people from that time in my life who didn't ostracize Daro. He always seemed interested in him, even if it was from a more academic standpoint than a personal one."

"If you have a contact at the Lyceum, you should go see him. Most of them may be stodgy old curmudgeons, but a friend in the Lyceum can be a powerful thing. They have resources neither Rogan nor I have."

Cecily hesitated. "I haven't been there in so long. They're just as likely to throw me out as let me in."

"It has to be better than sitting around here, waiting for Rogan to throw us some crumbs. Besides, the library is open to anyone. They can't toss you out of there unless you threaten to start a fire. Not that I would know."

Cecily shook her head. She could only imagine Callum walking through the stacks of books and rolls of parchment, shouting, "Fire!"

She looked back out the window. Callum was right—she didn't want to sit around waiting for anyone, even the king. "I guess I'll take my chances at the Lyceum." She looked back at Callum. "Care to join me?"

He smirked. "Not if you want to get past the front gates. They still haven't forgiven me for the last time I visited."

## 16 : THE LYCEUM

Cecily walked through the gates of the Lyceum, past two guards standing at attention on either side of the entrance. The wide, tree-lined walkway was flanked by small courtyards and gardens that led into the grounds. The smell of lilies and lavender carried on the breeze. She passed one of the four dormitories, tall buildings of gray stone that curved in wide arcs around the center of the grounds. They were flanked by conical towers and the walls were inlaid with marble and dotted with numerous paned windows. Small groups of students lounged on benches or under the shade of trees, others walking with brisk steps to and from the dormitory entrances.

At the heart of the Lyceum was the great library, touted as the largest in the world. The round building was topped with a dome, a tall spire rising from its peak. Thick marble columns and a sturdy stone base contrasted with the delicacy of the detailed stonework and etched glass windows. Surrounding the library were the lecture halls, four rectangular buildings that jutted out from the center like spokes on a wheel, each with a tower at the far end. From afar, the lecture halls looked identical, but up close there were variations in the stonework that indicated which wing of the Lyceum they belonged to.

Cecily headed for the Lyceum of Vision, the wing of the Lyceum that trained Wielders. The other three wings were for Shapers. The Lyceum of Stone trained those who worked with stone, ores and gems, teaching craftsmen and artisans. The Lyceum of Seed specialized in Shapers working with plant life, including gardeners, woodworkers and those skilled in creating various remedies and potions. The Lyceum of Blood primarily trained Serum Shapers, people with the ability to treat the sick and injured.

The Lyceum of Vision was on the far side, so Cecily cut through the library. She walked up the smooth steps to the paneled wooden doors. They were arched at the top, coming to a point in the center. Gripping the thick iron handle she pulled, and the well-oiled door swung out on heavy black hinges.

Her boots clicked on the shining marble floor. As she looked up to the dome above, she could see floors upon floors of books, jutting out in rings around the outer wall, leaving the center open to the ceiling high above. The dome itself was lined with gilded beams, painted to look like leaves on a vine.

With a sigh, she walked through the library and up one of the many staircases. The musty smell of leather and worn pages brought back a flood of memories from her days as a student. She circled around the second floor and paused to run her fingers across the leather spines of several books on a sturdy shelf.

The second-floor door led out from the library across a raised walkway to the Lyceum of Vision. Once inside, she passed classrooms and lecture halls with students bustling about as they made their way to and from their classes. She wasn't sure if Magister Brunell would be in a class, but she assumed she could check at his office. Her stomach fluttered with nervousness. She hadn't been through these halls since before the war. She had burned a lot of bridges when she'd left the Lyceum.

Although the Lyceum was ostensibly divided into the four schools, there was the also Lyceum of Power, a far more secretive division. It didn't have its own tower, but operated largely out of floors deep underneath the library. The faculty, however, had offices that were integrated with the other Lyceum buildings, further blurring the lines between the covert Lyceum of Power and the rest of the school. Cecily hadn't known Magister Brunell was part of the Lyceum of Power until she herself had been initiated into it. He had recommended her to the Paragon, the head of the institution, based on her set of abilities. Initially she had been ecstatic; proud of her accomplishments, she had looked forward to an exciting and prosperous future.

But her life in the Lyceum of Power had turned out to be far different from what she'd envisioned. The training had been brutal, long days spent honing her Wielding abilities to a fine point. Magister Brunell had taken her under his wing and taught her to do things with her ability she hadn't realized were possible. It hadn't been long before King Hadran had taken an interest in her, and she'd found herself executing his personal orders, under the direction of her Magisters.

She paused outside the open door of a classroom. A Magister stood at the far end, delivering a lecture to a group of about fifty students. The rows of seats bowed around the stage at the front, most holding students in varying states of attentiveness. Some slumped in their chairs, while others leaned forward, appearing to hang on every word. Cecily had once imagined she would someday be standing in front of a crowded lecture hall filled with bright-eyed students such as these.

Magister Brunell's office was on the sixth floor of the Vision Tower. She trekked up the winding staircase, her shoulders tight with growing anxiety. The stairs ended at an open landing, a slatted wood railing along the edge. Beyond was a hallway with doors on each side, some leading into offices, others to smaller libraries and study rooms.

Although a bit unsure of her memory, she walked directly to the Magister's office and found his name etched on a brass plate on the closed door. She knocked and waited with a pounding heart for the sound of an answer. No one responded, and she knocked again, louder this time, in case her first had been too timid. She hoped she wasn't interrupting something important.

No answer came. She paused, her fist held up as if to knock again, but opened her Awareness and peered into the room. It was empty. Her hand moved to the doorknob, and she twisted it back and forth, to no avail. It was locked. With a quick glance up and down the hallway, she focused her Awareness on the lock and probed the insides. She Wielded a small slice of Pressure to disengage the lock with a click.

The office looked exactly as she remembered it. Heavy curtains were pulled shut, shrouding the room in gloomy darkness. A thick burgundy carpet covered the floor, woven with swirls of green and gold. His desk stood off to the side, piled high with books, papers, and scrolls that created a cozy mess. Two large bookshelves lined the walls, filled with stacks of books piled two deep. Another small table had diagrams spread out, weighed down with shiny, black paperweights.

The air was stale and musty. She crept in and closed the door behind her with a gentle hand. She reached with a finger and swept it across the surface of his desk, then rubbed her fingers together. A light layer of dust covered everything. *He hasn't been here in a while.*

She walked around the office and peered at his stacks of books, rolled scrolls and diagrams. Magister Brunell had always struck Cecily as an avid academic. Some Magisters seemed to love their life of teaching, passionate about guiding the next generation. Magister Brunell seemed to teach his classes in order to have access to the Lyceum's resources for research and learning. He'd told Cecily many times that he believed there was significant potential in many Wielders that remained hidden, and he was determined to find a way to unlock it. He'd pushed Cecily relentlessly in her training and sent her off to work closely with King Hadran, always insisting on detailed descriptions of how she'd accomplished her tasks. She wondered how many of the clutter of books on his shelves held accounts of her doings while she was his student.

A noise outside the office made her neck prickle with anxiety. She didn't want someone to find her here. Her Awareness told her someone walked by, but was moving down the hallway. She waited until they had gone before she stole out the door and snapped the lock shut again.

If it hadn't been for the dust, she'd have assumed he was simply occupied elsewhere. But it was clear he hadn't been in his office recently. She decided to go down to the entry hall of the Vision Tower. There would be clerks and secretaries working and she could ask about Magister Brunell.

The ground floor was as busy as the classroom wing had been. Students, clerks, messengers and other staff came and went, everyone in a hurry. A clerk sat at a long desk facing the front door, scratching something on a piece of parchment with a quill. He was the only person who wasn't rushing off to one task or another, so Cecily approached the desk.

"Excuse me?" she said, resolve winning out over any lingering nervousness. "I'm looking for a Magister. He wasn't in his office."

The clerk stopped writing and slowly raised his eyes, his head still pointed down at his work. "Then he's probably teaching a class."

Cecily glanced around and wondered how to press the issue without admitting she'd been in his deserted office. "Yes, but I don't know where his class would be. Could you tell me where I might find Magister Brunell?"

The clerk's eyes rose again, quickly this time. He looked her up and down. "What business do you have with Magister Brunell?"

Cecily hesitated. "I'm Cecily Imaran. I used to be one of his students."

He narrowed his eyes at her as he stood. "Wait here."

Cecily crossed her arms and glanced around as she waited. After what felt like an eternity, the clerk returned. "Follow me." He turned and walked away without looking to see if she followed.

He led her back up the stairs to the third floor and stopped outside an office. Her heart sank when she saw the name etched on the brass nameplate. *Magister Evan*. After waving her in, the clerk turned and left, his swift stride taking him quickly out of sight.

Magister Evan's office was bathed in light from a large window overlooking the library. It was as neat and orderly as Brunell's office had been cluttered and dusty. Every book was tucked carefully in place and even his small collection of statues was precisely arrayed on a shelf. Evan himself sat behind a polished wood desk. He had a wisp of gray hair, and round spectacles perched on his small, upturned nose. Lines creased his forehead and the corners of his eyes, and his bony shoulders were enveloped in a dark green robe.

He looked up at her over the rims of his glasses. "This is unexpected."

"Yes, I apologize for dropping in on you like this," Cecily said. Magister Evan had been another of her teachers during her time at the Lyceum and had been particularly critical when she had left. "I was hoping to speak with Magister Brunell."

"What do you want with Magister Brunell?" he asked, as he pitched his fingertips together.

Cecily paused, unsure of how to answer. She glanced over her shoulder at the sound of footsteps. Two Lyceum Guards placed themselves in the doorway behind her. "I had business with him, of a personal nature."

"Magister Brunell is unavailable," Evan said. He adjusted his spectacles. "He is currently on sabbatical. You may leave a message with a clerk downstairs."

"Sabbatical? I was in contact with Magister Brunell recently and he didn't mention anything about going on sabbatical."

"He has taken an extended leave of absence. Whether or not he notified you is none of my concern. If you will excuse me, I am extremely busy and must return to my duties." Evan waved a hand and the two guards stepped up beside Cecily. "Odlem, Vanhem, please see Lady Imaran to the outer gates."

One of the guards put his hand on her elbow and she pulled her arm away, shrugging him off. Her heart pounded and her stomach fluttered with a surge of adrenaline but she knew there was nothing she could do. She turned and glided past the guards with her chin held high, hoping to leave with at least a shred of her dignity intact.

"Lady Cecily," Evan's voice came from behind her. She stopped and looked back over her shoulder. "You've spent a number of years avoiding our hallowed institution. I highly suggest that henceforth, you keep it that way."

Cecily shot him a poisonous glare, but he looked back down at his desk, robbing her of the satisfaction of a sharp look.

The guards followed her brisk pace all the way to the outer gate. She didn't bother turning to see if they watched her leave. Frustration boiled inside as she replayed the scene with Evan in her mind. Should she have pressed harder? She wanted to kick herself for letting him run her off so quickly. She should have at least tried to get him to speak with her. Even if he couldn't locate Magister Brunell, he might have been able to tell her something that would help her find Daro.

She turned south, heading down the hill to the lower part of the city, and fought down a sick feeling in the pit of her stomach.

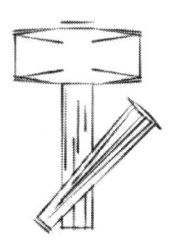

## 17 : CONDITIONING

Daro sucked in a breath and opened his eyes. Fear flooded through him as he remembered where he was. The room was dark, but he could see. He carefully tested his limbs, wiggling his fingers and toes. Relief crept in as his eyes and body responded. He moved his arms and legs, relishing the sensation. Sindre often left him paralyzed, unable to move or see. He would wake up, gasping as if he'd been drowning, shaking and drenched in sweat.

His breath felt hot against his face, and he realized he still wore the mask. He sat up, pulled the mask off, and tossed it aside. He tried not to think about what Sindre would do when she came back as his hand strayed to the back of his neck. The stone was still there, as it always was, embedded in his skin. He brushed his fingers across its smooth surface, feeling the edges. The line from the stone to his upper back was smooth, as if it had always been there. There was a symbol etched into it, but he couldn't make out what it might be.

Someone had left a plate of food, the smell of pungent herbs drifting into the air. He got up, tested the door, and found it locked. No surprise there. He'd have been wary if it opened, assuming some kind of trap. He decided to eat, if only to keep up his strength, then sat on the edge of the bed to wait.

It was difficult to track the passage of time. There were no windows, no way to see the rising and setting of the sun. He was often left in his room, alone for what felt like days. He tried to keep track, scratching a mark under his bed each time he thought it was morning. He reached down and scratched another mark, then carefully picked the bits of wood from his fingernail so Sindre wouldn't notice what he had done.

His thoughts strayed to Cecily and he wondered where she was. He half expected to hear the clicking of the lock, only to have his wife appear at the door. He imagined her face, flushed with exertion, her dark hair windswept and wild, urging him to come. She'd hand him his sword and they'd fight their way out, passing the unconscious forms of the guards who never saw her coming. She would lead him back out into the sun where their horses awaited and they would ride off together, leaving this terrible place behind.

It was a nice fantasy. He leaned back against the wall, closed his eyes, and allowed his mind to focus on her face. He could see every detail with such clarity: the curve of her chin, her brown eyes. He kept the vision firmly in his mind, resolving to return to it whenever he was threatened.

His mind strayed to Sindre, the hungry look in her color-mingled eyes. She possessed an inordinate amount of power over him and the thought made him sick. The pain he could handle, but the way she rendered him blind and paralyzed was terrifying. She'd taken his body from him and locked him inside. What else could she do? He tried to imagine the possibilities, to prepare himself. Could she control his body and make him do what she wished? What about his mind? That thought terrified him further. Could she control his thoughts? So far it didn't appear that she could, but he felt he needed to be prepared for anything.

He waited, trying to keep his mind firmly on Cecily. His discipline faded as time passed and restlessness set in. The walls of the room seemed to close in, the air getting warm and stale. His nervous energy built as he sat. When he could no longer sit still, he got up and paced about the small room. He brought his wife back into his mind, doing his best to be calm. His muscles twitched and he thought about trying to kick the door open.

The lock clicked. He stopped his pacing and turned to face the door. Sindre entered, her marbled stone necklace hanging loose around her neck. She closed the door behind her and Daro thought he could hear the shuffling of feet on the other side. Guards, perhaps?

He stood still and stared at her like a frightened deer. A knot of fear clenched his stomach as he wondered if she would incapacitate him again.

"Here we are again," she said with a cold smile. "But I see we still have some work to do." She looked around the room and gestured to the corner with the mask crumpled on the floor. "There it is." She picked it up and smoothed it out. "I assure you, this is only a tool to help you. Now let us see if we have learned anything." She held it out to him. "Put it on."

His breath caught in his throat. Giving in was not an option, but he knew exactly what was coming. He steeled himself for her retaliation and said, "No."

She sighed and took a step closer to him. "I had hoped we understood each other." He flinched as she held out the mask. Her voice shifted from cold to soothing, as if she were speaking to a small child. "Such a simple thing. Let's not fight over such a simple thing."

Daro remained still and silent, his back clenched with dread.

"No?" she said. "Very well. On your knees."

A jolt of pain shot down his back and despite his attempt to stay standing, he crumpled under the strain. The pain lessened but still pressed at him, an aching knot in his back.

"Knees," she said. The pain spiked again and he struggled to his knees, gritting his teeth. "Good," she said and knelt in front of him, still holding the mask. "I am a very patient woman." The pain spiked again. He grunted and leaned forward, his hands balled into tight fists. "Still, we have spent enough time on this one task and it is time we move on."

The pain continued and he cried out. As it disappeared, he was left panting and resting his forehead on the hard floor. He sat up, taking a few steadying breaths, and tried desperately to keep the image of Cecily in his mind. He could feel his heart thumping, his pulse pounding in his temples. The woman moved and he flinched, waiting for pain to strike again.

"You know what I can do to you if you refuse me," she said. "I can leave you here, lying on the floor, unable to move. How long do you think it will take before you put the mask on? How many days of lying prostrate on the floor, in the black, with nothing but rats to keep you company? You see, I can leave you helpless," she said. Daro's body went limp, and he crumpled to the floor. "But I can allow you your senses." She pushed him onto his back and ran her fingers up and down his chest. "You can feel this, but you can do nothing to stop me," she said and traced her fingers lightly down his arm.

Daro's breath quickened and he squeezed his eyes shut, desperate to move, but his body refused. Calm eluded him and panic began to rise. "No!" he shouted, and the word cut off as he realized he was able to speak.

The woman smiled and stroked him gently. "Ah, my darling, I can make everything better." She rubbed his chest and let her fingers trail down his stomach. "You are an enticing specimen, I must say." She leaned in close and whispered in his ear. "There is so much we could discover together. This," she said as she clutched her necklace, "allows me to do far more than cause you pain. This connects us. I can give you more pleasure than you ever dreamed."

The pain fell away and a warm sensation spread through his body. He wanted to fight, to turn away, to take control, but he was helpless. His body tingled and he railed against the sensation. "No."

"No?" she asked and leaned in so her mouth brushed his ear. His body twitched as the sensation heightened. "This could be a far more pleasant way to work together. Close your eyes, relax. You have been through so much." She rubbed his chest again, then ran her hand down his stomach and nearly brushed his groin. Her head tilted into his field of vision, and she licked her lips and smiled. "My poor darling," she said, caressing his face with her fingers, "let me make everything better."

Daro ground his teeth together and fought against the growing arousal. "Stop this," he said through his teeth.

"Stop? Oh, you don't really want me to stop." She ran her hand up his chest and curled her fingers, gripping his shirt and nearly scratching him. "I would much prefer to do things this way. Strictly speaking, I am not supposed to. But it can be our little secret, yes?"

He squeezed his eyes shut and breathed heavily. The sensation heightened, hovering between pleasure and pain. His eyes rolled back and he let out a low moan.

"Yes," she said, her breath hot on his neck. "That's it."

His legs twitched and he curled his fingers. Something in the back of his mind told him he could move again, but the sensations washed over him with such strength, he couldn't bring himself to. Sindre pressed her hands to his chest and leaned over him as she threw her leg over his hips and came to rest, straddling him. She ground into his groin, her body warm, and pleasure tingled through his limbs.

He took a shuddering breath and his eyes fluttered open. Sindre's eyes were narrowed, her mouth curled in a smile. "Yes," she said again, "this is what you want."

He shook his head, fighting the arousal. "No," he said, barely able to manage a whisper.

She leaned into his face, her mouth next to his ear. "Don't fight it. You want this." She nipped at his ear with her teeth and his body shuddered.

"No," he said again, his voice rising a little. "No. I don't want this. My wife…"

The woman laughed, a low purring sound. "You don't have a wife. Not anymore. Not here. She's dead."

Daro's eyes shot open and he grabbed Sindre's wrists. He sat up as he pushed her onto the ground. He squeezed her wrists and held her down on the floor as he spoke through gritted teeth. "My wife is not dead."

"Interesting." Her eyes were bright and she showed no fear. "It doesn't matter anymore. Dead or alive, you have no wife here. You only have me."

"Damn you," he growled. "Damn all of you."

"You will let me go."

Daro gripped her wrists tighter until pain exploded through him. It knocked him backward and sent him reeling to the floor. He called out, unable to check himself, his will nearly exhausted. He beat his fists against the floor as the agony drove through him, pulsing from his back into his limbs.

As the pain retreated he heaved his tired body up to rest on his knees. Sweat trickled down his back. The woman held the mask out to him again.

"Put it on."

Daro looked up at her through the hair falling across his face. "No."

The pain knocked him over again and he writhed on the floor. He gasped for breath as the sensation abruptly changed to pleasure. He curled onto his side and fought the betrayal of his body. She lashed pain at him again, and the sensation hit him like the crack of a whip. His body burned and he cried out as the heat built in his groin. Arousal washed over him and she struck him with pain, the sensations mingling, making his body shudder. He lay on his back, unable to think. "Please," he said, "stop this."

The pain heightened and he arched his back, roaring with the intensity of it. As suddenly as they had begun, the sensations disappeared and he lay there, his chest heaving.

"I can continue as long as necessary," she said, her voice casual. "Or you can cooperate and we can move on."

Daro ignored her and steeled himself for her next attack. She hit him with pain again and he rolled to his side, grunting. The pain vanished quickly. "Perhaps you are right about one thing," she said in a low voice. "Your wife may still be alive. But believe me when I tell you she will not be for long."

With a flash of anger, he reached out to grab her throat Agony pierced through him before he could connect, and he fell backward, yelling in rage.

The pain dulled and he turned onto his side. She leaned in close. "But perhaps you can still do something about that. I can see to it that she is not harmed. But only if you cooperate with me."

His body ached and he was terrified she would leave him paralyzed again. He knew he could not trust her, but his fear for Cecily grew. Whoever these people were, they had orchestrated an attack and succeeded. They had him and he could see no way out, not while he wore the stone implant. Visions of his wife coming to his rescue faded, replaced by an image of her lying on the ground, blood trickling from her mouth. They had nearly killed her once; he had little doubt they could do it again.

"How can you protect her? And why should I believe you?" he said, his voice hoarse from yelling.

"You are an important subject and it is my task to ensure your cooperation. The sooner you are made ready, the more my work is appreciated." She brushed his hair away from his face. "The men who brought you here take orders from me. I can ensure they leave your wife alone, as long as you continue to comply."

He looked up at Sindre, her strange eyes intent. "Promise me," he said. "Promise me she will not be harmed."

One side of the woman's mouth curled in a smile and she held out the mask. "You have my word."

Daro reached out, took the mask, and pulled the slick fabric over his head.

## 18 : BLACK MASKS

THE WIND PICKED UP and tugged at Cecily's cloak. She pulled it tight around her shoulders and clutched the clasp in one hand. It was midday, but the sun was hidden behind low-hanging clouds. It was unseasonably cold, even for autumn, the crisp air tingling against her skin. She wandered past the crowded market near the Life Tree and circled wide so she wouldn't come within sight of the beautiful Imaran sculpture. It reminded her too much of Daro.

The days drifted by and none of the leads they followed turned up any clues. Callum tracked down families of missing men and women, but none of them could shed any light on Daro's disappearance. They found no patterns, no indications of why he may have been taken, or where.

It was a long walk from the market to the Boar's Head, but she welcomed the reprieve despite the chill air. She veered west to take the Lyceum Span across the river. Each of the three spans were unique.

The westernmost, and most heavily traveled, was the Merchant Span. It was wide enough for two carriages or wagons to pass, leaving room to spare on each side. The walls were waist high and made of thick stone. The entire structure felt immovable, even at the center, high above the wide water below.

The eastern span was known as the Royal Span, named for its proximity to the palace and the exclusivity of its use. Only bearers of a royal seal could use the Royal Span. It was narrow and glimmering white, the delicate walls carved in detailed relief, depicting the first kings of Halthas.

Despite the fact that it was open to anyone, the center span was the least used of the three. Known as the Lyceum Span, its shiny black surface gleamed like ice and there were no walls to prevent a fall. Youths often dared each other to cross the Lyceum Span, goading each other closer to the sheer drop off the side. Most travelers who chose the Lyceum Span were careful to stay close to the middle as they crossed.

Cecily approached the Lyceum Span and walked onto the shining black tiles without hesitation. She loved the Lyceum Span and had crossed it often when she'd still lived in the city. No one else was on the north side of the bridge, so she slowed and wandered out onto the span with measured steps. The wind brushed her hair from her face, and the cold air smelled fresh. She crept as close to the edge as she dared, to peek out over the side to the river far below. There had been a time when she would have walked all the way to the edge and sat, her legs dangling over the side. She had a greater sense of her own mortality now and shook her head at the foolish girl she had once been.

A light drizzle began to fall as Cecily made her way through the southern city toward her inn. The streets were crowded, a slew of people walking in either direction, others milling about in doorways or stopping to buy fresh food from the open tents and carts placed haphazardly on street corners. The smell of roasted meat wafted through the air, mingling with the scents of leather and horses.

She looked up and a man dressed in black caught her eye. He walked toward her, his head buried in a deep cowl, but his eyes shone from inside, unnaturally bright. Her breath caught in her throat. She slowed and peered toward him. She couldn't be sure, but his face appeared to be covered in a black mask. But it was his eyes, multicolored and shining with an abnormal brightness, that made her adrenaline surge. They looked like the eyes of the man who had taken Daro.

She stepped toward him and his strange eyes widened as he looked at her. He brushed past, hurried his step through the crowd, and crossed to the other side of the street. She whipped her head around and turned to follow, trying to nudge her way past the throng of people. He turned a corner and she pushed people out of her way, ignoring their protests. She turned the corner and caught another glimpse of him. He ducked through the crowd and turned down another side street.

She opened her Awareness and zeroed in on his moving form. The outlines of people pressed at her, an overwhelming shock of movement. It was difficult to track a single person in the throng of bodies, but she honed her Awareness in front of her to sharpen the images and kept the man within her range.

She followed, moving as fast as the crowd would allow, as questions floated through her mind. Was he as dangerous as the ones who had attacked them? Had she imagined the eyes? What would she do if she caught him? She pushed the questions away. This man might know something about Daro.

She turned down the side street, not much more than a narrow alley with walls that drew close together. Cecily had to turn to squeeze out the other side. The street beyond was bustling with people, but she kept her mind on her target and felt him dart in and out of the crowd. A flash of black caught her eye and she dashed into the street after him.

Someone bumped into her, knocking into her shoulder. He shouted something unintelligible as she pushed past him, his voice quickly lost in the din of the crowded street. Her target flashed a quick glance over his shoulder before ducking into another alley.

She chased after him but couldn't close the distance in the crowd. She held her Awareness on him and felt his movements as he tried to lose her. He pushed onward, moving in and out of the groups of people traveling down the street. He spared another glance behind and made an abrupt turn. Cecily darted to the side, trying to avoid the crowd by hugging the sides of the buildings. A door flew open in front of her, and a woman carrying a basket emerged. Cecily nearly slammed into the door. She jumped to the side and spun around as she narrowly avoided crashing into the woman.

The man moved on, cutting across another street before turning. Cecily held him in her Awareness despite the distracting push from the throng of people milling about the streets. He picked up speed and dashed away. Cecily rushed forward in time to see him duck through a doorway partway down the narrow road. Hardly more than an alley, the street was nearly empty. Cecily hastened to the opening and peeked around the corner.

It led to an interior courtyard full of trailing vines and potted plants. Flowers bloomed on balconies overhead, spilling their soft fragrance into the air. Cecily slowed and stepped in carefully. Although it felt empty, she was wary of an ambush. She pushed out her Awareness and caught a glimpse of the man as he darted out of another opening on the other side.

The doorway led to another busy street, a confusing press of noise and people. The scent of fish told her she must be nearing the docks and riverfront warehouses. She wondered if the man was running at random or if he was making for a particular destination. The throng of people prevented her from moving fast. She pushed her way through, zigzagging across the road, and darted through any gap she could find.

The man burst forward and she nearly lost him as he dashed away. She pushed her way through the people until she was able to run, keeping sight of him as he sprinted. He turned another corner and she veered toward him but he ran faster. She nearly stumbled as she turned, her feet slipping on the wet stones. Holding out her arms for balance, she skidded forward, her awkward steps slowing her.

She stopped, only just keeping her balance. The street was nearly empty. The man ran ahead, but with a quick glance around to make sure she wouldn't draw attention, she dropped her Awareness and Wielded, sending out a tendril of energy to grab his ankle. She Pulled and his leg flew backward, sending him sprawling out over the stones. He struggled to his feet but she grabbed his other leg, Pulling hard, and he crashed to the ground again.

He rolled to his back, sat up, and backed away slowly. Cecily Pushed, heaving Pressure on his chest. He leaned backward, unable to hold himself up against her Push. "Who are you?" she called as she crossed the distance toward him. He held his arm up over his face and turned his head to the side. Cecily Pushed harder and he grunted as the Pressure grew heavier on his chest.

Something Pushed back against Cecily's Wielding Energy, the shock of it throwing her backward. She lost hold of her target. He scrambled to his feet and ran down the narrow street. Cecily tried to Wield, but something blocked her, like an invisible wall. She darted forward and slammed her Awareness against the wall. It opened, but as she turned the corner, the man was nowhere in sight, nor could she sense his presence. Only a handful of people moved up and down the open street, but there was no sign of the man dressed in black. She pushed her Awareness open further, probing the alleys and side streets that branched away. He was gone. It was as if he'd disappeared into thin air.

Her breath caught in her throat and she put her back to one of the buildings. The Sensor. Could he be here, Shielding the man? Was it him who had snapped her Wielding Energy clean off like an axe through a piece of wood?

She looked up and down the street but saw no sign of either the Sensor or her target. In the midst of the city, she'd never be able to sense a ripple in the Sensor's Shield, even if she knew which direction they had gone.

Her heart sank. She wasn't going to find him and the chances of running into him again seemed slim. But who was he and why was he in the city? She opened her Awareness again to orient herself and find her way back to her inn. Her mind flashed back to the Sensor, standing on the edge of the ravine as the rushing water took her out of sight. Had he assumed her dead? If that had been him, slamming her with that Shield, he now knew she was still alive. Would he be back to finish her off?

Her back prickled as she walked to her inn through the rain, her hair hanging limp around her face. Despite her Awareness telling her no one followed, she couldn't help glancing behind, sure she'd see a man with a black mask peeking around every corner.

## 19 : SMOKE AND HINGES

"Cecily, you should go to bed," Serv said. He leaned his elbow on the table and fingered the handle of his mug.

She blinked, her eyes locked on the table. "Is it past nightfall?"

"The sun went down hours ago," Griff said with a laugh, his voice slurring.

She glanced to the side. Edson had his head down on the table, his eyes shut. His shoulders rose and fell with his slow breath. Griff leaned back in his chair, resting his hands on his belly, and his eyes drifted closed. Serv sat across from her, his eyes clear.

She looked down at her empty cup. She hadn't meant to drink herself into a stupor, but her mind swam with wine and exhaustion. After telling her friends about chasing the man with the strange eyes several days before, Griff and Serv, along with Edson, had taken up rooms at the Boar's Head, insisting they needed to stay close to her.

Although their search for Daro had come to a grinding halt, she welcomed their company. Merrick came in and out of Halthas, Beau always at his heels, checking in on her. She wasn't sure where he stayed when he left, but she didn't blame him. He wasn't used to spending so much time in the city.

She rose from her seat on trembling legs, pushed back her chair, and gripped the table. "You'll be okay?" she asked Serv. Her voice sounded thick and strange.

He stood and helped her to the stairs. "I'll make sure everyone finds their beds. You go get some rest." She climbed the stairs, clutching the railing for balance. Her legs felt awkward and she wobbled in front of her door and fumbled with the latch before finally the door swung open.

She flopped onto her bed and nearly hit her head on the low ceiling. She'd chosen a little attic room at the top of the stairs, the roof pitched to a point in the center, low on the sides. Dim light filtered in through a tiny window, set high near the rafters, at the point of the ceiling. Cecily felt safer there, high above street level with no way in except the door.

She closed her eyes and her head felt fuzzy. Had she really had so much wine? She only remembered drinking two cups. Her thoughts drifted and she couldn't focus. Her limbs felt heavy and her arm dropped to hang over the edge of the bed. She tried to roll over but didn't seem to have the strength. She had a fleeting thought that she shouldn't be this tired, but it swam away as she sank into the darkness of an exhausted sleep.

A noise made her jump and she felt something hard against her back. Her neck was tight and uncomfortable. The bed felt like the floor. Her eyes fluttered open and she sucked in a breath. Something was wrong. She tried to move her arms but they were held above her head. She pulled and heard the clank and scrape of metal as something hard bit into her wrists. Her eyes darted around, but all was black, not a sliver of light piercing the darkness. She tried to pull her arms again, but they wouldn't respond. Her legs felt like dead weight and her head lolled to the side. Her breathing quickened and she tried to lift her head, but it wouldn't budge.

She squeezed her eyes shut and willed her body to move. Where was she? How had she been chained? Why couldn't she move? Confusion swirled in her mind and she forced her eyes open again. Light assaulted her, and tears sprang to her eyes. She squinted against the brightness and raised her hands to cover her face. *Where are the chains?* Her body felt suddenly hot and sweat sprang out on her forehead, trickling down her temples. Something bit at the back of her neck. She tried to swipe it away but somehow she couldn't reach. A face swirled before her eyes, hazy and indistinct, a smile curling its lips and the eyes a turbulent mix of color, brown melding into blue around a pinprick of black in the center.

She gasped, her eyes flying open. The room was dark. Only the faint glow from the streetlamps enabled her to see the shadowy shapes of her room. The ceiling slanted above her, the wooden beams meeting in the middle. Her eyes felt heavy and she blinked hard as she struggled to wake herself up. She rubbed her wrists but found no sign of the chains, no redness or chafing. *I must have been dreaming.*

Her eyes drifted closed; it was impossible to keep them open. Her breathing slowed and she felt herself sink again. Something in the back of her mind told her to wake up and check her room, but she couldn't find consciousness. She felt as if she was moving, slowly rocking to the motion of waves, the steady rhythm calling her down, into the release of sleep.

Noises intruded on the edge of her perception. She wondered vaguely if she was dreaming again. A loud crack jolted her eyes open and she thought she could hear voices. Was it morning already? Her room was still dark, the dull light from the window hazy and muddled. Her mind felt slow, as if her thoughts traveled through thick mud before reaching the surface. She blinked again and tried to force herself awake. Her eyes stung and she coughed, her throat dry and burning.

She took another breath and something in her mind clicked back into place. *Smoke.* The noises outside her room took shape and she realized it was shouting. She heard another crash, followed by screaming. Her room was quickly filling with smoke, a thick haze in the warm air. She pulled her tunic up over her mouth and nose and squinted, as her eyes watered. *The building is on fire.*

Shaking her head to clear it, she scurried off the bed and kept low to the ground. The shouting below was more distinct—cries for help, and someone yelling instructions. She crawled over to the door and felt it with the back of her hand. Smoke trickled in through the cracks, but the door was cool to the touch. She got up and tried to unlock it, but the lock wouldn't budge. She pulled on the latch, but it was stuck tight. She pulled again, shaking the door, but it wouldn't open.

She shook the door again, and her heartbeat rose. The smoke made her cough and she held her tunic to her face to breathe through it. She tried kicking the door, to no avail; she wasn't strong enough to kick it open.

Whirling around, she eyed the window. It was tiny and set high in the wall, just below the center of the pitched ceiling. No one could get in through that window, but she couldn't get out either, even if she could climb high enough to reach it. Cursing her choice of room, she turned her attention back to the door.

Using her Awareness, she probed the lock. The mechanism was melted on the inside, the moving parts stuck, and the latch was bonded to the doorjamb. There was nothing for her to move, no way for her to free the lock. Running her hand along the door, she focused her Awareness on the grain of the wood, searching for cracks or weaknesses. *The hinges!* She gasped, but the flood of relief was short-lived. The hinges were melted, fused to the fasteners in the doorway. The door was welded shut.

She crouched down low and pounded on the door for help. Tears streamed from her eyes as she coughed and choked. She looked back to find the window was lost in the haze, the room filling quickly. She clutched the fabric of her tunic to her face, coughing with every breath. As she cowered lower onto the floor, her eyes burned, her mouth bitter with the taste of ash. As the heat grew, sweat beaded on her forehead and ran down her back. She pounded on the door with her fist, unable to get enough air to cry out.

*I wonder if I'll suffocate before I burn.* A sob climbed her throat and she coughed again. She kicked at the door, but it made little noise. Her head felt as hazy as the room, as if her mind was filling with smoke. She squeezed her eyes closed as tears ran down her cheeks. The shouting outside stopped, replaced by a loud roar. Another crash rang out and the building shuddered. She pounded on the door again, hitting it with her free hand. Every breath was painful, like pulling sharp gravel down her throat. The smoke seared her lungs and her coughs came in uncontrollable spasms.

*Daro, I'm so sorry.*

Something hit the door with a loud crack, and the force reverberated through her body. She rolled away, desperately wishing for unconsciousness before the flames came to take her. Crack! Another bang came from the door, making Cecily jerk as she lay on the floor. Something assaulted the door again and through the smoke she thought she could see movement in the center of the door. Another bang and the door erupted in splinters of wood, the sharp edge of an axe sticking through.

Scrambling to her feet, she kept clear and squinted against the smoke as she breathed through the fabric. The axe hit again and pulled to the side, opening a hole in the wood. The pounding continued and the center of the door dissolved into splinters. A head poked through, a swath of fabric tied around the face up to the eyes. A hand reached through the hole. Cecily grasped and stepped through the ruined door.

Hands pulled her through as the heat assaulted her, beating at her in waves.

Her rescuer pressed gently down on her head, beckoning her to stay low, and led her by the hand down the stairs. Cecily coughed, keeping the fabric up to her face, and crouched low as she walked. The inn was an inferno. Flames licked the walls and wood beams glowed bright red. Smoke filled the building and heat pounded against her, evaporating the sweat off her body instantly.

She stumbled at the bottom of the stairs and nearly tripped on a piece of burning debris. Her rescuer grabbed her arms to keep her steady and pulled her forward. A loud crash from above sent sparks and ash raining down on them as they sprinted for an opening in the wall. The building shuddered and another crash rang out behind them as they dived out into the street.

"Cecily!" a voice called out as she lay gasping, the stones cold and hard under her face. Someone grabbed under her arms and pulled her forward, away from the burning inn as she coughed and sputtered, struggling for air. They turned her over on her back, and cradled her head.

A cool cloth pressed gently to her eyes and forehead, more wet cloth on her arms. She breathed deep of the clean air as her coughs subsided. Footsteps fell around her, people moving quickly. The sounds of yelling and commotion shifted into focus as her mind cleared. She coughed again and pressed the fabric to her eyes to wipe the burning tears.

A billowing black cloud of smoke shrouded the stars as the Boar's Head raged with fire. Orange and yellow flames spit out the windows and engulfed the walls and roof. The entire building was a roaring blaze. A fire brigade had arrived; Wielders Pulled water through a long tube and sprayed it on the flames.

Someone took the cloth from her and dipped it in a bucket before handing it back to her. She squinted, her eyes still burning from the smoke, to find her head in Griff's lap. His face was smudged with soot, but he smiled and helped her sit up.

"What happened? Did everyone get out?" she asked, her voice hoarse and her throat dry.

Griff nodded to the side and Cecily looked over to find Serv seated on the ground nearby, a strip of fabric bunched around his neck. Edson sat next to him and rubbed his eyes and face. Serv's forehead was black, his cheeks flushed and red.

"Can't say I remember making it back to my room after dinner," Griff said. "But I woke up choking on smoke. We all got out and realized you must still be inside. Before any of us could form a thought, Serv burst in there." He gestured at the ruined building. "He was gone for what felt like hours. I thought for sure the two of you weren't coming out." He took a shuddering breath and blew it out through pursed lips. "Damn amazing thing, seeing you two come flying out of that inferno."

Edson came over and crouched in front of her. "Are you hurt?" he asked, worry plain on his face.

Cecily looked down at herself. The skin on her arms was red and raw, but she didn't see any serious burns. "No, I think I'm okay." He handed her a waterskin and she drank deeply of the cool liquid. It soothed her dry throat, but it still hurt to breathe.

Serv turned his head and met her gaze. Tears sprang to her eyes as she stared at him, and the enormity of what he had done washed over her. He rose and helped her to her feet. She opened her mouth, but didn't know what to say or how she could possibly thank him. He pressed his lips in a small smile and shook his head. Still holding her hand, he raised it and covered it with his other hand.

"Thank you," she whispered. He let go of her hand and gave her a small nod.

The Wielders appeared to be winning the battle. The flames died down as the building billowed smoke into the night sky. People milled about watching, some tending to the wounded while others stood in pairs, holding each other as they watched the inn burn.

Griff stood up next to her and gently lifted her hand to inspect the burns on her arm. "These will sting something fierce, but you don't look too bad," he said.

She nodded. "How did this happen?"

He shrugged. "The fire started downstairs, probably in the kitchen. Spread through the building quick. Cecily, I'm sorry, I didn't think we'd had quite so much wine. I still feel all muddled, but I suppose that could be the smoke."

"It wasn't the smoke, or the wine," Serv said, his voice quiet. He turned toward them. "We were drugged."

Cecily's eyes shot toward her friend. "How do you know?"

"Where I come from, these things are common. Many of my warrior brothers and I took it upon ourselves to build immunity to such narcotics, to protect us from these cowardly attacks. I'm familiar with the effects. I only wish I had realized it sooner."

"But why, and who… and how?" Griff sputtered.

Serv shook his head. "The likely answer is in our wine. As to who or why, that I don't know."

"My door was welded shut," Cecily said. Serv looked at her, his brow furrowed. "That's why I couldn't get out. The lock, the doorknob, and the hinges, they were all melted. There's no way the fire was hot enough to do that."

"What do you mean?" Griff asked.

"I think I can answer the question of why. Someone is trying to kill me."

## 20 : THE QUARRY

"You should have told me," Callum said.

Cecily looked up. "What?"

Callum rolled his eyes. "You haven't heard a word I said, have you?" He paced around the room, agitated, and gestured as he spoke. "You didn't tell me about the man you saw, the one who ran from you. That was days ago. Were you planning on saying anything? And last night you buried yourself in wine. I realize things aren't exactly going well, but drinking yourself into a stupor isn't going to help."

Cecily sighed and rubbed her eyes. Her head felt heavy, her thoughts thick and slow. She hadn't slept much after the fire, and although it was midmorning the next day, the effect of the drug was still in her system. "I didn't bury myself in wine. Someone drugged me, unless you'd like to doubt Serv's word." Her eyes flicked to Serv, who sat on a barrel at the edge of the gray stone room, sharpening his sword. Callum raised his eyebrows at her. No one doubted Serv's word, not even Callum. "I can't even be sure of who I saw. I only saw him for a moment, but I could have sworn his eyes looked like the eyes of the man who attacked me after Daro was taken."

"But he obviously ran from you and someone helped him escape," Sumara said gently. She had arrived in the middle of the night. Cecily still wasn't sure how she'd gotten word of the fire. Their other companions had trickled in throughout the morning, each expressing their alarm at what had happened and their relief that none of them had been seriously hurt.

"This is all connected," Callum said and wagged his finger as he walked back and forth across the stone floor. "The men you saw, the fire, and I am telling you, the damn smugglers. They are all connected." Callum had appeared at the scene of the fire, melting out of the shadows, and quietly ushered them away. Cecily had only a vague memory of following Callum, but she'd woken up after a few fitful hours of sleep realizing he had taken her to the Quarry.

Deep beneath southern Halthas, the Quarry was a labyrinth of stone tunnels and rooms. Stone Shapers had extracted a great mass of stone south of the river to rebuild the city walls and defenses after the Attalonian invasion. As they'd quarried the stone, they'd created a series of tunnels to preserve the land above. When work was complete, the entrances had been sealed and the tunnel system faded into obscurity. Cecily didn't know who had rediscovered the underground complex, but Callum and others in the Underground used it extensively. During the war it had been an indispensable location, offering them protection and concealment. It was unnerving listening to their voices echo off the stone walls, feeling the damp air on her skin. It reminded her too keenly of their days fighting Hadran.

"I think we all agree on the connection," said Sumara. "Someone clearly isn't pleased that you made it out of the woods after Daro was taken."

Cecily shook her head. "I wonder if he knew I was still alive, or if he thought I drowned in that river." *And does he know I got out of the inn?*

"How can you be certain it was the same men who attacked you after Daro was taken?" Alastair cut in. "You only saw the one, and you said yourself, you can't be sure his eyes were different. We don't have very much to go on."

"Do you know any Wielders who can push back on someone's ability like that?" Cecily snapped. Her head ached. "He can Shield like no one I've ever encountered. What are the chances there are two men out there who can do that?"

"That may be a fair point, but you don't seem particularly sure of yourself, Cecily," Alastair said.

Callum's head whipped toward Alastair. "She was almost killed last night. You could cut her a little slack."

"I was merely pointing out that, by Cecily's own admission, she can't be certain the man she saw in the city was connected to Daro's disappearance. And we don't know that the fire was an attempt on her life."

Callum's mouth opened and he paused to look around the room at the others. "Are you serious? Palace life is turning you into an idiot, Alastair. She had to chase this guy through the streets. What was he running from? I think he knew who she was. How could he not be connected to Daro? Do you know a lot of folks with eyes like that? Because I don't, and I know a lot of people. Then a Sensor shows up and Shields long enough for them to disappear. I know the strength of Cecily's Wielding isn't supposed to be common knowledge, but we all know how strong she is. No one else can Shield that well, not against her."

Alastair opened his mouth to answer, but Callum pressed on. "As if that weren't enough, someone just tried to kill her; and it almost worked." He walked across the room again, ticking points off on his finger. "Paid someone to drug them. Melted the damn hinges. By the gods, Alastair, what more do you want before we act? You want to pull her body out of an alley before we do something about this?"

Cecily's heart rate rose and a sudden shot of adrenaline made her jittery. Sumara shifted in her seat, and Alastair sat across from her with his jaw rigid. The tension in the room was thick, anger bubbling behind everyone's eyes.

She stood up and put her hand on Callum's shoulder. "You're Projecting," she said quietly. Callum met her eyes, then looked around the room. Most had clenched fists, their necks and shoulders tight with strain. Only Serv seemed relaxed, although he'd stopped sliding the stone down his blade and cast wary eyes at his companions.

Callum took a deep breath and the tension melted. Cecily's heart stopped pounding quite so furiously and her friends shifted in their seats and breathed away the strain.

"Sorry," Callum muttered. He ran a hand through his hair and took a seat. It was rare for Callum to let his ability leak out without intent. He leaned back in his chair and stared at the table.

"They hit you quickly," said Serv. Everyone's eyes swung to him. He slid the stone down his blade as he spoke, the soft metallic swish barely audible above his gentle voice. "My bet is the Sensor isn't the one in charge. He realized you're still alive, and he didn't want his boss to find out. So he tried to get rid of you by making it look like an accident. That way his boss doesn't ever have to know you walked out of those woods."

"Interesting theory," said Alastair. "But you make a lot of assumptions."

Serv shrugged. "Assassinations are complicated, particularly failed ones. If they knew she escaped the first time, it is unlikely they would have gone this long before making another attempt. She's been in the city long enough—they should have tried to hit her before this. It leads me to the conclusion that prior to her encounter the other day, they thought her dead. And the attempt on her life came soon after. This tells me they acted rashly, arranging an attack as quickly as possible. It was hasty. Nearly successful, but hasty nonetheless."

Callum cocked his head at Serv. "You never cease to surprise me. How is it you know so much about assassinating someone?"

Serv gave Callum a small smile and went back to sharpening his sword.

"Fine, keep your silence," Callum said and waved him off. "The question is, what do we do about this?"

Cecily rubbed her face with her hands. It was hard to stay alert.

"The fire will of course be reported to the proper authorities," Alastair said. "King Rogan will—"

"King Rogan will what?" Callum cut him off. "Ride in on a stallion with a gleaming sword, ready to lead us to victory? I, for one, am rather tired of hearing that Rogan will save the day. What is Rogan actually doing? Where is he?"

Alastair's face grew red as Callum spoke. "His Majesty is pursuing the problem with all his resources."

"And he wants us to wait, is that it?"

"Your involvement now would compromise the Crown's investigation," Alastair said.

Callum narrowed his eyes. "What does he know? Has he found something?"

"You know I'm not at liberty to say."

"He doesn't have anything, does he? All those resources, and he hasn't gotten any farther than we have." Callum leaned back and crossed his arms. "Either that, or he isn't telling you anything." Alastair's mouth hung open. "So that's it. He's brushing you off."

"Callum, I'm sure Rogan has his reasons," Cecily said. She was sick of listening to Callum and Alastair argue. "He isn't brushing anyone off. We haven't had any luck. Is it so surprising that Rogan would be hitting similar walls?"

Callum shrugged. "As you say. But I'll tell you one thing. You're staying down here with me. Those people were willing to torch an entire inn in the middle of the city. You're not safe out there."

"Cecily, I am under orders to bring you back to the palace, with Mira as your escort and personal guard," Alastair said, in his best authoritative voice.

Cecily groaned inside. Another pointless issue for everyone to argue over. She put her hands up to stop both Callum and Alastair from speaking. "I will stay here," she said. The thought of being confined to the palace made her twitch. Alastair opened his mouth to speak, but she continued. "I appreciate Rogan's concern, and Mira is welcome to stay with me. But I won't stay in the palace."

Alastair closed his mouth and pursed his lips as he rose from his chair. "Very well. With that, I must return to the palace." Cecily rose. He turned toward her and put a gentle hand on her shoulder. "Be careful," he said, his voice quiet. "I wish you would come with me."

"I know. But you and I both know I can't sit around the palace with people waiting on me. Not now."

Callum rose from his chair, put a hand on her elbow, and led her out into the stone hallway. He looked up and down the corridor before he leaned in, keeping his voice low. "I have a lead on something that I think is connected to Daro. But I could really use your help."

Cecily narrowed her eyes. *Why is he whispering?* "Help with what?"

He glanced around again. "I have reason to believe someone high up is connected to the smugglers. They are getting in, past the inspectors, and I have a feeling I know why."

She kept her voice quiet, but it was hard to conceal her annoyance. "I understand you don't like these smugglers encroaching on your territory. But what does this have to do with Daro?"

"This isn't personal. I think whoever has Daro is the one importing the slaves."

"Why? Because you have a hunch that it is all connected?"

"Listen, I know it sounds like I'm making things up because it's convenient, but I'm telling you, I know these smugglers are involved. I can't prove it yet. That's why I need you."

What Callum was asking for slowly dawned on Cecily. "No, Callum. If you're asking me to do what I think you're asking, I can't do it. I swore I was done with that."

"I'm not asking you to find dirt on someone so a king can string them up outside the palace. These are slavers, and kidnappers, and we need to find out who is involved. It would just be a little late-night peek. No need to leave any bodies behind."

"No. I can't do it."

Callum's lips lifted in a crooked smile. "Come on, this won't even be that difficult. We've done worse."

"You're not dragging me into this."

Callum sighed and looked away. "Have it your way. But this would be far easier, and faster, if you'd help."

Another boy trotted down the corridor and stopped in front of Callum. He handed him a folded slip of paper before turning on his heel and running back up the hallway. Callum gazed at the note, his brow furrowing as he read the contents.

"I have to go," he said as he crumpled the note in his hand.

Cecily was used to seeing Callum's messengers delivering missives, but he usually dismissed their importance and tucked the notes away. "Is everything okay?" she asked.

"Not really," he said. "I have to go take care of something. If you're content to sit around and wait for Rogan, be my guest. But I'm not."

She watched him walk up the corridor, and his footsteps echoed off the stone walls. A wave of exhaustion rolled over her and she swayed on her feet. She put a hand on the wall to steady herself. Still nothing from Rogan, and Callum was chasing smugglers. She closed her eyes and brought an image of Daro to her mind. *Where are you?* Every time her thoughts strayed to her husband she had the sickening feeling that, wherever he was, something horrible was happening to him.

She called to Mira to let her know she was heading to her room, one of the small sleeping quarters down another hallway in the Quarry. If she was going to be able to think straight, she needed more sleep.

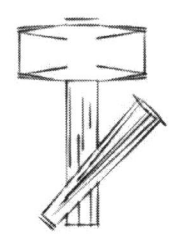

## 21 : TRANSFERENCE

Daro reached under his bed and felt the scratches in the wood. Thirty-four, thirty-five. Had he missed one? He tried to mark the day each morning when he woke, but his memory felt disorganized. The days blended together, a never-ending haze of visits from Sindre. She came to him daily now, always dressed the same, wearing that accursed medallion. Each day she wore him down, as she insisted on some small task. Whether it was kneeling before her, putting on his mask, or following simple instructions, she assaulted him mercilessly until he relented. Many nights he had fallen into unconsciousness, railing against paralysis, his body limp and useless on the floor, his hatred the only thing keeping him sane.

He began to find it easier to follow her instructions and feign obedience. He imagined his wife hovering just behind his shoulder, whispering in his ear. He would do what Sindre asked, but always with

Cecily in his mind. His thoughts were all he had left, the only thing he could control. She would not take his mind, but outwardly, he would comply.

The lock clicked and Daro pulled on his mask. It was easier to begin this way. They dressed him in black, a pair of loose-fitting pants and a long-sleeved shirt. He didn't know where his own clothes were—long gone, he supposed. The mask covered his head down to his shoulders, the only opening across his eyes. It was uncomfortable at first, but he soon took refuge in the anonymity. He hid behind the mask, retreating into the recesses of his mind.

Sindre entered, but this time she left the door ajar. He looked past her, curious to see if someone else would enter. Thus far the only people he had seen were the woman and a hooded and masked person who brought his food, emptied his chamber pot and helped him wash each morning. Judging by the hands, he thought it was a small man, but he couldn't be sure. He'd stopped trying to engage the person in conversation after the first few days. He never got so much as a nod in response.

"Follow me," Sindre said. She turned and walked out the door.

Daro hesitated. He hadn't left the room since his arrival. The four walls had become his world. Adrenaline made his stomach flutter and his limbs tingle. He took a few steps and peeked out the door, unexpectedly anxious. It was a long hallway with bare wooden floors and several other doors on both sides. The walls were paneled with dull and cracked wainscoting and sconces with oil lamps lined the hallway, in a style Daro had only seen on some of the older buildings in Halthas. The air had a musty smell to it, the mild scent of decay.

Sindre stopped and looked over her shoulder. "Come."

She walked down the hallway and Daro followed. His eyes darted around and drunk in the newness after so many days of being locked in his cell. He quickly lost his sense of direction as the twisting hallways branched off in different directions, one set of stairs leading up, another leading back down. He wondered if she was walking him in circles simply to confuse him.

He passed sections of dark, heavy drapes and he wondered if they hid windows. He would have given much for a glimpse outside, some indication of where he was. Sindre pressed on and he quickened his step to keep up with her, his bare feet padding after the sharp click of her boots.

She turned left, through a doorway that led down another hall. The thick door stood open and Daro noticed a series of locks. He followed her to another door on the right, noticing several people hovering near the opening as he stepped inside.

It opened into a large windowless room, a mess of shelves and cabinets along the walls. In the center was a square wooden table, thick legs supporting a heavy tabletop. Atop the table stood a large stone, almost triangular in shape, resembling a miniaturized mountain. It was white speckled with green, and as Daro gazed at it, the colors seemed to shift and meld together. Something about it reminded him of the Life Tree in Halthas, but as he looked closer, it appeared to be made of the same stone as Sindre's medallion.

Off to the side, a man sat at a desk, writing on a piece of parchment. He looked to be in his fifties, clean shaven with closely cropped dark hair. Black robes hung from his frame, much like those worn by the Magisters of the Lyceum. He nodded to Sindre and looked at Daro as he slowly rose from his seat.

"Come in," Sindre commanded, motioning for Daro to enter. He hesitated, then took a small step as his eyes darted between the two people. Something about that stone made him increasingly anxious and he didn't want to get near it.

"Impressive," the man said as he took a few steps closer to Daro and looked him up and down. His eyes reminded Daro of the woman's, a strange mix of color, his a swirl of blue and green. "I see you have accomplished much with him, Sindre."

"Yes," she replied. "His will is strong, but I believe we will find that to our advantage."

He nodded, still looking at Daro as one might inspect wares at a market. "You deem him ready?"

"I would have preferred more time, but yes."

"Ready for what?" Daro asked, his voice low.

The man cast a sidelong glance at Sindre. "You haven't given me as much time as the others," she said. "Another week and he would be more compliant."

He turned back to Daro and rubbed his hands together. He wore supple leather gloves. "Of course. Patience has been difficult with this one, I admit. I am anxious to see the results."

"As am I," said Sindre. "I have put a great deal of work into this one."

"Who are you?" Daro growled. Fear made his neck twitch, the muscles in his back tense. He clenched his fists and took a step forward.

Sindre stepped toward him but the man held up his hand. "No, Sindre, not yet. I suppose you were right; perhaps you needed more time." He peered into the slit in Daro's mask. "I've grown used to working with subjects who are more... pliable. But I think this is good." He gestured to the table behind him and stepped out of the way. "Come, sit."

Daro looked from the man to Sindre. She raised her eyebrows at him.

"Sit in the chair," she said, her voice lilting as if she spoke to a child.

Daro closed his eyes and thought of his wife. He hesitated another moment, expecting a spark of pain to drop him at any second. He knew Sindre would force him to her will, regardless of how long he held out. It was the same every single day. With a deep breath, he opened his eyes and obeyed.

"Good," she purred and rubbed his shoulders with a light touch.

Daro decided on a bit of boldness. "Who are you? What do you want from me?"

Sindre's fingers dug into his shoulders, but the man put his hand up. "Fair questions. We have kept you in the dark for quite some time." He pulled up a chair and sat next to Daro. "I am Nihil, and you might call this my laboratory. I have spent many years researching the possibilities hidden within Wielders and have had some great success unlocking their potential. I am a seeker of knowledge, really. I delve into the depths of Wielding energies."

"What does this have to do with me? I'm no Wielder."

"No?" Nihil asked. "Not in the Halthian sense, that is probably true. But if I am not mistaken, you have Imaran blood."

Daro nodded, but he didn't understand. *What does my father have to do with this?*

"I have long believed that Imarans manipulate energy in a manner similar to Wielders. It is difficult to study, as the Imarans live such an isolated existence. We know very little about their abilities or how they work. Of course, I'd have preferred a full-blooded Imaran to work with, but I was unsuccessful at procuring one. Then, my associates brought you to my attention. I don't know why it hadn't occurred to me sooner. I spend too much time here, I suppose. But you, the war hero, a half-blooded Imaran, living the life of a Halthian. I am very interested to see what you can show me."

Nihil turned and beckoned to someone near the door. "Bring the Stone Shaper."

Sindre kept her hands on Daro's shoulders, her gentle pressure enough to hold him down. His anxiety rose but he knew it would be useless to try to escape. His breathing quickened as someone led a man into the laboratory. His hands were bound and his head covered with a brown sack. He was led to a chair opposite Daro, across the table on the other side of the strange rock.

"You see, I was born in Attalon," Nihil said. "I'm sure you've heard the stories. Terrible place to be a Wielder." He shook his head and clicked his tongue. "When my father realized what I was, well, he did his best. We fled to Sahaar, where I wouldn't have to hide my abilities. When I was old enough, I came to Halthas." He moved about the room and gathered a leather-bound book, ink and a quill. "Ah, Halthas. City of Wonders, they called it, home of the famed Lyceum. It was a wonder, I admit. So much beauty, so many accomplishments. So modern. The Lyceum itself was less impressive, I'm afraid." He tugged on the fingers of his gloves and slipped them off. "But my work hasn't suffered without their patronage. In fact, I think they would have held me back."

The hooded man shook in his seat and whimpered quietly. As he looked closely, Daro could see bruises on his arms. His tattered clothing was dirty and hung off his bony frame. Sindre's grip tightened on Daro's shoulders and his implant tingled.

"The other thing about those fascinating Imarans is their Arcstone," Nihil continued, gesturing at the marbled stone on the table. "Arcstone has some amazing properties. I've been able to do miraculous things with my subjects using this stone."

He sat back in his seat and gestured to the man who stood behind the prisoner. He took the man's bound hands and pulled them toward the Arcstone, putting his palms on the stone, and used a length of rope to tie them fast. The prisoner made a futile attempt at resistance, tugging against his bonds and muttering something unintelligible as his head lolled to the side.

"I will warn you ahead of time, this experience will be unsettling at first. It is best to relax and let the energies swell within you. Pushing back is only painful and ultimately destructive. I have been looking forward to working with you for quite some time. I would hate to lose you on the first pass." He gestured toward the stone. "Place your hands on the stone."

Daro stared at the Arcstone. It appeared solid, yet the colors seemed to move the longer he watched it. The prisoner moaned softly, his arms still feebly straining. Daro's heart pounded and his breath came in shallow gasps. Of all the things he had endured, somehow this terrified him the most. The feel of Sindre's hands on his shoulders reminded him who was in control. He desperately wanted to resist, but as his eyes darted around the room, he could see no way out.

Nihil spoke. "Sindre."

A jolt of electricity shot down Daro's back. It was a familiar sensation; she had taught him what would be next. He gritted his teeth and clenched his fists as he waited for the next hit. Another jolt hit him, stronger than the first.

She leaned down to whisper in his ear. "Put your hands on the stone."

Nihil made a note in his notebook and looked back up at Daro, his eyes dispassionate. The other prisoner began to sob, his low moans shaking his scrawny shoulders.

Panic rose, a knot of fear building in Daro's gut. His breath came fast, and every fiber of his being screamed at him to get up and run. Sindre hit him with pain again, and he leaned forward as he tucked his arms into his body and groaned. His body felt as if it were on fire, the skin burning to a cinder and flaking off. She let the pain dissipate and spoke into his ear again. "We both know how this ends. I can only protect your wife for so long. We must show Nihil that we are working well together, or her life will be in danger."

Pain surged through him again. He leaned his head back and roared in pain. "Stop!" he cried. The pain ended abruptly, and he sat, panting, and held his hands up in front of him. "Stop," he whispered between breaths. "I will."

Sindre lifted her hands from his shoulders. Clenching his teeth, he reached his hands toward the Arcstone. The prisoner sobbed and Daro flinched. Nihil leaned in, his brow pinched, his eyes hungry, his own hands hovering above the stone.

Daro surged forward, as one might jump into a pool of cold water, anxious for the initial shock to be over. He pressed his hands onto the sides of the Arcstone. Light exploded in front of his eyes, a multicolored flash of brilliance that nearly blinded him. He felt as if he were rushing down a tunnel, the walls a streaming mass of radiance, pushing him forward. Images began to fly past his vision, scenes of people moving too quickly for him to make out. He felt dangerously hot, as if he were sitting too close to a fire. Visions darted by, overwhelming his senses. He struggled to breathe, heat and light and air rushing at him in a torrent.

The images slowed and he began to see them clearly as they drifted past. He could see a woman working in a shop, placing things on a shelf. He felt a sudden affection for this woman, the emotion passing as the illusion floated away. More visions appeared and sped past him, borne along the brilliant tunnel as the glare assaulted him. Each vision brought with it a passing feeling, like a long-forgotten memory triggered by a familiar scent. The visions grew darker as they slowed, the edges tinged with red. Daro felt a spike of fear as he saw men and women in a boat, dressed in rags and tied with rope. The image faded and was replaced by a dark cell, crowded with people. The sense of hopelessness nearly overwhelmed him. The tunnel continued, rushing at him with heat and brilliant white light, until he felt he might shatter, the pieces of himself streaming away into nothing.

A thunderclap of sound splintered the light. He flew backward and hit the floor. He lay on top of the broken chair and gasped for breath, his body warm and full, tingling with energy. Nihil and Sindre leaned over him, their eyes wide. Sindre spoke, but her words were broken, her face obscured by blinding flashes as if the sun shone behind her. Nihil put his gloved hand on Daro's forehead, touching his face through the mask. Everything looked sluggish, as if moving in slow motion.

Daro turned and pushed himself up with his arms to get to his feet, blinking and shaking his head. Visions and memories swirled in his mind and he struggled to decipher what was real. He looked down at the broken chair. The table still stood in the center of the room, the Arcstone unchanged. The other prisoner lay face down on the table, his hands still bound to the stone, his body withered and dry. Above the rope his wrist cracked and his hand crumbled, spilling dust out over the table.

Daro took a step backward. Nihil and Sindre were in front of him, holding their hands out, speaking in soothing tones. His body felt saturated, every inch pulsing with energy. His breath came easily and he felt as if he could chase the sun across the continent without stopping.

Nihil peered into his eyes. "Can you hear me?"

Daro looked down at his hands. He nodded to Nihil and marveled in the way he felt. He could barely stand still, his body full to bursting.

A wicked smile crept over Nihil's face as he gazed up at Daro. He nodded slowly as he looked him up and down. "Success," he said, a tone of lust in his voice. "You are Number Fourteen."

## 22 : NEWS UNEXPECTED

Cecily rubbed her hands to massage the warmth back into them. She sat at the back of the Ale Stone, at Callum's usual table. A messenger had pressed a folded note into her hand, a hastily scrawled message from Callum with instructions to meet him.

Mira sat next to her and scanned the tables. Although Rogan had failed to contact her since Alastair had insisted she return to the palace, Mira had stayed with Cecily to offer protection. Cecily tired of the constant presence of her friend, although she knew Mira meant well. And she had to admit, no one had tried to kill her since the fire at the inn, so perhaps it was a good thing the tall woman followed her everywhere.

She slumped back in her chair. It bothered her that she felt so tired all the time. She understood her friends' insistence that she remain hidden while they searched for signs of Daro. The fire had scared them all. However, the incessant waiting was slowly driving her mad. The weeks dragged on and she itched to hear from Rogan, clinging to the hope of a breakthrough.

"Have you been having nightmares lately?" Mira asked, her voice jolting Cecily from her thoughts.

Cecily looked askance at her friend. "Why?"

"I check on you in the night and it's obvious you're dreaming. I get the feeling they aren't pleasant."

Her face warmed with embarrassment. She wondered what she said while she was sleeping. "You're right, they aren't pleasant. I can't make sense of them most of the time." She paused, not sure how much she wished to share, although there was a measure of relief in talking about it. "Sometimes I see things, like I'm in another place. I see faces, people I don't recognize, but they seem real. The worst dreams have a light, like I'm traveling through a tunnel. I see all these images and it feels"—she paused and searched for the words—"it feels as if I'm falling through someone else's emotions. They're like sheets hung out to dry, blowing in the wind, and I'm running through them, feeling them brush against me as I pass. But they aren't sheets—they're someone else's feelings and memories. It's awful."

Mira's nose screwed up in a look of distaste. "That is awful. I thought maybe you were dreaming of Daro."

"I think I am," she said, her voice quiet.

Callum dropped into a chair facing them. His hair was messier than usual and his shirt looked rumpled. He tossed a thick gold coin on the table and blew out a breath in obvious frustration.

"What happened?" Cecily asked.

Callum rubbed his face with his hands and shook his head. His mouth was tight, and his whole body looked tense. "The bloody bastard."

Cecily could feel Callum's anger. It reminded her of the wash of emotions in her dreams. "Callum, be careful, you're Projecting again."

He pressed a hand to his eyes. "I know, I'm sorry." He glanced over both shoulders and leaned across the table. "I honestly don't know how to tell you this, but it's Rogan."

Cecily's heart jumped in her chest and her stomach tightened. She felt Mira stiffen next to her. "What happened? Is he okay?"

He let out another breath. "Oh no, nothing happened to him. Not yet, at least." He raked his hand through his hair. "Cecily, he knows who has Daro."

Cecily's breath caught in her throat. Her mind swam with the possibilities. "He found him? Where is he? What do we need to do?"

"You don't understand what I mean. He didn't find Daro. He always knew who took him."

Cecily leaned away. "I don't understand what you're saying. That isn't possible."

"I found out who has Daro. I heard about him a couple of months ago, but at the time I wasn't sure he was behind the abductions. His name is Nihil and I think he's been abducting people for years. And I was right—he's working with smugglers from Sahaar."

"What does this have to do with Rogan?" Cecily asked.

"From what I can gather, Rogan's been supplying this guy for years. He probably knows right where he is, and he's kept it from us the entire time."

"You can't be serious," Mira said, her voice sharp. "Rogan wouldn't lie to us."

"I didn't want to believe it either. I've had my frustrations with Rogan, but this... I didn't see this coming."

Mira shook her head. "What proof do you have? You expect us to take your word over that of the king?"

Callum leaned back in his chair and crossed one leg over his knee. "I have plenty of proof. Most of it is chained up in a dark hole, but I can take you there if you really want to hear it for yourself."

"I don't understand," Cecily said.

"A few months ago, some of my people found a building, an old manor house of some minor lord. It looked abandoned, but they saw people going in, big groups of them, although no one ever came out. I kept eyes on the building and finally we saw someone leave. It was just one man, but it was something. I managed to grab him a few weeks ago. He couldn't tell me much, but it was enough to start putting the pieces together." He took a deep breath and continued. "His job was to get the shipments into the house. He claimed not to know what happened to them after that, and after everything I did to him, he probably doesn't."

"By shipments, what exactly do you mean?" Mira asked.

"Slaves," Callum said. The word fell heavy on their ears. "I tracked down the owner of the manor, someone named Nihil Suor. He's using it as a waypoint to traffic people into Halthas. The only thing I still can't find is where they go from there. But that isn't all. Nihil sends men with the shipments, to get them through the city. My prisoner had some very interesting things to say about Wielders with unnatural abilities and eyes that are a swirl of different colors." He paused to let it sink in. "I was right. This Nihil bastard is buying slaves, and he must be the one who has Daro. Unless you know someone else with eyes like that."

They sat for a moment as Cecily considered what Callum told her. Her mind was a knot of confusion.

"We need to be careful here," Callum continued, "Nihil's men are dangerous. The guy I captured is terrified. He practically begged me to keep him hidden. But he isn't only afraid his bosses will find out he talked. He's afraid of Nihil."

"None of this has anything to do with Rogan," said Mira.

"It would seem so," he said. He produced a folded piece of paper, seemingly out of nowhere, grasped between two fingers. "Except for this." He flicked it onto the table.

Cecily picked up the note and unfolded it with trembling hands.

R ~

*We have come too far to back out now. I assure you, you will be enormously pleased with the progress I have made. Do not trouble yourself with the details. I am attending to everything.*

*I advise you to wait patiently for the fruits of our labor. Anything less will lead to, shall I say, unfortunate consequences.*

N

She dropped the note on the table. Mira snatched it up and read the contents. It took her a moment to process what she had read. *The fruits of our labor?* "How do you know this is for Rogan? 'R' could mean anyone."

"I got it before it reached the palace," Callum said. "The messenger had instructions to deliver it to the king, and only the king. I had to be extremely persuasive to get even that much out of him."

Cecily looked around. She didn't want to meet Callum's eyes. She could feel his gentle prodding, a slight uplift in her emotions, but it did nothing to stave off the empty chasm that opened inside her. She felt as if someone had pushed her off a cliff and she was free-falling into darkness.

"This is madness," she whispered as she looked up to meet Callum's eyes. Mira remained silent at her side.

He shook his head. "I don't know. This is why I rarely trust anyone. People are capable of anything."

"He knew?" she said, not asking anyone in particular.

"No," Mira said. "That isn't the Rogan I know."

"We all knew him," said Callum. "Or we thought we did." He shrugged.

Cecily reached for the note again, hesitating as if it might burn her fingers. She spread it out on the table and read it over again. "You make it a habit of intercepting Rogan's missives?"

"Not usually. I had reason to believe Rogan might be involved. I've been looking into it for weeks now." He paused and looked down. "I know I've been keeping this from you. But it's Rogan. I couldn't tell you I suspected him until I knew for sure."

Something began to fill the dark void inside her. For the first time in weeks, her mind began to clear as the haze of fear and despair lifted. She sat up straight as anger, hot and bright, filled her. She had spent so much time waiting, hoping, despairing. She'd put her faith in a lie and her heart raged at the time she had lost.

"You said you intercepted this before it reached Rogan?"

Callum nodded. "That's right."

"Which means he hasn't seen it yet?"

"True," he said and tilted his head. "Why do you ask?"

"I think it's time someone delivered it," she answered as she folded the note and tucked it away.

## 23 : CONFRONTATION

Cecily stood outside the doors to Rogan's study, arms crossed and chin held high. Mira hovered next to her. They'd been silent the entire ride to the palace, despite Mira's attempts to speak to her. For the first time since Daro disappeared, her mind felt clear. The haze of desperation lifted, burned away by white-hot anger and clarity of purpose.

The door opened and the guard nodded her in. Mira stepped with her but Cecily held up her hand. "Stay out here. I need to see him alone." Mira opened her mouth to protest, but Cecily walked into the study and shut the door behind her before Mira could follow.

The king stood behind his desk, conferring with Alastair over some paperwork. They both looked up at her abrupt entrance and Alastair dropped something to the floor.

She crossed the distance to the pair and looked at Alastair. His eyes were wide and he fumbled, apparently trying to decide if he should pick up the papers he'd dropped. She stopped in front of him and raised her chin. "I need to see Rogan. Alone."

His mouth opened and he looked back and forth between Cecily and the king. "Excuse me?"

Rogan's shoulders were set and his brow furrowed. "It's okay, Alastair. Allow me to speak with Cecily for a moment. Please." He gestured to the door.

Alastair looked to Cecily again, confusion plain on his face. She was past caring. He walked away and she waited for the click of the door as it closed behind him.

She stood across the desk from Rogan and pulled out the note Callum had given her. She tossed it on the desk, recrossed her arms, and stared at Rogan.

He picked up the note and his brow furrowed as he read the contents. "Where did you get this?" he asked as he folded the note and tucked it into his doublet.

"I hardly think that matters. Who is Nihil?"

Rogan looked down for a moment before answering. "Nihil is... a mess I am trying to clean up."

Cecily narrowed her eyes. "Do you admit you've been working with him?"

Rogan's face was unreadable. "In a manner of speaking, yes. But it is a relationship that has not been without difficulties."

"Does Nihil have Daro?" She paused and held his gaze. "Do not lie to me."

Rogan's face remained composed. He pulled out the chair from behind his desk and sat down. Cecily remained standing, her eyes fixed on her king.

After a long pause, he looked up at her and spoke. "Yes."

Cecily's neck stiffened and her voice was low. "How long have you known?"

"It's complicated."

Her hands trembled and her heart raced. She struggled to keep her voice even. "Complicated? How can this be complicated? I came to you looking like I'd lost a tavern brawl after they tried to kill me. You said you'd help. But you knew? Damn you, Rogan."

He held a hand up. "I only suspected Nihil at that point. I didn't know anything for certain."

"You should have told me. You could have at least given me his name, given me something to go on. We've been working for months, trying to find out who did this."

"I wanted to get to Nihil myself. My hope was that he would release Daro to me and we could resolve this quietly."

Cecily's anger burned hot, but as much as she wanted to hurl obscenities at Rogan, she needed to find out what he knew. "Who is he? Why did he take Daro?"

Rogan pitched his fingers together under his chin. "Nihil is something I inherited from my predecessor. He was working for Hadran, and when the dust settled after the war, he came to me and explained his work. He was researching Wielding Energy and claimed to have found a way to increase a Wielder's power. He convinced me of the importance of what he was doing, and my position was still so tenuous. I let him continue."

"Why would he have been working with Hadran? Isn't that something the Lyceum would oversee?"

"Quite honestly, I don't know. My greatest mistake in all this is failing to find out enough about Nihil's background. One of my contacts at the Lyceum recently told me he may have been denied entrance. And if what I suspect about his work is true, the Lyceum would never have allowed it."

"I still don't understand why he would want Daro. He isn't a Wielder."

Rogan shook his head. "I don't know the answer to that either."

Cecily walked over to the window and looked out over the gardens below. The plants looked gray and tired, weighed down by the rain. "Please tell me you know where to find him."

"I'm afraid I don't," Rogan said. "I haven't been successful at finding his location. The men I sent haven't returned."

Cecily felt hollow. "How could you let this happen?"

Rogan rose from his seat and stood behind her. "I didn't realize what Nihil was doing until it was too late. I thought…" He paused. "I don't know what I thought. I have been so wrapped up in other things, I let Nihil go about his business and didn't ask very many questions."

Cecily turned to look at him. "Busy? That's your reason? You were too busy?"

"I am the king. Every day I make decisions that affect the life of every person in this kingdom. I still have nobles plotting behind my back and the Lyceum trying to grab power out from under me, not to mention threats from outside the kingdom. You have no idea the pressures I am under." He pressed his fingers to his eyes. "Damn it, Cecily, I've needed you and Daro here. You never should have left Halthas in the first place."

Her mouth dropped open. "So this is my fault because I left Halthas?"

"That's not what I'm saying. I just..." He trailed off and turned back toward the window. "You have no idea what's coming. It's been generations since we had to fight anyone but ourselves. The nobles all think we're impenetrable, but they're wrong. This palace, the Lyceum, all the trade that flows in and out of our city, it all makes us a target. It's only a matter of time before someone shows up on our doorstep with an army we didn't see coming, and we won't be prepared. I can't let that happen."

She narrowed her eyes, as her anger rose again. "That's why you let Nihil continue working, isn't it? You weren't too busy to handle it. Whatever it is he's doing, you want what he's promised you. And if you take Daro back, he might not give you what you want."

"It isn't that simple."

"No, nothing is simple with kings, is it?" she said. "I knew Hadran, and what he was capable of. I would have expected something like this from him. But you? I thought you were different."

Rogan's eyes widened and his hand drifted absently to his chest. "I'm not Hadran," he said, his voice cold. "You don't understand what it is to be the king."

"I suppose now you're going to tell me it was all for the good of the kingdom."

"And what if it was?" he said, his voice rising. "We both know what it is to do things that are in the best interest of the kingdom, even at a hazard to ourselves."

She laughed, a short clipped sound with little humor in it. "You colluded with the men who took my husband and lied to me about it. And now you want me to believe you did it for the good of the kingdom? Very noble of you."

"Ah yes, noble," he said. "How noble we were, as we hid under the depths of the city and plotted treason. I don't recall either of us worrying about nobility in those days."

She whirled on him. "That treason made you king, in case you hadn't noticed."

"Yes, it did. And now we're hailed as heroes."

"There's only one difference between a traitor and a hero." She looked up and met his eyes. "Whether he ends up on the winning side."

Rogan sighed. "Be that as it may, you know as well as I do, there is nothing simple about the lives we lead. I always have to work for the good of the kingdom. This was no different."

"It's completely different! Nihil has been abducting people for years. Let's pretend for a moment that it wasn't Daro—forget that he was your friend. These are still your subjects. People's lives are being destroyed."

He shook his head. "Yes, and I'm sure someone like you wouldn't ever be a party to destroying lives."

Her heart raced and her fingers tingled. She spoke through clenched teeth. "What is that supposed to mean?"

"You know exactly what I mean. You hide it so well, but I know who you were. I know how you helped Hadran. You want to talk of destroying lives? How many did you destroy for him?"

"I never would have betrayed someone I cared for."

His eyes rose. "So there's nothing wrong with what you did for Hadran because they weren't people you cared about?"

Her voice rose to a shout. "I never once said there was nothing wrong with what I did. I have to live with it every single day of my life.

That, and more. You want to talk of pressure? You have no idea how much blood I have on my hands."

"Then stop lecturing me about what's right," he snapped.

Her anger began to boil over. She clenched her fists and dug her nails into her palms. "You want to talk about the past? Fine, let's talk about the past. How many times did Daro save your life? How many times, when we thought we were done for, did he bring us back from the brink? I don't care what has happened since then. I don't care about the threats you see or the pressures you're under. There is nothing that makes this right."

Rogan reached a hand out to her. "Cecily, please."

"No," she said, and the word sliced the air between them. "This is your fault. You let this happen. You always wanted us to come back. How do I know you didn't plan this from the beginning? How do I know Nihil isn't getting ready to deliver Daro right back into your hands?"

"You can't believe that."

"I don't know what to believe." Her voice rose again. "I trusted you. I trusted you with his life. His life, Rogan. You were supposed help me, with all your resources. Do you have any idea what I would do for him? What I have done for him?" Her hands trembled. She walked toward him and stopped just inches from his face. "I have done the worst of things to keep him safe. And I wouldn't hesitate to do it again."

Rogan's eyes widened, and he leaned back. He opened his mouth, but no words came.

"I want you to understand something," she said, her voice low. "There is only one reason you will live past this moment. If I kill you now, your guards outside will probably kill me. And if I die today, no one will save Daro." She held his gaze and watched his eyes look her up and down.

He took a step backward. "Cecily, you're angry. You shouldn't say such things."

"Why not?" she said, her voice hushed. "I killed a king before. I could do it again." The words escaped her lips and hung between them, thick like fog.

"What are you saying? You didn't kill Hadran."

She drew in a breath. Her heart beat fast and her shoulders knotted with tension. She'd never spoken the words aloud, not even to Daro. "Yes, I did. I killed Hadran."

Rogan shook his head. "No, you didn't. It was Nolan. They killed each other. Nolan sacrificed himself for all of us."

"I let you believe that. But I was there. I was supposed to keep Nolan hidden. You remember the plan. It failed. We failed. Hadran saw him coming and sucked the heat out of him. His body was blue and stiff before he hit the floor." Visions of that terrible night floated through her mind. She had promised herself she would take the truth to her grave, but there was something freeing about saying the words aloud, even in anger. "So I killed him."

"How?" he asked in a half whisper, as if he wasn't certain he wanted to know.

"I Reached into his chest and found his heart. I wrapped my Energy around it and I squeezed." She looked up and met Rogan's eyes. "I gripped it with Pressure until it burst. I could feel the blood pour out and drain into his chest. It felt like it was all over me, like my hands should be covered in it."

Rogan's mouth hung open, his eyes wide. He stepped backward. "Oh gods, Cecily," he whispered. He put his hand to his mouth and turned away. Cecily stared at the floor, trembling. The enormity of her admission stunned her into silence.

He turned back to face her. "There's no shame in what you did," he said, his voice firm. "It was war. We all did what had to be done. It is as simple as that."

"For the good of the kingdom," she said.

Rogan nodded. "Yes, exactly. For the good of the kingdom."

Cecily shook her head, a slow back and forth motion. She broke her gaze from the floor and looked up at her king. "I didn't do it for the good of the kingdom. I did it because I knew if Hadran lived to draw one more breath, he would call for his guards. And I knew Daro was in the hallway, just outside. If the guards came, there was no way he would get out alive. I didn't kill Hadran to make you king, or to save our kingdom. I killed him to save Daro."

Rogan stared at her, his mouth open. His face softened and some of the warmth returned to his eyes. He almost looked like the man she remembered.

"There was a time I would have followed you anywhere," she said. Her chest felt tight and her hands still trembled. "The only thing you need to do now is stay out of my way."

She spun around, walked to the door, and threw it open. The two guards outside had to stumble out of the way. Mira and Alastair both waited outside, but she ignored them and strode down the hallway without a word.

Cecily sat at Callum's table in the Ale Stone and folded her hands in front of her. She sat up straight, her shoulders relaxed and eyes clear. She had found one of Callum's young messengers and sent him off with a folded note, telling Callum to meet her. The buzz of a dozen conversations hovered in the air, an occasional voice carrying over the din. A pair of men sat nearby, tossing cards onto the table, pushing around small piles of coins. It seemed to Cecily they kept passing the same stack of coins back and forth as each won the next hand.

Callum arrived, tossing a quick glance over his shoulder, and dropped into a chair. "I'm surprised you're back so soon. What did our magnanimous king have to say for himself?"

Cecily's voice was crisp, her mind resolved. "Nothing worth repeating. Whoever Nihil is, he does indeed have Daro. Now we just have to find out where they are."

"Rogan didn't know?"

"No. Rogan's been lying to cover his tracks, but I don't think he was lying about that. It's up to us, now."

One corner of Callum's mouth curled in a smirk and he raised his eyebrows. "What'd you do to him?"

"Nothing." Callum's face sank with disappointment. "Believe me, part of me wanted to. But I thought it best I get out of the palace today. I can't help Daro if I'm stuck on the sharp end of a spear."

"Fair point. Okay, you tell me. What's our move?"

"You were already on the right track. We find out where the smugglers are taking their shipments, we find Nihil. The question is, how do we do that?"

He raised a finger and pointed at her. "That I can help you with. I have reason to believe a certain Guildmaster is taking bribes to turn a blind eye to their shipments and let them in through the river." He paused and brushed his hair from his eyes. "We're going to have to go in, and his estate will be guarded. You sure you're up for this?"

Her lips turned up in a smile that held no warmth. "Absolutely."

## 24 : FINDING CONTROL

The brisk air in the courtyard made Number One's skin prickle. He sat on a slab of stone and the cold soaked in through his pants. The air smelled wet with recent rain, the plants drinking it up eagerly, as the moss and ferns spread through the cracks in the stone. He resisted the sudden urge to remove his mask and let the cold air brush his face.

He plucked a fern frond and trailed his fingers across the leaf to feel the life pulsing through the plant. It was almost warm against his cold touch. He glanced around to make sure no one was watching, then turned back to the leaf. It began to wilt as the ends of each frond curled toward the center, turning brown and dry. He felt the plant's energy trickle into him, a tiny green line that seeped into his body. He pulled more and a crackling frost spread over the leaf as he took its heat. He crumpled it in his hand, and the frosted, dead leaf disintegrated between his fingers, falling like dust to the cobblestones below.

The others milled about the cobblestone courtyard, all dressed as he was, in black with masked faces. A few practiced with weapons. They slashed at each other with swords or shot targets with arrows. Number Four sat cross-legged on the ground, picking up small stones. He squeezed them until they glowed red hot, then threw them into a puddle. They hissed as they hit the water, curls of steam rising into the air, then popped with a loud crack. Number Six stood with his back to the others and ran his hands up and down a thick bramble that trailed along the wall. Number One watched as he coaxed it higher. The vines grew thick as he ran his hands up and down the plant. The thorns grew, black spikes protruding from the thickening vines, and the largest ones leaked a glistening drop of liquid from their tips. He dabbed the liquid with his finger and plucked the largest thorns, twisting them until they broke free, and collected them in a pouch.

Number One stood at the sound of footsteps behind him. Sindre sauntered toward him, her predatory eyes shining in the gray daylight. He saw Sindre less and less as time went on, but the sight of her always made his implant tingle. The others all stopped what they were doing and watched as she led a tall man, masked and dressed in black as they all were, toward Number One.

The man stopped as Sindre did, halting a few steps behind her. His eyes darted around the courtyard and his hands twitched at his sides. The other subjects began to meander toward her; Sindre drew them like a warm fire on a freezing night.

Number One peered at the man. He was well over a head taller than Sindre, his wide shoulders dwarfing the woman. As he looked carefully, Number One could see swirling colors in the man's eyes, silver mixed with streaks of brown and blue. Silver. This was him, then.

"Number One," Sindre said, her voice a purr that sent shivers down his spine, "this is Number Fourteen. It is Nihil's wish that you work with him, help him to harness and utilize his new abilities." She turned to Number Fourteen. His hands twitched and his eyes flicked from Sindre to Number One. "I am leaving you in the hands of Number One. I will return for you later."

Number Fourteen nodded, and his eyes followed her as she left the courtyard through one of the large wooden doors. The rest of the subjects watched her leave, pausing as she walked past. As the doors closed behind her, they drifted back to their tasks. Fourteen's gaze swung back to Number One and he stood silently, fingers twitching at his sides.

Number One's mind brimmed with curiosity. This was the man Nihil had sent him after; the one traveling with the woman. Something about her had tickled his memory, but he shoved that feeling down before he could give a name to her face. Memories were too dangerous.

He stared at the man's eyes. He could tell he'd been to see Nihil more than once, although it was hard to tell how many times he had been forced to lay his hands on the stone. Three, perhaps four? A twinge of sympathy struck him; such a foreign feeling. He searched it, stretched it out and prodded it, considering what it meant to feel such a thing for another person. It had been a long time since he had such an experience. Certainly none of Nihil's other subjects ever engendered such a response. Why was he feeling such a strange emotion for this newcomer?

Number Fourteen's eyes darted around the courtyard again, flicking toward the others.

"It's okay," Number One said. "They'll leave us alone for a time. She isn't watching."

Fourteen's eyes turned back to Number One. He glanced over his shoulder again before he nodded.

"Sit down," Number One said. "We should see what they've done with you."

Fourteen sat on the stone bench, in front of the cracked and broken fountain. Number One sat next to him and wondered how he should approach this man. He had helped with most of Nihil's other subjects, teaching them to wrestle with the effects of Nihil's work. He had been the first to survive the process and Nihil had labeled him Number One. More had followed; most died, usually after going mad. Those that survived with their minds more or less intact were given a number as he had been. Number One was often instructed to help these subjects, working with them to gain mastery of their new endowments, and the madness that threatened to overtake them.

He leaned toward Fourteen and felt the heat emanating from him. It came in waves, sheets of energy surging through the man. Number One tingled at the possibility of it. He could see why Nihil had been excited about this one.

"How do you feel?" Number One asked. Fourteen spread his hands, palms up, and looked down at them. He seemed to want to speak, but remained silent. "I can help you."

"I haven't spoken to anyone in so long," Fourteen said, his voice quiet.

*How long has he been here?* Number One had stopped counting the days a long time ago, so he wasn't always sure of the passage of time. But it had to have been months. He looked up at the grey sky, the steely clouds low and threatening rain. The air was cold, coming close to freezing. Late fall, almost winter. Had it been late summer when Fourteen had arrived? That felt right. That little sliver of sympathy curled open, if only a touch.

"Sindre isn't much of a conversationalist," he said. Sindre was a difficult topic amongst the other subjects. A few seemed to hate her, but their deep-seated fear kept them quiet. Most developed a twisted sort of love for her. One of them had even tried to kill another subject once, simply for mentioning her by name. Granted, he had died soon after, the madness too much for his mind to bear. But Number One had never understood those who grew to love her so. His hatred for Sindre burned hot, deep within his chest. The only time his dreams didn't descend into nightmares were the nights he dreamt of killing her, sucking the life out of her and watching her body wither away to nothing. As he always did, he pushed those thoughts away quickly, fear always winning out over hatred. He reached back and scratched the skin around his implant.

Fourteen looked up at him. His wariness seemed to be melting. It was hard to see much through the mask, but his eyes softened. "No, she isn't."

"You don't have to fear me," Number One said. "They put us together so I can help you."

"I still don't understand why I'm here. My wife…"

"No!" Number One said and held his hand up to stop him. "No, don't talk about that. Believe me, it will be better if you accept things the way they are. It's easier that way." Fourteen's eyes narrowed, tension showing in his arms and shoulders. Number One leaned away. He didn't know what Nihil had done to this one. He would have to tread lightly, not risk angering him. Better to build trust first. It wouldn't be the first time Number One had been attacked by another subject. "What Nihil has been doing, it will change things," he said, hoping to shift the subject. "What sort of Wielder were you when you came here?"

"I'm not a Wielder."

Number One paused to look at him carefully. Not a Wielder? All Nihil's subjects were Wielders. "A Shaper, then?"

"No."

This was unusual. Number One looked down. Fourteen pressed his hands into the bench and the stone crumbled beneath his fingers. Bits of rock rattled to the ground.

Fourteen pulled his hands up quickly, leaving finger-shaped cracks in the bench. He looked at his hands, turning them over in front of him. "I keep breaking things without meaning to." His voice was troubled and he rubbed his eyes with a sharp exhale. "I'm losing my mind."

"If you do go mad, you won't be the first," Number One answered. Fourteen's face jerked toward him and Number One shrugged. "Dealing with the madness isn't easy, but it can be done. Embrace it. Embrace the chaos, embrace the pain. Own them, and they will no longer own you."

He grabbed a piece of rock from the ground and handed it to Fourteen. The man hesitated, then reached out with a shaking hand. Number One dropped the stone into his hand and continued. "You need to learn control. You have to take all that energy swirling inside of you and focus it, use it. Hold the rock, but don't break it yet."

Fourteen gripped the rock and held it out in front of him. Number One watched as dust leaked from his fingers and small bits of stone scattered to the ground.

"Slow down," Number One said. The pulses of energy coming off Fourteen were palpable. "Slow your breathing, and regain control."

Fourteen gripped what was left of the stone and threw it against the far wall. It hit with a crack and shattered, shards of rock flying. The other subjects looked over. Several started to walk toward them, but Number One put his hand up to keep them back.

"That's okay," he said to Fourteen. "Control takes time."

"I have no control," Fourteen said, his voice a low growl. "I have no control over anything. I can't sleep, I can't sit still. I don't do anything unless they tell me. Unless she tells me. I tolerate it all, for what? So she won't hurt me again? She will anyway. So they might let me go? I know they aren't letting me go. I don't know what they've done to me, but the voices won't stop." He gripped his head with his hands. "I have memories that aren't mine and I'm starting to lose track of what is real."

Number One nodded along as he spoke. He remembered the days when the voices screamed in his head, so loud he could have sworn they were real. "Time will help."

Fourteen stood and tugged at his mask. He paced back and forth in front of the fountain, his head clutched in his hands. "I feel like I'm going to burst apart. I close my eyes and I see the light, rushing past me, rushing into me. It's too much. I can't hold it all." He stopped in front of Number One, briefly rocking from his toes to his heels before he turned and resumed his walk. "I can't hold it all," he said again.

Number One watched him pace and felt the energy emanating from him each time he got close. He was holding an enormous amount. All that energy was very tempting, an endless reservoir of power pulsing through the other man. Number One wondered how much of it he could hold. If he reached out and touched him now, how much could he Absorb? In his mind's eye he saw an image of himself, pulling in all that energy, the excess of it bursting from his fingertips, lighting up his eyes. What would it to do him? More importantly, what could he do with it?

He cast a quick glance around and beckoned for Fourteen to follow him around to the other side of the fountain. His heart began to accelerate. Would he be punished for this? Would this be what brought Sindre back to his room? Fourteen stopped just a step away and Number One felt the pulses of energy emanating from him.

"You need an outlet for all that energy," he said, keeping his voice low. "Somewhere to put it or it will drive you mad. Every time Nihil works on you, he forces someone else's energy into you. That's what the stone does. You get their power, but you get something else too. You get a piece of who they are, or who they were."

Fourteen stopped, his hands still twitching, his eyes intent. Number One took another step toward him. The other man's eyes were bright, the silver almost glowing. He looked more Imaran than Number One remembered, the gleaming silver muddled with shades of brown and blue swirling around his black pupil.

Number One leaned in close, his voice barely above a whisper. "That something else that comes through the stone, those voices you hear—that is the madness. You have to force them away, deep inside, or they will consume you. The farther you push it all down, the longer it will stay away."

Fourteen swayed, and his eyelids drooped. "I can't... make them... stop," he whispered. Sweat glistened on his brow just below the seam of his mask.

*Do it. Take it.* Number One didn't know if that was a voice reaching up from the depths of his mind, or if it was his own. The heat from Fourteen beckoned to him. *All that power. An endless reservoir.* He reached out with a trembling hand. "I can help," he said, so quiet the words barely left his lips.

Fourteen stood still, and his eyes drifted closed. Number One reached his hand toward him and gripped his arm. He felt Fourteen's sharp intake of breath as he began to Absorb his energy. Number One's ability had always been Absorption, but as a youth his power had been weak. Nihil had done many things to him, endowed him with the abilities of other Wielders. He struggled with the essences of other men in his mind, but he relished the power. Where once he could scarcely cool a hot cup of tea, now he could suck the life out of anything. He siphoned energy from Fourteen, and it came into him like a raging river. There was so much. His eyes fluttered and sweat ran in rivulets down his back. Fourteen's power seemed endless, a bottomless well. Number One's mind burned with the possibilities.

Images flashed through his consciousness. It wasn't only power he drew from Fourteen. Something else came across. His vision blurred, his view of the courtyard twisting and spiraling, replaced by a tunnel of blinding light. His chest tightened as emotions hit him in quick succession. Waves of fear, loss and confusion pounded him, nearly knocking him backward. He stumbled and clung to Fourteen to keep from falling.

An image coalesced into clarity—a face. She moved, looking up, and her gaze met his own. Dark hair, clear brown eyes. Her mouth lifted in a smile and Number One gasped as if the breath had been knocked out of him. She was like the ground under his feet, a cool breeze blowing across his skin. He was drowning in an ocean and she reached down, pulling him to safety. She was home.

He jerked his hand away, gasping for breath. Power surged under his skin, flowing through him like a tempest. The face disappeared, but something lingered, and a sensation took root in his mind. He didn't push it down to bury it under layers of memories, only some of which were his own. He held it, turning it over, recalling not just her face, but the solidity he felt when he saw her. He didn't want to let it go.

Fourteen sat on the ground, breathing heavily, and rubbed his eyes. Number One lowered himself to the ground and sat cross-legged, trembling with all the energy he had Absorbed.

Fourteen looked up, meeting his eyes, and nodded slowly. "Thank you."

Number One let the energy surge through him as he lay on his bed. He relished the feeling of power as it pulsed through him. Where it had made Number Fourteen seem jittery and anxious, it soothed Number One, like rolling over ocean waves on a clear day. Powerful was something he had not felt in a very long time. He jealously hoarded the feeling, even as the energy dissipated, radiating into the air. He couldn't hold it forever.

Fear crept in at the margins. They would take it from him if they knew. His implant prickled and he resisted the urge to try to pull it out. With as much power as he held, perhaps he would be successful this time. Worry began to sour his exhilaration as he imagined Sindre striding into his room. She would incapacitate him and leave him paralyzed on the floor, his mind a torrent of hatred and terror. He didn't know what would happen if he ripped the implant from his neck, but he realized he feared Sindre's punishment more than he feared the possibility of it killing him.

He let out a slow breath and recalled the face he had seen through Number Fourteen. His body relaxed as he imagined her. He saw her eyes crinkle and her lips draw up in a smile. Warmth spread over him and something awoke deep inside. He thought of her, this woman from Fourteen's mind, and felt something entirely foreign blossom inside. It was a feeling as unfamiliar as it was unmistakable.

He loved her.

## 25 : GUILDMASTER STELLAN

Cecily walked with Callum down the quiet street, her hand tucked in his arm. The sun had long since set and the air hung heavy with a misty rain. Water beaded on her cloak and the drizzle clung to her hair. A city guard eyed them as they walked past and Cecily leaned heavily on Callum, stumbling a little and giggling. He steadied her and laughed as the guard walked by. *That's right, we're just a couple on our way home after a little too much wine.*

Dressed in his usual blacks, Callum wore a cloak to keep off the rain. Cecily's dark blue cloak looked black in the darkness. Underneath she wore a pair of tight-fitting black leggings and a soft black tunic. She'd taken off her necklace and belt and left them back in her room. If things went bad, she didn't want to lose them.

They cut across the street and turned up a hill, veering south. Guildmaster Stellan's estate was on the south side of the city, not far from the Merchant Span. They'd spent the last several days combing the area, walking around the perimeter of the estate and scoping out the defenses. It had been years since Cecily had tried to break into a secured estate. She was surprised at how quickly it came back to her. They watched the guards, noting the pattern of their movements, and kept tabs on the lights in the estate windows. Messengers came and went during the daylight hours, but at night, things appeared quiet. They had seen a light in one window, on the third floor, burning later into the night than the others. Cecily suspected that was where they would find Stellan's study.

They stopped across from the estate and stashed their cloaks in a bush. Callum had found a spot on one side of the property where a large tree bent its branches over the Shaper-wrought fence. The bars were too narrow to squeeze between, and the lowest branch was just out of her grasp. Waiting until her Awareness told her no one was near, she used Reach to Pull on the branch, lowering it enough that she could grasp it with her hands. The leaves rustled and splashed water on them as they clambered up into the tree and dropped down on the other side.

Cecily nodded that the way was clear. They darted to the side of the building and pressed themselves against the wall. Callum took a quick look around and smirked at her, raising his eyebrows. "Just like the good old days, eh?"

She smiled but rolled her eyes at him, holding her finger to her lips so he would stay quiet. With a deep breath, she closed her eyes and spread her Awareness in a wide circle. Two guards patrolled the gate at the front of the estate. They stood, slumping against the thick posts, their spears leaning against the fence nearby. On the far side of the property, another two guards lingered around what was probably a back door. She could sense them sitting, rolling something around in their hands and tossing it. Playing dice. Certainly not expecting anything.

Sensing no one else outside the building, Cecily turned her attention to the interior and felt out the hallways, windows, walls, and doors. She quickly made a mental map of the layout, noting where she could sense people or movement. The ground floor appeared to be empty. A large kitchen stretched out on the back side of the building, but the bakers hadn't yet arisen to their early morning work. She sensed no movement in the various parlors and sitting rooms, nor in the large entry foyer. The second floor seemed to be mostly bedrooms, several with still forms lying in their beds. No one appeared to be awake.

She guessed the attic held the servants' quarters, based on the small rooms with multiple beds in each. But it was the third floor that had the signs she was looking for. It was completely empty of people, except for one hallway, where two men sat at a small round table just outside a door. She felt the outline of a sword at one man's hip. The other had taken his off, leaving it leaning against the wall. Judging by the location, she surmised it was the room they had seen lit well into the night as they'd watched the estate from afar. It was empty now. Stellan's study.

"I have it," she whispered. "We go in through the back. Two guards in back, and two in front of his study. Third floor."

They crept around the outside of the building, keeping close to the wall. As they rounded the corner, Cecily could see the two guards. They huddled next to the building, taking shelter from the rain under the eaves, hoods pulled down over their faces. A covered glowstone lamp bathed them in a circle of light. One man cupped his hands and blew into them, whether for luck with his dice, or to warm them, Cecily couldn't be sure. He tossed the dice onto their makeshift table and groaned as they came to rest.

Cecily looked at Callum, who nodded. She Reached across the grounds and grabbed a twig, using Pressure to make it crack. The guards' heads swung toward the noise. She waited, her hand on Callum's chest to keep him back. The sound of their conversation drifted over, but she couldn't make out the words. She Pulled on a branch, making the leaves rustle, then cracked another twig. One of the guards got up and adjusted his cloak before he stomped off in the direction of the noises. She Reached again, snapping twigs farther into the grounds to lead the guard away. *That's one.*

Callum nudged her with his elbow and winked. He looked over at the remaining guard and tilted his head. Cecily knew how to keep from feeling Callum's Projections, but the spike of fear he sent was so strong it made the hair on her neck stand on end. The guard jumped to his feet, and his head jerked around. Clutching his cloak at his throat with one hand, he turned in a quick circle, his other hand splayed out in front of him as if to ward off an attack. He took a few steps backward, away from the building, then turned and ran, heading in the direction of the other guard. *That's two.*

Cecily and Callum darted for the door, staying as quiet as possible. Cecily's heart pounded. She knew they only had a moment before the guards would come back to their post. She put her hand on the door and prodded the lock with her Awareness, following each piece of the mechanism to see how it operated. With a precise and tiny Pull the lock opened with a satisfying click. She pushed the door open and they both hastened inside, then quietly closed and locked it behind them. Callum pulled out a rag and they dried their shoes.

The door led directly into the kitchens. It was gloomy and dark, the curtains all pulled shut; not even the faint light from the lamp outside cut through the darkness. Cecily led Callum through, avoiding the large wooden counter and a stack of flour sacks. They crept up a narrow stairway that led from the kitchens, stepping carefully on each stair to avoid making noise, and emerged on the third floor. Cecily paused and scanned with her Awareness to ensure nothing had changed. The figures still slumbered in their beds on the floor below and the two guards outside Stellan's study were engaged in a game of cards.

Callum leaned close to her ear, his voice a whisper. "What I wouldn't give to see what you can see."

"Two. Both have swords close at hand. They're playing cards."

She felt him nod. "We take them out, then?"

Cecily stiffened. "Killing people wasn't part of the plan."

Callum pulled her back into the stairwell. He turned to face her, backed her into the corner, and kept his voice low. "We can't exactly scare them away, can we? We have to get in that room."

Cecily raised an eyebrow and tilted her head. "Has it been so long since we've done this? I can get in that room without leaving a trail of bodies. Besides, dead guards are going to alert Stellan that someone was here. I'll take care of the guards. Just get them nice and relaxed. I'll do the rest."

They crept along the hallway until they came to a corner. Cecily could feel the guards, leaning in toward each other, as they tossed cards onto the table. She got the impression they were bored. Cecily felt the shimmer of Callum's Projection slide past her, like a wave of tiredness at the end of a long day. He couldn't actually put people to sleep, but he was very adept at manipulating people's mental states. Cecily had once watched him relax someone so thoroughly, the man had fallen asleep with his face in his dinner.

One of the guards put down his cards and rubbed his eyes. The other rested his chin on his hand, his eyes heavy. Cecily Reached toward them and felt out their airways. She applied the slightest bit of Pressure and narrowed their windpipes very gradually. One man started to sway in his seat. The other blinked slowly. Callum kept them deeply relaxed so they failed to notice the shallowness of their breathing. Cecily knew she had to knock them both out at once. If one fell before the other lost consciousness, she risked one of them realizing something was wrong. She felt for the bundle of nerves on the side of their necks, just below the jaw. With a swift jolt of Pressure, she jabbed the nerve bundles and sent them both sliding to the floor. Pushing a whiff of air underneath them so they wouldn't fall too hard, she laid them silently down in front of the door.

"I love it when you get all clever on me," Callum whispered as they stepped over the unconscious guards.

The study door had a more complicated lock, but Cecily soon heard the click as it disengaged. They carefully opened the door and closed it shut behind them.

"You know, you need to be careful not to let too many people see what you can do. If word got out about what the Lyceum taught you, I don't think many people would be as impressed as I am," Callum said as he began rifling through stacks of books on Stellan's desk. "I forgot how good you are at picking locks."

"The Magisters emphasized the need for secrecy, yes. The list of people I trust with what I can do is very short. It doesn't even include my own family."

He stopped and looked up at her. "They don't know?"

"No, although I don't think they would believe me if I told them."

"You are a rarity. How long do you think we have before the guards come to?"

"Five minutes or so. Not long."

She focused her Awareness on the room itself and left Callum to sort through the desk. She drew her Awareness in, giving her a clearer picture of the room's contents.

"Were you planning on helping me here, or is turning in slow circles in the center of the room your idea of searching?"

She closed her eyes and felt out the walls. Putting up a hand, she said, "Wait." As she probed the wall on the right side, she felt an inconsistency. "There," she said and pointed. There was a heavy tapestry hanging from a dowel. She moved it aside, Callum at her back, and found a small door with a tiny keyhole. She imagined Stellan sleeping below, a key fastened securely around his neck. Smiling to herself, she probed the lock and was rewarded with a click. She pulled open the door as Callum held the tapestry aside.

"Like I said, the Lyceum is lucky most people don't know about you. I bet a lot of locksmiths would be out of a job," Callum said.

Inside were several leather-bound books. They pulled them out and quickly scanned their contents.

"Shipping schedules," Callum said. "They look just like the ones on his desk."

Cecily flipped through the topmost volume. It was only a quarter of the way filled out, a thick section of blank pages at the back. She ran her fingers up and down the list and tried to make sense of the notes.

Callum looked over her shoulder. He reached around and pointed. "There. Some of these entries have notes in the margins. 'Strike from record.'" He flipped the page. "Here it is again. You realize what he's doing? He's letting them in. No wonder he can afford this place." He took the book and flipped through a few more pages. "There are dozens of them in here. I wonder how much they're paying him." He shook his head as he looked through the log.

The last page was only half full. "Look at this—the date on this one is next week, but it has the same note in the margin."

A smile spread across Callum's face. "And we have them," he said.

Cecily thought about the guards outside the door. Her Awareness told her they were still unconscious, but they didn't have much time.

She scooped up the logbooks and placed them back in the hidden cabinet, closed the door, and Wielded the lock back into place.

Spreading her Awareness open to check the rest of the estate, she clutched Callum's arm. "Someone's awake."

He whipped his head toward her. "Where?"

Cecily's heart began to beat faster. "The main stairway. They're coming."

"We have to get out. Now." He pulled her toward the door.

The figure reached the landing on the third floor. The hallway made a turn before the study, but they only had seconds before the figure would see the unconscious guards. "We can't get out that way."

"Damn."

Cecily dashed to one of the windows on the far wall. She threw it open and looked down. The height was dizzying. She tossed one leg out the window and felt around for a foothold. Blessing the Shaper who had designed the rough stone facade, she inched her way out. Her toes gripped through her boots and her fingers held tight to the gaps in the stone.

Callum followed her out and found purchase on the other side of the window. He closed the window and she Reached in to click the latch closed.

The rain picked up and pelted her back with drops, making the wall slick. Her fingers already ached from holding on. "Try to go down," she said and kept her head resting tight against the wall. She restrained herself from looking down.

"Oh, you think?" Callum said, his voice strained.

The window lit up behind the curtains. Cecily pressed herself against the wall, hoping no one noticed that someone had been in the study. Had Callum rifled through the desk? Was the tapestry askew? She inched her foot down, feeling for another foothold, her chest knotted with fear.

Gripping the rough stone with her hands, she lowered herself down. It wasn't the first time she'd scaled a wall, and the memory made her stomach turn. Magister Brunell had first taught her how, when she'd studied at the Lyceum of Power. He'd shared her Awareness ability and had trained her to expand and contract the image, allowing her to spread it wide, or focus on a smaller area to sharpen the image. Using her Awareness, she easily found the handholds and gaps in the wall and she used them to quickly make it to the ground.

Callum wasn't far behind. He shook out his hands, wincing. "That could have been worse, I suppose."

A noise from above made them both look up. Someone opened the window. With a quick glance at each other, they dashed off in different directions. Cecily heard a yell from the window as she bolted toward the fence and threw open her Awareness. The interior of the estate was a bustle of activity, but the guards outside were slow to respond. One was heading her direction, but she scrambled into one of the trees lining the fence. A branch scratched her cheek and another snagged her shirt. She clung to the branch as the guard came near, desperately hoping the foliage would hide her.

The guard walked with his spear held out, as if expecting someone to jump out of the shadows. Cecily held her breath and willed him to keep his gaze on the ground. He crept under the tree as his head swiveled from side to side. In her Awareness, she could sense the second guard scope the perimeter on the other side of the estate. Callum had already cleared the fence and was circling around toward her. She felt the distinct feeling of Callum's fear Projection and the guard spun, his spear whipping around in a wide arc. He took a few backward steps, then turned again and sprinted off around the corner.

Cecily waited until he was out of earshot, making sure the other guard wasn't too close. She scrambled down out of the tree, and Callum reached up to help her from the other side of the fence. They stole down the street to where they had stashed their cloaks, then hurried for the Ale Stone, where they could gain access to the Quarry.

Callum lifted Cecily's chin and dabbed a wet cloth on the scratch on her cheek. He tossed his head and blew the hair out of his eyes. "It isn't bad," he said.

She sat cross-legged on a small table in Callum's underground quarters. They had made it back without incident, the dimly lit streets empty this late at night. "So they know someone broke in. Do you think they'll know why?"

Callum pursed his lips. "Hard to say. A man like Stellan is going to be a target for any number of reasons. He won't know who we were." He paused and gave her a small smile. "Besides, I may have left him a little present that should help throw him off our trail."

Cecily smiled. "I should have thought of that myself."

He stepped back to regard her. "Maybe so. But that was a nice trick with those guards. I forgot you could do that."

She shrugged. "My specialty was getting in and out without killing anyone. Hadran had no problems with killing people, but even he had to admit, it was easier to cover our tracks without dead bodies left behind."

"That's why you left the Lyceum, isn't it? Hadran wasn't satisfied with you just finding evidence of treason, or even planting it. He wanted you to kill for him."

Cecily nodded. "You can be alarmingly perceptive. I was young and naive. For a while, I believed what they told me, Hadran and even the Magisters. I thought Hadran was trying to protect his people. Of course the truth was, he was paranoid and thought everyone was out to usurp his power."

"I remember," Callum said. "I hate the fact that I ever worked for Hadran. I didn't always know it was him I was working for, mind you. He was as good as the Count at hiding who the orders were coming from."

"At least you didn't know. I knew exactly what I was doing. It never sat well with me, but I let it go for too long," she said.

"I never believed the story that you left to run off with Daro. Or at least I knew it wasn't the full story. You weren't some silly, lovesick girl."

"They didn't give me the chance to be a silly girl," she said. "I was good at playing one in front of people, but it wasn't who I was."

"Well, at least we got what we went in for. We know when their next shipment is coming, and the name of the ship. Whatever is on that ship, they want to keep clear of the inspectors. Now we just have to watch, and follow. Maybe we'll finally get somewhere."

Cecily nodded as a blossom of hope opened inside. Her dreams were getting worse and the stress of being without her husband mounted. But now they had something. After months of floundering, she finally had hope that they would track down Daro. She willed him to stay alive long enough for them to find him.

## 26 : INTO MIST

CECILY SQUATTED NEAR THE edge of the roof, her head tilted to one side. "Which one is it?"

Mira crouched down next to her and handed her the spyglass. "There," she said, pointing to the outer slip on one of the central docks. "The one out on the end, with the deep hull and single mast."

Positioned atop a warehouse roof, Cecily and Mira overlooked the docks on the south side of the river. The section of riverbank was wide and low, a bar of sand and well-worn river rock with a mass of docks jutting out into the water. The docks sprawled up and down the river, a tangle of ships pulling into the slips or launching out to set sail again. The vast majority of trade in and out of Halthas came through the south docks. Ships of every size, from huge seagoing vessels to smaller riverboats, tied up to unload their cargo and pay their taxes.

Cecily peered through the spyglass. The movements on the dock looked jerky and exaggerated through the lens. Sailors and workmen unloaded goods and hauled crates toward waiting carts on the shore. She focused on the ship noted in Stellan's logbook. A few sailors walked around the deck, appearing to work, but nothing was being loaded on or off.

"It's been there for hours and no one has come on or off," Mira said. She'd been on the rooftop, watching since daybreak. Griff and Serv loitered around the docks, wandering up and down and looking for any signs of the smugglers. Merrick was near the water on the east end of the docks with a small boat at hand, ready to follow in case the ship left unexpectedly. Sumara had a spot atop another warehouse a few buildings away, giving them another viewpoint. Cecily had insisted Edson stay behind, in the Quarry, despite his protestations. She didn't want him in harm's way. Callum had assured them he would meet them as soon as he could. One of his messengers had pressed a note in his hand as they were preparing to leave, and he'd run off in a hurry, muttering curses under his breath.

"Stellan is earning his pay," Cecily said. "He's certainly keeping the inspectors and the tax collectors away." She peeked through the spyglass again, wondering if the cargo hold actually held people. The thought made her stomach turn. She was too far away for her Awareness to cut through the mass of activity to give her any clarity on the contents of the ship, but the idea of finding it full of slaves was unnerving.

Cecily shivered and hunkered down in her cloak. The air was cold but it was blessedly dry. A low bank of gray clouds hovered over the city, but it hadn't rained since the day before. Atop the warehouse roof, fresh air mingled with the pungent scent of fish wafting up from the docks.

The day passed with mind-numbing slowness. Sumara, Griff, and Serv checked in at regular intervals. They had all observed the same thing; the ship sat with no activity save that of the occasional sailor on deck.

As the sun set, the docks began to quiet. The bustle of activity slowed to a trickle, a handful of sailors making their way into town for the night after securing their ships. A massive riverboat churned its way past the line of ships, finally tying up at the westernmost dock. The waves made by the huge wheel lapped against the shore and made the docked vessels rock back and forth.

Griff, Serv, and Sumara climbed the ladder to the roof. The temperature dropped quickly as the sun set, and they rubbed their hands together and breathed on them to keep warm.

"They seem to be staying for the night," Sumara said. "Perhaps it's best if we come back in the morning. If we're here at first light, we might see something."

Cecily glanced back over the docks, gray and faded in the waning light. She shook her head. "They might start unloading at night. If they actually have people on that ship, they'll need the cover of darkness to get everyone off."

A sharp whistle carried over the still air. *Merrick*. It was the all-clear signal. Cecily shivered. The last time she'd heard that call, they'd been fighting a war.

"Where in the name of the gods is Callum?" Griff asked as he produced a steaming loaf of bread and tore off thick chunks.

Cecily took a piece of bread. The crust was crisp, the inside warm and soft. She was starving. They'd brought provisions, but it was no substitute for a decent meal. "He didn't show up. He left in a hurry this morning after getting one of his notes." She took a bite of the bread, and the soft insides melted in her mouth. "Where did you get this? It's amazing."

Griff laughed. "Oh, I have my sources. You forget, this is our neighborhood."

Serv walked over to the edge of the roof. "We won't be able to see anything from here in the dark. If we want to keep watching, we'll have to move in closer."

They agreed and made their way down, cutting between the warehouses to keep out of sight. Serv led them upriver, where they still had a clear view of the dock activity. The river meandered in huge curves, and just east of the docks they had an unobstructed view of their target.

Fatigue set in as Cecily leaned back against a stone building. Across the river, the massive city wall jutted straight up out of the water, an impenetrable facade of thick stone. The water looked inky black and the hypnotic sound of the flowing river made it hard to stay awake.

"Cecily." Serv's voice was an urgent whisper. "Something's happening on the ship."

He crept out onto the rocky sandbar and motioned for her to follow. He paused, peering through the spyglass, then jogged toward the water, partially bent over to stay low. Cecily followed, staying as low as she could. She stubbed her toe on a rock and bit her lip to keep from crying out.

Serv handed her the spyglass and pointed. "Look—on the far side of the ship."

Cecily raised the spyglass to her eye and looked. A smaller row boat, long enough to have five or six rows of benches, was tied up on the river side of the larger vessel. She crept closer to the water to get a better view. A lantern swinging from the deck above bathed the side of the ship with a weak yellow light, illuminating a man in the smaller vessel. He put down his oars, and as he turned toward the larger ship, he raised his arms.

Cecily squinted to make out what he was doing. Mist built around the smaller boat and a large circle in the side of the ship shimmered, the grain of the wood almost sparkling to translucency. She focused the spyglass on the circle and could see the side of the ship fade, revealing the cargo hold inside. A man stuck his head through what was now a hole and Cecily nearly jumped back in shock. She handed the spyglass back to Serv and used her Awareness. Quickly plotting the structure of the ship, she could sense a massive disruption on the river side. The hole was like a gaping wound in the ship itself, the flows of energy stretched and distorted.

Inside the ship, a knot of people were jammed together in the cargo hold. Narrowing her focus, she could feel the ropes tying their wrists. These were not free passengers; they must be slaves.

A man inside the boat pushed people, one at a time, through the unnatural hole. He grabbed them and lowered them into the vessel waiting outside.

"Do you see this?" Cecily asked, her voice low. "They're masked. Like the ones who took Daro."

"I can't see much through that mist, but it looks like one of them opened up the side of the ship," Serv answered.

Cecily had never heard of a Wielder who could do such a thing. It was almost like the melding of a Wielding ability and a Shaper talent. "It's like he made it insubstantial. He's holding it open, I can feel it."

The others had crept up behind them. Serv passed the spyglass to Mira and they all took a brief turn, watching the slaves being unloaded into the smaller boat.

"Can't see a blasted thing through that mist. What do we do?" Griff's attempt at a whisper made Cecily cringe at the noise.

She turned to Serv. "Signal Merrick. They must be going upriver. We need to be ready to follow."

Sumara held the spyglass to her eye. "They aren't going upriver. They're going across to the wall."

Cecily swung her attention back to the ship. Sumara was right. Though the mist made it hard to see, the smaller vessel had disengaged from the larger and rowed across the river. Two men pulled oars while their cargo of slaves huddled down in the center.

"Where are they going?" Griff whispered. "There's nothing over there."

"Up the wall?" Mira suggested. "Maybe they have someone at the top who will lower ropes."

The group crept down the riverbank, closer to the docks, and watched the boat row across the inky black water. Cecily locked the ship in her Awareness and expanded her circle to check the wall. "The wall is empty. There's no one up there."

Cecily probed the wall near the water. "There's a stormwater drain over there. I bet it's big enough for the boat." As the boat neared the wall, she felt the shimmering effect of the strange Wielder's power. "He's dissolving the iron bars of the grate. They're going to go right underneath the city." She paused and took a quick look up and down the riverbank. "Signal Merrick. We need to follow."

She dashed down the riverbank, heading toward the docks, and heard the sound of her friends' footfalls behind her. Her mind raced, trying to formulate a plan, but she couldn't think clearly. The thought of letting the boat out of her sight made her panicky. These men might lead her right to Daro.

She reached the docks and skidded to a halt. Throwing a glance over her shoulder, she thought she could see the faint outline of Merrick's boat gliding through the water. The other boat was already disappearing into the storm drain. Merrick wouldn't reach it in time. She thought about trying to disrupt the Wielder, but her accuracy was poor at such a distance. The river was too wide.

"Damn it, where is Callum?" she asked, speaking more to herself than anyone else. If anyone might know where that storm drain went, it would be Callum. She looked up at the Merchant Span, high above, and thought about how long it would take to get to the north side of the river.

The ground seemed to explode and Cecily flew forward, sand and rocks flying. She landed on her stomach with a groan. As she rose to her knees, her back stung where rocks had pelted her. Out of instinct, her Awareness flew open and she checked on the others. Griff, Serv and Mira were moving, struggling to their feet. Sumara appeared to have taken the brunt of the attack; she remained sprawled on the sand, and although she didn't move, Cecily could sense her breathing. Another figure loomed behind. She turned and got to her feet as the figure walked toward her.

Her heart caught in her throat and her adrenaline surged as the figure emerged from the darkness, dressed in black, a mask obscuring the face.

"Cecily Graymere?" the figure said. It was a woman, her voice sneering with contempt. "This is a surprise. You should have stayed dead, little bird."

She knew that voice. She hadn't been called "little bird" in years, but there was no mistaking it. "Isley?"

"No," Isley growled. She held her hand in front of her and a knife coalesced, a shining blade with a narrow handle. It dropped into her hand and her fingers curled around the handle.

"What are you doing here, Isley?" Cecily asked and held her hands up in front of her. Isley had been a fellow student at the Lyceum. A

Light Wielder, her specialty had been Illusion. They had worked together in the Lyceum of Power, collaborating on some of Hadran's assignments. She looked at the knife in Isley's hand. She knew it was an illusion, but it looked eerily real.

"That isn't who I am," she said, "not anymore." She threw the knife at Cecily.

Instinctively, Cecily Wielded to Push the knife off course. Her Reach went right through. She jumped out of the way, even as she told herself it was only an illusion. The knife shot past and she heard the sound of fabric tearing.

Looking down at her clothes, she put her fingers through the hole the knife had made. *That's not possible.* Her eyes flew back to Isley. There were knives in both of her hands. Cecily threw herself down onto the ground.

She looked up and saw Serv and Griff rush in to attack. The knives disappeared and Isley's hands flew up in front of her, creating a stone wall. Griff slammed right into it and flew backward as if he had launched himself into solid stone. Serv sidestepped and turned, missing the wall, and it dissipated as Griff hit. Serv attacked, his curved blade flashing in the weak lamplight. A sword materialized in Isley's hand and she blocked Serv's attack. The blade vanished as it hit Serv's sword. A stone block materialized in front of Isley and she pushed it toward Serv. It hit him in the chest and knocked him backward.

Cecily got to her feet as an arrow sliced through the air. *Mira.* Isley blocked it with a shield that scattered apart as the arrow pierced it, leaving the arrow to clatter onto the rocky ground. Mira shot several more, but Isley threw up shield after shield, blocking each arrow before it could reach her. Cecily Wielded, grabbing Isley's knees with Pressure, but she had to let go as Isley threw more knives at her. One grazed her thigh and her leg blossomed with pain as blood trickled down and soaked into her leggings.

Isley created a massive stone boulder and sent it flying at Mira with terrifying speed. Cecily Reached, trying to Push Mira out of the way, but the stone smashed into her and sent her sprawling onto the sand.

Cecily Pushed air at Isley, trying to knock her off balance, but an axe came flying and she hit the ground again. She rolled back to her feet as a wall of rock rushed at her. She threw her arms over her head and turned so her shoulder took the brunt of the impact. The rock hit and Cecily's back and shoulder exploded with pain as she crashed to the ground.

Coughing and gasping, Cecily struggled to fill her lungs with air. She tucked her right arm under her body and tried to get to her feet. Sumara was near. She pushed herself up with her arms and shook her head as if to clear it. Cecily turned to see Serv being thrown back by one of Isley's impossibly solid illusions. Griff attacked from the other side, but Isley created another wall of rock and smashed it into Griff. He hit the ground and rolled to his side, struggling to his knees before he collapsed facedown on the ground.

Cecily met Sumara's eyes and they nodded. If they could attack her together, they might have a chance. Serv went in for another blow, visibly limping. Gritting her teeth against the pain in her shoulder and thigh, Cecily Wielded, Reaching for Isley's arms. She tugged them apart in opposite directions, hoping it would stop her from creating another illusion. She used Pressure to hold on, squeezing as Isley struggled against her.

"Serv, clear!" Sumara shouted. A bolt of lightning shot from her fingertips toward Isley. Serv jumped out of the way as the bolt hit and sent Isley flying backward. Cecily Wielded with all the strength she had left to Push Isley over the water. The lightning jolted around her body, and for a split second she hovered above the water, electricity crackling through her. Cecily let go and Isley splashed into the river, the aftereffects of Sumara's blast making the water blink and glow in the darkness.

"I hope that was enough," Sumara said, as she got to her feet. "I won't be able to do that again for a while."

She reached down and helped Cecily up. Despite the pounding he had taken, Griff ran to Mira and scooped her up in his arms. She had a bloody gash on her forehead and her eyes remained closed.

"We have to get out of here," Cecily said. "We don't know if Isley is dead or whether someone else is coming." A few sailors peeked out from the docked ships. She whistled again for Merrick, signaling retreat. The answer came from across the river.

They limped back to the entrance to the Quarry at the Ale Stone to find Edson waiting for them. A messenger dashed by and Edson stood. He looked Cecily up and down, his eyes wide and his mouth open.

"We need a Serum Shaper for Mira," Cecily said. Her leg was soaked with blood and she could barely move her arm for the pain in her shoulder and back, but Mira remained unconscious.

"They're already here," Edson said. "Someone tried to kill Callum."

## 27 : KEYS

"Get off, get off, I'm fine." Callum's voice carried through the stone hallway.

Cecily peeked around the doorway. Callum was in bed, propped up on pillows. Both eyes were black and swollen, his cheeks a mess of purpling bruises. Cecily entered, keeping her hurt arm tucked close to her body. A Serum Shaper had probed her to assess her injuries, concluding she hadn't broken any bones. The small woman had wrapped the wound on her leg and assured her that her shoulder and back were merely bruised, though they would be painful for a while.

The Serum Shaper rolled her eyes at Callum. "Very well, you know best," she said, her long skirts swishing as she walked out of the room.

Cecily sank into a chair next to the bed. Her body ached and she longed for sleep. Another Serum Shaper had been sent to help Mira, with Griff and Serv promising to stay by her side. At Cecily's insistence,

Sumara had gone to find rest. Merrick hadn't returned, and she desperately hoped he was somehow following the smugglers' trail.

"What happened?" she asked and gestured to his mangled face. "You look terrible."

Callum shook his head. "Remember that house I found, where my prisoner said the slaves were being taken?" Cecily nodded. "I left this morning because I got word it burned to the ground. By the time I got there, the fire brigade had put it out, but it was gone. Nothing left but ash and some smoldering timbers. I'd been hoping to get inside, see if we could find anything, but it's gone."

Cecily sighed. It felt as if every time they made the slightest bit of progress, they were jerked back to the start again.

"That isn't the worst of it," Callum continued. "Someone killed my prisoner while I was at the site of the fire."

"What?" Cecily breathed. Callum had secret locations stashed all over the city. Few people who weren't of high rank in the Underground knew about the Quarry, and Cecily knew Callum had plenty of other places at his disposal.

Callum winced and touched the bandage at his neck. "The lock was all warped, as if it had been heated and broken. They didn't just kill him. They left pieces of him all over the cell. I had that place guarded like a vault full of gold, and whoever did this tore through everybody."

"The lock on my room at the inn was melted shut. Heated."

He nodded. "Exactly."

"What about all that?" she said, gesturing at his face.

"Two of the smugglers' men jumped me. Apparently they took it a little personally that I'd gotten one of theirs. They threw a bag over my head, tied me up and beat me quite nicely." He shifted, groaning as he moved. "It was rather effective, I have to give them that. Then they hauled me up on top of the wall, manacled me with weighted chains and tossed me into the river."

Cecily's mouth dropped open. "You can't be serious. How did you survive?"

Callum smiled. He drew out a chain from around his neck and jingled a key. "Swiped this off one of them before they dropped me. Not exactly a trick I'd care to repeat, but it worked out okay for me in the end." He tucked the key back under his shirt. "You look almost as bad as I do," he said, raising an eyebrow. "I take it things didn't go so well down at the docks."

"You could say that," she said and winced as she stretched out her leg. She told him what they had seen: the mist, the man who'd dissipated the side of the boat, the route through the drain system, and their attacker.

"The woman who attacked you, this Isley. You said you knew her?" Callum asked.

"I did. I'd know that voice anywhere. She was the bane of my existence at the Lyceum." She rubbed her aching eyes. "She was a Light Wielder, an Illusionist. Her illusions were impressive, but she had a reputation for practical jokes, mean ones. She was disciplined quite a few times when her tricks wound up hurting people. I had to work with her sometimes, when I was in the Lyceum of Power. Hadran thought we made a good team."

"I bet you did," Callum said.

"She was masked, like the men who took Daro. It was Isley, but she wasn't the same. Her illusions had substance. She was beating us to pieces with them. It shouldn't be possible."

"At this point, I'm going with the assumption that nothing is impossible anymore," Callum said in a low voice. "Nihil seems to be doing something to people, changing their abilities. I'm worried he's done something to Daro."

"I am too," Cecily said, her voice quiet.

"We don't know where they took that shipment of slaves tonight. The manor house is still a smoldering pile of ash and broken timbers. We won't find anything there. Our only break will be if Merrick manages to follow that boat through the storm drains and figure out where they wind up."

A thought coalesced in Cecily's mind. "There's one thing we've been missing in all this," she said. "The Lyceum."

Callum raised his eyebrows. "What about the Lyceum?"

"Something has been going on up there. My old professor sent me a note and after everything that has happened, it sounds an awful lot like a warning, and maybe a goodbye. Then he went missing. They claim he's on sabbatical, but that man hasn't taken a break from his work in his life, as far as I know." She paused, and the pieces clicked together in her mind like a children's puzzle. "We keep getting attacked by men with impossible Wielding abilities. And one of them was one of my cohorts at the Lyceum of Power."

"You think the Lyceum is behind this?"

"Who else would be putting out Wielders with bizarre abilities? I kept assuming it couldn't be the Lyceum, but why not? The Lyceum of Power is notorious for bending the rules, if not outright breaking them. Goodness knows I did plenty of it when I was there. Nihil must be part of the Lyceum of Power."

"You don't think Daro is there, do you?"

Cecily shook her head. "Probably not. But the Lyceum of Power operates out of the lower levels of the library. If I can get in there, I can probably find out how they're involved, and hopefully where to find him."

"Getting in will be touchy. Didn't they escort you out the last time you were there?"

Cecily gave him a tired smile. "There's a certain irony in breaking into the place where I learned how to do it, isn't there?"

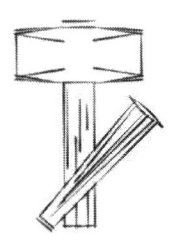

## 28 : WATCHTOWER

Daro crouched behind a boulder and stared up at the watchtower that loomed over the mountain pass. Built of massive stone bricks, the circular tower provided a lookout and means of defense for the main pass into the northern kingdom of Thaya. It was connected to a gate that joined to the rock on the other side, with a wide parapet above. A heavy portcullis could be lowered, sealing the gate if necessary. Daro seemed to remember traveling this way, but it seemed like a life that belonged to another person, the memories faded and weak.

The wind whipped through the pass, creating a high-pitched whistle. Snow topped the peaks, and the cold air pressed against his eyes and forehead. The rest of his face stayed warm under his mask, and he pulled the top of it down closer to his eyes.

Number One squatted next to Daro. "Nihil is expecting an important shipment from Thaya," he said. "Our job is simple: we need to make sure the shipment gets through. It won't be brought through the main gate, but the garrison sends out regular patrols of the surrounding area. We need to create enough of a distraction that the garrison won't send out a patrol for a few days."

Daro chose not to wonder about what sort of shipment Nihil was expecting that had to be smuggled through an alternate route. It was best not to consider such questions.

"Only a small garrison of men is stationed here, especially in winter," Number One said. "This will be quick and easy. Number Four and Number Twelve will start a fire in the bunkhouse over there." He pointed to a squat rectangular building near the tower and turned to Daro. "Your job is to get up into the tower and disable their beacon. It will be in the center, up there on top, a set of mirrors facing out that their Light Wielder can use to signal the next tower. We don't want them able to call for help."

Daro nodded, but something deep inside prickled at the instructions. What was he doing here? His heart began to beat faster and his body tingled with anticipation. He reached down and touched the hilt of his sword. He'd been training with it daily and found solace in the work. He could lose himself in his forms, letting his mind go blank as he practiced. Number One encouraged him to direct the flow of energy within him into the sword. Daro found himself swinging faster and harder than ever before. But he held back, keeping a tight rein on himself, fearful of letting all that power loose.

Number One had taught him to contain his power so he maintained a greater degree of control. There was a raging flood within him, and the only thing that truly helped was when Number One Absorbed some of his energy. The other man had incredible Absorption power. He could draw on Daro's seemingly endless well of energy, pulling it from Daro and offering respite, if only briefly.

Daro's fingers twitched as he looked back up at the tower. It seemed to grow taller before his eyes. He pushed down the fear and buried it under the burning energy. Fear was always present; he was learning to live with it, to own it, as Number One said. His implant itched and he resisted the urge to reach back and scratch it.

Number One was still talking. "There shouldn't be more than one or two men up there, so you won't have much trouble," he said. "I'll be down here, to make sure everything goes according to plan and take care of any loose ends."

The sun was already low on the horizon, disappearing behind the peaks, and the light faded to twilight. Daro was anxious to complete their mission and get back to the compound. Sindre had warned him before they left that his implant was designed to kill him if she didn't trigger it regularly. He would have six days, perhaps a week, before it hit, but in the end, he would die a slow, painful death. She said they had designed it that way to ensure the subjects' continuing cooperation. He thought about asking Number One whether it was true, but in the end he decided it felt like too personal a question somehow.

They waited for darkness to settle. A few torches on the tower and on the barracks wall gave the only light. The sky was thick with clouds, obscuring the stars. Daro narrowed his eyes and thought about seeing better, feeling some of his well of energy flow to his eyes. The landscape sharpened and the tower stood out against the black mountains behind.

Number One gave the signal, and Daro crept toward the tower, circling around to the back. He made sure his sword was secure at his belt, found his first footholds, and hoisted himself up onto the wall face. The bricks were large, rough stones with plenty of places to grip. The higher he climbed, the more he felt his power swell within him. He scrambled up the side of the wall, surprising himself with his strength. He almost felt as if he could pull with his arms and simply launch himself all the way to the top.

The wind whipped at his face, pulling at his mask, and his clothes rustled against his body. He felt warm, as if heat radiated from within. He climbed closer to the lookout ledge and his heart pounded faster. He brought his image of Cecily to his mind, but her face was hazy, beginning to fade. Clinging to the side of a tower, high above the ground, the mountain wind beating at him, he tried to focus and find calm. The torrent of voices, some whispers, some screams, tore at him from inside. He clung to the faint vision of his wife, grasping at the only stability he had left.

He pushed emotion aside and opened his eyes to focus on his task. He couldn't let distractions in. A small curl of fear unraveled itself in his belly as he thought about what would happen if he failed his mission. Sindre would certainly punish him, but he worried more about what Nihil would do.

He got a higher foothold and pulled himself up so he could see over the ledge. The tower culminated in a round chamber with a lookout balcony running around the circumference. The chamber had a few chairs and a small fireplace, allowing the guard on duty to keep warm. The beacon stood on a pedestal in the center of the chamber, right where Number One had said it would be. Made of curved mirrors, the beacon would reflect light and shine it over a great distance. The guards at each guard post on the borders of the kingdom were trained in a code, using flashes of light to communicate messages across great distances.

One of the chairs was occupied by a guard, who dozed in his seat. He sat with his legs stretched out in front, his sword leaning against the wall next to him. A small fire crackled in the fireplace and the remains of what appeared to be his dinner sat on a stool next to the fire.

Daro hoisted himself over the ledge and landed with soft feet on the balcony. He paused, keeping his hands on the ledge behind him, and waited to see if the guard would stir. The guard took a shuddering breath and let out a low snore as his chin fell to his chest.

A measure of relief trickled into Daro's mind. He would be able to get the beacon and steal back down the wall without any confrontation, as long as the guard slept. With a quick glance around to make sure he hadn't missed anything, he crept toward the beacon. It was secured to the pedestal with iron bolts, but Daro easily lifted it, snapping the bolts with a quick pop. He cringed and looked back to the guard, who slept on. Daro let out a breath and turned, wondering how he was going to disable the beacon without waking the guard.

He crept back to the balcony and peered toward the barracks. He could smell a faint wisp of smoke beginning to taint the air. It wouldn't be long before the barracks were in full blaze. That should keep the guards busy for a while as they made repairs to their buildings.

A sound behind him made his back and shoulders clench. Although he felt as if he could see for miles, he realized his ears were muffled, as if stuffed with cotton. He turned to find a second guard, staring at him wide-eyed with his mouth hanging open. It only took a second for Daro to react. He tossed the beacon off the ledge and drew his sword.

The first guard scrambled to his feet and struggled to get his sword from its resting place against the wall. The other guard said something, but Daro couldn't make out his words. His lips seemed to say, "Stop," and "Who are you?" but Daro couldn't be sure. All he knew was that he couldn't get down the wall fast enough to avoid their blades, so there was nothing left to do but engage his enemy.

With the raging torrent of energy welling up inside him, he felt as if his former skills as a swordsman had been nothing but a child pretending. He swung his sword, feeling the recoil of contact with his enemy, and relished the vibrations reverberating through his arms. He was vaguely aware of the guards yelling, and in the back of his mind he realized more would be coming. He swung right and checked the blow of the second guard before turning to strike at the other. Their swords clashed, the metallic ring singing out into the night.

His arms felt loose as he swung, his muscles tightening for impact. He flowed with his sword as the energy surged through him. He closed with the guards, driving them back, and his sword cut the air in an arc between them. They slashed at him, one strike after another, but he was faster. He blocked each one and pressed them backward, away from the protected chamber and out into the wind. Their cloaks whipped at their backs and Daro pushed them until they were wedged against the ledge of the balcony.

One of the guard's eyes flicked past Daro, and he heard the footfalls of more guards rushing up the stairs behind him. He turned, holding his sword with both hands, and pointed it at his enemies. The first guard stopped, and his eyes widened. Daro advanced, striking at his new opponent, then swung his sword back over his shoulder to deflect a blow from behind. The guard behind stepped closer and Daro kicked, hitting him in the gut and sending him staggering backward.

Three more guards emerged from the stairs, swords drawn. Daro circled, keeping his sword out in front, and stared at each guardsman as his gaze swept past. Two rushed in toward him, the confined space forcing the others to stay back. Daro switched back and forth between them, his sword clashing with theirs as they both attacked. He kept his foes at bay, but with six men surrounding him, he couldn't take the offensive. He fought to keep the well of power inside from bursting forth, like a man pushing against a dam to hold back the water.

He struck, pushing one of the guards backward, and sent him stumbling into a chair. Two more guards pressed him from behind as he moved into the center of the chamber. He blocked their strikes. His sword sliced through the air and hit with a satisfying clang. His arms tightened with each strike, the force reverberating through his body.

The guards shouted to one another, trying to coordinate their attacks. Daro's sword flew between them and stopped their attempts to hit him. They pressed him harder but he moved faster, ducking, spinning, blocking, striking. His strength felt endless and a strange sort of ecstasy overtook him. His mind felt clear, the voices quiet for the first time in months. The energy he fought so hard to contain felt like liquid silver running through his veins, hot and seductive.

The guards pressed in, attacking from all sides. Daro let go and allowed the well of energy to explode inside him. The dam broke and power rushed through him, white hot and terrifying. His mind soared with euphoria as he beat back his attackers. Blood splattered across the wall as he sliced through one of the guards. The body hit the floor and he kicked it aside, as he reached back with his sword to deflect the next attack. He turned, his body a whirl of motion, and plunged his sword through the man's neck. A spray of hot blood splashed his face.

He spun again and sliced through the man behind him, sending another spray of blood across the stones. His arms pulsed with blazing power. It saturated his limbs, making him astonishingly fast and stronger than he thought possible. A heady exhilaration spread through him as he cut down another guard, his sword turning in a wide arc to cut deep into the man's neck. More guards poured up the stairs, but he didn't care. He wanted them to come.

He drew in more energy, feeling as if it were coming from the stones themselves. It was endless, feeding him with fury and elation. He cut through the guard in front of him, his sword an extension of his rage.

The guards rushed him, their swords slashing at him from all directions. He parried and spun to slice through one man's chest. The next guard thrust toward him, but he blocked, then kicked another guard next to him. They pushed their attack, driving at him from all sides.

He pulled more energy, and it flooded through his body. He let it flow, no longer attempting to curb its advance. His hands and feet were almost numb with the strength and heat coursing through him. He deflected two more strikes but the guards kept coming, surrounding him. Someone scored a hit on his arm. The slice hardly registered as pain through the torrent of energy pulsing inside.

The sound of his heart pounding echoed in his head, drowning the clash of metal. The rush of power felt as if it might burn him from the inside out. He killed another guard, but they kept coming, his sword flying to keep their blows at bay. Using his sword to protect his head, he felt himself beat down, and he crouched toward the floor as the guards tried to end him.

His breathing quickened as another sword sliced down his back. His anger boiled, hot and dangerous, and he drew in more energy, as much as he could hold. He heaved upward, unleashing all his fury, all his hatred, and let his power erupt.

The top of the tower burst open as if something exploded. The blast erupted outward, launching Daro, and he soared through the air. His vision began to go dark, and a hazy realization that he was going to hit the ground flickered through his mind. The wind buffeted him as he arched downward, and the ground raced toward him. He hit with a heavy crack as rock and dust flew up around him. Something told him he should feel pain, but darkness flowed through his mind and he let it envelop him like a warm blanket.

A sound crowded into his solace, a voice calling him from the depths of relief. "Fourteen." It was muffled and hazy, as if heard through a thick wall. "Fourteen, can you hear me?"

He blinked and reached up to rub his eyes. The darkness was interrupted by an orange glow in the distance. The smell of smoke and the feel of the rocky ground beneath reminded him of where he was.

"Fourteen," the voice said again. It was Number One. Of course it was. Who else would it be?

Daro eased himself up to a sitting position. His arm stung and his back was a tight mass of agony. He reached up to check his mask and found it torn, hanging off his face.

Number One was looking at him with wide eyes. Daro glanced behind him and saw the tower, or what remained of it. The roof was on the opposite side of the pass, turned upside down as if it had been blown off and landed there. The rest of the tower tilted wildly, threatening to crumble and fall down completely. The barracks nearby burned in a blaze of orange and yellow flame, throwing billows of black smoke up into the night sky.

"What happened?" he asked.

Number One stared at him a moment longer. "That's what I was going to ask you," he said, his eyes still wide. "You nearly destroyed the whole tower."

Daro's limbs felt heavy and he wondered if he'd be able to walk. The darkness of exhaustion intruded upon the margins of his vision, calling to him, trying to pull him under. He furrowed his brow and looked from Number One to the teetering tower behind. He could see guards running around the barracks, trying to contain the blaze.

Images flashed through his mind: his sword slicing and cutting through men, blood splattering on the stones. He remembered the feeling of ecstasy as he'd let the power swell through him, opening himself and giving in to the white-hot energy. His sword had run through their bodies as if they offered no resistance, his mind glorying in the rush of the fight. He looked down at his hands, stained with blood and spattered with dirt. He had killed those men. And it had felt good.

He stared at his hands and wondered who they belonged to. Were they Daro's, or Number Fourteen's? He looked up at Number One, his voice a hoarse whisper. "What have I done?"

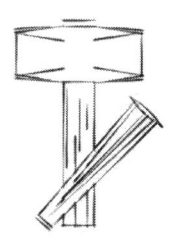

## 29 : XIV

Daro sat with his hands on the table, his mind heavy with dread. He stared at the Arcstone, the veins of green snaking up through the cream stone, tiny spots glinting in the lamplight. Nihil usually seated him on one side of the table across from a person with their head covered, what Nihil referred to as a source. Nihil seemed to have an endless supply of them, men and women dressed in rags, their hands bound. Every time he subjected Daro to the stone, another source would be brought in and Daro would be forced to absorb their energy. With each session, his soul felt as if it would fracture into shards like glass breaking on the ground. His strength increased and he was able to do things he'd never thought possible, but the echoes of the men he absorbed threatened to drive him mad.

Since the watchtower, he lived in constant fear of losing control. The sensation of power rushing through him had been hypnotic, burying the realities of his captivity and silencing the voices, but only for a time. He feared his grip on himself was faltering. Only Number One seemed able to help him, Absorbing enough of his wild energy to keep him at least partially sane.

Today another man occupied Daro's usual chair. Number One sat rigid, his back straight, his eyes down. His hands were spread wide on the table before him, the tendons straining. Sindre stood behind him, holding her hands behind her back. A source sat across from Number One, a tall man with bony arms. Anxiety fluttered in Daro's stomach. This was new, and the novelty was worrisome.

Nihil wore his customary black robe and gloves as he gathered a few supplies. He set down a small leather-bound notebook, a pot of ink, and a large feathered quill. The source swayed in his seat. Nihil looked up, flicking his hand to the side, and a man scurried over. He tied the source around the chest, securing him to his chair.

"Number Fourteen, you have been a most interesting test subject," Nihil began as he dipped his quill into the ink and scratched a few notes in his book. He flipped back through the pages, tilting his head as he read over his notes. "Your Imaran heritage makes you as fascinating as I had hoped. More so, as a matter of fact."

Daro glanced at Number One. He held still, as if he were made of the same stone that sat on the table, the only movement the rising and falling of his chest as he breathed.

Nihil continued. "When we first brought you here, you believed yourself to be devoid of any Wielding ability, isn't that right?" He didn't look up to see if Daro would answer. "I had my suspicions about Imarans, and I believe you have proven my theories correct. We may not see the Imarans as having the powers of Wielders and Shapers. In fact, my colleagues at the Lyceum seem to believe your father's people are something entirely different from us, a race with their own abilities, completely separate from the understood principles of Wielding. I, however"—he raised his eyes to Daro, pointing with his quill—"have long believed that the Imarans are not so different as we think. They simply possess a different flavor of Wielding ability, and you have inherited this ability from your father."

Daro shifted in his seat. It was unnerving to hear Nihil speak of his father. Sindre tortured him mercilessly whenever he mentioned his past, trying to drive any memory of his former life from his mind. He found those thoughts fading into obscurity, bubbling to the surface only occasionally. The only image he still clung to was that of his wife, a vision of her face, her hand reaching out to him, holding him steady.

"What ability?" he said, daring to ask a question. Number One didn't react to his voice, his eyes still locked on the table.

"Augmentation," Nihil replied, "considered to be the rarest form of Wielding by standard definitions. The Lyceum has long believed Augmentation to be so rare, it may as well not even exist. We only know of it based on some very old writings brought over from the Attalonian Empire." He paused again to write in his notebook. "But I surmised the truth. Augmentation may be a rare trait amongst Halthians, even with the astonishing number of Wielders in the kingdom. But Imarans are natural Augmenters. I theorize that nearly every one of them has some degree of the ability, although I certainly can't prove it, not from afar. But you, Number Fourteen, even with only half Imaran blood, you are filled with the capacity to Augment. We simply had to unlock it."

Memories of the watchtower, of power flooding his body, came crashing back. His well of energy had saturated his body, making him stronger and faster. Was that what was happening? He was Augmenting?

Nihil had allowed him a question. Perhaps he would answer more. "What is the stone?"

"Ah, yes, the Arcstone," Nihil said as he closed his book and put down his quill. "As you may have surmised from our time working together, I was born with the abilities of a Sensory Wielder. My gift allowed me to sense abilities in others, learning much about who they were. I was weak, not strong enough to gain entry into the Lyceum. I had thought I would find my place at the famed institution of learning. My father was Attalonian, and he abhorred Wielding in all its forms. The Lyceum was supposed to be my salvation, the one place a young man like me would be accepted, nay, celebrated for my contribution to the world. Alas, they did not believe I had what it took to be a candidate." Nihil's voice remained even, but Daro could sense the bitterness flowing beneath the surface. "I am a man who believes in progress above all else. I did not let the Lyceum's rejection deter me. I simply found other ways to further my learning, and later, my research. I discovered this amazing piece of stone, deep in the catacombs beneath the Great Library, and it changed the course of my research. One could even say it changed the course of my life."

He ran his gloved hand over the stone, an almost loving gesture. "This shard of Arcstone was left over from the days when the Imarans built the Life Tree. An incredible thing, Arcstone. Have you ever seen the Imarans bringing it upriver? It floats. It feels as dense as iron and it is incredibly heavy, yet it floats on the water. I can't explain it. I suspect the Imarans have an enormous supply of the stuff. Most of the goods they bring to trade in Halthas are made of Arcstone. And if my theory is correct, they use their ability to Augment the stone, imbuing it with many interesting properties."

Nihil paused again and looked over the stone at Daro. He guessed Nihil was considering how much to tell him. "Not all Arcstone is the same. The Imarans who built the Life Tree did something to their stone that made that incredible sculpture. But there is so much more to this wonderful stone. I discovered that I could enhance my ability with it. And it led me to the discovery that I could transfer abilities through it. I could greatly enhance the strength of a Wielder by imbuing them with the energy of another." His eyes shone. "The possibilities are endless. And you, Number Fourteen, have unlocked more of the stone's mysteries for me. So for that, I have to thank you."

He pulled off a glove and laid it carefully on the table. "I brought you here today to test another of my theories." He pulled off the other glove and laid it on top of its mate. "My ability is what facilitates the transfer. With the Arcstone as a conduit, I can draw the energy and ability of one into the body of another. There are limitations to this process, however, and I suspect my results will be even stronger with your help."

He turned to his assistant and flicked his hand toward the source sitting in the chair. The man picked up the source's arms and laid them on the Arcstone, using a length of narrow rope to tie his hands in place. The man's head lolled to the side, but he didn't resist. "Number One here has been one of my greatest achievements. He was the first to survive the process and has proven to be an excellent asset. His once-weak Absorption ability has been enhanced and modified to a generous degree."

Number One's eyes slowly rose to look at Nihil. His face was expressionless, but Daro could sense a great deal of tension in the other man.

"Today," Nihil continued, "I intend to see if we can use your capacity for Augmentation to aid in the transference process, and if we can Augment Number One's ability even further."

Daro's stomach clenched and his heart pounded. Number One continued to stare at Nihil, and his white-knuckled hands gripped the surface of the table.

"Number Fourteen, when I tell you, you will place your hands on the stone," Nihil said, his hard voice allowing no room for protest.

Number One's breathing was heavy. Sindre leaned down to whisper something in his ear. He flinched, his eyes blinking, and his shoulders clenched tight.

Nihil nodded to Daro and held his hands up, close to the stone. Every fiber of Daro's being wanted to lash out against this, but Sindre flashed a look at him. He felt a jolt down his back from his implant. His hands trembled as they hovered over the stone. Number One's shaking hands rose slowly, and his lips curled back in a grimace as he moved them forward.

"Now," Nihil commanded and Daro felt unable to resist. He pressed his hands against the stone.

The blinding tunnel of light surged past him, but this time he felt as if he were caught in the side of the tunnel, rather than at its head. Energy flooded through him, flowing from the source into Number One. He could see the images and emotions rushing past, gliding through him as they passed quickly into Number One. Daro was hit with memories so strong he couldn't separate them from his own. Emotions passed through him like translucent ghosts, rushing by and leaving him reeling.

He could feel his own energy being sucked along the river, pulled through him in a swirl of chaos. Echoes bounced back from Number One, the voices and memories assaulting him. He could hear the rending of the source's soul, the energy forced into Number One. It was as if a great cry poured forth and lashed through Daro's mind.

He cast around for an anchor, something to hold onto. He was drowning in a sea of turmoil. As he had done before when invaded with energy through the Arcstone, he imagined himself in a boat. He built the sides, the sturdy bottom, and hunkered down, letting the waves toss him.

Above him he could see Cecily. Her smile steadied him, a light in the turmoil. Through the madness, she reached down and called to him, assuring him she would pull him out of his misery.

Something bashed into him, like a piece of driftwood hurled by a wave. His vision blurred. Cecily reached her other hand out to him and called his name. His link to her felt weak, trembling as if it would tear apart. The voices tore at him, threatening to fracture his very being to pieces. He gasped for breath and clung to the sides of his boat. It was the only solid thing in the tempest that surrounded him.

Cecily's mouth moved as if she called to him, but he couldn't hear the words through the screams. Terror gripped him and he grasped the sides of his boat as the storm tossed him about. He crouched further down as the energy rushed past and nearly tore him apart.

He was losing his grip on himself. Cecily reached down, but he shrank away from her and clung to the sides of his boat. A wave crashed over him, freezing and boiling hot all at once. He couldn't reach for her, couldn't risk leaving the solidity of his boat. The voices pressed at him, calling him away. He covered his ears and sunk down, closing his eyes against the turmoil, to no avail. The voices only grew louder the harder he tried to shut them out. The energy surged past, as images from both the source and Number One beat against him, ripping him apart.

He hunkered down in his boat and took one last look at his image of Cecily. She called his name and reached out her hand, but he couldn't take it. Instead, he held to the boat and turned away, shutting out everything outside. A roof materialized, snapping into place, cutting him off from the terror outside. He slammed up the wall, building himself into a box. The darkness was thick and he still felt the waves of chaos try to toss him about. He made the walls thicker until the voices no longer carried through, burying himself deep enough to escape the tempest and hold together the pieces of his fracturing psyche.

Everything crashed into deafening silence. His breath echoed in his ears and he felt as if he sat alone, in a room buried in darkness. The voices were silent, the pandemonium within replaced with a numb stillness. He felt no emotion, no surges of pain, or anger, or loss. He felt nothing.

He opened his eyes and found himself in Nihil's laboratory. Number One writhed on the floor, moaning, as Sindre stood above him. Nihil sat in his seat, breathing heavily, and looked at Daro with wide eyes. He pulled on his gloves and reached a trembling hand toward his quill to write something in his notebook.

Daro's body felt fatigued and his reservoir of power was nearly dry, the constant stream of energy temporarily abated. His mind had gone somewhere beyond clear. He had very little thought at all. Emptiness filled him and he embraced it, letting the void fill him.

The last traces of his former life drifted away. He had once been a man named Daro, but he let that man go, like a drowned corpse carried away by the sea.

He was Number Fourteen.

## 30 : BREAKOUT

The pattering rain was a blessing, giving Cecily a reason to keep the cowl of her cloak over her head as she stole onto the Lyceum grounds. She wasn't sure if Magister Evan would have the guards stop her at the gate, but she didn't want to take the chance. She had learned in her days working for Hadran that often the best way to get into a place without being challenged was to act as if you had every right to be there. She strode right past the guards with her back straight, heading for the library without hesitation, and breathed a sigh of relief when no one stopped her.

The Great Library was open to the public during the afternoon hours, giving her access to the Lyceum grounds. She crept around the bookshelves, steering clear of any guards. There weren't many and it was easy to blend into the throngs of students, staff, and magisters milling about the books. Her back and shoulder still ached from their encounter at the docks, but true to the healer's word, she was beginning to feel better.

She knew the Lyceum of Power operated out of the lower levels of the library. There were at least six floors underground, plunging into the rock beneath the domed building. Most were for storage, books, and scrolls that were either very delicate, or considered very dangerous. The public wasn't permitted in any of the lower levels without special permission. She had decided to come alone, knowing the difficulty of even one person stealing into the lower library. She didn't think she'd be able to get anyone else down with her.

As the closing hour approached, she crept down the stairs. It took her several tries before she was able to make it past the guards and librarians. Twice she had Wielded, attempting to create a distraction, only to attract more librarians and clerks to the area. Finally the way cleared and she was able to make her way down.

Using her Awareness, she crept around, tucking into corners and around dusty shelves to avoid the clerks and librarians as they closed the library for the night. She crouched down between two large shelves, both heaped with scrolls and dusty stacks of parchment. The air was stale and dry, the scent of decaying parchment and dust heavy in the air. She leaned her head back against the wall and waited. She wanted to be sure she wouldn't run into anyone.

Her heart thumped wildly and her limbs tingled with anxiety. Her dreams had gotten worse, leaving her jittery during the day. At first they had been choppy and confusing. It was easy to attribute them to the stress she was under. She was worried about Daro, so she dreamed of him. But lately she was beginning to think there was something else behind these disturbing dreams. She no longer dreamt only of Daro. Another face intruded on her, almost as if he was watching her sleep. She would jerk awake, half expecting to find someone standing above her, watching.

A growing feeling of dread built. She feared something terrible had happened to Daro. Since he'd disappeared, she had gone to bed each night secure in the knowledge that he was alive, somewhere. She could feel their bond like something warm, a mingling of his presence with hers. Even when her dreams were at their worst, she always woke up and felt the link to his soul.

For the last several days, the link they shared felt different. She could no more explain what had happened than she could explain the bond itself. But deep inside, she knew something was terribly wrong. He might be still alive, but for how much longer, she couldn't be sure.

With a calming breath to steady herself, she opened her Awareness and focused first on her floor. She was two levels below the ground and could tell that she was alone. She expanded and probed the floors below. The next level opened in her mind, and a picture of the layout grew from the ceiling down to the floor. She found nothing but bookshelves filled with stacks of books, scrolls, and parchments, no doubt just as dusty and dry.

The next level appeared to be similarly deserted, but as her Awareness expanded it made the image hazy. She decided to head downward so she could get a clearer picture. She felt out the fifth and sixth floors, the ones she knew held the secret offices and laboratories of the Lyceum of Power.

She was surprised to find them nearly empty. In her days with the Lyceum, the underground levels were active at all hours of the day or night. Magisters came below to work on covert projects and research, or to train their students. Cecily had done much of her training in those very rooms. Several magisters even had quarters there, spending their nights sleeping with their work piled around them. With her Awareness open, she could feel the various rooms, but most of them were deserted.

She could sense two people on the sixth level. One seemed to be sitting outside the door to a room, and there was a figure inside, behind a closed door. A prisoner, with a guard outside. It wouldn't be the first time the Lyceum of Power had held someone in those rooms. She thought back to her last visit, to Magister Evan's explanation for

Magister Brunell's absence. She hadn't believed he was on sabbatical. Perhaps she'd just found him.

The sixth level was secured with a complicated lock. It took her several minutes to release the mechanism, allowing her to open the door. She crept along the hallway, keeping her footfalls as soft as possible. Focusing on the guard seated outside the room, she used her Reach to seal off his airway and apply a sharp jab of pressure to the nerves at the base of his jaw. He slumped over and she could feel him take a heaving breath, even as he lay unconscious.

The lock shocked her with a spark as she tried to Wield it open. She sucked in a breath and shook her hand, opening and closing her fingers as the pain dissipated. Gently searching the guard, she found a key around his neck. She unlocked the door to find a small room with a mattress on the floor next to a small table and chair. Magister Brunell stood in the center of the room, and his eyes went wide as she entered.

"Cecily," he said, and his mouth hung slightly open. "You are the last person I expected to see here."

Cecily glanced around. "I'm sure. This place is practically deserted."

"Help me with this," Brunell said as he pulled at something around his neck.

Cecily pulled the chain around his neck and looked for the clasp. It was a braided silver necklace with four circular pendants set at close intervals on one side. Each pendant held a small silvery-green stone, polished to a shine. It was an Absorption collar, a device designed to keep a Wielder from using their power. Cecily knew they existed but had never come into contact with one.

"I don't know how to open it," she said. There was no obvious clasp, but it was far too small to fit around his head.

"There's a lock, underneath the pendants," Brunell said.

Cecily probed it and found the tiny locking mechanism. It was as complicated as it was small and she wondered whose hands had created such a thing. After several minutes, she was able to delve in with a slice of Pressure to release the lock. The necklace fell into her hands.

Cecily shot a quick glance behind her. "Let's go. We need to get out of here."

Brunell started to reach for the absorber, but Cecily tucked it away. His gray magister's robes hung over his stout frame, and he'd aged since Cecily had last seen him, more gray peppering his dark hair and thick beard. They stepped over the unconscious guard and closed the door softly behind them. Cecily locked the door and carefully replaced the key around the guard's neck.

Brunell followed her up to the first underground level and they stopped in the stairwell leading to the main library. "There will be a few guards patrolling the grounds," Brunell said. He paused, closing his eyes. He possessed similar Wielding abilities to Cecily's, including an Awareness much like hers. He opened his eyes again. "We should be clear. Head for the north door and we'll turn west. There is a side gate that is rarely used. There might be a guard nearby, but we should be able to distract him long enough to get out."

Cecily nodded and let him lead the way. They crept through the main library and back out onto the wet grounds. Ducking behind a stand of trees, they watched a Lyceum Guard pass by. Cecily found herself wishing Callum was there to send the guard running with a quick brush of fear.

They made it to the side gate, and stole out into the street beyond. The sun had set, leaving the street bathed in lamplight, illuminating the driving rain. She pulled her cowl further down over her face and tucked her hand in Magister Brunell's arm. They walked down the hill, south toward the main part of the city, where they found a covered carriage to take them over the Merchant Span. They walked the last winding streets to the Ale Stone and down into the Quarry, and she led him down into the depths of the Underground.

Cecily and Brunell sat at a large table with Griff, Serv, Sumara, and Edson. Callum arrived, wincing as he lowered himself into a chair. Mira was still recovering from her injuries. The blow to the head had been severe and the Serum Shapers said it would be a few more days before she would be able to get out of bed. Merrick stood in the doorway, Beau seated nearby. He'd attempted to follow the trail through the storm drain for two days before returning to the Quarry in frustration.

Cecily nursed a cup of hot tea, the warmth seeping into her hands. Brunell hadn't told her much on the way back from the Lyceum. He seemed rather shocked to find himself suddenly free of his captivity, and he let her do most of the talking. She'd told him what happened to Daro and what they'd managed to discover so far. He'd nodded along as she spoke, asking an occasional question. She was anxious to find out why he'd been held captive and what he might know about the Lyceum's involvement in Daro's abduction.

"I hate to put you on the spot like this, after everything you've been through. But I'm hoping you'll be able to help us," Cecily said.

Brunell nodded and reached up to scratch his beard. "You'll have to forgive me if I appear rather bewildered," he said, his voice a deep rumble. "I've been held captive for several months now. My contact with the outside world has been limited. And I certainly wasn't expecting such a heroic rescue."

"Why did they imprison you?" Cecily asked.

"Ah, well," he said, resting his hands on his belly. "That is unfortunately what happens when you find out too much about what others wish to keep hidden. You already know that Nihil is behind these abductions. I do know Nihil. He's been working with the Lyceum of Power for years now. I didn't realize the truth of what he was doing until recently. And when I found out, well..." He paused and held up his hands. "They made sure I would stay out of the way."

"What is he doing, exactly?" Callum asked, as he watched Brunell through narrowed eyes.

Brunell took a deep breath. "From what I understand, he is conducting experiments, trying to make Wielders stronger. Cecily, I hate to say this, but if he has Daro, I fear the worst for him. He is experimenting on people. It is highly illegal and there is no telling what he is doing to them."

"We've seen some of his handiwork," Callum said.

Cecily's shoulders tightened. "Do you know where Nihil is?"

He shook his head. "I'm afraid I don't. I found out some of what he was doing, but I don't know from where he operates."

Callum tossed his hands up in the air. "No one seems to know, do they? No matter how many stones we turn over, none of them have anything useful to tell us."

Brunell held up a finger. "I might actually be able to help you. I may have been locked away in the Lyceum, but I was not completely cut off from the outside. I have spies of my own, still loyal to me, and they've been feeding me information during my captivity. I kept up on Nihil's activities as best as I could. If I am not mistaken, next week is the Feast of the Solstice?" he asked. The others nodded. "I happen to know something big is happening in Wesfell, a town on the river not far from Halthas. I'm not sure what, but I know some of Nihil's men will be there."

Cecily sat back in her chair and stared at an empty spot on the wall. She knew all too well how dangerous Nihil's men were. But if they didn't know they were coming, perhaps Cecily could at least follow them. Nihil's men could lead her to Daro.

"We have to be there next week," Cecily said. Callum opened his mouth, but she didn't let him interject. "Yes, I realize it is dangerous. I'm not suggesting we openly attack. We can't fight them. But what if they don't know we are there? They won't be expecting us. We can hang back, just watch. If we follow them, they'll lead us straight to Daro."

Callum scowled but her other friends were nodding.

"This is the best chance we've had yet," Cecily continued. "We didn't expect anyone to attack us at the docks, so we weren't prepared. This time, we know what we're up against and we will be ready."

"No one else seems to know how to find Nihil," Sumara said. "It seems foolish to miss out on a chance like this."

Callum shook his head. "Mira is still hurt, and I'm not fit for travel either. We won't be at full strength. You faced one of them and she could have killed all of you. We'd be crazy to go after them."

Cecily leveled her gaze at Callum. "What do you suggest we do, hide down here and wait? How long do you think it will be before they find us? They found your prisoner, they got the drop on us at the docks. They know we're looking for them. We've been searching for months and Daro is still missing. I won't sit here, licking my wounds, when I have a chance to find him."

Serv's quiet voice cut across the room. "I'll go."

Griff banged his hand on the table. "As will I," he bellowed.

"I want the chance to track them down," Merrick said as he scratched Beau behind the ears.

Edson spoke up. "Then I'm going too." Cecily opened her mouth to disagree, but he held a hand up. "I know you don't want me getting hurt, Miss Cecily, but I won't stay behind again."

Sumara nodded. Callum sighed and tossed his gold coin on the table. "I guess I better go pack."

"No," Cecily said and held up her hand. "You are right about one thing. You're hurt and you need to stay here until you recover. You and Mira will stay. The rest of us will go."

Callum brushed his hair from his face. The swelling around his eyes had diminished, but his face was still a mess of purple and yellow. "I don't like this."

Brunell spoke up. "I will be here to lend whatever assistance I can offer. After your help freeing me today, it's the least I can do."

She nodded to him and laid a hand on his arm. Gratitude swelled in her heart. They were finally getting somewhere.

# 31 : ABSORPTION

GRIT AND SWEAT MINGLED on Number One's forehead. The air was thick with dust and debris, illuminated by the swinging glowstone lamp. He and Number Fourteen were deep underground in the tunnel system that led away from the compound. It led straight to the city, the original entrance deep underneath the palace. He had found the tunnels, back in another life, and told Nihil where to find them. He and the other subjects had worked for years to expand the underground complex, burrowing under the city. The physical work seemed to keep them stable, to help them cope with the chaos threatening to take their sanity. Number One found some solace in the labor, as his burning muscles drew attention away from the tempest in his mind.

Number Fourteen stood nearby, picking up huge rocks and moving them to the side as if they weighed nothing. His movements were monotonous, his eyes empty. He hadn't spoken on their trek underground, although Number One could tell he still buzzed with too much energy. He glanced over at the big man, his black clothes turned gray with dust. Fourteen dropped a rock into a pile, pausing to stare, and his body hovered as if momentarily frozen. He looked down at his hands and shuddered before turning back to his work.

Fourteen had seemed different ever since Nihil had used him in Number One's last transference. Number One had desperately wanted to avoid enduring another session with the stone. It had been so long, he'd come to believe Nihil was finished working on him. When Sindre had led him to Nihil's laboratory, his stomach clenched with fear. It had taken a number of prods with Sindre's amulet to get him to sit in the chair. He scarcely remembered what Nihil had said. The voices in his mind had risen to a fevered pitch.

The transference itself had been far more intense than the others, the assault of energy battering him. He had felt Number Fourteen's presence in the process, the energy bouncing back and forth between them like echoes of sound on a canyon wall.

He had emerged from the transference stronger than before. It had taken him days to gain control over his ability. He'd accidentally killed a servant just by brushing past him in the hallway as Sindre led him back to his room. The man had shriveled up, his skin crusting with ice almost instantly. The effects had diminished after the first few days, and Sindre had drilled him mercilessly until he was able to keep control over his ability. A swath of death no longer followed him, but he could feel the power churn within, begging to be let out.

He picked up another rock, pulling its heat, and let it crust over with frost. The woman from Fourteen's memory haunted his mind. He dreamt of her nightly, her face hovering before his vision. He longed for those dreams, so calm and serene. Calling forth her image helped him rein in his powers. She was like an anchor holding his mind in place while a storm raged through him. Each time he absorbed energy from Fourteen, his vision of her grew stronger, coalescing into a memory he could almost believe was his own. He dared to whisper her name to himself, late at night when he knew no one would hear. *Cecily.*

Fourteen worked faster, tossing rocks behind him, and pushed forward down the tunnel. He had seemed increasingly erratic since the last transference and Number One was beginning to fear he wouldn't last much longer. He had seen it before. Nihil would push too hard, force them through one transference too many, and their mind would break. It was too much to be inundated with the life energy of another, forced to carry a piece of them with you. It took a certain type of strength to survive.

He was strangely concerned for Fourteen. He had worked with the others, watched many of them die, but he had never felt any kinship to them. Perhaps he saw them as Nihil did, as test subjects to be used and discarded when they failed. His connection to Fourteen, and to the woman in his mind, brought out feelings like distant memories, emotions from a past he could not find the courage to recall.

Fourteen stopped his work and crouched down. His shoulders rose and fell with heavy breaths. Number One squatted next to him to look at the other man's eyes. He found himself wondering what he looked like without his mask. The silver in his eyes had gone dull, mingling with the browns, greens and blues that were the telltale sign of Nihil's tampering.

"You're getting shaky again," Number One said.

Fourteen held up his hands. They trembled. He clutched them together, his breathing still heavy, and nodded. Number One wondered if he'd ever speak again.

The first time Number One had absorbed Fourteen's energy, he had been hesitant. In the weeks since, he had found himself craving the surge of power and the mingling of his mind with Fourteen's. His vision of Cecily always improved when he was connected to Fourteen. She constantly intruded into his thoughts like an itch he couldn't scratch. He told himself he was only helping his cohort, but deep inside, he knew he craved the connection.

He placed his hand on Fourteen's forearm and Absorbed. Fourteen's swell of energy surged into Number One and filled him almost instantly. The power reverberated through his body and spread warmth to his usually cold hands. He relished the feeling of exhilaration and strength. His life was not his own, but when filled with this much energy, he felt in command, as if he could control his own fate.

Number Fourteen's outward lack of emotion ran deeper than Number One had anticipated. He braced himself for the assault of feeling, the anger and fear that ran through Fourteen's being. It was gone. It was as if he drew energy through nothing but emptiness. There were no visions, nor pulses of emotion. His alarm grew as he realized Cecily was not there. He cast about for her, struggling to find even an echo of her image, but there was nothing. It was as if Fourteen was gone, and he'd taken his very essence with him.

Number One continued to Absorb, frantically searching for some sign of Cecily in Fourteen's mind. It was like walking through an abandoned building. He pulled harder, determined to find a trace of her, some glimmer of emotion.

A hand clasped his other arm and the flow of energy suddenly reversed. He opened his eyes and saw Fourteen grabbing his arm, his cold eyes boring into him. Number One's heart began to race as he realized Fourteen was Absorbing energy from him. Cold spread over him and he shivered, fear growing in his belly.

"Too much," Fourteen growled before he released his arm. He held his eyes a moment longer, then stood and reached down to grab another stone.

Number One stood and backed away. Nihil seemed to think Number Fourteen was his greatest triumph, but Number One was beginning to wonder what he had made.

The debris from the tunnel once again clear, Number One and Number Fourteen stood in the courtyard along with several of the others. Nihil strode in, Sindre at his side, and the men fell in line, military style, hands behind their backs and eyes straight ahead. Number One's arm still throbbed from Fourteen's grasp, like a burn that was beginning to heal.

Nihil wore his customary black robes. "We have an opportunity," he began. "My work has come under an intolerable level of scrutiny of late. I have made entirely too many breakthroughs to be interrupted now. There are still loose ends that continue to plague us, despite my very explicit instructions to tie them up." He wandered in front of the line of his subjects and glanced up and down at each of them. "A rather simple fix has been presented. I have need of some of you elsewhere, but Number One, I need you to take Number Four, Number Six, Number Nine and Number Fourteen with you. The trap will be laid; you will simply need to proceed once it has been sprung. Sindre will give Number One the details. The rest of you are to obey his orders as if they were from my own lips."

He stopped in front of Number One and looked him in the eyes as Sindre hovered behind him. "Let me be very clear about this. I want them all dead. Every last one of them."

Number One nodded, a quick up and down of his chin. Despite his burning antipathy, a strange sense of gratification spread over him at Nihil's implicit trust. *Obey his orders...*

Nihil turned to the others. "Very good. You are dismissed."

Number One turned to go, but Nihil put a hand on his shoulder. He stood there, silent, until the other subjects had left.

"I have a secondary job for you," Nihil said and leaned in close. "This will be an interesting test for Number Fourteen. I am intentionally putting him in a position that will tell me a great deal about the results of our work on him. I want you to observe him closely and report his reactions back to me, every detail. If he deviates from orders, you are to neutralize him immediately. I would send Sindre with you, but I need her here. I want him back alive, but do not under any circumstances allow him to depart. Is that understood?"

Number One nodded again as Nihil lifted his hand from his shoulder and walked away, leaving him alone in the courtyard. A light rain began to fall, droplets settling on his mask. He stood still a moment longer, wondering what test Nihil had in mind for Number Fourteen and whether he realized the full extent of Fourteen's alterations.

It appeared it was now his job to find out.

## 32 : REVELATIONS

Cecily crouched, wedged in a tiny alley, and scanned the street. Most of Wesfell was quiet and empty, the residents down by the river, dancing around the bonfires to celebrate the solstice. The sounds of their merriment drifted over the town. Griff, Serv, Edson, and Merrick were scattered around the area, similarly hidden. They had yet to see any sign of Nihil's men, but the last shadows of dusk were still stretching and fading into darkness.

Stars began to twinkle in the clear sky. The frigid air stung her cheeks, and her breath misted in front of her. She pulled her cowl down lower and tucked her hands into her cloak. Her Awareness was spread wide, looking for any signs of movement.

Serv appeared from behind, stealing through the alley on light feet. "Anything?" he asked, his voice a whisper.

She shook her head. "Only townspeople."

He nodded. "We haven't seen them either. I would suggest we move closer to the docks, but I have my doubts we'd find them dancing around a bonfire on the riverbank."

Cecily smiled and let out a breathy laugh. He nodded to her and crept back the way he had come.

She closed her eyes and traced the streets in her mind. *Where are you?* Her heart beat quickly and she felt the telltale tingle in her limbs as her adrenaline rose. She tapped the toes of one foot inside her boot, careful not to make any noise. It was hard to keep still.

A lone figure crossed into her circle of Awareness. This one wasn't heading for the river, but cutting across the town. She slowly stood, melting into the shadow of the alley, and kept her back pressed against the rough wood wall. The figure came within sight as he walked down the street and cast glances all around. He was dressed all in black, his dark clothes blending into the night. Cecily had to stop herself from gasping. He was hooded and masked.

She let him pass, his quick stride taking him down the street toward the center of town. She narrowed her Awareness and pointed it in his direction to make sure they didn't lose him. She didn't want to follow too closely; she had no intention of discovering what unnatural abilities this man possessed. She stepped out of her hiding place and kept close to the building, signaling Merrick with a quick flick of her hand.

Creeping along the street, keeping to the shadows, she pursued the masked figure, her friends following along behind. His movements seemed wary, as if he was trying to remain unseen. He turned up and down several streets, stopping at corners, and took time to look up and down the empty street before emerging.

He proceeded to the central town square and stopped before what felt to Cecily like a stone fountain. She waved her friends along, turned down a side street, and edged into an alley. They gathered behind her and she crept to the end, a clear view of the town plaza in front of her.

The figure walked around the other side of the fountain and suddenly disappeared from her mental sight. Cecily gasped and drew her Awareness back to sharpen the image of the plaza. He was simply gone, as if he'd never been there.

She leaned toward Serv at her shoulder and whispered, "He's gone."

His brow furrowed and he leaned out to scan the area. He glanced back over his shoulder and tilted his head toward the fountain. They emerged from the alley into the plaza. Large wooden buildings rose up from the cobblestone, arranged in a circle around the fountain. Streets and alleys snaked off in all directions, stretching out from the center. They crept out into the open, turning, as everyone looked for some sign of Nihil's men. Griff and Serv stood to her right, Sumara and Merrick on her left, Edson at the far end. Other than the six of them, the entire square was empty. *Where did he go?*

The soft scratch of feet on the ground whispered behind her and Cecily whipped around. Two men, masked and dressed in black, stood behind them. She turned again and found three more facing her. Her stomach clenched with fear as she watched them from underneath her cowl. They had barely escaped their last encounter with one of these masked Wielders, and there had only been one. With five surrounding them she had the sinking feeling they weren't getting out of this town alive.

Anger at the prospect of death burned away her fear. "Town Guard, Edson. Go!" she shouted and he took off running, back through the streets toward the river. Serv drew his sword and Griff hefted his heavy axe. Sumara's fingers crackled with power and Merrick nocked an arrow into the string of his bow.

A laugh came from the masked man in the center. She glanced at the two behind her. One looked poised to spring and follow Edson.

"Let him go. He's nothing but a child." It was the man in the center. He took a step forward and cocked his head to the side. "This will be over soon enough." Cecily hesitated and shrunk back at his voice. "Fourteen, you take the swordsman and the brute with the axe. Four, the bowman and the dark woman. Six and Nine, guard the rear and keep them from escaping. I'll have a little chat with the lady in the center."

He sauntered toward Cecily as the other two men spread out toward her companions. A trail of sparkling ice crystals spread out from his feet as he walked, as if he was absorbing the heat from the ground. *Maybe he is.* He stopped a few feet in front of her as the clang of metal rang out next to her.

She glanced to the side and saw Griff and Serv close with one of the men. He was a head taller than they were and swung an enormous sword through the darkness. Merrick had retreated back as far as he could to rain arrows at the man approaching him. The masked man threw something at each arrow, exploding them midair. Sumara's fingertips crackled with lightning and she let loose, unleashing a bolt into his chest. He stumbled and threw something at Sumara that burst into flames at her feet.

Cecily looked back at her opponent. Cold emanated from him as he drew close. She Reached, hitting him with Pressure, and attacked his knees. He paused to look down, and his eyes rose again to meet hers. Even in the darkness she could see the unnerving multicolored swirl, an unnatural blend of bright colors surrounding his black pupil.

Her breathing quickened and her heart pounded. The big one clashed with Griff and Serv, flashes of metal glinting in the weak lamplight. The third kept his distance from Merrick and Sumara and threw burning chunks of rock that burst upon impact. Sumara flung herself to the side and hit the hard ground to avoid a blast of flame.

Merrick's cloak had caught fire. He whipped it off and tossed it to the side.

"You didn't come here thinking you could win, did you?" The cold man in front of her spoke, his voice unnervingly familiar. Something tugged at her memory, like an echo of a dream.

Cecily attacked again, grabbing his throat with Pressure. Such a precise Wield was difficult when her opponent was ready to defend against her. He lifted his hand and the air sucked out of her lungs. Her limbs went cold and her back clenched. It felt as if he was pulling the life out of her.

Her hood fell back, leaving her hair loose and blowing in the wind. Her opponent's strange eyes went wide and the pulling sensation instantly left her. Clutching her throat, she stepped backward as his round eyes stared. She caught her breath and looked around as the man backed away. Griff and Serv still fought the tall one, but Sumara was in trouble. Her opponent had her nearly surrounded with burning chunks of rock and Merrick was out of arrows. Cecily could see her trying to gather enough strength to fire lightning at him again. Cecily Pushed, tossing the burning rocks away, and gave Sumara some space. Merrick rushed in, his short sword drawn, but the man hit him with another projectile that burst at his chest and knocked him back.

The sound of footsteps grew from the street behind them. *Thank the gods, Edson!* The Town Guard was coming. She glanced back at the two men guarding the other side of the square. One dug into his pouch and poured something into his hands. The other reached his arms out and the ground around him began to rumble, pebbles and dirt rattling as if the ground was vibrating. Chunks of cobblestone ripped free from the ground and flew up to surround his body, piece by piece. Her mouth dropped open as she watched him construct armor from the very rocks in the ground. He beat his fists together, rolled his arms, and stretched out his legs.

The Town Guard poured into the square. Cecily's relief was short-lived as one man threw something into the air that hung like a cloud of dust. The Guards in the front began choking, doubling over and gasping for breath. The stone man bellowed, and his howl reverberated off the buildings. He charged into the Guards, swung his heavy arms and knocked men in all directions.

Cecily glanced at the man shrouded in cold. He didn't attack, but backed away, his eyes still wide. She turned back to the rock Wielder and Pushed, trying to throw him off balance with a blast of air. He stumbled to the side but turned and threw a pebble toward her. It ignited as it flew, a lick of flame bursting from the top like a rider on a horse. Cecily Pushed it and easily knocked it to the side. He threw more, one after another, and she Pushed to send them flying in all directions. They exploded with a loud pop every time they hit the ground.

Sumara threw lightning at the rock Wielder again, but her bolt lacked strength. The stone man cut through the Town Guard, and the other tossed something that stuck into their legs and made them buckle. The big man knocked Griff backward and sent him sprawling onto his back. He turned and clashed swords with Serv. His unnatural speed and obvious strength sent Serv stumbling backward. Serv recovered his feet and his sword sliced through the air, but the big man countered. Their swords hit with a metallic ring and the big man's blade flew from his hand. Serv struck again, but the big man dodged and backhanded him hard across the face. He fell and both he and Griff lay on the ground, unmoving.

Cecily turned back to the cold man. He stood back, looking bewildered as he stared at her, his eyes still wide. She turned to attack the rock Wielder, but a rumble behind her made her whip around. The big man ran for her at full speed. In a panic, she lashed out at him, trying to grip his throat with Pressure. He reached her first and wrapped his big hand around her neck.

He lifted her up, his hand at her throat, and her feet dangled in the air. She gasped, trying to suck in a breath, but his grip was iron. As she looked down, her heart nearly burst. Through the mask, she could see his eyes, the telltale swirl of color surrounding a black pupil. Streaks of silver gray melded with brown, green and blue. She knew those eyes, that face, his hands and the set of his shoulders.

"Daro." The word came out as nothing more than a croak, the last of her breath gone as he choked her. Tears sprang to her eyes and poured down her cheeks as her feet flailed in the air. She thought she heard someone calling her name. "Please," she tried to say, but there was no air left. Her vision began to go dark. *Daro, I'm so sorry. I was too late.*

"Stop!" The word rang in her ears and a blast of cold hit her from the side, like a rush of freezing wind. The grip on her throat released and she dropped to the ground. She wheezed, sucking in air, and gripped her throat. Her neck throbbed as she got up to her knees, her breath coming in panicked gasps. *Not Daro, please it can't be Daro.*

She looked up to see the big man standing tall above her. There was no way she could deny it was him. The mask covered most of his face, but the way he stood, the shape of his arms, his shoulders, the set of his chin. It was Daro. He was silent, staring down at her without a shred of recognition. "No." Her mouth moved, but no sound would come, and she let out a choked sob.

A wide swath of ice shimmered across the courtyard. The cold man stood above it, his arms stretched out wide to each side. He looked at Cecily, as his shoulders heaved. He drew in his arms and stood tall. "We're done here," he called out, his voice heavy with authority. The other masked men shifted on their feet and looked around at each other.

Sumara was crouched on the ground, helping Merrick sit up. Griff and Serv both struggled to their feet. Edson stood on the far side of the square, favoring one leg, his sword still gripped tight in his hand. A number of the Town Guard lay still on the ground. Others had come around from different streets. They stood with swords in hand, eyes squinting against the dark.

"Go," the cold man yelled again as ice spread from his feet. "That's an order."

The stone man dropped his armor, and the cobblestones clattered to the ground. He and the other two turned and jogged out of the courtyard, heading west toward the edge of town. Daro hesitated and looked down at Cecily before turning to follow.

"Daro!" Cecily gasped and reached out for him. Tears streaked down her cheeks and her throat closed in a heaving sob. He didn't stop, but moved into the shadows and disappeared from sight.

The cold man crouched down, his face still obscured by his mask, and reached out a hand toward Cecily. She recoiled and scooted backward. Her mind raced as she looked back to where Daro had disappeared.

"No, wait," the man said as he held his hand toward her. The line of ice he had made glinted in the starlight.

Cecily froze, her heart racing. The voice sounded so familiar. It reminded her of the face in her dreams.

He crept toward her, staying low. "It's okay," he said, his voice quiet. He reached up to his throat and pulled his mask up over his face to reveal his sharp cheekbones and clean-shaven jaw, his straight blond hair pulled back to the nape of his neck. His voice was gentle. "I would never hurt you."

Her breath caught in her throat, and her heart felt as if it had stopped as recognition washed over her. It wasn't possible. "Pathius?" she said.

He leaned back as if the word stung, his eyes wide. The world seemed to slow, the water that shot up from the fountain hanging in the air, the sound of the others in the square drifting away as if carried off by the wind. "Pathius." She mouthed the name again, no sound escaping her lips. The Prince, son of King Hadran, presumed dead since the war.

He looked around wildly as he stood. Then he turned and ran in the direction of the others without glancing behind, his black mask clutched in his hand.

Cecily's friends drifted toward her as she struggled to her feet, her hand gripping her throat. Her heart felt as if would burst, her stomach in a tight knot. Tears ran unchecked down her face. He had been right here.

*Daro. What have they done to you?*

## 33 : TRUTHS

C͟ECILY WALKED UP THE road from the dock, her eyes focused on nothing. They had fled Wesfell and taken their small riverboat back to Halthas in the dark of night. Merrick had attempted to pick up the trail of Nihil's men, but as before, they had Swept it clean. They were gone without a trace.

Sumara and Merrick had suffered minor burns, and Edson had a swollen wound in his leg where one of the men had pierced him with a two-inch thorn. Griff and Serv were battered from their fight with Daro, or the man who had once been Daro. Cecily's hand stole to her throat, still sore and no doubt bruised. The image of Daro's face flooded back into her mind, his hard stare as he choked the life out of her. His eyes weren't simply changed; they were dead, lifeless. There had been no recognition, no sign that he knew who she was. Her link to him was weak, a mere whisper of what it had once been.

Another face passed through her memory. Pathius. She was beginning to believe there was no such thing as the impossible. Pathius was dead. He'd died in the war. Everyone knew that. Cecily remembered the prince from a life that seemed ages ago. She was practically a child. She had been presented to the prince by her father, with King Hadran looking down from his throne. Her mother had insisted she wear blue. She remembered dipping in a curtsy, feeling bewildered and confused. No one had asked whether she might wish to marry the prince. They'd simply pushed her along, expecting her to fall in line with their plans. They'd brought her to the parties and banquets at the palace, expecting her to smile and play their games.

It had been years since she'd seen Pathius, but there was no mistaking that face. He looked just like his father. Thinking about Hadran made her nauseous stomach worse. How could Pathius be alive? More importantly, if he was one of Nihil's men, why did he stop Daro?

As the companions walked in silence, she caught them stealing furtive glances her way. They'd all seen Daro, watched him try to kill her. She was grateful they didn't push her with questions. Her limbs felt heavy, as if she could barely put one foot in front of the other, and her chest felt empty. She needed time to understand what had happened and couldn't stop the tears that poured down her face.

They found the entrance to the Quarry and descended down the long staircase. Cecily wanted nothing more than to fall into bed and shut out the world. She stared down at her feet and shuffled along as she let Serv lead her gently by the elbow.

As they turned down the stone hallway at the bottom of the stairs, Serv gripped her arm and pushed her behind him. She blinked, feeling as if awakening from a heavy sleep. Serv drew his sword, and her other companions fanned out around her and looked around with weapons ready. Sound drifted back into her attention and she realized it was fighting, coming from deeper in the Quarry.

They crept down the hallway toward Callum's rooms, as the noise grew. Cecily looked down, disbelieving her own eyes. *Is that a body?* Callum's door was covered in scratches and dents, as if someone had been beating on it. Serv tried the latch, but it was stuck. He looked up and down the hallway and called into the door. "Callum?"

He pressed his ear to the door and furrowed his brow. Cecily moved forward but Griff held his arm out to keep her back. Serv called through the door again and they heard a faint answer.

"Serv, is that you?" It was Mira, her voice muffled through the door.

"Yes, we're here," Serv replied. "What's going on? Are you okay in there?"

"Hold on," she said. The low sound of something heavy scraping across the ground came from behind the door. "Thank the gods," Mira said through the door. "I don't think I can get the door open. We broke the lock."

Serv twisted and tugged at the latch. "Sumara?"

Sumara held her hand up to the lock and jolted it with electricity. The metal sparked and sizzled and soon the door loosened. Serv pushed against it a few times with his shoulder and managed to wedge it open.

Mira poked her head out and looked around, before ushering them inside. "Get in, quick."

They crowded into the room to find the furniture in disarray. Several pieces stood on end near the door. Callum winced as he stood. "I don't think I've ever been happier to see anyone in my life," he said, his voice breathless.

Cecily stared, her gaze flicking from Callum to Mira. Callum's purpling bruises were starting to fade but he held his arm against his body. Mira still had a bandage across her head, and a fresh cut on her upper arm dripped blood.

"What happened?" Griff asked as he gestured around the room.

"Oh, you know, the usual for us lately. People trying to kill us," Callum said.

"Who tried to kill you? The smugglers again?" Griff asked.

"That bastard Brunell. Luckily Mira was still here or you'd be permanently deprived of my charm. We managed to barricade ourselves in here. Mira was kind enough to dismantle the lock and move some furniture in front of the door. You Reach Wielders are too bloody crafty. It wasn't easy keeping him out. He yelled at us for a while, told us the lot of you were dead."

Cecily stared at Callum, her mouth open. "Brunell?"

"I'm afraid so. After a while it got quiet. We were thinking about breaking ourselves out when he came back, and he brought friends with him. They weren't far from breaking down the door, I expect, when a funny thing happened. We heard a lot of shouting and what sounded like a great deal of dying. We were quite content to stay in here and wait it out."

"Lyceum Guards," Serv said and glanced out into the hall. "There's one out there in the hallway. The other body looks like a mercenary."

Callum walked over and peeked out the door. "Looks like one of the smugglers, judging by his clothes. Sahaaran." He turned back to Cecily. "I'm so glad you took the time to break the venerable Magister out of his cell. And I can't help but feel we owe the Lyceum a bit of an apology."

Cecily reached up and rubbed her face. "I don't understand. Brunell tried to kill you? And he said we were dead?" She looked around at her friends as confusion swirled through her mind.

"I think Brunell set you up. He sent you into a trap. I don't think Nihil is working with the Lyceum. I think Nihil is working with Brunell. And he just tried to get rid of all of us. The Lyceum is down there, trying to clean up our mess."

Cecily clutched her stomach and staggered backward. She felt as if she'd been kicked in the gut. Sumara and Serv reached out to steady her. "No," she whispered. "This doesn't make sense. Brunell, he…"

"I'm sorry, Cecily, but Callum is telling the truth," Mira said. "Brunell attacked us. I think he wants us all dead. The Lyceum is trying to stop him."

"Is anyone else concerned that there's still fighting going on out there?" Griff asked as he hefted his axe up over his shoulder.

Cecily's fatigue fell away, her mind suddenly clear. She blinked, pulled her shoulders back, and stood tall. With a glance at her companions, she turned without a word and threw open the door, then walked down the hallway toward the sound of the fighting.

She could hear her companions as they followed, calling her name. She didn't care. Her feet moved quickly down the hallway. Something had burst inside her, driving out her fear and doubt. Rage, searing and pure, filled her veins.

The noise grew louder and the stinging scent of smoke drifted in the air. She had to step over bodies as she stalked down the hallway, deeper into the Quarry, but they didn't slow her down. Cecily turned a corner to where the hallway opened into a wide room. Stacks of barrels and wooden boxes stood along the walls, and a black streak marred the stone ceiling. A body lay on the floor in a pool of blood, his clothes half burnt. Two uniformed Lyceum Guards fought three other men in the center of the room, their swords clashing with a metallic ring.

She felt her friends catch up behind her just as she spotted Brunell, hunkered down behind a stack of boxes on the far side of the room.

"Brunell!" Cecily's voice rang out, echoing off the stone wall. The men fighting hesitated and turned toward her, their swords still raised.

Brunell's head peeked out from behind the boxes and his eyes went wide. He stood, slowly rising from his hiding place, his eyebrows raised and mouth hanging open. He held his hands up and the three men took a step back from the Lyceum Guards, keeping their swords up to ward off an attack. The Guards glanced behind them and kept their swords ready.

The sight of Brunell made Cecily's rage burn hotter. The beating of her heart sent her anger roiling through her limbs in a rhythmic surge.

"You weren't supposed to return," Brunell said.

"Unfortunately for you, I did," she said. "Was Wesfell a trap?"

He held up his hands and tilted his head to the side. "Please, Cecily, let me explain."

"Yes, please explain. Explain how you sent us right into Nihil's hands and stayed behind to kill my friends. Explain why I should believe that it was the Lyceum working with Nihil, and not you."

Brunell licked his lips. "This is far more complicated than you realize. The work Nihil is doing, it is extraordinary. The progress we've made…"

Her voice was ice. "No." She glanced over her shoulder and her hand flicked toward the three smugglers. "Kill those ones. Leave Brunell to me."

Brunell's mouth dropped open again as Merrick pulled back on his bow and shot one of the men through the eye. He dropped to the ground, twitching as he died, blood leaking from his face. The Lyceum Guards backed up to the wall, making way for Griff and Serv. Griff swung his axe, and the man staggered under the force of the blow. Serv closed with the final man. He lifted his sword and blocked Serv's first strike.

Griff pounded at his foe again and sent his sword flying across the ground. Swinging his axe around again, he struck the man through the throat and sent a thick spray of blood onto the stone floor. Serv reached his hand out and the other man leaned forward, his feet stuck to the floor. His mouth dropped open as Serv's sword arced around like a streak of light and ran the man through. His sword clattered to the ground as the body dropped. Serv stepped back and whipped out a cloth to wipe the blood from his blade.

Cecily walked over to Brunell, who stood gaping at the bodies of his men. His eyes rose to meet hers. She Reached into him and put Pressure on his throat. "You sent us into a trap." He gripped his neck, as his eyes widened. "Nihil doesn't work for the Lyceum, does he?"

Brunell stared at her for a moment, holding his throat. "No," he gasped.

"You work for Nihil." Her voice was monotone. She kept Pressure on his throat, allowing him just enough air to speak.

His eyes cast about the room. "We have an arrangement, yes," he said, his voice a croak.

She Pressed his throat tighter. She thought back to his last letter. *In the name of progress...* "Did you arrange Daro's abduction?" Brunell's mouth opened wordlessly. She stepped toward him. "Did you?"

His head nodded up and down and she let the Pressure go. He doubled over and gasped in a heaving breath. Rubbing his throat as he straightened, he looked at her with confusion plain on his face.

She stepped forward and backhanded him, pounding him across the face and sending him staggering sideways. Ignoring the stinging pain in her hand, she reached out to grab his robes. She hauled him to his feet and felt his Wield, a surging crush of energy directed at her throat. She Pushed back and slammed him with all the energy she possessed. He staggered backward, nearly tripping over a wooden box.

"Cecily, please," he said as he held his hands up. "You must listen."

She turned away, breathing heavily. She waited for his next assault, but he kept speaking.

"You have to understand. It wasn't personal. Nihil is doing incredible things. He is rewriting the laws of Wielding as we know them. The Lyceum was too shortsighted to see it. But the progress, it was incredible. I had to be a part of it. And Daro, with his Imaran ancestry—"

"No." She turned and held out her hand. Slamming him with Pressure, she grabbed his airway in a crushing grip. Brunell's eyes widened as he struggled for breath. Cecily held his eyes, staring at him as she crushed his airway, her eyes narrowed and teeth clenched. His face turned purple and he kicked his feet against the wall as her Wielding Energy surged and she Pressed him with her power. With a final squeeze, she gripped her Pressure harder and felt his airway collapse inside his throat. His eyes rolled back in his head as she let go. Stepping backward, she let his body slump to the ground.

Cecily turned to face her companions, her shoulders heaving, and brushed the matted hair from the sweat on her face. Everyone stared at her, openmouthed, their eyes wide. She glanced around at the bodies littering the ground. Her energy leaked away, leaving her feeling hollow and spent.

She stepped over the bodies and walked down the hallway, without sparing a glance behind her.

## 34 : CONSEQUENCES

PATHIUS.

Number One closed his eyes and let the name echo in his mind like a lover's whisper. He had buried that name, and the man it had once belonged to, deep below the surface of his consciousness. He had done it to survive. It was easier that way.

He no longer cared what was easy.

He stood alone in Nihil's laboratory, and the Arcstone pulled at his attention. It lingered in the corner of his eye, a hulking presence in the room despite its lack of size. He knew precisely why they had left him there. Fear. He feared the Arcstone as much as Sindre and her accursed medallion. Both dominated his life, had created the thing he had become. But he had been someone before, and despite his efforts to bury that man, he felt Pathius rise to the surface, wanting to reclaim his life. *Should I let him?*

Footsteps shuffled by, but the door did not open. They would leave him for a while, give him time to think about what he had done, like a disobedient child.

Wesfell had been a nightmare. It should have been so simple; the group had walked right into their trap. Even with the Town Guard on their heels, they should have been able to dispatch them easily. He had been ready to kill the woman himself, and the others would have been close behind.

Until he saw her face.

What Fourteen felt for Cecily ran so deep, it saturated Number One each time he extracted energy from him. It was more than love. Fourteen was connected to her on a level that Number One couldn't comprehend. He had never really experienced love, not that he could recall. It was a heady and turbulent thing, and the knowledge that the feeling was not his own did not diminish its power. He told himself it wasn't him that loved this woman. It was Fourteen.

Of course, Fourteen had tried to kill her.

He closed his eyes and the sound of his breathing echoed in his ears. Seeing her face had been a shock, like something from a dream suddenly coming to life. But watching Fourteen choke her, her feet struggling in the air, her face turning purple, had been more than he could bear. He knew Nihil wanted her dead. If he hadn't seen her face, he would have killed her himself. The thought made him shudder. His impulse to protect her was so strong, he had compromised everything to keep her safe. He had no doubt Nihil was going to make him pay for it.

The door opened and Sindre entered, followed closely by Nihil. Number One's stomach clenched as the door clicked shut. Nihil's robes swished along the floor as he took measured steps toward him. He stood in front of Number One, his face impassive.

"I sent you to Wesfell with simple instructions. Do you recall?" Nihil asked, his voice hard.

"Yes," Number One answered.

"You were to kill them. All of them," Nihil said as he held Number One's gaze. "It seems I put too much faith in you, Number One. I assumed you would execute your orders." He flicked his gaze toward Sindre and gave her a slight nod.

Pain exploded down Number One's back, radiating down in an agonizing wave. He doubled over, clenched his fists and ground his teeth to keep from crying out.

"Tell me," Nihil said as Number One stood, breathing heavily, "how does one receive such precise and specific orders and fail so completely to carry them out?"

Number One's back arched as another wave of pain made his muscles clench. It disappeared as quickly as it hit. "The Town Guard arrived too quickly," he said, his voice breathless. He knew the explanation wouldn't suffice. *How much do I tell him?*

"The Town Guard should not have been an issue."

A jolt of pain hit Number One. He grabbed his head and cried out until Sindre let go. "We weren't prepared to fight that many," he said through clenched teeth. Sindre hit him again and his legs buckled. He fell to his knees and held himself up with his hands. Sweat dripped off his brow onto the floor as he panted, his back and shoulders heaving.

"Your failure is going to cost me a great deal," Nihil said as he walked slowly around him.

Number One struggled to his feet, his breath coming in gasps. He glanced at Sindre from the corner of his eye. Her lips were curled in a tight smile and her eyes narrowed. *She enjoys this far too much.*

Nihil stopped in front of him and folded his arms, his gray robes hanging down. "I was told you ordered the others to leave."

"Yes," he said and braced himself for another blast of pain. Nihil raised his eyebrows. Number One's thoughts raced for an explanation. "We couldn't risk discovery. If we'd stayed any longer, the Town Guard might have overwhelmed one of us, and that could have led them here."

Nihil's eyes narrowed and his jaw clenched. "That was the wrong choice."

Number One buckled again as Sindre unleashed into him. He fell to his knees and cried out in agony. She kept the pain thick, driving him down onto the floor. When at last she relented, Number One was left gasping. The sudden absence of pain took his breath away.

"Up," Nihil said, the word a sharp command.

Rising to his feet, Number One stood and straightened his back. He breathed heavily as he stared past Nihil, his gaze fixed on the wall. The voices screamed, a swirling mass of chaos in his mind. He didn't push them down. He let them scream, the echoes of dead men feeding his fury.

Nihil stopped in front of him and Number One lost control. He surged toward Nihil, rage driving him forward. Nihil took a step back and Number One slammed into something solid. His body jerked back as if he'd struck a wall. He reached out and touched it, a slight shimmer in the air. A physical Shield.

Nihil's mouth curled into a smile. "You don't think I am without my own protections, do you? You aren't the only one to benefit from the Arcstone's gifts." He pulled at the fingers of his gloves, tugging at each, and slipped his hands out. He tucked the gloves under one arm and cocked his head at Number One. "And Sindre is not the only one who can ensure your obedience." The shimmer in the air dropped as Nihil stepped toward Number One and gripped his arm.

The energy inside Number One began to twist, as if Nihil had managed to grasp it and was tearing it from him. He cried out as he felt Nihil pull something inside of him. It felt as if Nihil would tear him apart. He wanted to move, to grasp Nihil and drain him dry, but Nihil may as well have held his beating heart in his hands. Pain burst through his body and he clenched his teeth, crying out in agony.

Nihil dropped his arm and stepped back. Number One gasped for breath, as he bent forward and clutched his stomach.

"Now," Nihil said as if nothing had happened, pulling his gloves back over his hands, "tell me about Fourteen. He struggled to contain himself at the Watchtower. How did he perform in Wesfell?"

A measure of relief washed over him. This he could answer. He straightened his back. "He followed orders precisely."

"This debacle, it was not the result of a failure on his part?"

Number One's breath caught in his throat. That was what this was all about. Nihil had sent Fourteen, knowing he would be facing his wife. He'd wanted to see what happened. "No," he said. "He fought as ordered."

Nihil narrowed his eyes again, as if trying to decide whether to believe him. After a long pause, he nodded. "Good." He clasped his hands behind his back. "An interesting thought occurred to me recently. I have never used a man that I have altered as a source. I wonder what would happen if I did?"

Number One's shoulders tensed as he imagined himself seated in that chair, his arms strapped to the stone as his life was drained away, his power ripped from his soul and imbued into someone else.

Nihil looked Number One up and down and glanced pointedly at the Arcstone. "If you continue to fail me, we may find out." He turned back toward the door and glanced over his shoulder at Sindre. "Make sure he doesn't disobey me again."

Number One's eyes flicked to Sindre. She smiled, one side of her mouth curling up, lust in her eyes.

Number One awoke in his room, the wooden floor rigid under his back. He had no memory of how he'd gotten there. Sindre had tortured him mercilessly until he'd passed out from exhaustion and pain. His body ached as if he'd been beaten. Sindre's work wouldn't injure directly, but the spasms of agony took their toll nonetheless.

He turned to his side and carefully pulled himself up, reaching up to the edge of his bed for stability. Crystals of ice crackled across the bed frame and fanned out on the floor from his feet. He felt jittery and raw, his command of his power unraveling. He took a few shuddering breaths and lowered himself down onto the bed.

He had survived Nihil's wrath. He wondered what the others had told him about Wesfell. It seemed they had been vague on the details. Nihil made no mention of Number One letting Cecily go, nor of him ordering Fourteen to stop when he could easily have killed her. Curious.

He let his aching back relax into the hard mattress. His mind was strangely clear, the voices quiet. Cecily had seen his face and said his name. He searched his mind and dug deep into Pathius's memories. Cecily was there, from a past he thought was dead. The memories were his own, vastly unlike the faded ghosts that Nihil had poured into his mind.

Number One had survived this long through obedience. But Pathius had been the son of the king, and princes did not have to obey.

## 35 : RETURN

THE DEEP BLUE SAPPHIRE sparkled as Cecily held it up, the lamplight glinting off its facets. It wasn't a large jewel, but the delicate silver surrounding it was a work of art. Daro's necklace. She couldn't bring herself to wear it over the bruises on her neck. She fingered the silver chain, the cool metal soft on her fingertips, and let tears fall unchecked down her cheeks. Her heart felt empty, broken as the memory of Daro's cold eyes flashed through her mind.

Callum had locked down the Quarry, calling in favors and bringing in a veritable army of men. The entire Halthian Underground was on alert. The Sahaaran smugglers were intruding on their territory, and news of Nihil and his aberrant Wielders had spread. Cecily had questioned the wisdom of trusting their protection to the sort of men Callum could call up, but he assured her there was now no safer place than the Quarry.

She heard footsteps behind her, echoing down the stone hallway. She quickly brushed the tears from her face and tucked her necklace away as Serv entered the small room. It was hardly more than a storage room, a few wooden chairs set around a makeshift table, a tall stack of wooden boxes in the corner.

Serv shifted his sword as he sat down. He looked at the table and sat with her in silence for a long moment before speaking. "Life often leads us down a path we would not have chosen. It hurts to lose one you love, even if the loss isn't in death."

A lump rose in Cecily's throat and she bit her lip to keep from crying. A tear broke free and ran down her cheek.

"We've all lived through tragedy at one time or another," Serv continued, putting a gentle hand on her arm. "The pain is not something you should bear alone."

Cecily reached up to wipe the tear from her face. "Where are the others?" She'd spent the last two days avoiding people, hoping to dodge their questions. A few days ago she would have been horrified if she had known she would kill Magister Brunell, let alone in a room full of her friends. Now she was simply glad he was dead.

"They're in the meeting room, trying to agree on a plan. When I left, Callum and Griff were eating everything in sight, and Merrick was stalking around the room like a caged animal."

With a breathy laugh, Cecily rose. "That sounds like it could get out of hand rather quickly. We wouldn't want them to run out of food."

She walked with Serv down the winding hallways, their footsteps echoing off the stone walls. The dim light of the glowstones and the weight of the earth above pressed at her. She was beginning to long for fresh air, and even the sun filtered through a cloudy, gray sky would have been a welcome change.

Callum sat hunched over the long rectangular table and picked at a plate of food. Merrick was indeed stalking around the room, walking with an anxious rhythm as Beau watched from a corner, his ears twitching. Sumara and Mira sat near each other, leaning close and speaking in low voices. Griff stood near his axe, which leaned blade-down against the wall. Edson huddled behind a small leather notebook, his quill scratching across the page.

They all looked up as Cecily entered. Callum leaned back in his chair and Merrick stopped his pacing.

Cecily took a deep breath. "I'll be honest. I don't know what to do next." Her friends glanced at each other. "The only thing I know is that I can't give up."

"Give up. Bah!" Griff said.

"We're not giving up either," Callum said. "But in all our collective brilliance, we haven't come up with much of a plan."

A young messenger ducked past Cecily and darted forward to hand Callum a note. Callum's brow furrowed as he read and he looked up at the boy. "Is this true?"

"Dunno," the boy said. "I just deliver 'em."

Callum rose from his seat, still looking at the note. He crumpled it in his hand and tucked it away before Cecily could see where it had gone. "Wait here," he said, his voice sounding bewildered. "I'll be right back."

Cecily watched as Callum and the boy left the room. She wandered to the back, too restless to sit down. Beau trotted over and looked up at her expectantly. She crouched down and scratched his head as he wagged his bushy tail. He leaned forward and sniffed her face, his wet nose rubbing her cheek.

Mira let out a quiet gasp and Cecily heard the chairs scrape across the floor as everyone got to their feet. A hushed silence filled the room and she turned around to find Callum, followed closely by Alastair. Cecily slowly stood and her gaze drifted past Alastair's shoulder.

King Rogan walked into the room. He was absent his kingly raiment, dressed in an unadorned doublet, his crown nowhere to be found. A hush fell over the room and Cecily's heart felt as if it had skipped a beat.

He stopped just inside the doorway, and his eyes locked on her. "Cecily," he said, his voice soft.

Anger rose in Cecily's chest and spread through her limbs like a crashing wave. She clenched her teeth and stalked across the room, the sound of her racing heart echoing in her ears. As she stopped in front of Rogan, she swung and slapped him, hitting him hard across the face with a loud smack. Rogan's head flew to the side and he reached up to hold his cheek as the room erupted with commotion. Alastair's mouth was open, his eyes raised in horror. Someone grabbed her arm, trying to drag her away, but she pulled against them and kept her eyes locked on the king, the palm of her hand burning.

Rogan held up his hands. "No, no, it's okay. The gods know, I deserved that."

The hand let go of Cecily's arm and she could hear her friends murmuring behind her. Alastair crossed his arms and glared at her.

Rogan rubbed his cheek. "You were right, Cecily. I suspected Nihil abducted Daro from the moment you came to me. I kept it from you because if it was true, it meant I was at least partially to blame. I not only allowed Nihil to work with my blessing, I funded him. I let him convince me his work was too valuable to interrupt. I believed he was working for the benefit of the kingdom, that he would deliver me the means to ensure the security of my reign. I told myself that, as king, I had to make difficult choices. That much is true. Unfortunately, I chose wrong. I swear to you, I would do anything to change what I've done. I should have come to you, all of you," he said as his eyes swept the room. "We should have faced this together."

Serv placed a calming hand on Cecily's shoulder. She looked up at her king and saw the man who had once been her friend. His eyes pleaded with her and she felt her anger diminish.

"We all owe our lives to Daro, in one way or another," Rogan continued. "None of us would be where we are today without him." He stepped forward, sank down on one knee, and reached up to hold her hands in his.

Cecily gasped. "Rogan, you don't have to do that. Please." Her gaze flicked around the room and her friends were staring, openmouthed. Alastair reached out as if to haul Rogan back up to his feet.

Rogan shook his head as he looked up at her. "If a man cannot admit when he has done wrong, he has no business leading others. Until Daro is returned to you, I am no longer the king. I am yours to command and I will help fight to get him back, to my last breath if that is what it takes."

Tears sprung to Cecily's eyes, and her anger melted away like ice on a hot stone. She gripped his hands and nodded, struggling to find words as he stood. "You're right, we should face this together."

Alastair leaned toward Rogan, his voice a hoarse whisper. "Majesty, with all due respect, do you really deem it wise to speak so rashly? You can't simply renounce your throne for the sake of one man. Even if that man is Daro."

"Calm yourself, Alastair," Rogan said, as he straightened his clothes. "My reign is not worth the ruin of a man's soul." He looked around at their companions. "I owe all of you an apology. I shouldn't have forgotten why I was king. It was because of all of you. I betrayed your faith in me, and for that, I am truly sorry."

Her companions nodded to Rogan, and even Callum managed a begrudging bob of his head.

Rogan took a seat and Cecily followed. They explained to him what they knew. He cringed as Callum told him of the Sahaaran smugglers trafficking slaves. They told him about their attempts to find Nihil's location and their run-ins with his Wielders. Cecily described, with as even a voice as possible, their encounter in Wesfell.

"She's right, it was Daro," Griff said. "Hard as it is to admit. Even with that mask, any of us would have recognized him."

"Well, he is a bit hard to miss," Callum said.

"Are you sure the other man was Pathius?" Rogan asked.

An image of his face drifted through Cecily's mind. "I'm positive. He looked somewhat different from what I remember, but I have no doubt it was him. And I'm fairly certain he recognized me."

"What did he say to you?" Sumara asked. "I saw him speak to you, after he ordered the others away."

Cecily looked away, and her hand drifted up to rub her sore neck. "He said he'd never hurt me."

"That's..." Callum paused with his eyebrows raised. "...disturbing."

"What does this mean?" Alastair asked. "Pathius has been presumed dead since the war. If he is alive, it could create some very serious complications."

Rogan nodded. "True. We will have to face those questions later. Right now, our objective is to find and free Daro, and stop this madman from taking any more innocent lives. Any concerns about

Pathius will have to wait." He rubbed his cleanly trimmed beard. "What have you heard from the Lyceum? My contacts there have been mysteriously quiet of late."

"About that," Callum said, drawing out the words. "We may have made a bit of a mess. We were under the apparently mistaken impression that Nihil was working under the auspices of the Lyceum of Power. Cecily was kind enough to free her old Magister, a certain Magister Brunell, whom they'd been holding prisoner. Turns out, Brunell was the one working with Nihil, and I can't fault the Lyceum for locking him up. Caused a fair bit of trouble down here."

"Magister Brunell," Rogan said. "Yes, I know of him. Where is he now?"

Callum brushed his hair from his eyes. "After he tried to kill me and Mira, and admitted to arranging Daro's abduction, Cecily may or may not have deprived him of his ability to breathe."

Rogan blew out a breath. "Well, that takes care of that, I suppose. And it explains the heightened security down here."

"We got a little tired of people trying to kill us," Callum said. "Being dead is bad for business."

"Can't say I fault you for that," Rogan said. "I've grown rather fond of having an entire regiment of guards at hand."

Cecily's shoulders relaxed with relief. She had been concerned for how Rogan would react to their story. He may have come to them as an equal, but he was still the king, regardless of whether he wore his crown. Killing Lyceum Magisters, even rogue ones, was liable to land one in a very deep, dark cell, a place far worse than where she'd found Brunell.

"The problem is," Cecily said, "we know Daro is alive and we know Nihil has him. But we don't know where they are. They have proven to be extremely difficult to track down."

"That is where I can help," Rogan said.

Cecily drew in a quick breath. "You know where they are?"

Rogan nodded. "I do. I lost a number of men in the process, but I was able to find where Nihil is working. There is an old manor house, north of the city. It may have once been maintained as a fallback point for the royal family, in case of invasion. It was abandoned at least a century ago, maybe more. I wasn't aware it even existed until my men found it. They came away with enough information that I am certain this is where we will find Nihil."

Cecily's heart thumped in her chest and her fingers prickled with excitement. "We have to go. We have to get him out."

Callum held up a hand. "Slow down there. This the den of the beast you're talking about. That place will be crawling with his Wielders. They've proven themselves to be a bit difficult to handle, in case you're forgetting."

"Five of us faced just one and we barely made it out alive," Mira said, and her fingers brushed what was left of the wound on her head.

"The ones in Wesfell would have killed us all, if Pathius hadn't stopped them," Edson said.

"There's no doubt this will be extremely dangerous," Rogan said. "I can pull together a detachment of men, and if your experience in Wesfell is any indication, we'll need a sizeable force. That won't be a problem."

"We may need more than numbers," Griff said. "Fighting these men isn't going to be straightforward."

"And unfortunately, we have to be prepared for Daro to fight back," Serv added. "We'll need a way to neutralize him without hurting him."

Rogan scratched his chin and nodded to himself. "My force will be large enough to handle even a group of powerful Wielders. But I think we need to enlist the aid of the Lyceum. The Paragon may have more insight into how we can attack Nihil's men, and how to extract Daro."

Callum snorted. "I'm not sure that we're on the Lyceum's list of friends at the moment." He glanced to the side and shrugged. "Not that I was before."

"You and I will go," Cecily said to Rogan. "We can speak to the Paragon."

Rogan looked at her. "Are you certain that's a good idea? After Brunell?"

"The Paragon won't dare deny you entrance, even if I'm with you. This is a problem that concerns them. People are going to hear stories about these powerful Wielders, and they're going to come to the same conclusions we did, blaming the Lyceum. They will want to have a hand in neutralizing this problem. Besides, there are others in there, men and women Nihil took from their families, just like Daro. We can't abandon them all."

"This all sounds a bit impossible," Callum said.

Cecily continued. "We all stood together once and we accomplished the impossible. I'm certain we can do it again."

Her companions looked around at each other, nodding. Cecily was surprised to realize she believed what she said. With these people at her side, she was certain they would finally find Daro and bring him home.

## 36 : PARAGON

The muscles in Cecily's legs burned as she trudged up the stairs. The Paragon's office was on the top floor of the Great Library. It was rumored his living quarters had been moved there and he hadn't come down in years. Cecily could imagine why. The winding stairs seemed endless.

She and Rogan were flanked by four Lyceum Guards, two leading the way up the stairs, and two following close behind. As they emerged onto the top floor, the guards peeled off and took up their positions on either side of a set of double doors. The floor wound around the circumference of the building, jutting out above the floors of books, the domed ceiling high above.

A clerk scurried over, his back hunched and fingers stained with ink. He reached a bony hand and tapped on the door, the sound lost in the arching dome above. He leaned his balding head toward the door, nodded to himself, and waved for Rogan and Cecily to follow him inside.

The Paragon's office was at one end of a long, narrow room, the outer wall following the wide curve of the round building. Bookshelves lined the walls, dusty tomes and leather-bound books placed neatly along the shelves. An enormous desk with feet carved to look like the claws of a great beast sat near one wall. Willowy curtains divided the room and Cecily could see the shadowy outline of a great four-poster bed on the other side.

Seated at his desk, the Paragon was almost invisible behind the stacks of books and scrolls spread across the tabletop. He stood as they entered, standing straight and tall. His crisp dark blue robes hung from his thin frame and his sparse hair was pure white. His blue eyes shifted from Rogan to Cecily, and his serene face gave nothing away.

He gave a cursory bow to Rogan, his head declining in a nod, before he flicked his gaze toward Cecily. She lifted her chin and his right eye twitched. He turned pointedly toward Rogan. "Your Majesty. To what do I owe this great honor?"

Rogan dipped his head, a slight show of respect toward the Paragon. "Paragon Windsor, forgive me for barging in on you so abruptly. I suggest we dispense with the trouble of decorum and get straight to the urgent matter at hand." The Paragon raised his eyebrows. "A rogue Magister by the name of Nihil has been engaging in some most egregious acts: slavery, abduction and what appears to be human experimentation."

The Paragon pursed his lips. "Yes, we have been aware of Nihil's activities for quite some time. I must correct you on one point. He is not a Magister of the Lyceum. He was turned away many years ago. His Wielding ability was not particularly notable."

Cecily spoke up. "You mean the Lyceum misjudged Nihil and failed to identify a lunatic."

Windsor's faced snapped over to Cecily, his voice low and strained. "It is only out of respect for our sovereign that I will refrain from having you escorted off the grounds."

"Paragon Windsor, please," Rogan cut in.

"This woman is accused of very serious crimes," Windsor said. "She broke into a restricted area and released a man we had detained. And if the reports from my guards are correct, she later killed him."

Cecily held up a hand. "I do owe you an explanation. You're right, I broke in and set Magister Brunell free. At the time, I thought Nihil was connected to the Lyceum of Power and suspected Brunell had been imprisoned for uncovering the connection. I didn't realize it was the other way around. When I discovered the truth, well..." She trailed off.

The Paragon looked at her, his eyes narrowed. "Yes, I have the report from my guards," he said as he tapped on a piece of paper. "You put me in a difficult position, Lady Cecily. Magister Brunell still had vital information. Not only did you release him, allowing him to further his own plans, you then killed him, erasing all hope of finding out what he knew."

"I apologize for the intrusion, and no one wants information about Nihil more than I do. But I can't apologize for killing Brunell."

"Bold words from a woman one step from a prison cell herself," Windsor said. "You've caused us no small amount of trouble over the years. More than once I questioned the wisdom in letting you go."

Cecily fought down the flare of frustration. "I fail to see how my past choices are relevant."

"I fail to see why you are here," Windsor snapped back.

"Nihil has my husband," she said and held the Paragon's eyes.

Windsor opened his mouth as if to speak, but hesitated. "I see." He tucked his hands into the sleeves of his robe. "That does not bode well, I'm afraid."

"No, it doesn't," she said. "I've seen what they have done to him."

Windsor nodded and looked down at his desk. "There are others, as well. We believe he took at least one of ours."

"Isley Paven," Cecily said and Windsor's eyes went wide. "I saw her too. Her illusions were alarmingly solid."

"I feared as much. We don't fully understand the means Nihil is using to alter his subjects. But we know he is violating the fundamental laws of Wielding, and the results are devastating."

"You said you've been aware of Nihil's activities for some time. What have you discovered?" Cecily asked.

Windsor lowered himself into the chair behind his desk and motioned for them to sit. Rogan pulled up a chair for Cecily and himself, and they both sat down as Windsor shuffled the stacks on his desk. "We captured one of his altered Wielders," he said. "I lost a number of men in the process. He was exceedingly difficult to contain. He was violent, erratic, and terribly powerful. However, it was his mental instability that was particularly alarming. We tried to reach him, but he was gripped by madness we could not penetrate."

Cecily's stomach clenched. She thought of Daro's eyes, cold and lifeless, as his hand squeezed her throat.

"I had my best Sensor examine him to determine what Nihil had done to him. The Sensor's report was disturbing. What she described shouldn't be possible. The man had the power of not one Wielder, but several, as if his Wielding Energy had been melded with that of others. She reported seeing a swirl of energy mingling and merging within the man."

"Let us speak frankly, and in utter confidence," Rogan said. "Is there a precedent for this? Has the Lyceum ever observed such a thing?"

Windsor shook his head. "Not to my knowledge, and certainly not in my lifetime. We tried very hard to question the man and all we could get out of him was something about a stone. We assume it had to do with his implant."

Cecily shot forward in her seat. "Implant?"

Windsor nodded again, a slow bob of his head. His eyes flicked to the side as if he couldn't bring himself to meet hers. "The man had a piece of Imaran Arcstone implanted in the back of his neck. It must have something to do with the process of alteration."

Her mind raced. An implant could be the reason Daro was not himself. "Could they be controlling them with this implant? Making them do things?"

"Nothing would surprise me anymore," Windsor said. "Arcstone is a strange substance. Magisters have studied it extensively over the years and have never been able to unlock its secrets. The Imarans have ways of using the stone that are completely foreign to us. But it appears that Nihil has discovered a way to use it in his experiments. I was trying to get more out of Magister Brunell on the subject, but obviously that is no longer possible."

"Perhaps the Imarans themselves can be of assistance," Rogan said. "I will send word, alerting them of what has happened. They may be able to help us understand what Nihil has done. They may also wish to know that one of their own is involved. Does Daro have family in Imara?"

"He may, but he hasn't had contact with them for many years," Cecily said. "Paragon, this man you captured. Where is he now? May we see him?"

Windsor sighed. "Unfortunately, he died not long after we captured him. His violent and erratic behavior heightened as time went on and eventually he burned himself out. He killed and injured a number of men and women in the process."

"This begs the question," Rogan said and turned to Cecily, "what can we expect if we get Daro back?"

"Your Majesty, I'm afraid I am not clear on your purpose here. What is it you intend to do?" Winsor asked.

"We intend to get my husband back."

Windsor's gaze shifted between Rogan and Cecily. "This is a formidable foe you face."

"We're well aware of that," Rogan said. "That is why we are here. We need to bring the full force of the Lyceum to bear on this matter. The safety of our citizens, the legitimacy of our kingdom, and the power of the Lyceum are at risk."

Windsor let out a heavy sigh. "That will be more difficult than you realize. Nihil's list of atrocities is long. We don't know how many people he has abducted, nor how many he may have killed. He has likely been importing slaves for many years and I fear he is not using them for labor. What we saw in the man we captured—it led us to some extremely disturbing conclusions. I only pray that we are wrong about the possible death toll. It may number in the thousands."

"All the more reason to strike at him now and put an end to this," Cecily said.

"Of course Nihil must be stopped." Windsor paused and looked down at his hands with pursed lips. "Since we are speaking in strict confidence, I will be plain. Nihil's crimes do not end there. He has been using these aberrations to strike deep into the heart of the Lyceum. The outward facade of strength we show is a lie. Nihil has managed to decimate the Lyceum of Power. We have lost many good Magisters and powerful Wielders. Our strength is not what it once was. The Lyceum Guard is still intact, but contrary to what we say to outsiders, they are not our strongest. As Lady Cecily is already aware, our strongest Wielders work within the Lyceum of Power. Thanks to Brunell, Nihil has managed to destroy that strength. I fear we may not have the power to face him. Besides a few decrepit old Magisters like myself, Cecily is the most highly trained Wielder we have left."

Cecily's mouth hung open, and her mind reeled. Hundreds dead, maybe thousands. She thought about those deserted floors, deep underneath the library. How many people had he killed, how many lives ruined? She thought of Pathius, a man who had once been a prince. What was he now? An aberration, a monster? Was there hope for any of them?

Rogan rubbed his temples, his eyes squeezed shut. "We still need your help, Paragon. I can commit a sizeable force of men, but we will need a way to neutralize these Wielders."

Windsor looked up to meet their eyes. "We have ways of limiting a Wielder's power when necessary to contain them, but I can tell you from experience, the means are far less effective on these altered Wielders. But I will do what I can."

Rogan nodded and stood from his chair. Cecily followed and the Paragon stood as well. Rogan bowed, bending at the waist in a deep display of respect. The Paragon did the same. Rogan held out his hand and clasped the Paragon's. "Part of the blame for these atrocities is mine. I will do everything in my power to stop this man. We can work together to rebuild the Lyceum's power."

Windsor nodded, his sharp eyes shining. He turned to Cecily, offering his hand. She gripped it and he held it gently, placing his other hand on top. "Lady Cecily, my apologies for the hurt you have no doubt lived through."

They bowed to each other again and Cecily dipped into a proper curtsy before she turned and headed for the door.

Once outside, Rogan touched Cecily's elbow and led her away from the guards. "Troubling news," he said, his voice low.

Cecily fell into step beside him. The guards followed, at a respectful distance. "Troubling, yes," she said, "but with the Paragon's cooperation, our plan will work."

"I hope you're right," Rogan said.

Cecily's voice was just above a whisper. "Hope is all I have left."

## 37 : SENDING MESSAGES

PATHIUS STOOD OUTSIDE THE door to Nihil's study amidst a flurry of activity. A messenger burst from the room and bumped into him in his haste. The young man looked up at Pathius's mask and balked, his face contorting into a combination of terror and embarrassment. Pathius turned his gaze away as the messenger scurried on, standing straight with his arms crossed as he waited his turn.

The muffled sound of Nihil barking orders drifted through the half-closed door. Pathius leaned forward and listened. Although he couldn't make out the words, Nihil's voice sounded strained and angry. It piqued Pathius's curiosity. The entire compound had been a furor of activity all day and Pathius had still not been told what was happening.

Sindre threw open the door and stopped as her eyes met Pathius's. Her cheeks were flushed and the hair around her face hung in wisps, drifting in the air as if a breeze blew. She touched her chest, pressing the medallion to her skin, and narrowed her eyes at Pathius as her nostrils flared. Pathius braced himself for a shock of pain but she stalked off, brushing past him, and disappeared down the hall. Pathius let his shoulders relax and breathed out a sigh of relief.

"Number One," Nihil's voice bellowed from inside the study.

Pathius entered, pushed the door aside and stood at attention, his gaze fixed on the wall.

"Our location has been compromised and we are preparing to evacuate," Nihil said, his voice abrupt.

Pathius kept himself still despite the surprise that reverberated through him. This was unexpected.

"My sources in Halthas tell me that the king is preparing to attack the compound," Nihil continued. "He appears to be amassing a large force. It is possible we could face him, with our position fortified here, but it is a risk I am not willing to take." Nihil turned and walked over to a window, pacing almost aimlessly. "Rogan is forcing me to accelerate my timeline, but I will have to deal with him later. Right now our priority is to ensure my subjects, and the Arcstone, are evacuated safely. I cannot allow either to fall into enemy hands."

Pathius flicked his gaze to Nihil. The muscles in his jaw stood out and deep creases ran through his forehead. His hands were agitated, his robe swinging as he paced.

"You and a few others will remain here. I won't abandon our home to our enemies so easily. I am sending the rest on, into our underground stronghold under the city. Number Three will lead, and I will send Fourteen with them."

Pathius nodded once, a quick lift and dip of his chin. Possibilities flew through his mind, the voices in his head rising from the depths. He struggled to keep his face composed, and a flicker of fear trickled down his spine as his thoughts turned traitorous.

"I am planning a little surprise for Rogan for when he arrives. He reneged on our agreement and I am going to make him pay for it. My plan requires your particular talents. Once Rogan's force has been deterred and the compound destroyed, we will make our way through the tunnel into the city." Nihil turned back to his desk and touched a map, unrolled and held down by a polished rock in each corner. "After we secure our new location, the Lyceum will be within easy reach. We've already weakened them. A targeted strike and the Lyceum is sure to fall." He looked back at Pathius, his eyes intense. "With you and the others at my side, the Lyceum will have no choice but to submit to me. I will be Paragon and my work will no longer be in the shadows. With the power of the Lyceum behind me, there is no limit to what I will accomplish. We will make true progress."

Pathius pictured Nihil standing tall in the dark blue robes of the Paragon, surrounded by men with multicolored eyes. Would Pathius be standing at his side? Would he still wear the black mask, or was it a Lyceum Guard uniform he wore? Was this what he had become? He forced himself to speak. "What is my task?"

"You will deliver orders to Number Three. He is charged with leading the evacuation. We will meet them in our stronghold under the city once this location is secure," Nihil said. "Once we are out, you will wait here with Number Four and Number Five for Rogan's force. Put up a token defense, let them think we are ready to fight. Once you have drawn them in, you will destroy the compound. The cellars and tunnels below have already been cleared. You will freeze the pillars below to weaken them. Number Four will take care of the rest."

Pathius gave one last nod. He didn't trust himself to speak as Nihil dismissed him. He walked out the door as another servant scurried in and he could hear the sound of Nihil's voice rising again, as he walked down the hallway and turned the corner.

The voices in his mind stirred. What had Nihil created? A glorified servant? A crackling sound caught his attention and he glanced over his shoulder. A trail of glistening ice coated the floor as he walked, spreading out in sharp crystals from his feet. He no longer cared.

He wandered the hallways, his thoughts a blur. Many times in recent days he had thought of simply killing both Sindre and Nihil. Fear stayed his hand. He didn't know what would happen to him if Sindre died. His hand reached back to brush the cold stone on the back of his neck. He ran his fingers along the edges, to feel where the smooth stone met his skin. It almost felt seamless. Anger surged in his gut, a deep, raw sensation. He clenched his teeth and his lip quivered as he fingered the implant.

With a shuddering breath, he wiped the sheen of sweat from his brow. He glanced behind to ensure he was alone before he tugged his mask back into place. He walked down the hallway as an idea solidified in his mind.

Forcing his steps down the familiar hallway, he turned left toward Nihil's laboratory. He peered into the room, the Arcstone heavy on the square table. His heart raced and his mind swirled with visions of a tunnel of light streaking past. He shook his head and blinked as he pushed himself into the room. Finding Nihil's desk, he quickly pulled out a piece of paper, and dipped one of Nihil's quills into a bottle of ink. With a pounding heart, he wrote, the tip of the quill scratching across the surface of the paper. He flicked his eyes up repeatedly, sure he would look up to find Nihil or Sindre striding in. After drying the ink with a blotter, he replaced the stopper and laid the quill back in its place before scurrying out of the room.

He found Number Three in his room. The door was ajar and the other man sat on his bed, straight backed and still. His hands buzzed with static, tiny jolts of electricity jumping between his fingers. Pathius entered and Number Three's eyes rose, his body motionless.

Pathius reached back and closed the door with a soft click. "Nihil has orders," he said. "We are abandoning the compound and retreating through the tunnel. He orders you to lead the others. A few of us will remain behind and meet you when this location is secure."

Number Three nodded.

Pathius paused and rubbed his chin through his mask. His plan was beginning to solidify. It was probably madness. But they were all more than half mad as it was. "I have another task for you."

Number Three's eyes lifted again. "Yes?"

Pathius crouched down and rested his elbows on his knees. "I need you to take a message to someone." He reached into a pocket in his shirt and took out the paper, folded into a tight square. "This is not from Nihil." Wondering what was going on in the Number Three's mind, he watched his eyes.

"Is Nihil aware of this?" Number Three asked.

Pathius's heart quickened. Perhaps Number Three had been the wrong choice. Three was strong, but if Pathius acted quickly he could probably kill him first. "No."

Number Three's multicolored eyes drifted from Pathius to the note in his hand. "Where does it need to go?"

Pathius let out his breath. If Rogan was coming, it was likely Cecily would be with him. "The recipient is probably at the palace. You won't be able to get past the guards without attracting attention, and you must avoid that at all costs. Outside the palace, you'll be able to find a messenger or clerk to deliver this. Tell them to take it directly to a woman named Cecily, of the family Graymere. She'll be close to the king."

Number Three reached out and took the note. He turned it over and ran his fingers along the edges. "What does it say?"

Pathius looked into Number Three's eyes. He was in too deep to back out now. "Read it. Cecily is Number Fourteen's wife, from before." Number Three's eyes twitched. "I'm telling her where she can find him. I think she is part of the force that is coming for the compound. She is trying to get her husband back. I want to help her succeed."

"Why should I help you?"

Pathius leaned closer to Number Three and lowered his voice to a whisper. "Nihil is losing his grip. This may be our way out. If he loses Fourteen, all hell will break loose. If we work together, this could be our chance at freedom."

The word was so soft, Pathius could scarcely utter it. Number Three's eyes widened and he leaned away. Pathius held still, ignoring the voices swirling in his head. This was worse than rebellion. It was treason. Nihil would have Sindre torture him until his body gave out. His neck tightened and a knot of fear clenched in his belly. This was insanity.

Number Three rose from his bed and Pathius stood. Three's eyes were intense, his brow furrowed down. He looked up at Pathius and held his gaze. "I will see to it."

Elation poured into Pathius, dousing the fear. His lip curled up in a smile, and he reached out to grip Three's hand, giving him a nod of respect.

"Once you're at the fallback point, under the city, Cecily will come for Number Fourteen. I need you to make certain she succeeds."

Number Three nodded. "It shall be done."

## 38 : TRUST

CECILY WAITED IN THE courtyard, the palace towering above her. The tall spires gleamed in the early morning sun, the chill air crisp against her skin. The heady scent of gardenia from the Shaper gardens hung in the winter air, mixing with the musky smell of leather and horses.

The bulk of Rogan's force amassed on the other side of the palace in a makeshift staging area. They had decided on a force of a thousand men, including a number of Fire Wielders who usually manned the wall. None of them wanted to take any chances with Nihil's aberrant Wielders. True to his word, the Paragon had sent a contingent of Lyceum Guard from each of the four wings of the Lyceum, and more importantly, a supply of absorption collars. Cecily had one tucked in a small inside pocket, the weight a constant reminder of what she intended to do with it.

Griff and Serv were nearby, their horses saddled and ready. Serv ran his hands along the straps, checking his buckles. He caught Cecily's eye and gave her a small smile and a nod. His calm demeanor helped settle her nerves. Griff laughed at something a passing soldier said, his loud guffaw carrying over the din. He strode around the horses, eating a large piece of sausage.

"I don't know how you can eat right now," Cecily said.

Griff smiled. "I can always eat," he said with a wink, taking another bite as sausage juice ran into his auburn beard.

Mira and Sumara waited nearby, talking with Edson. Mira had changed out of her Royal Guard uniform, opting for a thigh-length tunic over black leggings and boots, her quiver and bow strapped to her back. Sumara's long white dress was covered by a full-length brown wool coat, with wide sleeves and a long hood that hung down her back. Edson stood to the side and nodded along with the conversation. His leather armor was secured with black straps and a green cloak hung down his back. A sliver of wistfulness cut through Cecily's apprehension as she looked at him. She wondered if this was how a mother felt, realizing her son was no longer a boy.

Merrick walked over to her, tugging on his brown leather gloves and flexing his fingers. His faded green cloak drifted behind him.

"Did you find anything?" she asked. Merrick had left the previous day to scout ahead.

"It looks clear. I got close to the complex, but there was little I could see. We will need to be prepared for anything," he said.

Cecily nodded. "I agree." Merrick reached out and squeezed her arm before walking away.

The back of her neck tingled and she turned to find Callum lounging against a stone pillar. "Kind of nice having the crown on our side this time, isn't it?" he asked and gestured to the activity in the courtyard.

Cecily took a few steps toward him. "We have the advantage in numbers," she said. "Unless he has an army of those Wielders hidden in his compound."

One corner of Callum's mouth turned up in a crooked smile. "If that's the case, there's not much hope for any of us. But I'm putting my money on us this time."

"This time?" she asked. "Have you been wagering against us?"

He lifted his shoulders in a lazy shrug. "There was a time when I wasn't so confident in our little band of rebels. The whole treason thing was a bit much, even for me. I am rather fond of my head staying attached to my neck."

"Aren't we all," said Griff as he clapped Cecily on the back.

The other companions wandered over, lingering near Cecily while they waited for Rogan and Alastair. The company was nearly ready to depart. Cecily's eyes roved around the courtyard and a calmness settled over her, heartened by the presence of her friends.

Rogan appeared on the palace steps, flanked by Alastair and several Royal Guard. Cecily sucked in a quick breath. He was dressed for travel, a dark shirt under leather armor, his black cloak cascading down his shoulders, a sword at his hip. He looked exactly as she remembered him from the war, a man not yet the king.

After quickly scanning the courtyard, Rogan walked over to Cecily, his hand resting on his sword hilt. "Everything is in order." He nodded to the others, meeting their eyes in turn.

Cecily tipped her head to him as her thoughts drifted to Daro. She didn't know what he would do when they arrived, or whether they would be able to contain him. She had to believe she could reach him this time, regardless of what they had done to him.

Thinking about Daro brought images of Pathius to her mind. It troubled her that his face drifted into her consciousness so often. He was like a blot of dark paint that drips into a lighter shade, permeating the color. She no longer dreamed of Daro, but woke in the night soaked in sweat, visions of Pathius still swimming in her mind.

Cecily turned and almost tripped over a young messenger boy. His hood was down, his cheeks pink with cold. He looked up at her with wide eyes, his mouth working as if to speak.

"I have a message for Cecily of the family Graymere," he said as his eyes darted between her, Sumara, and Mira. "Is one of you Miss Cecily?"

Cecily narrowed her eyes and looked around. She caught Callum's eyes and he shrugged; apparently the messenger wasn't one of his. "I am Cecily," she said. The boy held out the message, hovering with expectant eyes after she took it. She dug into a pocket and handed him a coin, and he scurried off, disappearing between the lines of horses.

As she opened the note and read, her throat clenched and she forced herself to swallow. She stood still, reading it several times while her friends shifted on their feet, looking back and forth between each other.

Callum spoke up. "The suspense is too much. What is it?"

Cecily tried to process what she read. She looked down at it again. The letters were slanted and messy, blots of ink dotting the margins. "It's from Pathius," she said.

Everyone erupted in a flurry of gasps and questions, leaning toward her, and some reached out to take the note. She clutched it to her chest as her mind reeled. "He says they are abandoning the compound. He and some others are still there, but they've sent Daro away. He's telling me where to find him, and how to get there."

She reached out and handed the note to Rogan. He read it over, his forehead creasing as his eyes flicked across the page. He lowered it as he finished. "This doesn't change anything," he said. "There's no way we can trust his word, and even if we could, this doesn't change our plans. We march for the compound."

"Agreed," Alastair said. "This must be some sort of trick."

He passed it to Serv, who read it with Griff and Sumara looking over his shoulder. "One thing is certain," Serv said as he looked up at the companions. "Nihil knows we're coming. We need to be prepared for the worst. And it is quite possible Daro won't be there by the time we get in."

Cecily's mind raced. There was much more at stake than one man's life. Nihil needed to be stopped and Rogan's force was the way to ensure that end. Serv handed her the note and she looked at it again. The pull of her bond with Daro stirred inside her, faded and weak. The words scrawled on the paper plucked at her. If they prevailed against Nihil, but Daro wasn't there, how would they find him? Her doubt solidified into firm resolve.

"I know this is madness," she said, "but I believe him. Pathius stopped Daro in Wesfell, and we know they had been sent to kill us. He must have put himself at great risk when he did that, and when he sent this." Her friends went silent, their eyes flicking around as if they waited for the others to react. "Rogan is right—this doesn't change the plan, except we have to assume Nihil knows we are coming and will have laid a trap. Merrick will take men to scout ahead and the rest of the force will attack the compound. Neutralize as many of his Wielders as possible; try not to kill them. I don't know if we will be able to help them, but we have to try. Remember, these are all men like Daro, taken from their families. We have to assume they are being controlled, and there may still be a way to set them free."

Callum brushed his hair from his eyes. "And what is it you're going to do, exactly?"

Cecily took a breath. "I'm going after Daro."

"Cecily, that's madness," Alastair cut in. "You can't possibly believe this message. If Nihil is setting a trap, this is most certainly it. This is suicide."

Serv's voice carried over Alastair. "I'll go with you."

Cecily's head whipped around to look at Serv. His face was serene, his blue eyes bright.

"We all admire your loyalty, Serv, but our plan is sound," Alastair said. "You can't go gallivanting off because of this. Be reasonable."

"I know, it doesn't make sense," Cecily said. "And I can't ask any of you to go with me based on my gut feeling. But I'm telling you, I know this is real. Pathius sent this, and he isn't lying. He's trying to help us."

Callum stepped forward, his head tilted to one side. "I'm in." Everyone's eyes swung to look at him. He shrugged. "If Cecily thinks this is what needs to be done, I'm inclined to believe her."

"You're not going anywhere without me," Griff said with a wide grin.

"I'm with you too," Edson said.

Rogan met her eyes and stared hard for a long moment. He gripped the hilt of his sword and pursed his lips. "Very well. Merrick will take Mira and a small group of my men to scout the compound. Alastair and I will lead the main force. The rest of you, go with Cecily. If this message is correct, you can intercept Daro and bring him to the Lyceum. If not, we will retrieve him from Nihil's compound. But," he said and paused with one finger raised, "be wary. I suspect we will all be walking into a trap." He reached out and gripped Cecily's hand. "I won't lie to you. I can't promise anything about the fate of Nihil's other Wielders. The Paragon was adamant that it would be far too dangerous to let them live, and I tend to agree. But I will keep your words in mind." He squeezed her hand. "Be safe."

She nodded. "You too."

He turned on his heel and walked away, and his purposeful steps took him quickly out of sight. Alastair followed, his sable cloak flowing behind him.

Mira leaned in and gave her a hug. "Be careful," she whispered.

Cecily squeezed her back. "You too."

Merrick nodded as he and Mira turned to follow Rogan and Alastair.

The rest of her friends looked at her. She glanced down at the note one last time before she folded it up and tucked it into a pocket. Her shoulders relaxed and her mind was clear. She couldn't explain why she knew this was right, but something deep inside told her to trust Pathius.

## 39 : COLLAPSE

THE STILLNESS OF THE forest was a lie. Violence dwelled beneath the branches of the trees, hiding in wait, ready to strike. Pathius couldn't see the king's force, but he knew it was coming. He strained his ears, anxious to hear some sign of the impending battle. The sun had crested past midday, the shadows growing long, yet there was still no sign of them.

From his vantage point atop the building, he couldn't see far into the forest. The trees were thick and there was no clear road or path leading to the compound. Rogan would have a difficult time bringing a large number of men through. No doubt the new king already knew the lay of the land. Pathius had not seen his scouts, but he was certain they had been there.

His mind drifted back to an earlier time, the before. He heard the voice of his father, lecturing him on tactics and strategies. He let the memory come, no longer trying to suppress his former self. He was

Pathius now, once a prince of Halthas. He was no longer Number One. Nihil just didn't know it yet.

He crouched down and kept his head low as the first of Rogan's forces appeared through the trees. They crept amongst the underbrush and took up their positions behind the tree line. Pathius could see the forest begin to shift as a great mass of men moved into place. His gaze swept from side to side, taking in the numbers. He couldn't tell for sure how many were coming, but it appeared to be a sizeable force. He laughed to himself as he thought about how few of Nihil's men were left in the compound. Rogan had come expecting a battle. Pathius would have to do his best to give him what he came for.

A voice called out from the trees and Pathius braced himself. A great roaring sound rose from the trees and a line of fireballs shot toward the building. *They brought Fire Wielders.* Excitement grew in Pathius as he stood, reached out his hands, and Absorbed the energy from the fire. The flames arced toward his hands, lines of fire reaching for him through the open air. The heat poured into his body, racing through his arms and filling his chest. He closed his eyes, arms spread wide, and let the heat sear through him.

Noises from below brought him back to the moment. There were shouts and commands as men scuffled through the trees. Another volley of fire flew into the air. Brilliant streaks of flame soared up, ready to come down and rain fire on the compound. Pathius paused, watching the raging orange balls flickering with heat and light. He gasped and a shudder ran through him. All that power. It was so beautiful.

He sucked in the energy from the fire, and the flames once again surged toward him. The heat burst into his body and nearly knocked him backward. He pulled in his arms, reveling in the scorching heat as it ripped through him. As he looked down at his hands, he could see shimmers of heat radiating away from his body. He couldn't hold this much energy; he let it dissipate, knowing there was plenty more to come.

A volley of flaming stones streaked toward the trees, each landing with a loud pop as it hit. Number Four was below, helping Pathius mount their token defense. He shot out another scattering of stones, and the explosions reverberated off the trees. Number Five was on the other side of the compound and Pathius saw arrows firing, bending around the trees to find their targets.

Another set of fireballs arced through the air, this time aimed at the far ends of the compound. Pathius managed to drain the two closest to him, but the others hit the building, making it shudder under his feet.

More men stepped forward from the tree line and raised bows. The Fire Wielders lit the arrows and at a yell from their commander, they let loose. The flaming arrows flew toward the compound, many of them pointed at Pathius. He ducked down behind the ledge, as some of the arrows stuck into the outer wall. A few clattered behind him and he pulled in their heat, leaving nothing but withered arrows trailing lines of black smoke into the air.

He looked over the ledge to find the archers preparing for another volley. Two archers went down in quick succession, hit by Number Five's arrows. Pathius centered on another one, reaching out his hand toward him. He concentrated, feeling the energy inside the man, and Reached for it. He got a hold of it and tugged, sucking in an abrupt burst of energy. The archer's head and arms rocked back as if he'd been hit in the chest, and his body slumped to the ground.

Pathius trembled with all the energy he had pulled, the air around him shimmering as it dissipated. He hit another archer with his energy drain, Absorbing his heat, and watched the man hit the ground. Rogan's men were shouting orders, pointing up at him. He ducked down and hurried across the roof, keeping low, and ran to the other side. Another clatter of arrows hit where he'd been standing.

Peeking out over the ledge, he could see Rogan's line push out of the trees, the men forming up in the clearing. Archers hit the building with their flaming arrows, but Pathius let them burn. He reached his hand toward the nearest archer. Heat from the man poured into Pathius, a line of energy streaking from the man's chest into Pathius's hand. The man stood frozen, his mouth open in a silent scream as his skin turned blue and frost spread out from his chest. A crackling sheen of ice coated him and he fell to the ground, stiff.

Pathius breathed hard, the heat sending rivulets of sweat dripping down his back. The men below were yelling, pointing up at him while exploding bits of stone popped and sent sprays of dirt into the air. Another ball of fire exploded against the far side of the compound. Pathius briefly wondered if Number Five had fallen back or if he was caught in the blast of flame.

More of Number Five's arrows streaked toward Rogan's force just then, answering his question. The men below held their line and sent more fire at the building. The blasts hit with a boom, the sharp crack of broken glass and splintering wood ringing out through the air. The outer wall of the building burned, black smoke muddling the air.

Pathius pulled energy from the flames, if only to glory in the heat raging through him. His head swam with euphoria and his body felt light, as if he could leap off the building and hover in the air. He pulled the energy from another blast of fire and let it sear through him. The mix of pain and exhilaration was intoxicating and he found himself laughing, his voice ringing out amidst the din of the attack.

Holding so much energy threatened to unmake him, but he didn't care. His skin tingled as the energy poured off him in waves and his hands almost seemed to glow. He reached out his hands and Pushed, feeling the heat rush through his body and out his fingertips. A blast hit the ground in front of Rogan's line, sending up a burst of dirt and rocks. Pathius looked at his hands, his eyes wide. *This is new.*

His mouth curled in a smile beneath his mask. He moved across the ledge and took up a new position. The flat roof was beginning to feel warm. He placed his hands on the roof and Absorbed the heat, sending a crackling circle of frost spreading around him. He sucked in a breath, glorying in the power that swelled within. Curious to see if he could do it again, he Pushed the energy out and let it surge from his fingertips. Another blast exploded in the clearing, sending rock and dirt flying.

His mind swirled with the elation of power that raged through him. The voices in his head seethed, their sounds mingling with the shouts of Rogan's men, the roar of flames and the surge of energy churning within him.

Pathius glanced down through the haze of smoke. The line of Rogan's force held strong. A man walked up and down the lines, shouting orders and encouragement. He wore no uniform, just leather armor with a black cloak streaming behind him. He held a sword aloft, pointing with the tip. He raised it and brought it down as the archers loosed, his head turning to watch the volley. *I know you.*

Rogan himself. The new king. Pathius knew his father was dead. Nihil had told him years ago, probably as a means to tighten his grip on Pathius's mind. It had been so long since Pathius had thought of himself as the prince that hearing of the new king had done little to affect him. But seeing him there in the flesh, standing tall amidst the battle and shouting orders at his men, made Pathius rage.

The building shuddered beneath him and Pathius had to stumble to keep his footing. The lower levels must be burning. It was almost time. He looked back over the side of the ledge. Rogan walked further down the line, his stride sure and his bearing tall. Pathius let him go. He wanted to face Rogan man to man, not strike at him from afar like a filthy assassin. His father would have railed at him for throwing away the chance to kill an enemy. But Pathius was not his father, nor did he wish to be.

The smoke thickened, obscuring Pathius's view of the force below. A clear whistle called out from the courtyard behind him, the signal to retreat. He stood up and threw his hands out to the sides, pulling heat from the ground just in front of Rogan's men. A thick line of cracking ice erupted, running across the ground in both directions. Sparkling frost spread as weeds and scrub withered and died along the line. Men shouted, jumping back to avoid the spreading ice and pulling each other out of the way.

Pathius turned, reluctant to leave the fray, still buzzing with energy. He ran toward the trapdoor in the floor of the roof, pulled it open, and dashed down the steps. Smoke crept into the interior of the building, billowing in from the front. Nihil would be pleased; the fire would make their job easier.

He raced through the courtyard to the other side of the compound and flew down a hallway that led to the cellar. Number Four and Number Five were ahead of him, already heading down the steps. Number Five peeled off, angling toward the lower stairs that led into the tunnel. Pathius followed Number Four into the cellar.

Originally a storage area designed to hold supplies, the now-empty cellars spread out beneath the compound. Nihil's men had already knocked down most of the walls, leaving the entire building held up by only a few beams. Pathius raced toward the far end and spun, looking out over the pillars that bore the weight of the building above. Number Four waited at the other side and gave him a quick nod.

Pathius darted forward and brushed his hands against each beam as he passed, Absorbing enough heat to send a snapping sheen of ice and frost spreading across them. The building above shuddered the pillars weakened, dust and debris clouding the air.

He raced past Number Four, leaving the rest to him, and flew down the stairs into the tunnel system. The passageway branched off, heading south toward the city. He'd be running directly beneath Rogan's army, but if he and Number Four did their job well, Rogan's forces would never be able to sift through the remains of the compound to find the tunnel entrance. Part of him wished he had a view from up above. He had to give Nihil credit—this was going to be spectacular.

Booms from above shook the ground and debris cascaded down from the roof of the tunnel. Pathius's heart raced as he staggered backward. Number Four darted down the stairs, tossing flaming stones behind him as he went. The ground shuddered again and Pathius moved back. He had no desire to be buried in rubble.

Nihil and the others had already fled down the tunnel, so he nodded to Number Four. Grabbing more pebbles from his pouch, Number Four heated them with his hand before he tossed them into the space under the building. Pathius backed up, his feet slipping on the rocky ground, as more dirt and dust fell from the ceiling. The pebbles popped, bright explosions hitting the supports. Number Four threw a few more, sending bright flashes of flame under the building as they backed away. The weakened pillars snapped as Pathius and Number Four fled further into the tunnel.

A great rending groan cut through the air and the ground shook. Dirt poured over them and they raced ahead, Pathius's heart beating wildly in his chest. His swell of energy diminished, but adrenaline pushed him forward as the supports cracked behind him. A loud boom echoed through the tunnel and he pushed Number Four to the ground. Pathius dove down and they both curled up, covering their heads, as a huge blast of dirt and rock surged through the tunnel. The sound of the collapse tore through his ears.

Pebbles clattered down from the sides of the tunnel and dust swirled in the air. Another creak sounded behind and a puff of dust blew around them. Pathius brushed the dirt and bits of rock from his hooded head and blinked against the grit in his eyes. He got to his feet and shook off the dirt. Number Four rose and brushed the dirt from his arms and head. Pathius shifted his mask back into place as his eyes watered.

The tunnel behind them was completely collapsed. A precarious wall of debris was stacked, floor to ceiling, cutting off the entrance to the compound. If they had done their job, the entire compound had caved in, crashing and sinking into the ground, leaving nothing but a gaping hole with a pile of smoking debris.

Pathius turned toward the city, away from what had been his home. A sense of buoyancy spread through him, despite the heaviness of his limbs as the last of his energy dissipated. Destroying the compound put another crack in the chains that bound him to Nihil. He had every intention of putting a wedge in that crack and pounding it until the chains finally shattered.

Number Four followed, trailing just behind his right shoulder. Pathius took his time, reveling in the booms that echoed down the tunnel, the aftershocks of the compound's collapse. He wondered if Cecily had managed to free Number Fourteen. Judging by Fourteen's demeanor of late, he doubted she would have much luck bringing him back to himself. He couldn't decide whether he hoped Cecily could help him recover or not. A part of him hated the thought of Cecily in the arms of another man, even if that man had once been her husband. But the blow it would cause Nihil to lose Number Fourteen was worth the pangs of jealousy. His only regret was that he was unlikely to make it to their stronghold before Nihil realized Number Fourteen was gone. The look on Nihil's face when he discovered his prized subject was missing was something Pathius would have loved to see.

The tunnel shuddered again and dust drifted from the ceiling. Pathius walked on as the next phase of his plan snapped into place in his mind. He glanced back at Number Four and knew the man would come to his side when the time came. Nihil had taught him to lead better than his father ever had. Soon he would no longer be taking orders from a man in a stolen magister's robe. He would be the one giving them.

## 40 : WHAT ONCE WAS LOST

DUST HUNG IN THE air, drifting through the pale light of glowstones. Cecily had led them through the interior of the palace, down into a deserted storage cellar deep below. The wide room was mostly empty, nothing but a stack of old barrels, a few crates, and some furniture covered with old cloths. Pathius's note had described the route, but as they stood in the dank room, Cecily wondered if she'd understood the directions correctly.

Callum turned in a slow circle, his nose crinkling. "Stinks down here."

The pungent scent of rot permeated the room. "He says there is a door leading down into a tunnel," Cecily said as she glanced down at the note again. "But he doesn't say where to find it."

"I'm having some doubts about this. I've never heard of a tunnel running under the palace, and underground hiding places are kind of my thing," Callum said.

"He says right here, it's a forgotten entrance. Besides, he grew up here. Maybe it was something the royal family kept hidden."

Callum shrugged and kept looking around. Griff grunted as he pushed a crate across the floor, and the bottom scraped with a loud groan, but he shook his head. Sumara and Serv walked around the perimeter, feeling out the wall and looking behind the cloth-covered furniture.

Dust spilled into the air as Edson pulled back a thick canvas. He waved his hand in front of his face and coughed. Cecily walked over and found he had uncovered a smooth wooden chest. The cover had kept it fairly clean and she ran her fingers across the dark filigree carved on the top. It looked Imaran. "Here, help me move this."

She and Edson pushed, moving the chest toward the center of the room. It sat on an old, threadbare carpet, the pattern faded and worn. Pulling back the carpet, Cecily found a square seam cut in the stone floor. In the middle was a brass circle, set deep into the stone, the center a swirling pattern of interlocking lines. She placed her hand over it and probed it with her Awareness.

"What is it?" Edson asked.

Cecily closed her eyes and concentrated. "A lock." She felt it out, letting her Awareness follow the lines of the mechanism. It was beautifully complex, without an obvious keyhole. She traced the lines of metal, caressing them with a slight touch of Pressure until she found the right spot. She Pushed to make the mechanism twist, snapping the lock open. A brass handle popped up into her hand and she turned it, the metal scraping together as she twisted it in a half circle. A puff of dust rose from the seams as the latch disengaged. She and Edson pulled, raising the heavy stone slab upwards on a hinge, until it leaned back against the floor on the other side. Looking into the hole, she could see a set of stairs plunging down into darkness.

"I hate tunnels," Callum said with a sigh. They all looked at him.

"Callum, you live underground," Serv said.

He shrugged. "I hate tunnels that aren't mine. I like knowing what's in them."

Cecily shook her head and laughed. Holding a glowstone in front of her, she made her way down the rickety wooden steps. The wood creaked and groaned as she walked, but they felt secure. Her companions followed and they gathered at the bottom.

The tunnel was bare stone, but large, easily twice as tall as she was and wide enough for several people to walk abreast. She held her glowstone aloft, illuminating the walls. "What is this place?"

Serv ran his hand along the wall. "Shaper-wrought," he said. "But old. I bet this tunnel is nearly as old as the palace itself."

"They dug this out of solid rock?" Sumara asked as she held her glowstone up and looked at the ceiling.

"Stone Shapers can do some pretty amazing things," Callum said. "This looks a lot like the Quarry, but older."

Cecily checked the note. Pathius had drawn a rough map of the tunnels, showing her where to go. The main tunnel ran north, with another tunnel branching off to the west. The westward tunnel would lead them to their destination, and it appeared to curve and wind, rather than traveling in a straight line.

She led them onward, and they held out their glowstones for light. The walls were smooth stone with empty iron sconces secured to the walls at regular intervals. Pillars stood in the center, spaced widely apart, bearing the weight of the stone above. The rock gradually changed from solid stone to a mix of stone and dirt, the floor littered with pebbles and crumbling debris. The iron sconces were placed on the pillars instead of the walls.

A tunnel branched off to the west and they turned. The new tunnel was much smaller, the roof closer to their heads, and the walls closed in.

Serv held his glowstone out to inspect the walls. "I would guess this tunnel is much newer."

Callum nodded. "Looks that way to me. I wonder if Nihil dug it."

"I don't know how far this goes," Cecily said, "but I think we're heading toward the Lyceum."

Cecily's Awareness told her the way was clear, but they looked carefully nonetheless. If Pathius was leading them into a trap, it was possible the Sensor would be Shielding, rendering her Awareness useless. There was no scale to the map, so they had no way of knowing how far they needed to go. They crept along with caution, listening for any sign of Nihil's men.

Cecily felt them with her Awareness just as they saw the glow of light up ahead. They stopped and shrank back, pocketing their glowstones to douse the light. A soft glow illuminated an opening on the right side of the tunnel, ahead of their position. Cecily closed her eyes, breathing in deep, and focused her Awareness. She could feel the wall of the tunnel opening into a wide doorway. Beyond were a series of open spaces, much like rooms, carved into the ground. She crept forward a few steps, her eyes closed. She meticulously probed the entire space to be sure she didn't miss anything, or anyone.

There were three figures in the first room; the rest were empty. Her heart began to beat harder. Focusing her Awareness tightly on each figure, she felt them up and down. Each wore a mask, their head covered with a hood. Nihil's men. One man had a slight frame and carried two blades strapped to his back. The second was about the size of Callum, tall and lean. He stood back from the other two, his back against the far wall. Her heart caught in her throat as she probed the last one. He was tall and thickly muscled with a wide sword at his hip. She reached for her link to Daro, willing herself to feel his presence, the broken piece of their bonded soul. She had to be sure.

Turning back to her friends, she whispered. "He's there." There was no doubt it was him. Her Awareness touched the outline of his form. She mentally ran her hands over the wide shoulders, the thick arms. She knew that body. Breathing in deeply, she felt their bond. It was shaky and tenuous, as if something stood in the way, blocking the energy from flowing between them. But it was not broken.

Anticipation rose in her gut and her limbs tingled. Her companions leaned close. "Three men, including Daro," she said. She fought to keep her voice a whisper, excitement threatening to overwhelm her. "They are all masked. I'm sure they're more of Nihil's men. Sumara, as soon as we're in range, hit the man on the right with as much lightning as you can muster. We take him out fast. Griff, keep Daro occupied for as long as you can while the rest of us deal with the second man. Sumara can circle around behind and jolt Daro enough to incapacitate him. We'll have to carry him out. The note shows the closest exit, and I don't think it's far."

Griff's eyes widened, his voice low. "Is that all? Perhaps we should have brought more of that army with us."

She looked around to meet everyone's eyes. They nodded. They spread out and crept along the tunnel walls to keep out of sight as long as possible. Serv and Edson walked with swords drawn, Griff hefting his heavy axe. Callum brandished knives in both hands. Cecily kept her Awareness open, feeling for any sign they had been spotted.

As they got close, Sumara stepped forward and turned to meet Cecily's eye. She nodded and Sumara darted in front of the opening, her long coat flinging out behind her. She sent a shock of lightning from her fingertips, the sound cracking open the silence as the rest of the companions followed.

Cecily turned the corner to find Sumara's target surging to his feet. Her heart sank as she realized the man took Sumara's blast. He stood, his masked face turning to look at his attackers. Reaching up, he pulled two short swords from behind his back and brandished them in front of him. They began to glow, shining streaks of orange pulsing from the hilts to the pointed tips.

Griff closed with Daro and held out his axe to keep him from joining the fight. Cecily could hear him speaking in reassuring tones. "Easy there, Daro. We're here to help, my friend."

Cecily hit the swordsman with Pressure, Reaching for his wrists to disarm him. He shook off her Wield and walked forward to attack. Serv and Edson stepped in front of Cecily and clashed swords with the man. Sparks flew from the hot metal as their swords clanged, the metallic ping ringing through the air. Serv stepped back and held out his hand, rooting the man's feet. He only managed to stick one and the man tugged at his stuck foot while he parried Edson's strike.

Callum threw a knife at the swordsman but he knocked it aside with his blade. He gripped his swords and let out a yell as he pulled his foot free. His swords glowed hotter, flashing bright in the dark tunnel. Serv attacked and he blocked, before spinning and swinging for Edson. Sparks flew as their swords hit and Edson had to jump back, them from his sleeve.

Daro swung at Griff, his eyes shining through his mask. Cecily Pushed at Daro, trying to keep him from hitting anyone. He felt heavy against her Push but she managed to make him stumble backward a few steps. Griff swung his axe, driving him back, still talking to him.

The third man hovered in the background. He was dressed like the others, in black from head to toe, his face hidden by a black mask.

He stood with his arms crossed, his eyes darting around watching the others, but he made no move to attack.

Cecily turned her attention to the swordsman. His blades gleamed hot in the dim light as he closed with Serv and Edson. Callum threw another knife and scored a hit; the small blade stuck into his leg. Cecily Reached and Pushed against the knife, driving it further into his flesh. He roared with pain as he swung his swords to block Serv and Edson. They pressed their attack, driving forward, and the swordsman limped backward. He fought back but favored his injured leg.

Sumara swung around behind, hovering near the far wall of the tunnel. Cecily knew she needed time to recharge. Daro clashed with Griff, and Cecily Pushed against Daro again, driving him backward. He swung, and his huge sword collided with Griff's axe. Griff stumbled backward under the weight of the attack, but kept his axe aloft to ward off another blow.

The swordsman's blades arced toward Serv and Edson. Serv spun and blocked but the other blade nicked Edson's shoulder. Flames erupted from his shirt and he jumped back, crying out as he tried to pat away the flames. Cecily ran to him, threw the edge of his cloak over his arm, and doused the fire. His face clenched with pain and she turned to see Serv pressing his attack. Two more knives flew from Callum's position, but the swordsman knocked them away with one blade as he battled Serv with the other.

Desperation rushed through Cecily, and she Reached for the swordsman with a surge of Pressure. She Pushed at the knife still sticking in his leg, and he yelled as the leg buckled beneath him. She held up her hand, gritting her teeth, and kept the Pressure thick. She let go long enough to attack one wrist with all her energy, and his blade clattered to the floor. The glow immediately subsided. Serv attacked, thrusting for his chest. The swordsman blocked, but Cecily Reached again, this time getting a grip on his other arm and Pulling it to the side. His next swing went wide as she Pulled, leaving his body open.

Stepping in, Serv plunged his blade through the man's chest. The swordsman's eyes went wide and he looked down as blood gurgled from his mouth. Serv slipped his blade from the body as it dropped and slumped on the floor in a heap of black.

Cecily turned to see Sumara creeping toward Daro. Griff yelled and swung his axe as Daro struck. Daro's head whipped toward Sumara and he swung with a fist, backhanding her against the wall. She collapsed onto the floor, then struggled up to her knees. Cecily Pushed against Daro again, driving him backward into the room. Griff held out his axe and Serv closed in. Daro's eyes flitted from one to the other, as if deciding who to attack first. Cecily gripped his wrists with Pressure, trying to get him to drop his sword, but he held fast and shook off her Wield as if it were a mere annoyance.

From the corner of her eye, Cecily could see the third man as he walked toward them. Her heartbeat quickened and she prepared to attack, wondering what dreadful powers this one possessed. He held up his hand as he walked behind Daro, and everyone hesitated. He placed his hands on Daro's shoulders and a bright flash filled the air. The crackling sound of electricity made Cecily's stomach lurch. Daro slumped backward into the man's grasp and he carefully lowered him to the ground.

Cecily's mouth dropped open and her eyes went wide. The man crouched next to Daro, his eyes traveling over Cecily and her companions. He stood and met Cecily's eyes. "Go," he said. "Now." His gaze followed them as he walked past, and he circled around, disappearing up the tunnel at a jog.

Cecily rushed to Daro and pulled out the collar. She wrapped it around his neck and locked it, hoping fervently it would be enough to contain his power when he awoke. His body twitched but his breathing was steady. She pulled off the mask, tugging it up over his head and tossing it onto the floor. Tears sprang to her eyes as she touched his cheek, running a finger along his jawline. She brushed the hair from his face with trembling hands and took a shuddering breath. "Daro," she whispered as she cupped his face in her shaking hands. His skin felt warm, his bare cheeks soft.

Serv crouched next to her and placed a gentle hand on her shoulder. "We have to go."

She nodded, resting a hand on Daro's chest, and wiped the tears from her eyes. She took another shaky breath and got to her feet as a mix of relief and fear swelled in her chest. Griff had sheathed his axe on his back and bent down to wrap his arms under Daro's shoulders. Callum and Serv lifted his legs. Together, they hefted him up, grunting under his weight.

"At least they were feeding him well," Callum said, his voice strained.

They backed out into the tunnel and continued on, the men struggling to carry Daro's unconscious form. Edson held his burned arm close to his body as he walked. Sumara winced and clutched her chest, but assured Cecily she was not severely hurt.

The exit Pathius had drawn on his hastily scrawled map wasn't far. A tunnel branched off, and they found it ended in a staircase, a slatted wood trapdoor at the top. Cecily's Awareness found the shape of a building above them, the door leading into a cellar. It felt empty, so Sumara jolted the locked door to blast it open.

Cecily peeked her head through, finding an empty storeroom. She crawled up out of the tunnel and moved aside for the rest of her companions. Sumara and Edson came first, followed by Griff, struggling up the stairs under the weight of Daro's upper body. Daro's head lolled to the side, his eyes still closed. They set him on the floor and pushed him out of the way while Callum and Serv climbed out.

She probed the building again to make certain it was deserted. They crept up the stairs, as the men lifted Daro again and hauled him up to the ground floor. Cecily did what she could to help, Pushing Daro up to help alleviate some of his weight.

The building looked like a residence, but it was completely empty, and a thick layer of dust covered the floor. They left tracks in the dust as they walked, kicking it up in little clouds as their feet shuffled through. Light filtered in through curtained windows. Cecily had forgotten it was daytime; the darkness of the tunnel made it feel as if must be night.

She made her way to the front of the house, peeked out through the front door, and squinted against the daylight. The street outside was little more than a narrow alley, lined with small dwellings. Looking up and down, she found the street deserted but could hear the din of a busier road close by. She poked her head out further and looked around, trying to orient herself. Looking up, she could see the Lyceum perched on a hill not far away.

She darted back to her companions. "We're near the Lyceum," she said. "Callum, go find a carriage, someone we can pay to keep quiet. We can't haul him up the hill like this, and I don't know how long we have before he wakes." Callum nodded and ran off. "Serv, make sure that trapdoor is sealed shut. I don't know what that was about back there, but we don't want anyone following us."

Serv and Griff ran back down into the cellar. Edson and Sumara offered to watch for Callum in the front, leaving her alone with the unconscious Daro.

She knelt next to him and reached out, almost afraid to touch him again. Resting her palm against his cheek, she closed her eyes and breathed in his scent. His skin was warm, almost feverish. She laid her other hand on his chest and felt it rise and fall with his breathing. It took all her self-control not to collapse onto him and sob. She didn't know who he would be when he awoke, so she reveled in the moment. Tears slid quietly down her cheeks and her hands trembled. He was here, in the flesh. She leaned forward and laid her forehead on him, her body shuddering as she breathed.

Her voice came out in a soft whisper. "I knew we would find you."

## 41 : CUTTING LOSSES

THE DAY WORE ON as Pathius and Number Four made the long walk through the tunnel. He estimated they had crossed beneath the northern city wall, although the tunnel itself never changed. He watched for signs of the turn that branched off, leading to their meeting point.

His arms and legs were heavy, his body sluggish and tired. He wondered if it was an aftereffect of Absorbing so much energy. His eyelids drooped as his feet stumbled along. He forced himself to keep his eyes open and stay awake. Even the voices in his head were quiet, nothing but a low hum that threatened to lull him to sleep on his feet.

Number Four walked a step behind, occasionally flipping a hot chip of rock to pop on the ground. Pathius blinked at the sharp cracks, the muscles in his back clenching. Thoughts of Cecily crept through his tired mind. He wondered if she had managed to get Fourteen out, and whether Nihil had discovered he was missing. Would Number

Three stay true to his word? What would Pathius find when he caught up with Nihil and Sindre?

Footsteps echoed down the tunnel. Someone was coming toward them. The sound jolted Pathius from his weary stupor. Three figures emerged from the gloom, masked and dressed in black. Pathius wasn't expecting anyone to come this direction. What had happened? Had Nihil sent men back to find them?

Pathius halted and held his hand out toward Number Four. The three men stopped ahead of them, standing side by side across the width of the tunnel. Number Five, Number Seventeen, and Number Eighteen. Pathius could tell each by their height and bearing. He'd become adept at recognizing his cohorts even though he had never seen any of their faces. A curious thought fluttered through his mind. What did they look like?

"Are we later than expected?" Pathius asked. He felt a brush of energy and his heart beat quickened. Was that Number Five, trying to put up a Shield against him?

"We have orders," Number Five said. "Number Four, you are to come back with us. Number One is finished."

A sheen of frost spread from Pathius's feet. "You don't have to do this," he said, his voice steady.

"Yes, we do," Number Five said. "We have our orders."

There was no point feigning loyalty now. "Don't you realize how powerful we have become? We don't have to take his orders anymore." Pathius could see their eyes shining in the dim light of their glowstones. Number Seventeen's gaze flicked from side to side. *He's unsure. Nihil hasn't had him long. Maybe I can reach him.* "Nihil's grip is weakening and his plans are falling apart. How hard did he work to defend our compound, only to have us destroy it and leave it behind? What else has Nihil lost?" *One of us already got away, didn't he?*

Number Eighteen turned his head and looked to Number Five. Number Four hovered behind Pathius and stepped to the side, closer to the wall. Number Seventeen clenched and unclenched his fists, as he looked back and forth between Pathius and Number Five.

"How much of this is your fault, Number One?" Number Five asked. "How long have you been betraying us?"

"I never betrayed you," Pathius said. "Don't let Nihil fill your head with his lies. Ask yourself, why should you believe him over me? Because he'll have Sindre torture you if you question him? They only control us because of these damned pieces of rock in our backs. But they can't keep us forever. Nihil took it too far. He made us into something else, something he can't control. We are too powerful now."

"Dangerous words, but not surprising for a traitor," Number Five said, his voice a growl.

Number Four spoke, his voice a low hiss. "You speak as if we have a choice. We all know what will happen if we run. Death will be our only escape, and it comes soon if we flee."

"Lies," Pathius said, letting his voice ring out, echoing off the tunnel walls. "Fourteen got out, didn't he? Do you think his implant will kill him? I don't. I think they tell us what they need us to hear so we won't run. Sindre can't torture us all. If we rose up against them, there would be nothing they could do. They control us with fear." He leached heat from the air, and his fingers crackled with frost. "I'm not afraid anymore."

"You should be," Number Five said. Daggers dropped into his hands and he threw them at Pathius, the blades flashing in the dim light.

Pathius reached out and Absorbed their energy. He stepped one foot back and to the side, letting the blades slice by him. Frost erupted across the metal and they clattered to the floor. He looked down at his hands. Those knives should have flown far beyond where they fell. *Did I just take the energy of their motion?*

His mouth curled into a smile as Number Five threw two more knives. He held up both hands and Absorbed the energy from the blades. They slowed, bending downward, and fell to the ground at his feet.

"What are you doing?" Number Five yelled at the others. "We have our orders."

Number Eighteen held out his hands and blinding light began to flash. Pathius held up an arm and squinted against the glare as the blaze pierced his vision. Invisible hands seemed to grab the front of his clothes, trying to pull him to the ground. He held his hand out toward Number Eighteen and Absorbed the energy from the flashes. The light streamed toward him, each burst filling him with power. He braced his feet against Number Seventeen's Pull, reaching to Absorb Number Seventeen's energy. The Pull on his clothes released and Number Seventeen slammed him with a Push, strong enough to deflect his energy drain. Number Eighteen doubled over but the afterglow of his flashes still burned in Pathius's vision.

Pathius's fatigue melted away as his body filled with power. Breathing deeply, he pulled in the ambient heat from the air. Frost formed on his brow and the cold bit into his skin. His breath misted out in a cloud, even through his mask. "We can break free from Nihil. It doesn't have to end this way."

"It does for you," Number Five said as he unsheathed his sword.

Pathius reached his hands toward Number Five, aiming to drain him dry. Number Seventeen Pulled his arms, yanking them sideways, and dislodged Pathius's grip. He darted his glance to the side. Number Four was still against the wall, watching with wide eyes. *At least he isn't attacking me.*

"What's Nihil going to do to you when you get back?" Pathius said, throwing his words at Number Four. "Assuming Number Five lets you live. How long before he destroys every one of us? But if we fight, we could have freedom." Number Four stayed frozen, backed against the wall, his eyes darting from Pathius to the others.

Number Five advanced and Pathius sent a blast of energy that sent him stumbling back. Reaching for his heat, he Absorbed his energy, feeling the warmth saturate his body. Number Five cried out and Number Eighteen stood, sending flashes of light and a pulse of energy that clouded Pathius's mind with pain and beat against his vision. He cringed, squeezing his eyes shut and covering his face with his hands. The light still burned behind his eyes and he lost his hold on Number Five.

Number Seventeen's Pull gripped Pathius and tossed him to the ground on his back. He hit the dirt with a thud, his eyes watering. A weight pressed him down as Number Seventeen Pushed on his chest. He could see Number Five from the corner of his eyes, the sword still in his hand. "Nihil is going to kill all of you," Pathius said, his voice a gasping croak. "But if we work together, we can be free."

Number Seventeen pressed harder and drove the air from his chest. Pathius lifted his head and reached out a hand to Pull Number Seventeen's energy. He began to Absorb and felt the man's heat pour through his arm, filling him with raging fire. Number Seventeen Pushed back, severing Pathius's hold, but he let go of the Pressure on his chest. Pathius sucked in a deep breath and surged to his feet, then reached out to hit Number Five with another power drain.

Number Seventeen gripped him again, and the Pressure held his legs. Number Eighteen moved closer, his flashing hands burning Pathius's eyes and flooding his head with agony. He knew he had only seconds left as Number Five approached with his blade. Spreading his hands, he Pulled all the energy he could reach, sucking it in as the air around him sparkled with frost. Snapping ice spread out along the surface of the tunnel, circling from the floor around the walls to the ceiling, as he Absorbed the heat energy into himself. This might be the end, but there was no way he was going to let Number Five be the one to kill him.

Number Five raised his sword, the ice and frost reflecting the light from Number Eighteen's hands. Number Seventeen gripped him with Pressure, holding him fast, his arms spread wide.

From the corner of his eye, Pathius could see Number Four spring into motion. He dug into his pouch and drew out a handful of pebbles. Pathius gasped in surprise as Number Four tossed them at the others and jumped toward Pathius with another handful of rocks. The rocks hit, bursting with loud pops, and sent dirt and shards of ice flying into the air. Number Four slammed into Pathius and pushed him backwards, away from the others. An explosion hit at Number Eighteen's feet and he flew back, hitting the floor of the tunnel. Number Seventeen lost his Pressure on Pathius as he threw his hands up over his face to block the spray of dirt and ice. Number Five turned a shoulder to the blasts and held up his arm to shield his face.

Number Four turned, digging his other hand into his pouch, and emerged with another handful of rocks. Both fists gripped tight, and Pathius could see the rocks glow in his grasp. He threw both handfuls up in the air, and the rocks exploded on impact as they struck the walls and ceiling. The tunnel shook as the ceiling cracked, rocks and dirt pouring down. Pathius scrambled backward, watching as the tunnel collapsed. Through the falling debris he could see Number Five stagger backward. Seventeen and Eighteen stumbled back but the rocks and dirt poured over them, burying them in a pile of rubble.

Another boom echoed from the other side of the collapse and the tunnel shook again, the air heavy with dust and debris. Pathius held his hands out and widened his feet for balance. Number Four looked up at him, his eyes wide as a crack snaked across the floor, the rock cracking with a loud groan. Pathius tried to run back up the tunnel but the ground shuddered and opened under his feet.

The debris from the tunnel fell alongside him as he plunged into icy cold water. It wasn't deep and he pushed against the bottom, his head lurching to the surface. The cold rocked his body like a beating and he felt the last of the energy he'd Absorbed leach out into the freezing torrent as the water swept him down.

The darkness was nearly impenetrable, and he struggled against panic. The voices in his head howled and his limbs grew stiff and heavy. Number Four yelled behind him, an incoherent bellow, choked with water. Pathius sputtered, coughing as the swift current carried them on. He thought about Absorbing energy from the water, but didn't want to wind up encased in ice.

A hand gripped the back of his shirt, and Pathius reached around to grasp Number Four's wrist. It was difficult to make his hands move, his fingers already numb with cold.

"Storm drain," Number Four yelled.

He was right. They were being swept along the storm drain system, pipes underneath the city streets that carried rainwater out to the river. If they were lucky, Shaper ingenuity would extend to practicality and there would be a walkway or a ledge leading to a way out. Pathius reached for the side of the narrow pipe, hoping to find a surface to grip. His hand came down on flat stone and he lobbed his other arm over, trying to hoist himself up on the side. Kicking his numb legs to propel him forward, he lurched up onto the narrow ledge and dragged his body out of the water.

He couldn't see for the darkness but he heard Number Four cough up water on the ledge further downstream. A dim orange light glowed and as Pathius crept closer, he could see it was a handful of glowing rocks, shining through Number Four's fingers.

Shuddering with cold, Pathius leaned his back against the wall, and his head drifted back to rest against the pipe. Number Four handed him a glowing hot rock. It burned Pathius's fingers but he Absorbed the energy and the glow faded to dullness. The warmth spread through him like a wood fire on a wintery day. He handed the cold rock back to Number Four and exchanged it for another searing pebble. He Absorbed the heat, letting it trail into him slowly, and cupped his hands around the stone to warm them.

His mind sharpened as his body warmed. A voice told him he should be afraid. He had done the unthinkable. Nihil would never let him go, and if he did, his implant was sure to kill him. Did he fight his way out only to endure a slow and painful death in a few days? He hadn't been lying when he told the others he didn't believe it. He knew Sindre had power over him when she was close, but her medallion had limits, as did her reach. He no more believed his implant was going to spontaneously kill him than he believed Nihil was a true Magister of the Lyceum.

"Thank you," Pathius said as he turned to look at Number Four.

Number Four nodded, water dripping from his mask. His face was ruddy in the orange glow of his rocks. "I'm tired of belonging to him."

"Nihil won't let us go," Pathius said. "He'll find out we're alive and he'll come for us."

Number Four was silent for a moment. "So what do we do?"

Pathius turned his head and looked Number Four in the eyes. "We come for him first."

## 42 : CHAINS

Cecily stood outside the locked room and pressed her hand against the door. She closed her eyes and felt the contents with her Awareness. The room was small and square, lined with fist-sized sunstones in a ring around the top of the wall, just below the ceiling. The room was a closely guarded secret of the Lyceum, a place reserved for containing powerful Wielders. The sunstones, normally used to store heat, had the ability to draw power from any source nearby. People typically set them out in the sun or near their fire to charge them, then dropped them in their bath to warm it. The enormous concentration of sunstones in this room had the ability to draw energy from a Wielder and weaken their power.

Daro lay in the center of the room, bound with thick chains. His arms were stretched wide, his legs wrapped in the sturdy coils, all of it bolted to the floor. They had tried to restrain him with leather straps, but he'd broken through them as if they were nothing but thread. Even with the absorption collar and room filled with sunstones, his strength was formidable.

Rogan approached and Cecily closed her Awareness, feeling the world come crashing in around her. She blinked and turned to him, her heart heavy.

"How is he?" Rogan asked.

"Quiet," she said. "He just lies there, staring at the ceiling."

Rogan shook his head. "I'm sorry, Cecily. I wish there was more I could do."

"What happened at the compound?" she asked. Rogan had returned with his force the day before. She hadn't had an opportunity to ask him for the details.

"They knew we were coming, as we suspected," he said. "It appears Pathius told the truth about Nihil abandoning it. At first they seemed to defend their position, but after a while they disappeared. Some of the men started cheering, thinking we'd won. That was when the building collapsed."

"It collapsed? The whole thing?"

Rogan nodded. "It came apart and sunk into a hole. We're lucky I hadn't yet sent any men inside. No one could have survived that. When it was over, there was nothing left but a pile of smoking debris."

"Was there anyone left?"

"Not that we found. It's possible whoever was left there to defend it got away somehow, but I don't know where. We searched the entire area and didn't find even the hint of a trail. Merrick is convinced there was a tunnel underground, but the entrance was completely buried."

"It probably connects to the tunnel where we found Daro." She turned to look at Rogan. "That one had an entrance to the palace. It clearly hadn't been used in years, but you need to make sure it's sealed off permanently."

Rogan nodded. "The Paragon already informed me. We're working on a plan to flood the tunnels. If there's anyone hiding down there, by tonight they'll be flushed out."

Paragon Windsor walked over and nodded to Rogan and Cecily in turn. "Have you seen any progress since yesterday?" he asked.

"No." Cecily had been there day and night, even sleeping in the hallway outside Daro's cell. The other companions camped out around the circular top floor of the library, taking turns sitting with her, all of them refusing to leave.

"My Sensors report the same thing they saw with the other one we captured," Windsor said. "He is burning with energy, but there's something else inside of him, something they can't explain. There is energy that clearly belongs to him, yet it is mixed with energy that appears to be from others."

"Other people?" Cecily asked.

"It would seem so. We suspected based on our other captive that Nihil had developed some sort of energy transference. If he found a way to draw the energy from one Wielder into another, it might explain what we're seeing."

"But Daro isn't a Wielder," she said. "He never had power of any kind."

"He appears to be one now," Windsor said. "Or something resembling one."

"How is that even possible?" Cecily asked. "You can't just turn someone with no abilities into a Wielder."

Rogan spoke up. "Perhaps it is something he inherited from his father."

"That is a possibility," Windsor said. "We have little understanding of the powers the Imarans possess. Perhaps he had something within for Nihil to manipulate."

The thought was sickening. Her stomach tightened every time she thought of what they had done to him. "We have to get that implant out of him," Cecily said.

Windsor sighed. "I agree with you. We tried with our previous captive. I don't know if we could take it out without killing him. And to be honest, I'm concerned about unchaining Daro, even to turn him over. The Serum Shapers had a difficult time sedating him enough to get him where he is now. If we try to remove that implant, I can't predict what he'll do." He turned to look Cecily in the eyes. "I fear the man is broken beyond repair."

"I respect your concern, Paragon, but I won't give up." She closed her eyes and took a deep breath. "I'm going in again."

"Very well," Windsor said and turned. His deep blue robes swished across the floor as he walked back to his study.

Rogan laid a hand on her arm. "Be careful. I know you look at him and see Daro, but the man in there isn't your husband. I hope Daro is still in there somewhere, but right now, he's dangerous. I don't like you going in there alone."

"I know," she said as she met Rogan's eyes. "But I have to keep trying."

Rogan unlocked the door and she stepped in, listening for the click of the lock behind her. The sunstones pulled at her power, leaving her feeling heavy and lethargic, like she'd had a big meal and too much wine. She sat down in the plain wooden chair and pulled it as close to Daro as she dared.

He lay sprawled on a thick carpet on the floor, his black clothes smudged with dirt and dust. His hair spilled out around his head and his jaw was set, his teeth clenched. Seeing her husband in chains was horrifying, but it was his eyes that made her heart pound and her stomach flutter. The multicolored swirl was unnatural and difficult to look at. She remembered them shining brightly when she had faced him in Wesfell, and in the tunnel where they'd captured him. Now they were dull, the colors muted and weak.

He stared at the ceiling and appeared to ignore her. The muscles in his jaw stood out and his breathing was even; his chest rose and fell in a slow rhythm. In a way it was an improvement over his first day in the cell. He had raged against his chains, snarling and shouting like a wild animal. She had called out his name, begged him to stop, sobbed as she watched him rail. If he had heard her voice then, he'd given no sign of recognition, nor did he now.

His newfound calm grew unnerving. She sat and watched him for a while, looking him up and down, and wondered what was going to become of him.

"This isn't how I imagined things," she said, her quiet voice cutting the silence. "We spent all that time trying to find you, but none of it has gone how I planned." Her hands began to tremble and her voice shook. "I was supposed to come charging in, all our friends at my side, cutting a path to your prison. We were supposed to be unstoppable, the companions together again. Rogan with his sword drawn, ready to throw fire. Alastair, reluctant as he may be to fight these days, would be there to fight for you. Serv would stick the feet of his unsuspecting foes to the floor while his sword cut them to ribbons. Griff would rush in, his axe cutting down everyone in his path. Sumara would dart through and jolt her enemies to send them sprawling. Callum would cover the whole place in a miasma of terror, sending half of them running for their lives. Mira would hang back, an arrow for everyone who ran. Even Edson would stand with us, charging in with his blade drawn."

She took another breath. "You would see me coming, and hope would give you strength. You'd pick up the sword of a fallen enemy and join us as we slayed everyone who was left. They would pay for what they had done to you and we'd leave no man alive." She sniffed and wiped the tears from her eyes. "When it was over, we would stand with our friends in triumph. You would wrap me in your arms and whisper in my ear how much you loved me." She shuddered and choked, hardly able to get the words out. "We would cry together and you'd refuse to let go of me for days."

Tears streamed down her cheeks. She let them fall. Daro stared at the ceiling, the tendons in his neck standing out. "But this," she continued, her voice barely above a whisper. "This was not how it was supposed to happen. I was supposed to get you back. But I still don't know where you are. And the worst part is, I have no idea where to look." She wiped the dripping tears from her cheek. "I thought you were hard to find before. Now I don't even know where to begin."

She paused, and her breath came in shaky gasps. She wiped her eyes again. "Daro, you have to help me. You have to give me something, some sign you're still in there. Because right now, I don't know who you are. You're just a man who looks an awful lot like my husband."

The tears came again and despair churned in her belly. "You have to fight this. You have to fight to get out. I don't know what they did to you. I don't know what you've been through. But I know that I can't fix this for you. I will try to reach you, until the end of my days if that is what it takes, but I'm out here, banging against a glass wall that won't break."

She took another shuddering breath. "Please, Daro. You have to be in there somewhere. You have to keep fighting."

"I can't." His voice scraped from his throat, like a knife across burnt bread.

Cecily gasped and her heart lurched. Leaning forward, she searched his face. "Yes, yes, you can. I know you're in there. Just keep coming, keep trying. Please, Daro." Her heart beat fast and her body thrilled with hope.

Scooting forward off the front of her chair, she crouched down low. She lifted a trembling hand and reached for Daro. His hands were balled up in tight fists and she sent her fingers out, daring to brush his hand with hers.

He threw himself against his chains and let out a guttural growl from his throat. His face turned toward her with a snarl. Cecily sprang back and caught herself with her arms behind her. His breathing was heavy and he pulled against his chains, lifting his head, as his body strained against his bonds. He laid his head back on the floor and took heaving breaths, his teeth clenched. His arms ripped up again and the chains clanked against the floor, before his eyes fixed on the ceiling and he lay still.

Cecily's mouth hung open as her heart pounded and she fought to keep the tears from flowing again. For that tiny moment, he had broken through. She knew that had been him; she just had to find a way to help him out of the prison that still caged him.

She stood and Reached for him with her Wielding Energy, letting it surround him. She spread it out and it drifted over him so she could feel the shape of his body underneath. She closed her eyes and Pushed, applying just the slightest touch of Pressure, and enveloped him in a soft caress. The sound of her heart echoed in her ears and she held her touch, squeezing him as if he was in her arms.

A little rivulet of energy traveled back along her Wield. Trailing up, it wove its way around her Reach, tentative like a new lover's hand. It stole into her and gave her a brush of Pressure as it passed through. It happened so quickly, she was almost uncertain she had felt it.

She opened her eyes. Daro lay still, his eyes still locked on the ceiling. It wasn't much, but it was something. She sat in the chair and settled herself in. Leaning back, she crossed her feet at the ankles and laid her hands in her lap. He was in there somewhere, and she would stay with him for as long as it took to find his way out.

Daro flinched as the silence of his refuge broke. The walls he had built were thick; they kept the voices outside where they couldn't touch him. He knew there was chaos out there, a swirling vortex of terrifying power. Outside, he had no control. The pieces of his mind would rip apart, torn away like red and brown leaves in an autumn windstorm. He crouched down and clutched at the pieces of himself, trying to hold them together.

A sensation drifted in and pressed at him, insistent but gentle. It wasn't fear, or pain. It was familiar, a voice that promised relief. A serene tendril of energy curled around him and wrapped him in a subtle embrace. Something had gone missing, leaving a gaping wound inside. The tendril filled it and began to piece it back together. The walls of his refuge held steady, but a slow fissure split across the roof, like crack in the ice of a frozen lake.

## 43 : TO WHATEVER END

A LOW RUMBLE WORKED its way into Cecily's consciousness and her eyes fluttered open. Daro lay on the floor, his eyes closed, the shackles spreading his arms wide. She sat up and stretched, her back sore from sitting on the hard chair. She must have fallen asleep. Boom. It was faint and distant. *Maybe a storm?*

She stood and looked around the room. It didn't sound like thunder. She glanced down at Daro and his eyes flew open. She startled and stepped away. He lay still, his eyes wide open and locked on the ceiling.

She decided to find out what was going on outside. Callum answered her knock and let her out. As she stood in the open foyer, a refreshing rush of energy radiated through her. The sunstones were saturated with Daro's seemingly endless well of energy, but they still pulled at her and left her feeling weak and tired. No wonder she had fallen asleep.

"What's going on? Is it a storm?" she asked.

Callum shrugged. "Could be. It's been raining all day."

"I feel like I've been shut away for days," Cecily said as she rubbed her eyes. "Anything new out here?"

"Rogan and Alastair have been in the Paragon's study for a while. It sounds like they rounded up some of the riverboat Wielders to divert storm water and flood the tunnels we found. I haven't heard if anyone got out."

"I don't think we'll be so lucky as to drown Nihil like a rat. But it is a satisfying thought."

Callum smiled, one side of his mouth curling up, and he raised his eyebrows. "It is, isn't it? In any case, the Paragon and Rogan have this place locked down like a vault. They cleared the library completely and the students are in their dormitories. Rogan brought a contingent of his own guard, and the Lyceum Guard are on full alert." He leaned in and lowered his voice. "I have some of my own men out there too. One can't be too careful."

The foyer of the top floor wound around the circumference of the building, a chest-high wall circling the interior. Rooms and offices were spaced around the outside, their windows facing the Lyceum grounds. Alcoves were interspersed between the rooms, with cushioned benches and outward facing windows. The foyer was dotted with beautifully polished tables and ornately cushioned seating, a place the highest ranking Magisters used at their leisure. Cecily and her friends had taken over the top floor, sleeping on the benches and lounging in the chairs. Guards were posted near the stairwell and several more stood at the doors to the Paragon's study.

Sumara got up from her perch on an upholstered bench. "I'm not sure I like the sound of that," she said and glanced up at the dome as another boom echoed through the building.

Edson wandered over, followed closely by Griff and Serv. Edson jerked at the next crack of sound and grabbed the hilt of his sword. "What's going on out there?"

"Thunder?" Griff asked.

A loud blast reverberated through the building. "That's not thunder," Serv said.

Rogan and Alastair emerged from the Paragon's office, Windsor close behind. A messenger burst through the door from the stairs and stopped to speak with the Paragon as Rogan and Alastair stood close.

Merrick and Mira trotted over, circling around the inside of the round foyer. "We're under attack," Merrick said.

"Someone is coming toward the library, and they're cutting through the guards like they're children," Mira said.

"Nihil," Cecily breathed. She wondered how many of those aberrant Wielders he had.

Rogan and Alastair hurried over. "Nihil is attacking," Rogan said. "Reports from below indicate he has a small force of men, but the guards haven't been able to hold them back."

"It doesn't matter that his force is small," Cecily said. "We know how powerful they are." She flinched as a loud boom echoed through the dome and the building shuddered. "We need to call up the guards from the lower levels. Once Nihil gets in, the guards downstairs won't be able to hold them back. We can make a stand here with a larger force."

Rogan nodded to Alastair, who ran to relay the order.

"Should we barricade the door?" Griff asked, pointing to the furniture placed around the foyer.

"No," Cecily said. "Barricade or no, they'll get through. Turn the furniture over to give us cover." The building shook and another loud boom sounded from below. Guards poured in from the stairwell on the far side of the foyer. "Station the archers around the railing on this side. They can fire at the door once they come in. And be careful of fire. Nihil's Wielders might try to light this place up like a torch." She cringed inside at the thought of all those books on the floors below.

"Merrick and Mira, take opposite sides," she continued. "Stay back and make every shot count. Sumara, don't hesitate to strike Nihil if you get a clear shot; give him everything you have. Otherwise, aim for the others and don't expend everything at once. And find yourself a weapon."

Sumara smiled and patted her hip. "I'm not without protection."

"Griff," she said as she looked up at the big man's eyes. "Charge in after the archers get off a few rounds. But don't forget, these aren't thieves and mercenaries. They've almost killed us more than once, and we've only faced a few of them. Don't get in over your head."

Griff smiled and lugged his axe onto his shoulder. "I look forward to removing some heads."

She turned to Serv and he pursed his lips in a small smile. "Just, be careful," she said. "And look out for Edson."

Serv nodded and Edson rested his hand on the hilt of his sword.

"If defending the library doesn't get you entrance into the Lyceum, I don't know what will," she said to Edson. "Rogan, with all due respect, you have to keep yourself out of the line of fire." She looked up at her king. "Halthas can't afford to lose a king tonight. Stay behind your guards and don't try to do anything heroic."

Rogan smiled with narrowed eyes. "Yes, sir."

Callum clasped his hands and turned his fingers inside out, cracking his knuckles. "I have some new tricks I've been dying to try out," he said, his voice flippant. "Of course, if I have anything to say about it, I won't be the one doing the dying."

Another boom crashed below. They'd be inside the library soon. "I know I brought you all into this," she said as she looked around at her friends. "This didn't have to be your fight." Boom, the building shook. "He's just one man, and I shouldn't have expected you to put yourselves in danger for him. But you did. Whatever happens, I want you all to know, I could never repay you for what you've done for us." She glanced back at the door to his cell. "And if they're coming for Daro, you can be damned sure they aren't getting him."

The companions began to spread out to take up their positions, turning over furniture to provide cover. Serv hung back and pulled out a narrow sword. The blade was fairly short, with the slight curve of Serv's own weapon. He held it out horizontally, placed the hilt in one hand, and rested the end of the blade on his other palm. "You might need this," he said and held it out to her.

Cecily smiled and grabbed the hilt. She swung it a few times, getting a feel for the weapon. She was certainly no expert swordswoman, but Daro had taught her to use a blade. "I could have used one of these a few times over the last few months," she said. "Thank you."

Serv nodded, put his hand to his chest, and gave her a shallow bow.

Cecily walked over to the railing and crouched down behind the half wall, away from the door to the stairs. She had a clear view of Daro's cell but didn't want to lead Nihil or his men straight to him. Her heart thumped with anticipation, an all-too-familiar feeling of the inevitable crashing toward her. She closed her eyes and took a deep breath. The coming battle filled her with apprehension, but she owned it and let determination rise to swallow her fear.

A great crash resonated from below, the sound of splintering wood and scraping metal echoing up into the dome. They were inside. Cecily waited, forcing herself to breathe slowly, and listened to the sounds of the guards left below mounting their defense. Metal clashed on metal, explosions rang out and men shouted orders, the noise drifting up from the lower levels. She wondered if Pathius was with them. Would he fight against her this time?

The din grew louder as the battle ranged up the stairs, climbing from level to level. Cecily glanced over at Callum. He smirked and gave her a wink. Shouting rang out and the noise grew, the pounding of feet on the stairs. Something hit the stairwell door, a loud bang that made Cecily blink. Another crash, and the door flew off its hinges and toppled to the floor. Cecily kept her back to the half wall and rose from her crouch, just enough to turn her head over her shoulder and see the door.

A blast of dust clouded the doorway. Men in masks, dressed in black from head to toe, burst onto the foyer and spread out quickly. The archers struck, sending a volley of arrows at the men coming in through the door. One of the masked men lifted a hand and some of the arrows burst into flames before they cleared the opening in the center of the foyer. The rest clattered against a wall that suddenly sprang up, dissipating as the arrows hit.

Behind the disappearing wall, one of the masked figures held out her hands and two shining blades shimmered into existence. *Damn, Isley is still alive.* Another circled around her, his black clothes obscured by stones, fitted together like armor around his body. An arrow bounced off the stone at his shoulder and he turned, his heavy stride making the floor shake.

Cecily waited as more arrows flew. She kept the sword clutched in one hand and glanced back at the door. *Are you here, or did you send your lackeys to do all the work for you?* She wanted Nihil.

A woman walked through the door, her face bare, dark blond hair pulled back in a low ponytail. She fell back to one side and lifted her hand to her chest to clutch something that hung from her neck. Her gaze swept the foyer and she called out, barking orders at the masked Wielders, and pointed with her other hand. One of the masked men stood in front of her, as if to shield her from attack.

Lightning bolts shot across the foyer, and the loud crack shocked Cecily's ears. One of the bolts hit a masked man in the shoulder and sent his upper body reeling backward. He righted himself and shook it off, rolling his shoulder and continuing into the foyer. Another bolt shot by and left a black streak on the wall.

The arrows continued, slicing through the air with a swish, bows twanging. Mira's arrows curved, darting up and down, only to be batted out of the air or bounce uselessly off the stone man. Another arrow shot toward Isley but she blocked it with a shield and the arrow clattered to the floor.

Two more men emerged from the doorway. One was masked like the others, but he wore a winding chain around his body that covered him like armor. It moved, coiling around him like a snake, the ends dripping from his hands like a living thing. He twirled the ends and swung them around in a wide circle as he stalked into the foyer. Behind him came a man with a bare face, clean shaven with short dark hair, peppered with gray. He wore long black robes, much like a Magister of the Lyceum. *That's him.*

Cecily Reached, a crushing grasp that headed for his throat. She felt her Wield take hold and she gripped, trying to use Pressure to seize his neck. A shimmer in the air appeared in front of him and her Wield dissipated. The Pressure bounced back and flung her arm away. She stared. She'd never encountered such a force before.

Nihil looked around, his head moving from side to side. Sumara's lightning strike shot toward him, but it hit the shimmering air and the jolts of electricity buzzed off in a cascade of sparks. Cecily Reached for him again, but it was like hitting solid stone. Her Wield couldn't get through.

The arrows diminished and she could hear the ring of swords being drawn behind her. Sumara stayed low and peeked out of her hiding spot while she recharged. Mira fell back, still raining arrows on the masked men. A few of them scored hits, but no one went down. The man with the stone armor charged across the foyer, knocking guards to the side. Griff ran forward and closed with him. His great axe clashed against the stones, sparks flying as it hit.

The man covered in chains darted forward but Serv reached out and stuck his feet, rooting them to the floor. The chain man pulled, trying to free his legs as his eyes darted around. As Serv approached, he roared and swung the chains in his hands. Serv blocked the first swing and the metal rang out against Serv's blade. Serv turned and struck again. His sword bounced off the chain as it coiled around the man's chest, moving to fill in the gaps.

Cecily looked across the foyer and saw another masked man, pulling back an arrow in his bow. *I know you.* It was the Sensor. She Reached for his bow and Pushed up on the bottom. His arrow flew up into the dome and arched down to fall harmlessly through the center to the marble tiles below. His head whipped around and Cecily ducked, her heart beating fast. She peeked over the ledge and saw him searching, another arrow nocked, the string pulled back. She focused on the bowstring and Pulled, then heard him yell as his arrow dropped to the floor.

The din grew louder as guardsmen from the Lyceum and the palace rushed in to fight Nihil's Wielders. Cecily hit the Sensor with Pressure again, this time aiming for his knees. She snaked her energy around his joints and squeezed with a slam of Pressure. He cried out and stumbled as he looked up and met her eyes. She Pressed harder but he knocked her back with the power of his own Push.

Callum was nearby, hiding behind an upturned bench. He peeked out over the top, his eyes focused on Isley. Cecily felt the brush of his Projection as it wafted by like a breeze through an open window. It skimmed against her outermost layer of consciousness, a deep ambivalence, thick with indecision and uncertainty. Woven throughout the Projection was a sizzle of fear, making the hair on the back of Cecily's neck stand on end. Isley stopped and looked down at her hands. Her head turned as if she suddenly couldn't remember why she was there.

Cecily looked up to find the Sensor rushing toward her. She grasped Serv's sword and shot to her feet. The Sensor no longer had his bow. He held a curved blade, slightly shorter than Cecily's and thicker at the tip, with a jagged point at the end. His multicolored eyes narrowed as he stalked around her, blinking as another jolt of lightning flashed. The sound of Serv's sword clashing with chain rang in Cecily's ears and Rogan's voice shouting orders cut through the din.

The Sensor darted in and struck with his blade. She felt the distinct Push of a Pressure Wield against her wrist. She Pushed back, dislodged the grip of his energy, and struck with her sword. He blocked, and the metal clashed with a sharp ring. She felt another hit of Pressure against her leg but she Pushed back. The Pressure dropped and she blocked his sword strike as she Reached out to hit him with a Push to the chest. He stumbled backward and his eyes narrowed.

Out of the corner of her eye, she could see Griff across the foyer, still locked in combat with the stone armored man. Mira had circled around closer to Cecily and fired arrows into the melee. Cecily worried she must be running out. The Sensor struck again and she grabbed his sword arm with Pressure, trying to hit the right pressure points to make him lose his grip. He shook her off and slammed her with a Push that sent her stumbling backward. She got back to her feet and added a Push to her sword to block his next strike.

The sound of a woman's voice shouting orders reached Cecily's ears. She blocked the Sensor's next strike and turned her wrist to whip his sword around as they clashed. A loud boom rang out behind her. She saw Callum dart from his hiding place and run to crouch behind the half wall in the center of the foyer. As he dashed by, the glint of metal appeared in his hands. He'd lifted a dagger off the Sensor. She'd have to thank him for that later.

Another crash pounded behind her. She Reached for the Sensor's throat but it was hard to get a grip when he was moving. She Pushed, heaving him away with all her strength. He staggered backward and nearly dropped his blade.

Cecily glanced over her shoulder and her heart lurched. Daro had broken the door of his cell wide open. The door hung loose on its hinges, half broken and crooked. His hair hung wild around his face and his eyes glowed bright, shining and terrifying. The remains of his shackles still hung from his wrists, the heavy chains snapped into jagged shards of metal, the absorption collar broken at his feet. His shoulders heaved with his breath and his teeth were clenched as his gaze swung around at the battle.

Daro clutched at the walls of the vessel he had created in his mind. He tried to shut out the chaos but he was tossed about on the waves of a storm. He felt like a caged animal, cornered and deeply threatened. Cracks ran across the roof of his stronghold, jagged lines of blinding light. Something on the outside had tried to get in, to reach him in his refuge, but the voices and the torrent of energy threatened to unmake him.

He railed against the confusion. Something pounded on the walls and surged through the emptiness, shock and pain determined to break in. He didn't know where he was or what was happening on the outside, and he shrank away from the breach, desperate to keep his mind intact.

Cecily whipped her head between Daro and the Sensor, unsure of what to do. She didn't know if Daro would attack, nor who would be the object of his rage. The Sensor shot forward and Cecily had to duck to keep from getting sliced open. She thrust her blade at him, Reached for his arms, and Pulled, trying to give herself an opening. He Pushed back and she lost her grip as his blade turned hers away. Her eyes darted to Daro. He stood still and breathed heavily, as his gaze roved over the foyer.

She closed with the Sensor again, their blades clashing as they Reached for each other with Pressure. She spun around, blocking another strike, and saw Rogan and Alastair, trying to get to Nihil. Paragon Windsor stood against a wall, surrounded by his guard, and fired jolts of lightning. The bolts hit the shimmer around Nihil and dissipated, the shafts of electricity snaking off as they traveled along the surface of the Shield.

The noise of the battle pounded in her ears and her arm burned with the effort of swinging her sword. Daro still stood outside the cell door. The sound of the woman's voice rose over the clamor and Daro's head whipped in her direction.

"Fourteen," she called. Cecily glanced at her. She'd moved around to the other side of the foyer and now stood almost directly across from Cecily. One of the masked men still stood in front of her, deflecting any attackers who got close. "Fourteen, you will attack them. That is an order." Her voice carried over the rest of the fighting and Daro recoiled. He stepped backward and glanced toward Cecily.

"Daro!" Cecily yelled, her voice giving out as she clashed with the Sensor. Daro gripped his head and doubled over. He cried out as if suddenly in pain.

Daro's body flooded with agony. It surged through his head, down his back, and into his limbs. He huddled down in his boat and tried to block out the pain. It seeped in through the walls and threatened to let the chaos in. His vessel rose and fell in the turmoil and the voices called to him. It was madness outside.

Orders. If he could just follow orders, the pain would stop. He should stand up and heed Sindre's command. Another voice warred for his attention, familiar and safe. As it called to him, it cut past the pain and leaked in through the walls, deep into his consciousness.

Cecily backed into an upturned chair and almost lost her footing. She threw a Push at the Sensor to give her enough time to recover. Movement caught her attention. Someone was coming at her from the other direction. She flicked her gaze to the side to see Nihil striding toward her through a gap in the fighting. His black robes drifted back, his unnerving eyes intense.

He held up his hand toward the Sensor. "This one is mine." His eyes moved back to Cecily. "You have been exceedingly difficult to kill. If I had seen to it myself in the very beginning, perhaps we could have avoided all this unpleasantness."

Cecily swung her blade and Reached for him with her Wield. Her Energy hit the shimmering wall, his Shield too thick to penetrate. Her blade smashed into his Shield as if she'd struck solid rock, and the recoil sent her arm flying backward. Her sword flew from her hand and dropped to the ground.

She lurched back to her feet and looked toward Daro. He stood upright and clutched his head. "Daro, please!" Cecily called. The woman yelled, repeating the number "fourteen," and Daro doubled over again, his voice a loud roar. Griff still battled the man covered in stone and the bodies of guardsmen littered the floor.

Nihil took two quick steps toward her. She held up her hand to Wield, but he reached out and grabbed her wrist. His grip felt like a hot wire wrapped around her arm. Something inside her began to twist, as if he plunged a dagger into her gut and wrenched it around. Her mouth dropped open and she tried to cry out, but the twisting ripped her voice from her throat. Her eyes shot down to her belly but here was nothing there. The feeling spread, spilling out into her chest and down her legs. She gasped for breath, her lungs caught in a crush she couldn't see. Nihil's teeth clenched and his eyes were wide. She felt the energy inside her, the source of her Wielding power writhing and cracking, as if Nihil grasped it and tore it apart.

Tears blurred her vision and she tried to dislodge his hand from her arm. She could barely move. He pulled her arm higher and the feeling intensified. Her Wielding Energy ripped like a piece of fabric. Her head lurched back and she cried out, calling for Daro. Her body felt as if it would break under the strain. "Daro!"

Another voice cut across the battle, but she couldn't understand the words. Nihil's grip relaxed and the tearing stopped. She turned her head to see two more men, both dressed in black. One wore a mask, but the other's face was bare. Long, pale blond hair streaked back from his face. *Pathius.*

The sight of him sent a thrill through her but she recoiled at the burst of emotion. Pathius ran toward them and a sheen of frost spread from each footfall. Nihil let go of her wrist and she collapsed to the floor, her legs unable to hold her weight.

Pathius slammed into Nihil's Shield with his hands and pushed against it with his palms open. Nihil stood still in the center, the air shimmering around him. "You're a fool, Number One," he said. "You were always a fool."

"That isn't my name," Pathius said through gritted teeth. His arms were spread wide, his palms pressed into the Shield. Frost sparkled in the air around him and Cecily's breath misted out in a fog.

"You don't have a name because you never deserved the one you had. You were weak. I made you what you are. Without me, you'd be nothing but a disappointment."

Pathius roared, his face contorted with rage as he shoved against Nihil's Shield.

Cecily got back to her feet on shaky legs and felt her strength returning. She turned her head back to Daro. He doubled over, his arms wrapped around his body. His face turned toward her, his lips curled back in a snarl, his eyes squeezed shut.

"Cecily!" Callum's voice rang out and she turned to see the Sensor bearing down on her. She threw herself to the side, and the Sensor's blade whipped past her ear. She rolled to the ground and picked up a sword. It wasn't hers. It felt heavy in her hands but she held it up as a surge of adrenaline poured through her.

"Daro!" she called as she blocked the Sensor's strike, holding the heavy sword with two hands. Their swords clanged. "Daro, you can't give in to them." Block, thrust. "Your name is Daro and you are a son of Imara." Turn, strike, sidestep. Daro clutched his head. "If they thought they could own you, they were wrong." Clash, block. The woman yelled something else at Daro and lightning flashed behind her. "They don't own you. Nobody owns you." Spin, block. "You have to come back, Daro. You have to fight." The woman yelled again and Daro cried out. Pathius beat against Nihil's shield and the Sensor struck at her again.

Cecily felt the brush of Callum's Empathy, and the Sensor blinked his eyes, hesitating. She struck again, hitting him with a Wield of Pressure, and he stepped backward. "I love you, Daro," she cried out. "I love you and I know you are still in there." She struck at the Sensor again, gripping his wrist with Pressure to send his next swing wide. "They thought they could break you, but they were wrong." She spun and her sword clashed, the hit reverberating through her exhausted limbs.

Recognition flashed through Daro like a spark. He knew that voice. It slipped through and poured over him, drenching him with warmth. Another crack tore across the roof of his vessel. The voices screamed at him, threatened to tear him apart. His body was saturated with energy; it pulsed through him like a tempest.

He turned toward the crack and tore the breach open. The way out was thick with pain and confusion but a steady hand reached for him. He stood and held out his own hand, but wavered, shrinking back from the chaos outside. The sound of his heartbeat echoed through his mind as he fought against the turmoil.

The Sensor grabbed Cecily's arm with Pressure and she stumbled. She tried to block his thrust but his blade sliced across the outside of her ribs and cut deep into her flesh. She screamed as the pain seared through her and she stumbled backward, grabbing her side with one arm. Anger raged through her and she gripped the Sensor's arm with Pressure. She threw his arm wide and thrust the sword through his chest. His eyes shot open and he staggered backward. She let go of the sword, leaving it sticking out of his body, as blood leaked out onto his black clothes. He looked down at the sword, his hands moving as if to grab it, his eyes wide in his masked face. He fell to his knees and slumped to the ground, the sword sticking out through his back.

Cecily clutched her ribs and staggered, trying to get her back to the wall. She backed into an upturned bench and lowered herself to the floor. She pressed her hand against the wound and felt blood leaking from her side. The noise of the battle was muted, as if she covered her ears with her hands. Time slowed as she looked around the foyer, everyone seeming to move as if caught in thick sap. Serv still fought the man in chains, his sword caught in a coil of metal. Rogan had Alastair at his side, but one of Nihil's men closed in on them. Cecily blinked again. Mira and Merrick fought back to back as two men pressed close. Edson stood over Sumara, his sword hefted in front of him. Sumara sat on the ground and reached around his leg, lightning building in her hand, as a masked figure ran to attack. Callum stood nearby, his hand raised as he sent another Projection across the foyer, blood dripping from the dagger in his other hand. Griff flew backward as a hit from the stone man sent him flying. Pathius raged against Nihil, the shimmering shield starting to blacken at the bottom like the edge of burning paper.

The world sped up and sound came rushing back. Daro roared in pain, hunched down on his knees. The woman yelled, her face contorted with fury, as she clutched a medallion that hung from her neck.

Cecily winced as she pushed at her wound to stop the bleeding. Vision blurring, she clenched her teeth and groaned. Daro clutched his head and chaos spun around her, the sounds of battle rushing by. *We aren't going to win.*

She blinked her eyes open and let calm resignation settle over her. Leaning her head back against the bench, she turned toward her husband. The clamor of the battle fell away and she called out to Daro, her voice weakening with every word. "*Mynas feorh signede ewoer cweoan mynas son.* My soul sings and yours answers my song. *Aet-samne wea a-feagen.* Together we become one. *Ge-treowsian o arian ealdor be-innan eowa.* I pledge to honor the life within you. *An-standan neah eower siid.* And stand by your side. *O aeg-hwaet endian.*" She took a shuddering breath. "To whatever end."

Something stirred inside Daro, like a piece of frayed rope winding itself back together. He shot his hand upward and grabbed onto the lifeline of Cecily's hand. He pushed the walls of his refuge away, and they dissipated into mist. Cecily's presence filled him through their bond, a deep well of peace and stability. His soul reached out to hers and their energy intertwined. It circled and twisted as the tendrils of their spirits connected, restoring their fractured bond.

His mind was clear. He pushed himself up to one knee and wiped the dribble of blood from his nose. The pain fell away as he blinked his eyes back into focus and rose to his feet. Sindre's jolt of pain shot down his back, but he let it wash over him. He swung his gaze to Sindre and met her eyes. Her lips drew back over clenched teeth and she shouted something at him as another spasm of pain shot through his body.

*No.*

He reached back and dug into the back of his neck around his implant. His body surged with power as he wedged his fingers beneath the stone. The blinding pain nearly brought him to his knees. He cried out, letting his voice rip from his throat in a roar. He clung to the strength of his bond and pushed away the torment as he pulled the stone from his flesh. Blood trickled down his back as held it, a pale, diamond-shaped shard. He squeezed his hand to crush it and shook the blood-soaked fragments to the floor.

His gaze swung to Sindre and she gaped at him, silent. He rushed toward her and reached out to grab her medallion. He wedged it out of her hand and her arms fell away, her eyes wide. He pulled her face close to his, his hand tight on her medallion. He felt her connection to the stone, a coiling line of Wielding Energy flowing into her. He seized it and poured everything into her: his pain, the torment of the victims forced into him through the Arcstone, the chaos and suffering of his ordeal. As he thrust his agony in, her jaw dropped open and her eyes bulged. A high-pitched scream crawled from her mouth, starting low and building as Daro held her. Blood ran from her nose and leaked out the corners of her eyes as her scream turned into a noiseless wail.

Her body slumped to the ground and the chain broke off in Daro's hand. He stood over her and watched her body as it twitched and shuddered, until she finally fell still. He looked down at the medallion in his hand and closed his grip, then squeezed and crushed it to powder. He opened his fist and let the remains pour out over Sindre's body in a cloud of dust and chips of rock.

Cecily realized she'd been holding her breath and exhaled. The masked Wielders all backed away, looking around at each other. A weapon crashed to the ground behind her. Cecily took another breath and the masked figures all turned and ran for the door, disappearing down the dark staircase.

"No!" Nihil yelled. Pathius still stood in front of him, pressing into the Shield. The edges looked withered and black. "Get back here! You can't run!" Nihil's lips curled back over his teeth and his eyes were wild. "You're mine!"

Pathius flung himself against Nihil's Shield, and his primal shout cut through the stunned silence of the foyer. Daro ran to him, the broken manacles still hanging from his wrists. He reached his arms out wide and slammed into the Shield with his fists. Cecily could see sparks of energy shooting out across the surface of the Shield and Nihil stumbled backward. Pathius and Daro pressed in, attacking the Shield with fury. Pathius gripped it, as snapping ice spread around his feet, the air heavy with sparkling frost. Daro beat against it again, slamming his hands into the Shield. Cracks snaked out across the surface and Nihil shouted something unintelligible. Daro hit it again and the Shield exploded like glass, ripping across the foyer in a burst of energy. Nihil flew backward and hit the ground with a loud thud. Daro stumbled away with the force of the blast.

Pathius lurched forward, grabbed Nihil by the throat, and hauled him to his feet. Blood dripped from Nihil's mouth. "You made me what I am," Pathius said, his voice a growl, "but you don't own me. This ends here."

Nihil's mouth hung open and his eyes goggled as Pathius gripped his throat. He clenched his teeth and scraped at Pathius's arms but Pathius held fast. Nihil's skin turned gray, his cheeks sunk in, and his body withered. His neck turned blue and frost crackled and spread out from his throat, turning his face to ice. Pathius's shoulders heaved and he held Nihil's body as the ice spread down to his fingertips. He let go and the body dropped, as stiff as if it had been cut from stone.

Cecily struggled to her feet and gripped her ribs. Serv sheathed his sword and rushed to her, limping as he ran. Callum stepped forward to stand at her other side. Edson helped Sumara to her feet and Merrick ran over to help Griff. Rogan hovered near the Paragon and Alastair still held out his sword. Mira had a cut across her cheek and held one arm tight to her body. They all looked around at each other, their eyes coming to rest on Cecily.

She looked over at Daro. He stared down at Nihil's body, Pathius at his side. Pathius looked up, and his gaze moved around the room. He brushed the hair from his face and turned to Daro. Their eyes met for a brief moment, and then Pathius turned to lock eyes with Cecily. The muscles in his face twitched like a spasm of pain and he closed his eyes before turning away. He walked across the foyer and disappeared through the door.

Alastair and Rogan both stepped forward and the Paragon started to shout an order, but Daro held up his hand. "No." All eyes swung to him and he shook his head. "Let him go."

Cecily turned toward Daro and met his eyes. They still swirled with unnatural color, but recognition was plain on his face. She walked toward him, still holding her ribs, the pain all but forgotten. He stepped toward her and they stopped, facing each other. Tears sprang to her eyes and she took a shuddering breath as he reached out to brush her face with his fingers. He cupped her cheek and she pressed her palm into the back of his warm hand. Her chest felt full, as if she might burst. She closed her eyes and tears trailed down her face. He wrapped a trembling hand gently behind her head and led her into his embrace. She leaned into his chest and felt his strong arms envelop her. She tucked her arms in and let herself collapse against him as they sank down to their knees. His warmth poured through her and she shuddered with a quiet sob.

"I love you," he whispered, his mouth close to her ear.

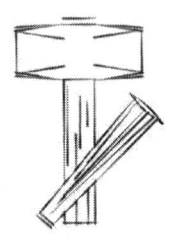

## 44 : AFTERMATH

THE WIND BLEW THROUGH Daro's hair, chill against his skin. He stood on the dock outside the *Lady Violet*, the riverboat's huge wheel rising high into the air. The wide river ran by, flowing into the midst of the city on its way out to sea. Gray clouds hung heavy in the sky, threatening snow, judging by the cold bite in the air.

Cecily stood on the dock just ahead, speaking with Callum and the riverboat captain. She wore a burgundy cloak, stitched with a pattern of dark swirls and lined with black fur. The hood lay down her back and her dark hair hung in a loose braid, tendrils blowing around her face in the wind. She spoke to the captain, nodding and gesturing, as she finalized the arrangements for their voyage to East Haven. The captain smiled, put his hand to his chest, and bowed before he walked away up the gangplank to board his ship.

Daro's memories were gradually returning, coalescing into recognition. He remembered his abduction and the early weeks of his captivity with vivid clarity. Most of it he wished he could forget. He knew he had spent months locked in Nihil's compound and recalled what they had done to him. His neck twitched as he thought of Sindre and her medallion, Nihil's cold eyes, the feel of the Arcstone under his hands.

His later memories grew muddled, hazy as if seen through an opaque piece of glass. He recalled destroying the watchtower, the thrill of strength as he unleashed his power. He closed his eyes as he thought of the blood of those innocent men, spilled by his hand. His sessions with the Arcstone blurred in a haze of violation, the feeling of other men's energy rending through him and defiling his soul. Nihil's experiments had pushed him past his limits. He remembered feeling as if he was caught in a storm at sea, the chaos raging around him. He'd closed himself off, buried his consciousness deep within the torrent, a desperate act of self-preservation.

He remembered the events leading up to the Lyceum, but it was difficult to distinguish which images were his and which belonged to the minds of the dead men Nihil had poured into him. He desperately wanted to believe he hadn't tried to kill Cecily, but deep down inside, he knew. He could still see her face, terrified and gasping. They hadn't spoken of it yet. Words of apology had lingered on his lips a hundred times over the last weeks, but he could never seem to get them out. How does a man apologize for trying to kill his wife? Her eyes told him he was already forgiven, but that only wrenched his guilt. He didn't know if he could forgive himself.

Griff, Serv, and Edson approached from the riverbank. They'd insisted on seeing them off. The others had said their goodbyes in the city over the last several days. Merrick had left first, saying he was anxious to get back to his cabin. Daro helped him load a horse with supplies to keep him stocked for the winter. Mira had suffered broken bones in one hand and would need time to heal before going back to her duties at the palace. Sumara had declared she needed a holiday and would be spending the next month in her patron's country manor outside Halthas.

"Well, my friend," Griff said as he clapped Daro on the back, "have a safe trip home."

He turned to them, marveling at their composure every time they saw his eyes. "I don't have the words to thank you," he said. He'd tried numerous times to express his gratitude to their companions, but words always fell short. "Not just for me, but for Cecily." He glanced over at his wife. "I can't imagine what she's been through. I'm so grateful you were there for her."

"It was our honor," Serv said and gave Daro a shallow bow.

Griff stood with his legs wide, his arms crossed over his broad chest. "We'll be heading east in a few months. We'll be sure to make it through Norgrost."

Cecily walked over to them, her pale cheeks blushing pink in the cold. "They're loading the last of their cargo and are almost ready to leave." She turned to Edson. "Are you certain you're ready for another adventure after all this?"

Edson smiled, a light stubble showing on his upper lip. "I don't know about adventures," he said, "but I'll be okay with them."

"Ha!" Griff said, bellowing a loud guffaw, "he'll be more than okay. Serv will make a swordsman of him yet. We have plenty of work to do. I suspect more than a few of our clients wonder where we've been. But don't worry, we'll have him back in time to hand him over to the Magisters. The Lyceum will get their turn with him next spring."

"The Paragon gave me my letter of acceptance himself," Edson said.

"I hoped I'd be able to help you with your admission," Cecily said. "But I didn't think it would be quite so dramatic."

The men each embraced Cecily in turn, and her eyes misted over with tears. Daro shook their hands, careful to keep his grasp gentle, lest he hurt them with his newfound strength. "Take care," he said as they walked away.

Callum hovered nearby. He sauntered over and brushed his hair from his eyes. "I suppose this is goodbye."

Cecily's mouth turned up in a warm smile. She opened her arms and Callum stepped in to embrace her. "Thank you again," she said, "for everything."

Callum lifted a crooked smile and shrugged. "What can I say? Even someone of my dubious heritage and questionable profession can do the right thing now and again."

"He doesn't give himself enough credit," Cecily said as she looked up at Daro. "We never would have found you without him."

"Well, I need to be off," Callum said and turned to head back to the riverbank. "My displays of valor must sadly come to an end. The Underground is in a bit of disarray at the moment, and I have to track down the rest of those Sahaaran smugglers."

"Will you be okay?" Cecily asked, her voice thick with concern.

Callum smiled as he flipped a coin into the air and caught it with deft fingers. "That I will. I've been through worse. Recently, in fact." He paused in front of Daro and leaned in, his voice low. "Be careful with her."

Daro met his eyes. He tried to sound confident. "I will."

Callum's gaze lingered for a brief moment, his eyes narrowed. He gave a quick nod and strolled off the dock. Daro knew the others must be wondering if he could be trusted. He wondered that himself.

"It's in your pocket," Callum called out over his shoulder.

Daro smiled as he reached into his pocket and pulled out Callum's coin. At least some things hadn't changed. Cecily put a hand on his arm and they turned to board the ship.

The sound of horses approached and they both turned back to the riverbank. Two Palace Guard reined in their horses. Rogan and Alastair pulled up behind them, followed by two more uniformed guardsmen on horseback. Alastair wore his doublet with the embroidered royal crest, looking tidy and official as ever. Rogan's circlet sat on his head, a heavy crimson cloak over his intricately embroidered beige doublet. He dismounted, pulled off his leather gloves, and reached out to grasp Daro's hand.

"You didn't think we would let you leave that easily?" Rogan said. He reached out to take Cecily's hand, lifted her fingers and placed his other hand on top. "I'm sad to see you go, Lady Cecily. I hope that all can be well between us."

Cecily covered his hand with hers. "Of course. Perhaps we'll see you next year when we visit."

Rogan smiled. "Yes, I think you will, barring any sweeping crises. It will be good to spend time with our companions." He turned back to Daro. "Are you certain you won't change your mind about staying? Those Wielders Nihil left behind are dangerous. We still don't know all they are capable of. I could use your help finding them." Daro opened his mouth to answer but Rogan put up a hand. "I know, you have been through a lot and I have no right to ask anything of you. You should go home. But do consider returning. I will always have a place for you and I know the Paragon would be beside himself if Cecily returned. Times have changed. This isn't Hadran's kingdom anymore."

"Thank you," Daro said. His head swam and he wished they could get on with their journey.

Alastair clasped his hand in turn. "It's good to have you back, my friend. I hope you won't stay away too long."

Daro nodded. His eyes began to twitch and he rubbed them, hoping no one noticed.

Cecily placed a hand on Daro's arm. Her touch was like a cool balm on his fevered skin. "Thank you for coming all the way down here to say goodbye," she said. "I'll send word once we're home."

The gangplank creaked under their feet as they boarded the *Lady Violet*. Cecily went aft to see to their cabin. Daro stayed on deck, enjoying the open air despite the cold. He hardly felt the chill in the air; the deep pool of energy within kept him warm. He hadn't even donned a cloak. The wound his implant had left behind itched and he reached up to scratch at his bandage.

Cecily came back to stand next to him and leaned her head on his arm. He placed his hands on the side of the boat, his breath coming out in a cloud, and savored the feeling of his wife at his side. A torrent of energy still ran through him, the voices called out, and his mind felt disorganized. But he took comfort in her, and the knowledge that she was taking him home.

## 45 : CHOICES

CECILY TUCKED HER SILVER necklace under her tunic as Daro wrapped her burgundy cloak around her shoulders and fastened the clasp at her throat. She brushed her hair back from her face and slipped her fingers into her supple leather gloves. They were in their room at the Float in East Haven, a cozy suite on the top floor with a four-poster bed topped with a soft handmade quilt.

"Where are you going?" Daro asked and touched his fingers to her cheek. His hands were warm.

"Probably to the bakery," she said. "I just need to get some fresh air."

He kissed the top of her head and smiled, then reached up to scratch the back of his neck. His eye twitched, and he blinked hard before rubbing it with his knuckle. He lay back on the bed and let his head drop onto the pillows. Cecily was growing accustomed to looking at his strange eyes, and they had spent long days at the Float, doing nothing but lying in each other's arms. She relished the feel of him, breathing in his familiar scent, and basked each night in the knowledge that he would be there, lying next to her when she awoke.

Their trip up the Bresne River had gone without incident. Daro had been quiet and kept away from the other passengers, but she could hardly blame him. They spent most of the trip locked away in their cabin and both looked forward to a brief stay at the Float before making the trip home. Their brief stay had lengthened, however. They'd been in East Haven for weeks.

Daro sucked in a quick breath and Cecily glanced over at him. "Are you sure you're okay?" she asked and picked up her small wicker basket.

He rubbed his hands down his face, but smiled. "Yes, I'm fine. I'll see you in a little while."

She left their room and made her way downstairs, through the common room and out onto the pier. A light snow fell, dusting the world with a brush of white. The river meandered lazily by, too deep and wide to succumb to ice, even in the dead of winter. She drew in a deep breath and let the cold air rush through her nose. The crisp, fresh air felt good, cold as it was. She was probably spending too much time shut up in their room.

She wandered down the street and kept her cloak wrapped tight around her shoulders. Her black boots kicked up the powdery snow as the chill air bit at her skin. The streets were almost empty; a few people scurried by, unwilling to loiter in the cold. Something tickled at her attention as she approached the bakery and she glanced over her shoulder. Two Imaran men stood outside a shop up the road. They wore thick hooded cloaks, but their tall stature and thick builds marked their heritage. She had seen them several times in recent days and couldn't get over the feeling that they were watching her. Shaking her head, she told herself it was just her imagination.

As she pulled open the door to the bakery, she savored the warm smell of freshly baked bread. She kicked the snow from her boots and smiled at the baker. His head was shiny bald and he wore an apron smudged with puffs of flour.

"Back again?" he said with a warm smile.

"My husband has grown rather fond of your apple tarts."

He wiped his hands on a towel. "He must have indeed. You are a good wife, braving the cold to come here for him."

Cecily shrugged. "They make him happy."

Since they'd left Halthas, Daro's moods had become unpredictable. He was often warm and affectionate, speaking to her in quiet tones and touching her with a gentle hand. But his mood could turn and he would drift into listlessness and distraction. He often woke in the night, covered in sweat and breathing hard. He wouldn't speak of his nightmares. The Paragon had urged them to remain in the city so the Lyceum's Serum Shapers could help him, but Daro had been adamant they go home. Cecily was beginning to wonder if they had made the right choice.

She paid the baker and tucked the tarts into her basket before heading back out into the cold. A few lonely snowflakes drifted from the clouds and the buildings were crusted with frost. Daro wouldn't mind if his pastries weren't hot, so she took her time, wandering through the shallow snow toward the river. Her cloak kept her warm enough and she thought the fresh air, and time alone, would do her some good.

There were benches by the river, surrounded by a stand of thick trees, just a short walk from the Float. She brushed off the dusting of snow and sat, tucking her cloak around her. She set her basket down, took a letter out of her pocket, and carefully unfolded it. The words were scrawled on crisp cream-colored paper, the letters smooth and precise.

>*Lady Cecily,*
>
>*Please accept my personal thanks for your role in stemming the tide of disaster that threatened the Lyceum and our fair city. The situation was rapidly deteriorating. Had you and your respected companions, along with our gracious sovereign, not stepped in, the damage from Nihil's attacks could have been far more extensive.*
>
>*I realize your relationship with our hallowed institution has been strained in the past. Under the former regime, you were expected to use your particular talents for nefarious purposes. As previously buried truths have come to light, I have realized your decision to leave the Lyceum of Power may not have been the flight of fancy of a lovestruck youth. I regret the rift that has formed between you and the Lyceum and I wish to extend the invitation to restore that relationship.*
>
>*You know better than anyone the danger Nihil's experiments pose to Halthas. He may be gone, but the Wielders he altered are at large, and this is a situation that is of grave concern to both the Lyceum and the Crown.*
>
>*I will also be forthright and tell you the Lyceum of Power was all but ruined by Nihil's assassins. They struck repeatedly and ruthlessly and we lost many good men and women. Thus far, we have managed to maintain the dignity of our institution to the public at large. The Magisters of the Lyceums of Vision, Stone, Blood, and Seed have all expressed their deep concern over this breach and there is a hole in our power that I cannot deny.*

*It is my hope that you will strongly consider returning to Halthas, when you are ready, and join us in rebuilding our honored establishment. I respect your need to withdraw to care for your husband as he recovers from his ordeal, but I implore you to consider a future here, at the Lyceum of Halthas.*

*With Respect,*

*Paragon Windsor*

She clutched the letter between her gloved fingers. She knew the Lyceum was in a difficult position and it was a relief to feel as if they were no longer her silent enemy. The Paragon's words tugged at her, calling forth images of a future she had thought impossible. *I implore you to consider a future here.* It was strange to imagine a different life, living in Halthas, working for the Lyceum. There was much that was tempting about the Paragon's offer, but it brought forth doubts as well. Would she have to live amongst high society, socialize with her family? Even if she wanted to go, would Daro agree?

Shivering, she picked up her basket and set it in her lap, letting the heat from the fresh pastries warm her. The tip of her nose burned with cold but she wasn't ready to go back to their room. She glanced down at the letter, and her thoughts drifted to Pathius. She could still see him as he stood over Nihil's body and looked at her as if he wished to speak. There had been such pain in his eyes.

She didn't understand why she felt anything for Pathius. When his father was still king, she had barely known him. He was the face of a future she didn't want, but wasn't sure how to escape. For years, she had believed him dead. If Nihil had done this much damage to Daro after months of captivity, what must he have done to Pathius over the course of those years? She shuddered at the thought.

The idea of Nihil's Wielders wandering through the kingdom was enormously troubling. Rogan and the Paragon were actively searching them out, but she didn't know if they were having any success. She tried to tell herself it wasn't their fight. She and Daro had done their part and they were going home. He had been through enough.

But the more she watched Daro, the more her sense of unease grew. She was filled with relief and gratitude to have him back, but he wasn't the same man who had set out for Halthas last summer. Nihil had altered him, and no amount of love or warm food was going to repair the damage. She and her companions had fought so hard to get him back. She wasn't sure what Daro needed to heal, but she knew she was going to find it.

She may have her husband back, but she was starting to realize she couldn't take him home. Not yet.

## 46 : WATCHING

Pathius ducked between the buildings and melted back into the shadows. The ground in the tight alleyway was dry, the tops of the buildings leaning toward each other, blocking the flakes of snow. He hung back, hardly daring to breathe, as his gloved hands pressed into the walls on either side.

Cecily emerged from a building across the street and pulled her fur-lined hood over her head. She carried a basket at her hip and the hem of her cloak swished through the shallow snow as she walked down the quiet street toward the river.

He waited and peeked his head around the corner as snowflakes drifted into his hair. When she was almost out of sight, he stole from his hiding place and pulled his cowl down low. The cold air brushed his face. He was still unaccustomed to the absence of his mask. How many years had he worn it? He didn't know.

He followed her toward the pier, thinking she was returning to her inn, but she turned down a footpath that led to the river's edge. Turning up another street, he hoped to circle around so as to stay out of sight. He emerged further upriver and peered around a building's edge. She sat on a bench near the flowing water, holding something in her hands.

Pathius crept toward the bank and stole close enough to feel the sheen of her energy, a smoldering warmth that called to him. A raw hunger grew inside him, a desire for something he couldn't name. It crept into his thoughts and lurked in his dreams. He slid behind a tree, pressed his hand to it, and pulled energy from within the towering timber. He felt the edge of hunger soften. But Absorbing energy from the things around him didn't satisfy the craving that had taken root. He wasn't sure what would.

Cecily picked up her basket and set it in her lap. Pathius crouched down and leaned forward to look at her. He wondered what would have happened if he had never Absorbed the energy from Fourteen that day in the courtyard. He should probably call him Daro now. He would never have developed this strange affection for Daro's wife. He would have killed Cecily in Wesfell. She wouldn't have lived to rally the new king, nor the Paragon, to fight against Nihil. No one would have marched on Nihil's compound and Pathius would still be masked, answering to a number instead of his name.

He reached back and scratched at the scab where his implant had been. It had come loose when Daro had crushed Sindre's medallion and killed her. It fell out of his neck, leaving a bloody wound behind. His only regret from that day at the Lyceum was that Sindre hadn't died at his hands. He pacified his irritation by remembering the satisfying feel of Nihil's energy as it poured into him, his body withered and frozen, falling to the floor.

But it wasn't gratitude for his freedom that made him follow Cecily across the kingdom. He didn't know what it was. He couldn't explain it, even to himself. Daro's deep love for his wife had been so ingrained in his soul, a piece of it had bled into Pathius when he Absorbed Daro's energy. And now he couldn't get rid of it.

He wasn't sure he wanted to.

He knew he couldn't follow Cecily forever. Every day he told himself it would be the last, he would tear himself away and go. But when he thought about where, a great barrenness stretched out before him. Where would he go? He had no life to return to. His father was dead, the throne in the hands of a new king. What life was left to him now?

Number Four waited for him at the edge of town, hunkered down in a room at a cheap inn. The man still couldn't tell Pathius his name. Pathius wasn't sure if it was because he was afraid, or because he truly didn't remember. Perhaps he would have to help him choose a new one.

He thought about the others who had suffered at Nihil's hands. They had scattered after Nihil's defeat. Only Number Four had waited for him, the rest disappearing into the city, and beyond. He had no doubt Rogan and the Lyceum would hunt them down, one by one, killing them like rabid animals. It was only a matter of time before someone came for him. Perhaps that held the answer to his quandary.

If they were going to survive, they would have to do it together.

## A NOTE FROM THE AUTHOR

Thank you so much for reading To Whatever End. I sincerely hope you enjoyed it! This is just the beginning for Daro, Cecily and Pathius. If you'd like to be the first to hear about new releases, please visit my website at www.clairefrankbooks.com and sign up for my newsletter.

I welcome feedback from readers. Please consider leaving a review at your favorite retailer, if you're so inclined.

You can also contact me by email at claire@clairefrankbooks.com or find me on Facebook and Twitter.

Until next time…

Made in the USA
Middletown, DE
15 March 2015